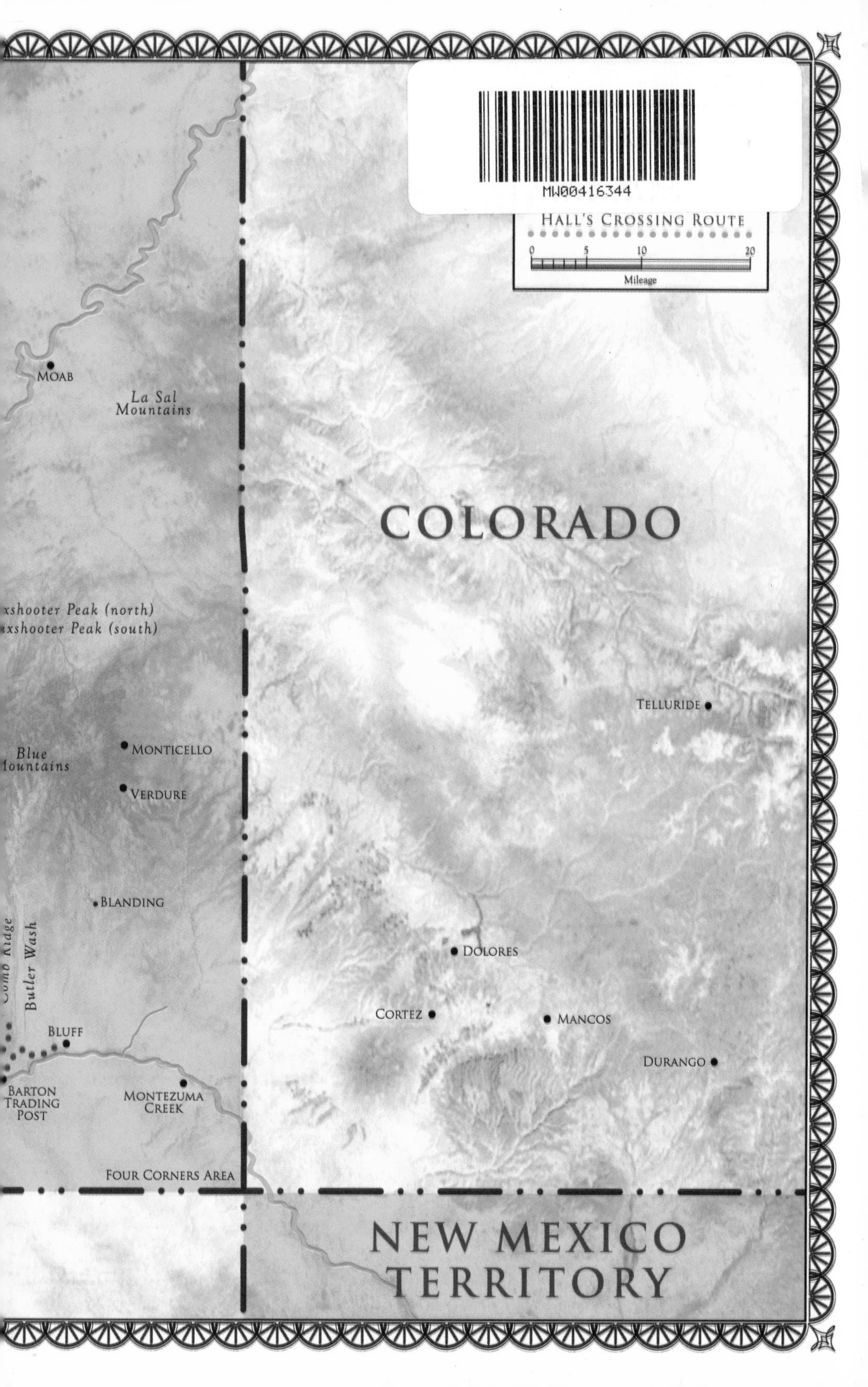

MW00416344
HALL'S CROSSING ROUTE
0
5
10
20
Mileage
MOAB
La Sal Mountains
COLORADO
xshooter Peak (north)
xshooter Peak (south)
TELLURIDE
Blue
Mountains
MONTICELLO
VERDURE
BLANDING
Comb Ridge
Butler Wash
DOLORES
CORTEZ
MANCOS
BLUFF
DURANGO
BARTON TRADING POST
MONTEZUMA CREEK
FOUR CORNERS AREA
NEW MEXICO TERRITORY

TO SOAR WITH EAGLES

TO SOAR WITH EAGLES

The Sequel to the Best-Seller ONLY THE BRAVE

GERALD N. LUND

SALT LAKE CITY, UTAH

This is a work of fiction. Characters and events in this book are products of the author's imagination or are represented fictitiously.

Visit us at DeseretBook.com

Library of Congress Cataloging-in-Publication Data

Names: Lund, Gerald N., author. | Lund, Gerald N.
Title: To soar with eagles / Gerald N. Lund.
Description: Salt Lake City, Utah : Deseret Book, [2016] | ?2016 | Includes bibliographical references.
Identifiers: LCCN 2016003330 (print) | LCCN 2016004082 (ebook) | ISBN 9781629722016 (hardbound : alk. paper) | ISBN 9781629734514 (ebook)
Subjects: LCSH: Mormon pioneers—Fiction. | Utah—History—19th century—Fiction. | Frontier and pioneer life—Fiction. | San Juan County (Utah)—History—Fiction. | San Juan County (Utah)—Fiction. | GSAFD: Christian fiction. | LCGFT: Historical fiction. | Romance fiction. | Novels.
Classification: LCC PS3562.U485 T63 2016 (print) | LCC PS3562.U485 (ebook) | DDC 813/.54—dc23
LC record available at http://lccn.loc.gov/2016003330

Printed in the United States of America
RR Donnelley, Harrisonburg, VA

10 9 8 7 6 5 4 3 2 1

"But they that wait upon the Lord
shall renew their strength;
they shall mount up with wings as eagles;
they shall run, and not be weary;
and they shall walk, and not faint."

—Isaiah 40:31

CHAPTER 1

April 4, 1888, 10:30 a.m.—Verdure Camp—South Montezuma Creek, San Juan County, Utah Territory

As Edna Rae Zimmer gradually awoke, three things registered in her consciousness, one right after the other.

The first was the brightness. When she had finally closed her eyes in sleep last night, the darkness in the wagon had been so complete that she couldn't see her hand when she put it in front of her face. Now the wagon was filled with a golden glow of light that penetrated even her closed eyelids. It felt wonderful. That had been one of the most frightening things about being lost in the blizzard: they couldn't even see the snowflakes that blew into their faces. For all they knew, they might have been going around in circles for hours.

The second thing was the warmth. Yesterday she had experienced a cold more bitter than she had thought was possible. It had penetrated to the very marrow of her bones. Even after the sisters had got them all into dry clothes, she had insisted on sleeping fully clothed except for her boots and outer coat. Even under two quilts, she shivered violently as she fell asleep. Now, a gentle, pervasive warmth filled every part of her body. Heaven could never be more wonderful than this. Light and warmth. She had never fully appreciated these two simple things before.

But wonderful as those two things were, the third was what hit her with the greatest impact. She was alive. And *safe*! Which was wonderful. But most wonderful of all was that Mitch had found her. Mitch had forgiven her. And he had asked her to marry him. And he had said all the right things in just the right way.

And then, in a flash that stiffened her whole body, the fear was back. She jerked upright and untangled herself from the quilts. What about Evelyn and Leona? Were they all right? She vaguely remembered the men bringing them to the wagons. Were they warm too? *And Nean!* What of the child? She had been so still last night when Mitch had laid her in Evelyn's arms in the back of the sleigh. *No, it couldn't be.* Evelyn had lost a baby last summer, a beautiful little girl who had lived only a few hours. She couldn't lose Nean, too.

As Edie sat there trembling, she became aware of the murmur of voices close by. She quickly combed at her tangle of thick hair with her fingers, crawled to the back of the wagon, and pulled back the cover. She gave a low cry as brilliant sunlight assaulted her eyes. She clamped them shut again, then gradually cracked one eye open, and then the other. The sun was about halfway toward its zenith, a blinding white ball in a wide expanse of azure blue sky. But that was only half of the glare. Sunlight was also reflecting off of dazzling white fields of snow. Strangely, it registered in her mind that the snow wasn't nearly as deep as it had been last night, and she wondered why.

"Hey," a gruff voice called out. "Look who we've got here." Edie turned, expecting it to be Mitch. But Brother Frederick I. Jones appeared, a huge smile on his face. A moment later, his wife, Mary, was beside him. She quickly pushed around her husband and came to Edie, reaching out to grasp both of her hands. "Good morning, dear. I'm so glad you were able to sleep."

"I . . . yes. I did sleep some. Uh . . . where am I?"

Husband and wife exchanged worried glances, and then

Brother Jones smiled even more broadly. “You are in our wagon. We’re in Verdure. And you are safe now.”

The relief was palpable, and Edie managed a wan smile as she looked past them. She saw other wagons and a couple of tents nearby. A creek about four or five feet wide cut a dark swath through the trampled snow. Then her eyes fell on a figure seated on a backless stool next to a low cooking fire. It was a woman. Her back was half turned to Edie, but she could see that it was Evelyn. She had two-year-old Nean on her lap. Evelyn was holding her daughter tightly, almost clinging to her, and humming to her as she rocked her back and forth, back and forth.

Edie looked at Mary Jones. “Is Nean all right?”

Mary squeezed Edie’s hands tightly, joyfully. “Nean is fine. In fact, she’s amazing. It’s like nothing happened to her. And thanks be to the Lord for that.”

Edie hardly dared ask. “What about Leona? Is Leona all right?”

Mary patted her hand. “Leona is fine too. She’s still sleeping.”

Edie sat back, starting to feel safe again. There couldn’t have been two better people to be greeting her at this moment. Fred and Mary Jones had been some of the first to be called to the Blue Mountain Mission and had come with their family the previous summer, so Edie knew them well. Brother Jones was a big man, probably six feet or more, with broad shoulders, a full head of hair, and piercing blue eyes. He also wore a full, untrimmed beard. He had been asked by President Hammond, San Juan’s stake president, to act as presiding elder over the little group of Blue Mountain pioneers, and so technically he was their priesthood leader.

Mary was somewhat of a plain woman, probably in her early thirties, who was a near-perfect match for her husband. Kindly, always cheerful, and quick to reach out to others, she had become like an older sister to Edie.

"You're alive," Brother Jones was saying quietly. "And that's no small miracle. You all have a couple of places where you have some mild frostbite, but nothing serious. Someone in heaven was watching out for the four of you, that's for sure."

"Yes," Edie finally said. "It is a miracle."

Still looking around, she saw more people, all of them watching her and smiling. Parley and Ency Butt were by another wagon with a cooking fire nearby. And there was Mons and Eliza Peterson—which surprised her. She knew Mons had determined to come up to the Blue Mountains with this first vanguard, but the last she'd heard, Eliza had planned to wait and come up with the rest of the families. But Edie was glad. Eliza was only three or four years older than she was and had always been friendly to her.

But she didn't see the one person she was looking for.

Edie felt a tug. "Come, dear," Mary was saying. "We've kept some breakfast warm for you."

"Is Mitch here?"

Brother Jones frowned. "Ah, no. He and George Adams left early this morning to go find the wagon and George's team."

Edie's disappointment was devastating. "How long will he be gone?"

"It's hard to say," Brother Jones replied. "It depends on where the horses are."

Watching the despair fill her friend's eyes, Mary put an arm around Edie and helped her down from the wagon. "Come, dear. You need to eat something. No more talk of last night."

"But what if Mitch can't find them? What if the snow's too deep?" Suddenly, she couldn't breathe. "What if he gets. . . ."

Her hands came up and covered her face as her whole body began to shake.

Fred Jones took Edie from his wife and pulled her into his embrace. "There, now," he soothed. "Mitch and George will be all right. The storm is gone. They're in a sleigh. They'll be fine. They've got to find those horses or they'll die."

Edie forced herself to push back the panic. Of course they did. Those two magnificent animals had saved her life. All of their lives. "Of course," she stammered. "I'm sorry."

Mary took her arm. "They left early. They'll be back soon. Come, Edie. You need to eat. Mitch made us promise to make sure you ate something."

12:45 p.m.

Edie reached out to take the tin plate off of Mitch's lap, but he immediately moved it out of her grasp and got to his feet instead. "Are you finished?"

"Yes." She was pushing at her food with her fork. It wasn't even half gone. But she handed the plate to him anyway. "I'm not very hungry. I ate breakfast just an hour or so ago."

"Then let me take it," he said. He took her cup and the fork and spoon as well and started for the wagon.

"Thank you," she murmured.

Mary Jones intercepted him and took the dishes from him. She glanced at Edie and quietly said, "Mitch, you take that girl of yours and go for a walk or something. We'll be fine here."

Mitch turned to look at Edie, whose head was down and who was drawing circles in the snow with one finger. "Are you sure?" he whispered.

Fred came over and joined them. "Yes. You'll find that the

snow has already melted off of the south-facing side of the creek. Get a saddle blanket from our wagon to sit on. The grass will still be wet."

"She needs time with you, Mitch," Mary said quietly. "Just the two of you." She hesitated. "Be gentle with her. She went through a horrible ordeal yesterday, and even though she doesn't see it, she's still in a state of shock."

Mitch nodded. He had watched Edie during their lunch and seen the tremors sweep through her. "All right. Thank you."

When he came back to Edie, he took both of her hands and pulled her up to face him. "Come. We're excused from cleanup. Orders of Sister Jones." He took her by the elbow. "Let's go find us a nice sunny place where we can talk."

She looked at him, momentarily torn, and then finally managed a thin smile. "Are they shooing us away so that the newly engaged couple can have time alone together?"

"Something like that. Is that a problem?"

"No. I think it sounds wonderful." She raised a hand and waved at the others. "Thank you."

"Supper's not for four more hours," Brother Jones called back. "Don't feel like you need to be in a hurry to come back."

1:00 p.m.—Near Verdure Camp

Mitch spread the saddle blanket out on a place where the grass was winter-brown but thick. It was a few yards back from the creek bank and left them in clear view of the camp. They had privacy, but they also were maintaining their propriety. On the hillside opposite, the one that faced north, there were still four or five inches of snow, but on their side it was all but gone. They sat quietly for a while. Mitch watched the gurgling rush of the stream, muddy now with the runoff from the melting snow. Edie stared at the ground. Twice she looked up at him and then quickly away again when he turned to meet her gaze. The third time, she reached up and gently removed his hat and set it on the grass. Then, catching him off guard, she raised one hand and combed her fingers through his hair. "It's getting long," she murmured. "You need a haircut."

"I know. But we're a little short on barbers up here."

"Want me to cut it?"

He gave a short laugh. "Can you cut hair?"

"Of course I can. You just get a pair of scissors and hack away."

Not sure if she was teasing him or not, Mitch asked, "Have you ever cut anyone else's hair?"

"No. But even the best barbers had a first time. So, will you let me cut yours?"

He hesitated for only a moment. "Sure."

That brought her clear around. "Are you serious?"

"Sure."

"It doesn't worry you what I'll do to it?"

"No. The way I figure it is this. Even if you do a terrible job, there are only about ten people up here to even notice. And besides, I'll just wear my hat at all times."

Edie nodded absently, and there was no hint of a smile. Her thoughts had left him again, just that fast. He reached out and took her hands. "You're getting cold. Want me to go get your mittens?"

To his surprise, she jerked away and thrust both of her hands into the pocket of her jacket. "No. Don't leave me, Mitch. Please!"

The ferocity with which she had said it startled him. "I won't, Edie. Not ever."

She visibly relaxed, somewhat embarrassed. "I. . . ."

"It's all right, Edie. I'm here. I'm right here." He could see the stress lines around her eyes and noticed that her fists were clenched inside her pockets. Seeing that he was watching her, she looked away. So he studied her face in profile, loving every curve and line—the high but soft cheekbones, the petite little curve to her nose, the soft lips and firm chin. Since she was sitting on his right, he was looking at her left cheek. He could see the faint mark where her dimple—her only one—would appear without warning when she smiled. And then he realized that he hadn't seen that dimple once today.

Be gentle. He was beginning to understand Sister Jones's counsel. He moved closer and put his arm around Edie's shoulders and pulled her close. "I love you, Edna Rae Zimmer," he whispered.

Her head jerked up and for a long moment, those deep brown eyes that he loved so much searched his. "And I love you too, Mitch," she finally replied. But to his surprise, that only seemed to cause her to withdraw further.

The silence stretched on for another minute or so. She stared at the creek, then at the trees. Her hands came out again and she started picking at the loose threads on the saddle blanket. As she did, Mitch saw the tremors again. He reached out and covered her hands with his. "Edie?"

She looked up at him.

"Do you want to talk about yesterday?"

A look of sheer panic twisted her face. "No!"

"Okay. It's all right." Another long, heavy silence, and then he tried again. "Would you like to talk about our wedding? Make some plans?"

She didn't move, keeping her head down, but the picking at the threads accelerated noticeably. She didn't look up when she finally spoke. "I . . . I wasn't sure if after yesterday you still wanted to marry me."

Mitch was genuinely shocked. "Of course I still want to marry you. Why wouldn't I?"

"Because I was stupid. Such an idiot."

He opened his mouth to protest, but stopped. *Let her talk. Don't say anything.* The thought came clearly and distinctly into his mind. So he clamped his mouth shut again and waited.

Edie half turned to him, her troubled eyes searching his face. Then, in a very low voice, she went on. "It was my fault, you know. Evelyn was the first to have the idea of coming up here early, to surprise George. But then she started having second thoughts. It was a crazy idea. We all knew that. Three women coming alone on a road that's barely passable in the summertime, and with a two-year-old child, too? But by that point, I wanted to see you so badly, to fall down before you and beg you to forgive me for being such a fool that night at the Swing Tree. So I pressed her. I told her that we could do it. Leona was anxious to get up here too, because she'd promised her father that she would cook for you men. So together we convinced Evelyn we could make it."

Mitch bit his lip, determined to say nothing yet, but he couldn't stop from shaking his head to show that he didn't agree with her.

"No, Mitch!" she burst out. "You have to be honest with me. You can't tell me that you think this was a wonderful idea. Not now. Not when we came so close to death. Can you?"

"I. . . ."

"Don't lie to me, Mitch. If you love me, please, please, don't lie to me."

"Okay," he sighed. "I understand why you and Evelyn and

Leona wanted to surprise us. And there was nothing wrong with that. It was quite sweet of you, actually."

"But stupid."

"You said that the weather was wonderful when you left."

"It was. In the low eighties, and no clouds anywhere. But we should have known it would be different up here."

"Why? Look, Edie. How many times have you been across the road between here and Bluff? Twice, right? Once when you came up last spring with the Deckers, and once last fall when you and I went back to Bluff. So you don't know this road well. You don't know this area well. You've never been up here in the winter. We left before first snow last year, as you will remember. So . . . lack of experience is not the same as being stupid. It would have been stupid if you had said, 'There's a blizzard up there, but we don't care. We're going anyway.'"

He could see that she was understanding him and that it was helping her. So he mustered every ounce of earnestness in him. "So, no, I don't believe that you were stupid. And I am certainly not disappointed in you. I'm just so glad that everything—"

Suddenly, Edie's head dropped and she buried her face in her hands. "I almost got us killed, Mitch," she sobbed. "It was unbelievably horrible. When the snow got so deep that the horses couldn't pull the wagon any farther, we knew we couldn't just stop. No one up here knew we were coming, and no one down there knew we were in trouble. Who knew how long it would be before someone even found us? A week? A month?"

Again Mitch pushed away the temptation to interrupt, to try to make it right for her.

Edie was staring at her hands, which were trembling badly now. When she spoke, her voice was a choked and barely audible whisper. "We decided to take the big horse and leave the other. We had no saddle, of course. So we took turns riding him. And whoever was on the horse held Nean. We went for what seemed like hours. One on the horse, clinging to Nean for dear life with one hand, clinging to the horse's mane with the other, the other two following behind, letting the horse break trail for us."

She finally looked at Mitch. "The snow was so deep. Above our knees. With our full skirts it was like we were pushing against. . . ."

A shudder shook her body and ran down her back, and tears sprang to her eyes. "And then—" She looked down at her hands, which were clenching and unclenching. It was as though she didn't even recognize that they belonged to her. "And then the horse just stopped. His legs were trembling with exhaustion. His stomach was heaving in and out. And then there was this soft sound, kind of like a deep, painful sigh."

Edie closed her eyes. "Oh, Mitch. I'll never forget that sound. And . . . and then he dropped to his front knees and just rolled over. Evelyn had to jump off or she would have been crushed."

Suddenly, she was back with him. "Are you sure he's all right?"

"Yes. Both of the horses are fine. They were exhausted, but they're going to be okay."

Had she heard him? Did it register with her? He couldn't tell for sure. "You don't have to talk about it now, Edie. Just rest for a minute."

She didn't seem to hear that, either. "When I was taking my turn on the horse, and trying to hold Nean, I was terrified that I was going to drop her. My arms would get so numb. And the snow was so deep. I kept saying to myself, over and over, 'Don't drop her! Don't drop her! Or . . . or. . . .'" Edie looked away.

"Or you'd never find her because the snow was so deep?" Mitch suggested in a low murmur.

"Yes." Edie straightened, brushing at the tears, fighting for control. "I know that sounds ridiculous now, but it was so real to me. Her being buried in the snow and. . . ."

Mitch took her gently in his arms and let her burrow her face into his shoulder. Edie continued talking. "Near the end, I thought she was dead. I thought our sweet, little, delightful, adorable Nean was dead. But I didn't dare tell Evelyn. And at that moment I wanted to die too, more fiercely than I've wanted anything else in my life." And then the sobs burst forth and her body began to shake.

For several minutes they just sat there, her pressed against him, him saying nothing but holding her tightly and rubbing his hand across her back over and over and over. Gradually the shudders subsided, and Mitch could feel Edie begin to calm. Still he said nothing. And still he held her close.

Finally, she pulled back and looked at him. She wiped at her runny nose with the back of her hand, barely aware that she was doing so. "I want to ask you a question, Mitch, and I want you to be honest with me."

"All right."

"Even if you think it's going to hurt me. I *need* you to be honest."

"I shall."

"This morning, when you and George left to find the animals and the wagon, did you . . . ?"

"Did I what?"

"Last night, after you rescued us, you asked me to marry you."

"Yes I did. And I—"

"This morning, after you realized what had really happened, that you had come across three silly women who nearly got themselves and a young child killed because they thought it would be fun to surprise their men, did you . . . ?"

"Did I change my mind?" he asked softly when she couldn't finish. When she nodded, for a moment he was so stunned that he just stared at her. Then he took her by the shoulders and shook her ever so gently. "No! Not for one second, Edie."

Finally sensing the full extent of her anguish and pain, he released her and gently took her face in his hands. He leaned in until their eyes were just inches apart. "Edie, look at me. Look into my eyes."

She sniffed again but did as she was asked.

"I swear to you, Edie. No such thought ever entered my mind. Just the opposite. I was awake half the night because I was so elated that I had you back—that I hadn't lost you. That you had forgiven *me* for being so stupid that night at the Swing Tree."

Her eyes were boring into his. "And you didn't once think, 'What kind of a girl is this Edie Zimmer? Do I really want to marry someone as flighty as that?'"

"No!" Mitch cried. He leaned even closer. "Just the opposite. I am in awe of what you women did last night. The courage that you and Evelyn and Leona had is astonishing. For every possible reason, you should have perished. But you didn't. By the sheer force of your will and courage, you prevailed. I figure you must have come almost ten miles through the snow. You were about three miles from the wagon and a mile farther on from where the horse collapsed. How you ever pushed that far in snow that deep, I'll never know. If you had stopped once, decided to just sit for a moment and rest, it would have been over."

He leaned in and laid his cheek against hers. "Hear me well, Edna Rae Zimmer. You are the most remarkable woman I have ever known." And to his surprise, tears sprang to his eyes and his voice caught in his throat. "And if you are still willing to marry me, then I consider myself the luckiest man in the whole world."

He kissed her softly on the lips. "And so," he said as he pulled back. "I ask you again. Will you, Edna Rae Zimmer, take me, Mitchell Arthur Westland, to be your lawfully wedded husband for this life and in the world to come?"

Edie's eyes were brimming with tears, but he saw now that they were tears of joy. "Yes!" she whispered. "And will you, Mitchell Arthur Westland, take me—"

"Yes! Yes! Yes! A thousand times yes."

CHAPTER 2

April 4, 1888, 3:30 p.m.—Near Verdure Camp

They sat there for a long time, shoulder to shoulder, holding hands, sometimes talking, sometimes content to be quiet with each other.

Finally, Edie turned and looked toward the camp. "We probably ought to be getting back."

"Are you ready to go?" Mitch asked.

"Yes," she replied. Then instantly, she changed her mind. "No. I do want to talk about our marriage, if that's all right."

"Of course."

"Do you remember what I said to you that night at the old Swing Tree?"

Mitch hooted softly. "Are you kidding? That will be burned into my brain forever. What specifically were you thinking of?"

She quoted herself softly. "'Mitch, if you only had worded your proposal of marriage a little differently, I would have thrown myself into your arms and cried, "Yes, Mitch. I will marry you. I will marry you today. I will marry you tomorrow. Or a year from now, or—"'"

"'Or twenty years from now,'" he finished for her. "Oh, yes, I remember it all very clearly." Then he gave her an impish look. "So . . . ?"

"So what?"

"Do you want to get married today? It's getting late, but I think maybe we could pull something together."

"Yes!" she cried.

He reared back, staring at her. "Really? I was just kidd—"

Laughing up at him, she gave him a little shove. "No, silly. I'm teasing you."

As Mitch looked into Edie's face, seeing the merriment and the pure joy in her eyes—and her dimple now on full display—he nearly started to cry. Suddenly he knew that while yesterday would haunt her for many years to come, she had found peace.

"So," he said again, "seriously, you and I once talked about your birthday and that—"

Edie's hand shot up and clamped over his mouth. "Not yet. There's one thing first."

"What?"

She cocked her head and gave him what he was coming to think of as *the look.* "Surely, I don't have to tell you everything, do I, Mister West—?"

His kiss cut her words off, but she recovered quickly and threw her arms around his neck and kissed him back. It was a long, lingering kiss filled with joy and hope and promise.

Suddenly, from behind them, they heard clapping. Mitch turned his head and then started to laugh as he pulled away from her. "Whoops. I forgot that we have an audience."

"Good!" Edie cried and waved at the small group by their wagons. Then she kissed him again. They were all applauding long and loudly now, and somebody was whistling. Edie cupped one hand to her mouth. "I told him yes," she called.

Parley Butt's voice came floating back to them. "Way to go, Westland. It's about time!"

Laughing and showing her full dimple now, Edie slipped an

arm through Mitch's. But as she did, a shadow briefly crossed her face.

"What is it, Edie? What's wrong?"

She sighed deeply. "I am suddenly completely and utterly exhausted."

"I can believe that." He stood and pulled her up and then retrieved the horse blanket. "Miss Zimmer, I am taking you back to the wagon, and you're going to take a nap before supper."

"I won't fight you on that," she said. And with that, they started back for the others. But ten steps later, she stopped again.

"What?"

"I do want to talk about when we should be married before we rejoin them. Is that all right?"

"Of course."

"Can we sit down? My legs are a little wobbly."

"Of course," he said again. He found a good spot a few feet away and laid out the blanket again. He wondered if that would bring another reaction from the others, but it didn't.

When they were seated again, Edie rubbed at her eyes. "Whew! I don't know what came over me all of a sudden."

"It's called emotional letdown."

She was suddenly teasing him with her eyes. "I think we agree that today is rushing it a little, but what if I said, 'Let's get married tomorrow'?"

Mitch was reeling a little. "That is possible. Are you serious?"

"I can't tell you how tempting that sounds, but no."

"We talked about getting married on your birthday. That's about"—he calculated quickly—"a little less than six weeks from now, and that's very doable."

But to his surprise, Edie shook her head. "I am crazy in love with you, Mitch Westland, but I'm not sure that means we should act crazy."

"So what do you suggest?"

"Well, two things. First, I do want to be married on my birthday."

"But—"

"Second, I want to be married in the temple first. Oh, I know we can go later, but I want to do it right."

"I totally agree. But will the Manti Temple be dedicated by then? We could go to St. George or Salt Lake, or—"

"Not this birthday, Mitch."

"*What?*"

"On my next birthday. A year from now. When the Manti Temple will be open."

Mitch's face fell. "No, Edie!" he exclaimed. "I don't want to wait *that* long."

She looked at him with deep satisfaction. "Now, that was the right answer. Keep it up, and I may kiss you again right out here for everyone to see."

"I'm serious, Edie."

"So am I. Think about it. As much as we both want to be married, we have to be practical, too. If we leave now, you'll be leaving right when you're needed the most here. A trip to Manti and back will take several weeks. Maybe more. You've got corrals to put up, a cabin to build, cows to brand. And remember, the reason I'm supposedly up here is to help Alvin and Emma Decker tend their children. And, as you know, Emma has a new baby. They plan to come in about another week, if the weather holds. I can't just leave them in the lurch."

"Yes, of course."

"Oh, and one other thing. If we're bringing *Oma* Zimmer to live with us—as you promised we would do—"

"I did, and I meant it."

"Well, we've got to build a separate room for her. I think it's going to take a year to get it all done."

For a long moment, Mitch looked at her, loving her more than he thought was possible. "Though I kick myself for saying this, you are right, dear Edie."

She laughed merrily. "Oh, yes. I think I like those four words almost as much as I like the phrase, 'I love you, dear.'"

"What four words?"

"'You are right, dear.'"

Mitch laughed. "I'll try to remember that."

"So we're agreed? A year from now, on the thirteenth of May?"

"Agreed, with one slight adjustment to your plans."

"What?"

"Well, several of the men here are going to be leaving in a week or so to go back to Bluff for their families."

"Yes."

"I hadn't planned to go with them."

Edie's eyes lit up. "Yeeessss," she said very slowly. "But . . . ?"

"You know what my mother will do to me if she hears about our engagement from someone other than me? She'll tan my hide and then slap a branding iron on it."

"And the last thing my mother said to me as I left was, 'Now Edie, if you go fixing things up with Mitch, the first thing you're going to do after that is turn right around and come back down here and tell me. I don't want to hear about it in a letter.'"

"Then that settles it. We'll both go down and tell them together."

Edie's mind was already racing off to something else. "Mama's always said she wants to make my wedding dress. She's an excellent seamstress, you know. And there is one other thing you've forgotten," she added.

"What?"

She snuggled in against him. "Thank you, Mitch," she said with great gravity. "Thank you for letting us talk about this now. Ten minutes ago I was a blubbering idiot; now I'm so happy I want to stand up and shout, but . . . you need to formally ask my father for my hand in marriage."

Mitch groaned. "Your father's never liked me."

"That's not true!" she cried. "He likes you a lot."

"Oh really? How is he able to hide it so well?"

"That's just Papa," she laughed. Then she leaned in closer, and her voice dropped to a conspiratorial whisper. "Actually, he was the one who told me to get myself up there to the Blue Mountains before you found some other girl that caught your fancy."

"Really?"

"Yes, really. He told me that you needed some rough edges knocked off, but I was just the woman to do it."

"*What?*" he cried.

His expression was so doleful that she burst out laughing.

"Gotcha!" she cried.

Edie jerked away as he howled and grabbed at her. "He did not say that."

"No," she said, unable to suppress a peal of giggles, "but he should have."

7:10 p.m.—Verdure Camp

After supper was over, Mitch and Edie offered to wash the dishes down at the creek while Evelyn and Eliza put their two little girls to bed. Because she had done most of the cooking, Leona was told she could sit back and relax. Working together,

Mitch and Edie finished the job quickly and now were seated around the fire with the other adults.

Talk was focused on when to go down to Bluff and get their families. Edie and Mitch explained their plans. She would go back with Mitch and stay with her family while he and his father and his brother Johnnie rounded up the cattle Mitch would bring back up with them.

Eliza Peterson leaned forward, looking at Edie. "So have you set the date yet?"

Edie nodded. "Next year. On my birthday. May thirteenth. In the Manti Temple."

That brought another round of congratulations. To his surprise, no one asked Mitch why they were waiting so long. He explained why anyway. And, to his surprise, that seemed especially to impress the men. There was not only understanding in their eyes, but admiration as well. Here was a young woman who understood the necessities of life on the frontier. That kind of sensibility carried a lot of weight with them, and it was clear that their opinion of her as a woman had gone up even more than before.

As things settled down again, Edie remembered something that had been forgotten in all of the hubbub of that day and the night before. She looked at Brother Jones. "Did Evelyn or Leona give you the news about stake conference?"

Evelyn, who still looked a little wan from their ordeal, was momentarily startled. "Oh! No, I didn't." She looked at her husband. "Sorry, dear. I totally forgot."

Leona Walton looked sheepish. "Me too."

"What about stake conference?" Brother Jones asked.

"Well," Evelyn said, "after we had stake conference in Bluff, you brethren left, but President Hammond stayed on in Bluff for a while to rest up. The day before he and Sister Hammond left for Mancos, they held a final meeting. President Hammond talked about the Blue Mountain Mission and how it needed the support of the whole stake. Then he announced that he had decided that our stake conference in August would be held here."

Brother Jones jerked forward. "Here?"

George Adams was equally shocked. "But . . . it's the first of May and we've barely started on our homes up here. We haven't even talked about a meetinghouse yet."

Evelyn looked at her husband. "That's what Bishop Nielson said too. But President Hammond just smiled and said he has great confidence that we can rise to the challenge."

Leona spoke up. "He emphasized that he wasn't expecting us to have everything perfect, but he did say that you brethren at some point would have to take some time off from your own projects to build a covered meetinghouse so we can have shelter in case of inclement weather."

Brother Jones nodded thoughtfully. "Brethren, if that's what the president wants, then we shall respond. Aside from the challenges, I think it's a wonderful idea. Think of it. The whole stake will see this marvelous place we have found. We could end up having dozens more want to move up here and join us—which is exactly what we need."

April 6, 1888, 2:40 p.m.—Westland Home Site—Monticello

Mitch dismounted from the wagon and tied the team to a cedar tree. He turned to help Edie down, but she had already hopped off. She came over to join him and slipped her arm through his. "All right, Mister Westland," she said, "show me this place you've picked out for us."

That surprised him. "You've been up here before."

"Twice," she agreed, "but all you did was wave your arm in the general direction of this line of cedar trees and say, 'Honey, this is where we're going to build our home.'"

"Ah," he said somberly. "So you want a little more detail than that?"

"I do," she said, letting go of his arm and walking out from the trees.

"Good thing I brought some stakes and some twine then, right?"

She turned back in surprise. "You're actually going to stake it out today?"

"I'd say it's time, wouldn't you?" He pointed to a stack of aspen logs they had cut last summer and some fresher ones he and Parley had cut up in Pole Canyon the day before.

Edie smiled, and then not waiting for him, strode farther out away from the trees. As she did, she looked out across the vast expanse that lay before them to the east, now fully illuminated by the afternoon sunshine. During the previous evening, scattered thunderstorms had come off the Blue Mountains, which lay just behind them. The gusty winds that had preceded the storms had whipped up billowing clouds of dust and filled the atmosphere with a reddish brown haze. During the night, the rain had come, heavy at first, but turning into rain showers that had lasted into the morning. Now, the last of the clouds had scudded off to the east. The air was astonishingly clear, and from where Edie stood—about a quarter of a mile above the town site—the view was quite breathtaking.

As Mitch came up to join her, he dropped the bundle of small wooden stakes, a roll of twine, and a small sledgehammer. "What do you think?"

"I think the view is astonishing. So where is the house going to be? Right here? I want it right here."

He laughed. "Whoa, woman. The answer is yes, right here. But I need your opinion on something first."

"All right. What?"

"Which way do you want the house to face?"

"What are my choices?"

"Well," he drawled, "think in terms of what view you want. He held up his hands, extending his thumbs and touching them together to form a partial square. "Just remember this. We are going to have a large picture window in the living room. And you'll sit there every day in your rocking chair and—"

"We don't have a rocking chair."

"That's going to be my wedding present to you."

"No! This—" she flung her hand out to include where they stood. "This is my wedding present, Mitch. This house will be the most wonderful wedding present I could ever hope for."

"Nope. There's gotta be a rocking chair."

"Why?"

"Because you're going to sit right here and look out on this view while you nurse our babies, all eleven of them."

She laughed right out loud. "Only eleven? Why not an even dozen?"

"All the better. I just want to make sure our children grow up loving this country as much as we do. And what better way to do that than to give them a view they'll never forget?"

That sobered her. He was right. How could anyone not fall in love with the land if this was the view every day?

"So, what's your preference? The La Sals or the San Juans?"

"The La Sals," Edie said without hesitation, looking to the northeast.

The La Sal Mountains were forty or forty-five miles away,

but in the crystal-clear air, they loomed up like you could reach out and touch them. With the recent storm, all of the peaks were glistening white. It was a stunning vista.

"You're sure?" Mitch asked. "On a day like today, the San Juans are pretty spectacular too." He was looking straight east. Off in the far distance there was a range of white peaks that seemed to fill half of the horizon. "They're a much higher range than the La Sals."

"Really? They don't look like it."

"That's because they're almost a hundred miles away. The La Sal Mountains have several peaks that are about twelve thousand feet high, but the San Juans have twenty-five peaks over twelve thousand feet high."

Edie was impressed. "How do you know all that?"

"Because I worked on the railroad in that area, remember?"

"Oh, of course."

"And someday, I'm going to take you to a little place called Telluride. I don't think there's a place on God's green earth more beautiful than Telluride. I was there once, scouting a route for a new spur line. I just stood in the middle of Main Street and gawked like a six-year-old kid. The town's in this little narrow valley, with the greenest mountains you've ever seen towering up on both sides. And you can stand in the middle of Main Street and see a waterfall about a mile east of town. Ah, Edie. That waterfall has a vertical drop of over four hundred feet. They call it Bridal Veil Falls. It is really something."

She was watching him, enchanted by the faraway look of wonder on his face. She had never heard him talk about the scenery around them before. It was just there. Part of where you lived.

"I'd love to see it," she murmured.

Mitch spun around. "I'll take you there on our honeymoon," he blurted.

She laughed merrily. "Come back down to earth, Mitch. Our honeymoon is going to be spent going to and coming back from the Manti Temple next May."

He sniffed loftily, pretending to be offended. "I know all of that," he said, "but I'm talking about our second honeymoon."

"Second honeymoon? My goodness. And when will that be?"

He gave a diffident shrug. "I have no idea. After the kids are grown and gone maybe. I don't know. But I am going to do it, Edie. A second honeymoon. Mark my words."

Smiling, she put an arm around his waist. "I like the way you think, cowboy, but until then, I want our view to be to the La Sals. Is that all right with you?"

"I totally agree." He took her by the hand and led her to where a boulder protruded from the red earth. "Have a seat. There's one more thing I want your opinion on."

"I like it when you ask my opinion."

After Edie was seated, Mitch looked around and found a stick about a foot long. He dropped into a crouch right in front of her and smoothed out a place in the soft dirt about two feet square. "All right," he said. Then, using the stick, he drew something quickly in the sand and stepped back. "Can you tell me what this is?"

"Of course. It's the Flying-W brand. Your brand. The Westland brand."

"That's right. For my cows and for Dad's. And that's the problem. I'm thinking we need our own brand now."

Edie was nodding. "I agree. And, by the way, I really like the word 'we.' So what are *we* thinking?"

Mitch grinned. He erased the brand with his hand and drew quickly again, then stepped back.

Edie's brow wrinkled a little. "The E-D brand?"

His grin broadened. "No, the *EDIE* brand."

"Ah," she drawled, leaning forward to study it more carefully. Finally, she looked up. "You're spoiling me rotten, you know."

"I hope so."

Then she shook her head. "I think it still needs to have a W in it."

"Easy enough." He quickly added a few lines, joining the letters together across the top.

Edie studied it thoughtfully for almost minute and then stood up. She lifted a foot and held it over his drawing. "May I?" When he nodded, she tamped the letters out, took the stick from him, and crouched down. She deliberately turned so as to block his view. Then she stood up and stepped back. "There."

Mitch leaned in and a smile played around the corners of his mouth. "A backwards E?"

"Do you like it?"

"I do. It's the Edie Westland brand for the EDW Ranch." He kissed her. "I like it a lot."

"I like it a lot too" she said with a smile.

He chuckled softly. "The brand or sealing it with a kiss?"

She blushed slightly. "I'm not sure."

He kissed her again. As he did so, she reached up and laid

her hand on his cheek. To her surprise, he winced and jerked away from her. "Ow!"

She fell back a step. "What? What did I do?"

Mitch shook his head as he gently rubbed his jaw. "Nothing. I . . . I think I've got a piece of meat lodged between my teeth. My gums are a little tender, that's all."

"A little?" Edie asked, giving him a hard look. "You need to have someone take a look at it."

Mitch snorted softly. "It's nothing," he said. "It'll work itself out."

She wasn't put off so easily. "If it doesn't, I've heard that Brother Ed Hyde has done some dentist work. Will you talk to him?"

Mitch shook his head. "I'll get it out when I get home tonight."

Edie just looked at him and shook her head. "Men," she muttered to herself.

Notes

Six families initially came up to the Blue Mountains in the spring of 1888. In early March 1888, a small group of men came up to prepare things. They fenced in more land and planted grain. Most had left their families back in Bluff until the weather softened some. The families were Frederick and Mary Jones, Parley and Ency Butt, Mons and Eliza Peterson, Charles E. and Jane Walton, George A. and Evelyn Adams, and Alvin and Emma Decker. The Deckers moved to Mancos later that summer. Together, those families had about two dozen children ranging in age from young babies to eighteen years. About two thirds of them were eight years or younger. As the summer wore on, several other families came (see Cornelia Adams Perkins, Marian Gardner Nielson, Lenora Butt Jones, *Saga of the San Juan* [San Juan County Daughters of Utah Pioneers, 1968], 99; Albert R. Lyman, *History of San Juan County 1879–1917* [1919], found at www.hirf.org/history_hist_san_juan_01-05.asp, 67).

CHAPTER 3

April 9, 1888, 8:10 a.m.—Alvin Decker Home Site—Monticello

As Mitch rode up to the Decker tent, Emma Decker and Edie stepped out together to greet him. Emma had week-old Nathan in her arms, and Edie held the tent flap open for the rest of the children. Jane, who was eleven and the oldest, was holding little Willie's hand. He was three. Adelia, or Della, followed behind. She was not quite five yet.

"Mornin'," Mitch said as he swung down from the saddle.

A chorus of "good mornings" followed.

"We've just finished breakfast," Emma said. "Got plenty more."

"Thanks anyway," Mitch replied, "but some of us are going up to Pole Canyon to bring down more logs and are meeting in a few minutes at the corral. I just stopped by to see if Alvin was available for a quick question."

The question seemed to catch Emma off guard. "Uh . . . actually, he and young Alvin left at dawn this morning. He's . . . uh . . . he's making a quick trip over to Mancos."

"Mancos?" Mitch replied. "He didn't say anything about that yesterday when I saw him."

"Yes . . . uh . . . he planned to go next week, but decided not to put it off. He should be back in four or five days."

Obviously disappointed, Mitch hesitated for a moment,

debating something in his head. Sensing that something was up, Emma turned to her children. "Come," she said. Then to Edie, "Mary Jones says she has a pattern for a quilt I can borrow. I could be an hour or more. Are you all right to stay with the baby, Edie?"

"Of course."

"Good." She waved to Mitch and then hurried away, herding the children ahead of her.

Once she was gone, Edie looked at Mitch. "Did you eat before you came here?"

"Um . . . not really. But I'm okay."

"Eggs and bacon or mush?" she said, moving toward the cooking fire, where a frying pan was nestled in the coals. "And don't tell me you have to go. You can take five minutes."

"Mush," he answered, obviously not happy.

Her head jerked up. "Mitch, you've got a long day ahead of you. Why not eggs and bacon?"

"Not that hungry. Mush with a little milk will be fine."

"With some brown sugar on it?" she asked.

"That would be great."

Edie was eying him closely "You want a piece of bread with it?"

"Uh . . . no. I'm all right."

When she had a large serving of oatmeal porridge before him, she sat down beside him. As he started to eat, she studied him out of the corner or her eye. Finally, she leaned in closer. "Mitch Westland. Is that tooth still bothering you?"

There was a startled look and then a quick shake of his head.

"Then why are you eating so . . . so . . . gingerly?"

"I'm just enjoying your company," he said. "I won't get to see you all day."

She hooted. "Oh, brother."

She reached up without warning and touched the lower part of his jaw. He jumped as though she had touched him with a hot iron. "Ow!"

"I knew it!" she cried. "It's that tooth, isn't it? What's it been now? Three or four days? And don't tell me that it's just meat stuck in your teeth. Something's wrong, Mitch."

Mitch took one last spoonful and got to his feet. "It's just a little tender. I've got to go."

Suddenly, Edie had a thought. "Were you looking for Alvin to get more laudanum?"

His expression darkened. "Never mind about Alvin. I've got to go." And he stood up. Edie was up in an instant too, glaring at him. "Open up. Let me see."

"If it's not better by Saturday, I'll talk to Brother Hyde."

"Saturday? And today's only Monday?"

"All right," he blurted, "Thursday. We're going up to Pole Canyon again on Wednesday."

Edie finally nodded and wagged a finger at him. "You think I'm going to forget, but I won't. It's Thursday, or else."

"Okay, but don't you talk to Brother Hyde. I'll do that."

"If you talk to him Thursday, then I won't have to, will I?" she snapped back.

April 11, 1888, 8:35 a.m.—Decker Tent and Home Site

Edie set her journal aside, careful not to make any noise. She rose from the cot that served as her bed and took two steps to the bassinet near the back of the tent. Her face softened as she looked down into the face of Nathaniel Cornelius Decker, now sleeping peacefully. As she watched, she saw his lips puckering rhythmically. She wondered if he was dreaming about nursing, and then wondered whether babies dreamed at all, especially at two months.

Either way, Nathaniel was asleep, which meant Edie was free to start mending the children's clothes and her own apron, which she had torn two days ago on a nail. Emma had taken the other children with her to see Mary Jones.

But Edie didn't move. She knelt down beside the small crib and reached out to softly stroke the baby's cheek with the back of one finger. His skin was so soft, so perfect. It looked as though someone had made his little nose by putting a dab of clay on his thumb and sticking it in place on the baby's face, flattening it a little to make it stick. He was so beautiful. So peaceful in sleep.

Edie heard footsteps outside. A moment later, Emma opened the flap and stepped inside.

"Well, that was fast," Edie said.

"Yes." Emma waved a paper. "Mary knew right where it was, and then she volunteered to keep my children there to play with hers."

Edie smiled. "Well, I was just going to start some mending, so why don't you try to take a quick nap while the baby is still sleeping?"

"Because I'd rather talk to you." A frown wrinkled Emma's brow. "Edie, there's something I need to tell you. Let's go outside and sit in the shade. It's quite a lovely morning."

Alvin Decker had chosen for their family's future cabin a site that had a cluster of cedar trees in one corner of it. He had pitched their tent beside the trees so that they always had morning shade. The two women sat down and removed their bonnets. It would be in the high seventies by afternoon, but now the air was cool and delightfully refreshing.

They sat quietly for a moment, enjoying the morning, but

then Edie noticed that Emma was avoiding eye contact. Edie leaned in. "What was it you had to tell me, Emma?"

Emma finally looked up, and her eyes were sad. "I feel awful about this, Edie. I know we asked you to come up with us again this year to help with the children, but. . . ."

"What?"

There was a long, painful sigh. "Alvin's gone to Mancos to tell his family that we will be moving there in a few weeks to join in their freighting and road construction business."

Edie's mouth dropped open as she stared at her friend. "You're moving?"

"I'm so sorry, Edie. I wanted to tell you sooner, but Alvin has really been torn about whether to accept their invitation or not. It's a wonderful opportunity for us, but this is our home, too."

"I . . ." Edie was reeling. This was a stunning revelation. Thoughts were rushing at her almost faster than she could process them. Edie lived with the Deckers, sleeping in their wagon and taking meals with them. It was her payment for helping Emma with the children. What would she do now? She and Mitch weren't going to be married for another year.

But those thoughts were quickly pushed aside by a sharp pang of sorrow that brought tears to her eyes. She and Emma were dear friends now. And the Decker children were the delight of her life. She loved them as though they were her own family. And now it was over? But all Edie said was, "Does anyone else know?"

"Brother Jones. Alvin told him that it was a possibility before we ever left Bluff. Alvin's family wanted him to come join them immediately, but Alvin told them that he'd made a commitment to the Blue Mountain Mission to come up this season. So we'll help get people settled here and help build as many cabins as possible before we go."

"When will that be?"

"Not until about the first of July."

"Well," Edie exclaimed, "that's a relief."

Emma reached out and clasped her friend's hand. She was very near to tears now. "Oh, Edie, I feel like we've betrayed you. We talk you into coming up with us another year, and then we abandon you. I'll do whatever I can to help you find a place to stay."

Laying her hand over Emma's, Edie shook her head. "I wasn't thinking about that, Emma. I'm relieved that I get another two months with the children." And that did it. The tears began to flow. "I'm going to miss them so much. Do they know yet?"

"No, and I dread telling them. They love you so, Edie. This will be very hard for them."

As if on cue, from inside the tent, they heard a faint cry. A moment later it came again, and then just that quickly it turned into a howl of protest.

"That's my little piglet," Emma said with a laugh as she got to her feet. "He opens his eyes, looks around, and starts hollering that he's hungry." She motioned for Edie to follow her. "Come in while I feed him. I've got an idea to share with you."

Once they were inside the tent and the baby was nursing contentedly, Edie looked at her friend. "So, what is your idea?"

"I feel awful about leaving you in the lurch after bringing you up here, especially since you have a year until you're married. So, what about the Waltons?" As Edie reared back in surprise, Emma rushed on. "Think about it. I know they're building two bedrooms in their cabin—one for Charles and Jane, and one for the girls. Charlie Jr. will sleep in the barn until they can build a lean-to out back. It will be crowded, but what if you shared a bedroom with Maggie and Leona?"

"I . . ."

"Maggie is only a year older than you, and Leona is a year younger. And you and Leona are already such good friends. I think it's a perfect solution."

"But, Emma, I . . . it would be such an imposition, and—"

"No, Edie. Think about it. Sister Jane has just been called as the stake Relief Society president. That means she will have to travel a lot just to visit the various wards and branches in the stake. And, as you know, Charles is buying that fancy new threshing machine, so he and Charlie will be gone a lot with the threshing crews come harvest time. I'll bet they'd jump at the chance to have you there with Maggie and Leona. I talked to Alvin about it last night, and he thought it was a wonderful idea."

She reached out and briefly touched Edie's arm. "We'd both feel so much better knowing that we weren't leaving you high and dry. If you'd like, I can broach the idea with Jane and see what her reaction is."

A little dazed by it all, Edie finally nodded. "It *would* be a wonderful solution."

"Then consider it done. I'll talk to her this afternoon while you and the kids are fixing dinner." Emma sat back, very pleased with herself. "And now, while I'm meddling in your affairs, there's one other thing."

Edie tossed back her head and laughed, causing Nathaniel to jerk awake and look as if he were going to cry. Emma cooed to him and got him eating again and then turned back to Edie. "It's really none of my business, but. . . ."

"Meddle away," Edie whispered with a smile.

Emma took a quick breath. "Okay, let's talk about your wedding."

"My wedding?" Edie exclaimed.

"Yes. Everyone agrees that it was wise of you and Mitch not

to try to marry right away. There's so much going on here right now, and he's got to go down and get his cattle, and—"

"And dig a ditch to bring water to our site, and cut enough hay for winter, and build some kind of shed for the cows, and. . . ."

"Yes, yes, yes," Emma responded. "All of that, too. But that will all be done by this fall, so why not marry in September or October?" Before Edie could answer, Emma had another thought. "Are you and Mitch staying up here for the winter?"

Edie nodded. "That's his plan."

"And what about your plan?"

"If he stays, I stay. He's not sure that's a good idea, but that's the way it is."

"So then why not marry before the fall? He can have enough done on the cabin by then that you'd have a place to stay."

Edie considered her question soberly. "Actually, I too have been having second thoughts about waiting a year." Her voice caught a little as she thought of the baby nestled in Emma's arms. "If we didn't wait, I could have a baby of my own by my birthday."

"Exactly," Emma said. "And since you are so worried about whether you can have babies, why not get started sooner?"

Edie's shoulders lifted and fell in a deep sigh. "Don't think I haven't asked myself that question over and over. I think about it all the time."

"I can only imagine what a burden that is for you."

Edie gave Emma a long look and then lowered her head. "More than you know," she said in a low voice. She drew a deep breath, debating for a moment, and then spoke. "I don't remember much about my brother," she began. "I was only three when he was born. They wouldn't let me see him. All I knew was that one day we were all excited about having a new baby in the house, and the next, there was this terrible dark cloud hanging over us. But I was eight years old when my little sister was born. I remember that day very clearly. She was so beautiful. Just like your little Cornelius. Perfectly formed, with tiny little fingers and dark blue eyes—" She couldn't finish.

"Oh, Edie," Emma cried, grasping her hand. "It's all right. You don't have to tell me."

"I want to!" she cried. "I need to. I've held this all in for so long." Edie took a handkerchief from her apron to wipe her eyes and then began again. "I got to hold her and rock her, and I was so happy. And then . . . and then, two days later, she was gone." A long silence, then, "And after that, no more came."

"But that doesn't mean it will happen to you, Edie. You can't lose faith."

Edie laughed in soft bitterness. "Do you know how many times I've told myself that? 'You have to have faith, Edie. You just have to have more faith.'"

Emma's face contorted and tears sprang to her eyes. "Oh, Edie, I'm sorry. I didn't mean it—"

"No, no, Emma. I'm not criticizing you. It's just that. . . ." She wiped her eyes again and blew her nose. "I was fourteen when my parents were called to come to the San Juan Mission. By that time I had been praying every morning and every night for years that I would be able to have a family of my own. And I decided I wanted my patriarchal blessing before we left. Richfield had a stake patriarch by then, but he knew our family so well that I was afraid he would just tell me what I wanted to hear."

Edie shook her head ruefully. "I know, I know. That was immature of me, but it meant so much to me. So Papa took me to Salt Lake City and I got my blessing from the Church patriarch.

Emma was surprised. "I didn't know that you've received your patriarchal blessing. How wonderful."

Edie barely heard her. "The patriarch's name was John Smith, and Mama and Papa were a little bit in awe, because he was the son of Hyrum Smith and nephew of Joseph Smith. But all I could think about was, 'Will he promise me that I'm going to have children?' Even when he put his hands on my head, I kept saying to myself, 'Please, please. Tell me I'm going to have children.'"

"And did he?" Emma asked, crying openly now too.

"No, not really. He said I would have a family, but that was all. Nothing more specific than that." There was a fleeting smile. "Except that he did talk about my husband. He promised me that if I would marry in the temple, I would find a faithful man who would make me the queen of his home."

"Well, I think that one is being fulfilled," Emma said with a smile. "Sometimes I laugh in open delight when I see how much Mitch loves you."

Edie managed to smile back. "Yes." Then the smile faded. "But there was no promise about children. I was so upset that I cried all the way back to Richfield. I needed more than that. I needed a promise I could hold on to, that I could cling to. But it wasn't there."

"Oh, Edie, Edie, Edie. My heart weeps for you. But just because Brother Smith didn't specifically talk about children doesn't mean that you won't have any. My father used to tell me that a patriarchal blessing is not a map that shows which roads we have to take, but more like a compass to show us the right direction. If the Lord promised you a family, that sounds like you'll have children of your own and. . . ." The look on Edie's face caused Emma to stop.

"I know, but . . . I was so hoping for a road map. I was hoping for something specific so that I could stop worrying about it."

Both women were silent as Edie finished. Edie couldn't look

at Emma. The guilt was back. Did she think she was the first woman in the world who had faced this problem? Her mother had endured it and found happiness. Her grandmother too.

Edie sighed and finally managed a wan smile. "But back to the original question. Why not get married in September or October?

"Yes, especially knowing all of that."

She sighed. "There are two main reasons to wait until spring."

"You want to be married on your birthday."

Edie chuckled and shook her head. "Ironically, that's more important to Mitch than it is to me. Not sure why, but he thinks it would be really special. But for me, it is a 'nice to,' not a 'have to.' But being married in the temple, and especially the Manti Temple, is very important to me. I was five years old when they announced that a temple was going to be built in Manti. Everyone in central Utah was ecstatic. A temple of our own. When I was seven, my parents took me to the groundbreaking. And while they were actually sticking the shovels into the ground to turn over the dirt, my Oma Zimmer laid a hand on my shoulder and whispered in my ear, 'Edna Rae, this is where you are going to be married. I want you to remember that.' And I felt this little thrill go through me, and I knew she was right."

"That's wonderful. But, Edie, they've announced that the Manti Temple will be dedicated next month. Not by your birthday this year, probably, but definitely by this fall."

"I know, but fall will be a really busy time for Mitch too, especially with getting the house ready for us to live in. Going to Manti and back will take two to three weeks. He can't just leave."

Emma's mind was racing. Surely there were answers to that problem.

"But there's a bigger problem," Edie continued, "and it also has to do with Oma Zimmer."

Emma's brow wrinkled in puzzlement.

"My grandparents on my father's side were born in Switzerland and then moved to Germany shortly after they were married. Actually, my father was born in Germany. They came to America when he was ten."

"I didn't know that. He doesn't speak with an accent."

"Oh, no, not Papa. When he first came to America the other boys made fun of his accent, so he changed his name from Franz to Frank and learned to speak English like a native. But anyway, when my grandfather died, Oma Zimmer came to live with my parents. I was six or seven, so basically I grew up with her as a second mother. I am very close to her. When my parents were called on a mission to come to Bluff, they had mixed emotions. Oma Zimmer has bad arthritis in her hands, and the doctors said that the hot, dry climate would be good for her. But they also knew that pioneer life would be very difficult for her, so she stayed in Richfield with my uncle. They planned to bring her out to live once things were settled, but it keeps getting postponed because my parents keep talking about going back to Richfield."

"I had heard that," Emma said.

"So one day, when I was talking about this whole thing with Mitch, he said, 'Well, why not let your grandmother live with us?' I was elated, and so was Oma Zimmer when I wrote to her. So that's our plan. We'll bring her back with us after the wedding next spring."

Emma was nodding now. "And you're afraid that if she comes here for the winter it will be too hard on her?"

"Maybe if we had the cabin completely finished, with her own bedroom . . ."

"Ah," Emma said, understanding at last.

"So as much as I would like to be married this fall," Edie concluded, "I . . ." Her shoulders lifted and fell. "It's not going to happen."

Notes

Nathaniel Alvin and Emma Morris Decker came to San Juan in the first pioneer company along with about twenty others in their extended family. They arrived in Bluff on April 6, 1880. Emma was in the early stages of pregnancy when they left Parowan in October 1879, but since the journey took six months instead of the predicted six weeks, she was in the last stages of her pregnancy for those last difficult two months. On April 12, 1880, just six days after their arrival at Bluff Fort, she gave birth to a baby boy in their wagon box. They named him Alvin Morris Decker (see David E. Miller, *Hole-in-the-Rock: An Epic in the Colonization of the Great American West* [Salt Lake City: University of Utah Press, 1966], 179; see also Decker Family Records). She went on to have seven more children, one about every two years. All but one lived long and prosperous lives. The boy born in the wagon box lived to be eighty-six.

Alvin and Emma Decker were one of the first families to settle in the Blue Mountain Mission. They came with the first group called in the summer of 1887 and then returned the following summer. But sometime during that second summer, they moved with their family to Mancos, Colorado. Alvin and Emma are both buried in the Weber Cemetery in Mancos (see *Saga,* 308, and Decker family history sheet on FamilySearch.org).

John Smith, son of Hyrum Smith, served as patriarch to the Church from 1855 until 1911 (see *Encyclopedia of Mormonism,* 3:1065).

The Manti Temple was announced on June 25, 1875. It was finished and opened to the public in May 1888 and dedicated on May 21. It was the third operating temple in Utah after the St. George (dedicated 1877) and Logan (dedicated 1884) temples.

CHAPTER 4

April 12, 1888, 8:05 a.m.—Westland Home Site—Monticello

Edie watched Mitch expertly work the ax and cut a notch in the end of a six-foot length of aspen log. The chips flew as he rhythmically swung. He stopped, brushed the chips away, and examined his work. He set the ax aside and reached for the draw knife.

"Are you sure I can't help you?" Edie asked as he began to smooth the cut.

"In a minute. Almost done."

She was seated on a stump a few feet away with her back to the morning sun. "I talked to Sister Walton this morning," she said after a moment.

He glanced up. "And?"

"Emma was right. She was pleased to have me stay with Maggie and Leona."

"That's good. I'm glad, Edie. That's a relief to have such a good solution."

"And the timing will be perfect, too. Jane is going to accompany the Deckers to Mancos and start the first of her visits to the branch Relief Societies. I'll move my stuff over to the Waltons' the night before they leave."

Bending down, Mitch blew the last of the chips from the notch, eyed it for a moment, and then straightened. "All the better," he said. He set the draw knife on a nearby log and walked a few steps to where the block and tackle hung from the sturdiest of the cedar trees. "All right," he said, pulling a pair of gloves from his back pocket. "If you can work the rope and lift one end of the log, I'll hoist the other end up. Put on my gloves, because the rope can burn your hands."

He showed her what to do and then looped the end of the rope with the iron hook on it around one end of the log a couple of times and cinched it tight. In three easy pulls, he lifted the end of the log about three feet off the ground. Then he handed Edie the rope. "Okay. Hold on to the rope. I'm going to lift the other end of the log. As I raise my end up, you raise yours to keep it mostly level. Then hold your end steady while I swing my end over and put it in place. Then I'll come and put your end in place and that will be it."

Edie was, of course, familiar with how a block and tackle worked. "I'm ready when you are."

It went exactly as Mitch described it, and in less than a minute, they had the log in place. Mitch let it drop into its slot with a satisfying *thunk* and then stepped back, grinning. "That finishes course number five," he said, eying his work with satisfaction. "What do you think, Sister Zimmer? Is it starting to look like a cabin yet?"

"Oh, yes, Mitch. And it's going to be wonderful."

"Unfortunately, from here on in, it will take three of us to lift the logs into those higher courses. The Waltons will be to that same stage by tomorrow, so we'll do them next. Then, Charles and Charlie and Mons will come and help me."

"Sounds wonderful," she replied. "I can hardly wait."

Mitch came and slipped an arm around Edie's waist. "I like it when you're up here with me."

"As do I," she said. But she wasn't smiling. She put her hands on her hips. "Mitch?"

"What?"

"It's Thursday, you know."

Mitch didn't look up, but grunted something unintelligible.

"You promised me, Mitch. Your tooth is not better. It's worse. Don't you think I can tell?"

He said nothing.

"Mitch? You promised me."

"We're going back up for another load of logs tomorrow, but I'll talk to Brother Hyde about it. He's going with us."

"You promised me you would do it today."

"Edie, sometimes things come up that you have no control over. I will tomorrow."

Her lips pressed tightly together. "Why are you being so stubborn?"

"If we don't get more logs cut and down here, all work on our cabins stops. It's only one more day."

"Fine," she snapped. "I told Emma I'd be back in time to help her with the laundry. Bye."

"Aw, come on, Edie. I'll do it Saturday. I have been pretty busy here, you know," he said petulantly. He came over and tried to put his arms around her.

She sidestepped him neatly and started away, flouncing her skirts. But she stopped and whirled on him. "Next Monday, we are supposed to leave for Bluff, and from there you go out after your cows for a week or more. Why is it that I'm the only one worrying about this?"

"All right, all right," he said. "As soon as I'm finished this evening, I'll talk to Ed."

She lifted her chin. "You do what you have to do, and I'll do what I have to do."

"Edie! You promised me you wouldn't talk to Brother Hyde before I do."

"And you promised me you'd talk to him today."

8:27 a.m.

On the quarter-mile walk back into town, Edie debated with herself whether to stop and talk with Brother Edward Hyde. She had promised Mitch to give him until Thursday. And it was still Thursday. But she was also worried. Despite all of his protestations to the contrary, she could tell that the tooth was taking a toll on him. He ate as though his food might be spiked with thorns, and he was even starting to mumble a little when he spoke.

As Edie approached the Hydes' place, she slowed her pace. Should she keep her word or not? She was just coming up on Mons Peterson's cabin, and she saw that he was on a ladder, working on the first of the rafters that would become the roof. Edie and Mitch had become good friends with Mons and Eliza Peterson, even though the Petersons were several years older than they were. And Mons owed Mitch a favor because he had been helping him. Perfect!

She changed direction slightly and walked over to the cabin. Mons saw her and looked down at her. "Mornin', Sister Edie."

She gave him one of her brightest smiles. "Good morning, Mons." She squinted at the first of the rafters. "Looks like you're making progress."

"Slow but sure. How are things looking up at your site? From here it looks like you and Mitch got another couple of courses up."

"We did, though I'm not much help."

"Every pair of hands is valuable." He was watching her curiously. "Are you looking for Eliza? She's down at the creek with the children."

"Actually, I was hoping I could talk with you for a moment."

"Oh?" He was clearly surprised, and he climbed down from the ladder. "How can I help you?"

She told him about Mitch's tooth. He grinned. "And he's toughing it out, right?"

"Exactly. He's been taking some laudanum for the pain, but it's not going away."

Frowning, Mons said, "If he's taking laudanum that says a lot. You need to get him to Ed. He hasn't had any formal training, but he's got a medical book and has helped quite a few people out. I think he's even pulled a few teeth."

"That's what I've heard. Mitch said that maybe he'll talk to him, but unless he's laid out flat on his back, I don't think he will."

Mons muttered something that sounded like "stubborn old cuss" and then half turned and looked across the street and down several lots to the Hyde home site. A large tent was there, and two or three courses of logs were behind it. Mons raised one hand and cupped it to his mouth. "Halloo, Ed." He waited a moment and then called again. "Brother Hyde. Are you there?"

For a moment, Edie nearly panicked. She hadn't expected something quite so direct and immediate. But then she thought, "Why not?" She *hadn't* talked to Brother Hyde; Mons had. She turned toward the Hyde tent.

William Edward Hyde had the same first name as his father, so he went by Edward or Ed. His parents now lived in Mancos, but Ed and Emma had decided to answer the call to settle the Blue Mountain Mission. The Hydes were in their midthirties and had six children ranging in age from about thirteen to a baby a year old.

A moment later, the tent flap opened and Ed Hyde stuck his head out and looked around.

"Over here, Ed," Mons called, waving a hand. "Do you have a minute?"

Brother Hyde waved a hand, ducked back in the tent, and a moment later reappeared with his hat on. He came and joined them. "Mornin', Sister Edie," he said, touching the brim of his hat.

"Good morning, Brother Hyde."

Mons quickly told him of the situation with Mitch. As he did so, Emma Hyde came out of their tent and came over to join them. "Is there a problem?" she asked Edie. Edie nodded, but again Mons quickly filled her in.

"His mouth is sore enough that he can barely eat anymore," Edie explained.

Brother Hyde grunted. "Which tooth is it, can you tell?"

Edie touched her left lower jaw. "It's right here, near the back."

"Yup. Bet you a nickel it's an impacted wisdom tooth," he said.

Edie swallowed quickly, not liking the sound of that.

Brother Hyde smiled wryly. "Not sure how much wisdom a seventeen-year-old has, but it's not uncommon for wisdom teeth to grow in crooked around that age. Sometimes the teeth get so crowded that the wisdom teeth can't break through. That's what impacted means, and I'm guessing that's what's bothering Brother Mitch."

"Will it go away on its own?"

"If it's just a wisdom tooth pushing straight up, once it cuts through the gum, the problem is solved. But if it's impacted and pushing on the other teeth, it can cause some real grief. I'm guessing it needs to come out."

Edie let out her breath in relief. She liked Brother Hyde. He was a big man with a squarish head that sat on a thick neck, giving him the look of a blacksmith. But he was affable, with a wry sense of humor, and his wife, who was a wisp of a woman compared to him, had been one of the many sisters who had taken to mothering Edie and preparing her for her upcoming marriage. She liked their family very much.

Ed turned to Mons. "Why don't you and I go up and I'll take a look at him? If I'm right, we'll bring him back down here." He grinned. "At the end of a rope, if we have to." Then to Edie and his wife, he said, "You two get things ready down here. Have the girls take the rest of the children off to play somewhere."

"You'll want a kettle of boiling water, right?" Emma asked.

"Yes. And bring one of the cots outside, along with our dressing table. We'll want as much light as possible."

"Thank you," Edie said softly. There was a wan smile. "I may hide for a while when you bring him down. He's not going to be happy with me."

"He won't be now," Emma agreed, "but he will be once it's out." Then to her husband, she added, "Mitch is strong as an ox. Do you want us to get another man or two?"

"Definitely. At least two more—one to hold his head still and one to help Mons stop him from flailing his arms and legs."

"I can help," Edie said, feeling a little sick at the thought of what was coming for Mitch.

Both men were shaking their heads. "Knowing Mitch," Mons said, "he's not going to want you around while this happens. This isn't going to be pretty."

"I don't care whether he wants me there or not," she retorted. "I'm staying right by his side."

9:45 a.m.

"No, Edie! Please!" Mitch, who was lying on the cot, turned his head. "Sister Hyde, see if you can talk some sense into her."

Emma looked at Edie. "He's right, Edie. It's better that you wait somewhere else."

Edie shook her head stubbornly. "I'm staying."

Emma looked to her husband as Mitch grumbled something under his breath. Ed shrugged. "You two are going to have to work that out between you. I have no objection if she stays."

They were outside of the tent, in the shade of one of the Hyde wagons. Because of the size of their family, the Hydes had two wagons and a spacious tent. Water was boiling in a kettle hanging over a bed of glowing coals. A small dressing table stood near the head of the cot and had several clean cloths on it, along with a bottle of medicine and a basin of cool water. Seven adults stood around the cot waiting for direction. Looking around, Ed seemed satisfied and started giving instructions.

"Emma, did you give Mitch some laudanum?"

"Yes. One dose as soon as he got here."

"Good, give him another." Then to Mitch, "The laudanum will only take the worst edge off the pain. It's going to feel like the fires of Hades when I cut open the gum to get at the tooth."

Edie blanched and swallowed hard. *Cut open the gum?* She hadn't considered that.

"I understand," Mitch said quietly. "I'm ready."

"Mons," Ed continued, "I want you to hold his head. Fred, you hold his feet. Charles, you take one arm, Emma, you take the other. He's going to be thrashing like a bucking bronco, but you have to hold him still while I'm working on him."

Brother Hyde looked over at Edie. "Sister Zimmer, bring that kettle of water over and put it beside the table within reach." He picked up a leather bag lying beside the cot that was filled with something heavy and clunked metallically as he lifted it. "We have to sterilize my instruments before we start working on him."

"All right." Edie grabbed one of the small hand towels, folded it twice, and went to the fire. Using the towel as a hot pad, she lifted the kettle off the fire and brought it back. Ed pointed to where he wanted it. As she set it down, Brother Hyde withdrew a two-foot-long pair of blacksmith's tongs from the bag and held them out to her. She almost shrank back. *What were those for? They were far too large to fit into Mitch's mouth.*

He nudged her gently. "Into the water. You'll use these to get the other things out, but it has to be sterilized too. But only the tongs, not the handles, okay?"

As she complied, Ed leaned over the kettle and dumped the contents of his bag into the steaming water. Edie gaped as she saw what he had meant by his "instruments." There was an ordinary pair of pliers like you saw in every tool box and a pair of needle-nose pliers. There was a miniature hammer made of chrome steel and three different-sized chisels. And lying on the top of it all was a pair of blacksmith's pincers, slightly larger than the pliers.

As Edie stared at them in the bottom of the kettle, her stomach lurched violently as she realized this was how Brother Hyde was going to get the tooth out. *Yank it out, to put it more accurately? Or knock it out with the hammer and chisel?*

Brother Hyde was watching her closely. "Are you all right?" he asked softly.

"Yes," she croaked. "I'm okay."

He studied her for another moment and then removed a hunting knife from the sheath on his belt. Its long, narrow blade gleamed in the light. Edie told herself to turn away, but she couldn't. Ed reached over and picked up a whetstone from the table and began putting a final edge on the blade. Back and forth, back and forth, the steel whispered softly as it was stroked across the stone. When he dropped that into the kettle too, Edie closed her eyes. *I can't do this.*

She opened her eyes again when she felt a hand on her arm. She was looking into the eyes of Emma Hyde. "Edie," Emma said, so softly she could barely be heard by the others, "there are some images that you are better off not to have in your head, because they stay with you for a lifetime. Go. We'll take care of Mitch, and we'll call you when we're done."

And with that, Edie whirled and bolted away. She didn't stop until she was out behind Mons Peterson's cabin, where she could not hear or see anything that was about to happen.

Notes

William and Angeline Hyde and their extended family were some of the first pioneers to come to the San Juan Mission. They came from Salt Lake City, where William had been on the police force. In addition to the small trading post he ran in Montezuma Creek, he had invested in the trading post out at the Rincon with his son-in-law, Amasa Barton, who was killed at the post.

William Edward Hyde and his wife, Emma Tolman, came to Bluff in 1887 and to the Blue Mountains in 1888. Of Edward, one historian wrote: "Edward Hyde set broken bones or extracted teeth when necessity arose, with any kind of crude instrument that would clamp over the teeth" (see *Saga*, 312).

CHAPTER 5

April 18, 1888, 7:40 p.m.—Arthur Westland Home —Bluff City, San Juan County

"Pa?"

"Yes, son?"

"What are you thinking you'll do with your cattle?"

Arthur Westland sat up straight in his chair. He had been slouching down, looking like he was ready to fall asleep. "Not sure what you mean, Mitch."

"You wanna sell the rest of them? Get out of the cattle business altogether?"

That got his attention. And also that of Mitch's mother, Gwen. She didn't say anything, but turned to watch her husband curiously.

"I . . . I dunno. Been thinking a little about going into partnership with a couple of other men here. Open up a mercantile store and do our own freighting, maybe do some freighting on the side. But that won't be this year."

Mitch glanced at his mother. "Sounds like you have decided that you're not moving back."

She frowned. "We decided that quite a while ago."

"I did promise your mother I'd take her back to Beaver to see the rest of the family."

"That's wonderful," Mitch said. "This summer?"

"Yes. In about a month." She beamed happily. "We were

holding off deciding until we learned whether there was going to be a wedding during our absence."

"I'm envious. I'll bet all the nieces and nephews have grown a foot by now. I hope they'll all come to the wedding next summer too."

"Of course they will," Gwen said. "I wrote them a letter this morning to tell them about your official announcement."

Mitch sat beside his father. "So are you going to try to keep the cows and do the other work too?"

"Probably not."

Mitch leaned forward. "Then why don't you let me take yours up to the Blues with mine? Saves you having to worry about them. Blue Mountain grass is pretty sweet, and there's more of it than there is down here. I'll fatten them up for you. Then come fall, I can take as many of yours as you want to sell and drive them up with mine to Thompson Springs. That's about ninety miles from Monticello. They say the big Midwest slaughterhouses are sending buyers out west this fall. Rumor is they'll be paying top dollar."

Mitch's mother picked up her chair and came and sat in front of them. "How many head do you think you have now, Mitch?" she asked.

"About sixty. Maybe sixty-five, if I can find them all." He looked at his father. "You?"

"Fifteen to twenty, if we can find them all."

"We'll find them."

Arthur shook his head. "Maybe not this year. But I'll get to that in a minute. How will the Carlisle bunch feel if you bring that many head back with you?"

Mitch shrugged. "They're running maybe two thousand head on about sixty square miles of landscape. Adding a hundred head into sixty squares miles is like putting water into the ocean with an eyedropper. They'll never notice, but if they do push us, we'll push back."

"Maybe I am interested then."

"If the price holds for on-the-hoof beef, I'll pay off the rest of what I owe you this fall."

"I'm not worried about that, son."

"I am. So why will there be more challenge than usual finding my cattle this year?"

"You haven't heard about the ELKM outfit?"

"No. Can't say that I have. Where do they come from?"

"Texas. Abilene, maybe Fort Worth. Not sure, exactly. But that's almost a thousand miles from here. That's a pretty impressive cattle drive. Especially when you consider that they brought over two thousand head with them."

Mitch gave a low whistle. "*Two thousand?*"

"Yes," Gwen spoke up. "You should have seen them. It took over two hours just to trail them through town."

Mitch was still trying to grasp the idea of what it would take to drive two thousand head of beef anywhere. "And where were they taking them?"

"Here."

"What?"

Arthur frowned. "The outfit's headquarters are at the Rincon. Using the old Barton Trading Post. They call themselves the ELKM Ranch. What does that tell you?"

Mitch gave a low cry as it clicked for him. "Elk Mountain?"

"That's right. And their animals are spread from the Rincon to Elk Mountain."

"But that's our grazing land."

Arthur shook his head in disgust. "They've already appropriated some of the best springs and grazing areas up on the mountain."

Mitch jumped to his feet. "They can't do that. We have that treaty with the Utes. That's our land, and. . . ." He stopped. Even as he spoke, he knew that wasn't exactly true.

"That's right," his father nodded. "We do have the treaty, and we continue to pay the Utes fifty dollars a year and give them a lot of free food, but technically, it's all public domain. We already share it with some of the other cattle outfits. Nothing deters this bunch. They've got a lot of cowboys, and some of them are pretty rough."

"Tell him the rest," Mitch's mother prodded.

"The rest?" Mitch said. He turned back to his father. "What else?"

"Every last one of those two thousand cows is a Texas Longhorn."

8:05 p.m.—Zimmer Home—Bluff City

Mitch was still fuming when he reached Edie's house and knocked on the door. She answered immediately, but to his surprise, she had a shawl around her shoulders and stepped out beside him, shutting the door behind her. The sun was low in the sky, but it was still full light.

He gave her a puzzled look, seeing that she was clearly troubled. But when he went to speak, she shook her head and motioned for them to move away from the house. Suddenly there was a little ping of anxiety in his mind. "You okay?" he asked.

"I told Mama and Papa that we wanted to go for a walk." Then she peered up at him more closely. "And what's the matter with you? You look furious."

"I am furious. But that can wait. You tell me first. Is something wrong?"

Edie took Mitch's elbow and started them toward the front gate. "Shall we go to our usual talking place, the old Swing Tree?"

"Fine," he agreed. The feeling that something was wrong was getting stronger. So as they reached the front gate, he stopped and turned to face her. "What is it, Edie? You're starting to worry me. Does going down to the Swing Tree mean I'm in trouble again?"

She took both of his hands and laughed. "No, Mitch. This isn't about us. No, no, no."

"Whew," he said as he started walking again. "My heart kind of dropped there for a second."

Edie smiled. "Nothing is coming between you and me ever, ever again."

"Good."

They passed a few people who called out congratulations on their way down to the river, but no one stopped to talk. Neither Mitch nor Edie spoke until they reached the Swing Tree. There were three girls in their young teens there, but when they saw them approaching, they quickly left.

"Do you want to swing?"

Edie shook her head. "Maybe in a few minutes. Let's just sit for now."

They went over to the same log they had used on the night when things once fell apart between them. Edie took Mitch's hand but didn't look at him. Instead, she stared out across the river. When she finally looked up, she let out a long and painful sigh. "My parents are going back to Richfield," she said without preamble.

That took him totally aback. "They are? Wow! When did they decide that?"

"About two weeks ago. Mama had actually written me a letter that she was going to send up with the other families, but when we came they told me in person."

"How soon?"

"The first week of June. Papa wants to make sure the mountain passes are open. They'll probably be traveling alone, so he doesn't want to take a chance of getting stuck somewhere."

Mitch nodded. That was just good sense. "But why now? I got the impression when we were with them last night that his freighting business was doing all right."

"It is. But Mama's never really been happy here. She loves the people, but the heat and the dust and the isolation—" Edie shook her head. "It's been hard on her. So that's not a surprise. But the clincher was that Papa has an offer from a freight outfit in Mancos. They want to buy him out— wagons, teams, and all."

"That'll be a blow to Bluff and to us up north."

"No, the buyers have committed to keep freighting in goods to the settlements here. And they should. It's been a profitable business for Papa. But now they can afford to return to Richfield and buy back in with his brothers in their freight business. They're doing really well."

"I'm so sorry, Edie." Monticello was about sixty miles from Bluff, which meant they already didn't get to see her parents very often, but it was a lot closer than Richfield.

"Oma Zimmer will be very pleased. She loves all her children, of course, but she's always been closest to Daddy. They'll buy a home big enough for her to live with them." Edie turned and looked at Mitch. "They waited until today to announce it because Mama refused to leave until she knew what was going on between you and me. And they are thrilled about the marriage. Mama's so happy for me. And Papa is too. Especially now."

"What will this mean for Oma Zimmer coming to live with us?"

Edie's face fell. "I asked that too. They're not sure. Her arthritis was particularly bad this last winter, so she really needs a dryer, warmer climate. But with my parents going back, it will mean she has to leave them if she comes here." She turned and faced Mitch squarely. "Would you mind terribly if I didn't go back up to Monticello with the other families next week? I think I need to stay and help Mama and Papa pack."

"Of course I don't mind. What about the Deckers?"

"Leona is helping Emma with the children. She can do that until I get back."

"Stay as long as you need to. There'll be other families coming up later. Or I'll come down for you whenever you like."

"Thank you," she said. "Now then, enough of my troubles. What has got you so riled up?"

Mitch harrumphed a little and then told her what he'd learned from his father. "Longhorns, if you can believe it. They brought in Texas Longhorns."

Edie seemed puzzled. "I should probably know this, but tell me, why are you so upset that they're Longhorns? Isn't a cow a cow?"

The look of horror on his face made her laugh. "Sorry. I take it the answer to that is no."

"There are huge differences between the various breeds, which I won't go into right now, but the Texas Longhorn looks like some kind of mistake on God's part."

"Mitch Westland!" she teased. "You shouldn't say things like that. It's sacrilegious."

"Wait until you see one, then you'll know what I mean.

They're a tough breed, I'll give you that. They do really well in arid climates like ours. That's why they like them in Texas, especially in West Texas. But they're not a really good beef cow. The meat tends to be tough and stringy. And they're just plain odd-looking. Their front quarters and the hind quarters are closer together than in other breeds. It's like they're all scrunched together. Then, to finish it off, they've got those awful horns that have as much as a three- or four-foot spread. Put it all together, and I'm telling you, you've got one ugly cow."

"I had no idea there was a beauty contest for cows. But you don't have to own them, so what does it matter to you?" Edie shrugged. "Just don't buy any of them."

Mitch gave her a sharp look. "Edie, these cattle are range cattle. They roam freely anywhere they can find grass." When she still just looked at him, he leaned in closer. "*As do my cows.*"

"Oooohhhhh."

"Yes, exactly. If I don't get my cattle out of there, and quickly, next spring I'm gonna have a whole bunch of half-breed calves." He took a deep breath and let it out slowly. "So, all of that is to say that Pa and I may take longer to round up our cows than I thought. So, it's good that you want to stay longer too. Not sure how long we'll be, but we can talk when I get back."

"How long would you guess?"

"At least a week. Maybe ten days. But at least you'll still be here when I get back."

"Yes, I'm glad for that. Will you come say good-bye before you leave tomorrow?"

He gave her a quizzical look. "We're leaving at dawn. Sure you want me to?"

"Uh. . . ." She smiled coyly. "It does feel so good to sleep in a real bed again instead of on a cot. Why don't you just kiss me good-bye right now?"

8:55 p.m.—Westland Home—Bluff City

As Mitch approached his parents' home, he noticed that the front door was half open. Through the curtains on the window he could see two men sitting with his parents, but their backs were to him, so he couldn't tell who they were. A little surprised to have visitors this late in the evening, he increased his pace.

When Mitch took off his hat and entered the home, he stopped short. There were actually three men sitting in the living room with his parents. Two he recognized instantly as they stood up. The first was Kumen Jones; the second was Lemuel H. Redd, or Lem, as everyone called him. Both were smiling broadly as Mitch's father said, "Ah, here he is."

Kumen Jones was closest and stepped forward, extending his hand. "Mary tells me I missed the big announcement last night," he said as they shook hands vigorously. "Congratulations."

"Thanks." He turned as Lemuel Redd came over, hand outstretched. "Evenin', Lem," Mitch said. "Good to see you again."

"And you, Mitch. Eliza and I extend our congratulations as well."

"Thank you."

Lem turned to the third man, who was right behind him. He was young, about Mitch's age. "Do you know Joe Hammond, from Mancos? President Hammond's boy?"

"Yeah," Mitch replied as they shook hands. "Ate at his table a few years back when I was over working on the railroad in Colorado. Good to see you again, Joe." Then Mitch turned to the two older men. "This brings back some memories. You're not going out after Moenkopi Mike again, I hope."

Lem chuckled. "Kumen and I were talking about that very thing on the way over. How long ago was that? Four years?"

"Yes," Mitch's mother said. "And we had been in the valley here only two or three days, as I remember. It wasn't the most auspicious beginning for our family, I might add."

Lem's smile quickly faded. "And I'm afraid we're here to ask if we can borrow both your husband and your son again, Sister Westland."

If his mother was surprised at that, she gave no sign. She only smiled and said, "I've got some oatmeal cookies I made earlier today. And some milk cooling in the well. Any takers?"

Five hands came up. "Ah, now, Sister Westland," Lem drawled as he slapped his stomach, "if you're gonna tempt me like that, you've gotta promise not to tell my Eliza on me."

"Promise," she said, clearly pleased. "Okay, cookies all around."

As she went into the kitchen, Lem turned to Mitch. "Your father was just telling us that he told you a little about the ELKM outfit."

"He did. And I'm still fuming. Whatever you've got in mind, count us in."

Kumen leaned forward and looked at Arthur. "How much have you told him?"

Arthur shook his head. "Not much. He had to go see Edie."

"Well then," he said to Mitch, "here's the situation. This is a big outfit. About forty riders. And half of them or more are running from the law.

Kumen spoke again. "They're ugly, mean, spoiling for a fight, and totally without scruples."

"And they hate the Mormons," Joe Hammond added.

Mitch pulled a face. "That sounds familiar. And they like it here because it is some of the most desolate, isolated country in the whole United States."

"Exactly," Joe Hammond came in, "which is convenient

if you're in the business of rustling other people's cattle and horses."

That got Mitch's full attention. "Is that what they're doing?" He looked at his father. "Is that what you meant about not finding our cows?"

"Yes," his father said grimly. "But we haven't been able to prove it."

Just then, Gwen came back with a tray of cookies on tin plates. "Mitch, Arthur, can you bring in the milk? It's on the table."

No one spoke until the cookies were served, but then, after a few compliments to the cook, the men immediately returned to their conversation, eating as they talked. Gwen sat down beside Arthur.

Kumen looked at Mitch. "Have you heard of the M-pole brand?"

Mitch shook his head.

Kumen's voice turned grim. "We started finding cattle—Herefords, not Texas Longhorns—that had these horrific branding scars that ran across the length of their bodies, some from the ears to the tail."

"What?" Mitch was stunned. "Why?"

"Well, first of all," Kumen went on, "we've been fighting isolated cases of rustling since we got here. There's always a cowpoke or two willing to put their brand on a sleeper calf, or even use a running iron to try to change one of our brands."

Before Mitch could respond, his mother interrupted. "I'm sorry, but what are sleeper calves and running irons?"

"A sleeper calf," Mitch is explained, "is an unbranded calf that has somehow gotten separated from its mother and is found wandering alone. Since it's hard to identify who it belongs to, the law of the open range is that the first man to find it and put his brand on it gets to legally keep it. That seems kind of harsh, but there's no way to prove who it belongs to, so. . . ." He shrugged. "But some cowboys will find a calf that's close to being weaned and cut it away from its mother. They drive it far enough away that the mother can't find it. After a few days, the mother gives up, and you have turned a supposed 'sleeper calf' into a calf that is now yours."

Lem picked it up from there. "As far as running irons, some cattle rustlers use a straight piece of iron, very much like a poker, to 'write over' someone else's brand. It's called a running iron because you can manipulate it any way you like, like drawing with a pencil. So, if you're clever, you come up with a new, larger brand that totally blots out the old brand."

Gwen was clearly shocked. She knew about rustling, of course, but she had never known the details of how it was actually done.

"In most cases out here in the West," Arthur spoke up, "being caught with a running iron in your bedroll is considered a hanging offense."

"That's horrible," Gwen exclaimed.

Kumen responded. "But this bunch has taken things to a new level. More and more cattlemen are branding their animals in two or three places to make it harder for rustlers to get away with branding over them. We'll brand on the back and the front haunches or on the neck. And we're starting to cut unique notches in the animals' ears to help identify them." Now he turned to Mitch. "But that doesn't stop this bunch. They came up with the M-pole brand. They use a much thicker running iron. Then they write 'ELKM' with it. Only they do it in huge letters, starting on the neck and taking it all the way back to the tail. That way they blot out any possible brand."

"That is ghastly," Gwen said with a shudder.

"Yes, it is," Lem replied. "And if the animal has a notched ear, they burn half the ear off."

"But that is so obvious," Mitch replied. "If they have an animal like that, just arrest them."

"These are bad men, Mitch, but they are not stupid. They brand their own cows in the same way, so there's no way to prove for sure what they're doing unless you catch them in the very act." Lem turned to Kumen. "Which brings us to why we're here."

Kumen leaned forward in his chair and spoke. "A bunch of us have been out in Comb Wash and Butler Wash rounding up our animals to take them up to summer pasture. Yesterday, near sundown, as I was out making one last sweep, I heard the lowing of cattle. When I followed the sound, I found three temporary holding corrals with about forty or fifty head in one of the side canyons."

Mitch nearly leaped out of his chair. "Our cattle?"

There was a grim nod. "No one was around, so I snuck down for a look. Some are ELKM cows, but most not." He glanced at Mitch and Arthur. "I counted more than a dozen with the Flying-W Brand."

Mitch felt his blood go hot. A dozen head was worth five or six hundred dollars.

Kumen continued. "They've obviously used this place before. There are several fire rings near the corrals, and I found running irons in the bedrolls there. I hid there waiting for an hour until they came back. There were five of them. They said they were going to spend two more days rounding up whatever they could find and then brand them before they take them up to Elk Mountain." He looked around the group. "When I heard that, I skittered out of there and rode all night and today to get back here. Got in about two hours ago."

"We've got to stop them," Mitch said, his voice trembling with anger.

Lem Redd actually grinned. "We thought you might say that." He turned to Hammond. "You take it from here, Joe."

Hammond was excited. "About two weeks ago, my pa—President Hammond—sent me to Salt Lake with a warrant to arrest unnamed rustlers operating in the areas west of Bluff. The marshal's office there immediately sent Deputy U.S. Marshal Joe Bush back with me. He's hired on two Navajo trackers to help him find the rustlers and see if we can't catch them in the act. That's important," he added, "because Bush says that no matter how incriminating the M-pole brand may look, it's not sufficient proof to stand up in court."

Arthur was excited by this. "And he's in town right now?"

Hammond's grin was slow and lazy. "Yup. Was getting ready to head out tomorrow when Kumen came riding in. He's ecstatic."

Lem came back in. "He's forming a posse. He's already deputized me, Kumen, and Joe. But he's hoping to get a couple more of the owners of the cows to join us."

Mitch leaped to his feet. "How soon do we leave?"

"At first light," Lem said. "We'd be right pleased to have you and Arthur with us."

Notes

While I have added a few details to support the narrative, this crisis brought on by the arrival of the Elk Mountain outfit is based on historical records. This includes the number of cattle they brought in, where they headquartered, the nature of the grotesque M-pole brand, and the shady ways that cowboys supplemented their own or their bosses' herds (see *Saga*, 78, 229–31; Norma Perkins Young, *Anchored Lariats on the San Juan Frontier* [Provo, UT: Community Press, 1985], 97–102; Albert R. Lyman, *Indians and Outlaws: Settling of the San Juan Frontier* [Salt Lake City: Bookcraft, Inc., 1962], 102–4; *History* 63–64, 70).

CHAPTER 6

April 19, 1888, 4:20 a.m.—Westland Cabin—Bluff City

Mitch turned as he heard a soft sound behind him. What he saw was not unexpected. "Mama, what are you doing up so early?"

"I wanted to say good-bye." She sighed. "Seems like I'm always doing that with you."

"I. . . ." Mitch shrugged. There was nothing to say to that.

Nodding, Gwen came and stood beside him and watched as he saddled his horse. "What did Edie say when you told her? You told her everything, I assume."

"I did. I feel bad. She had already gone to bed by the time I got back to her house. But I almost lost Edie once because I was treating her like she was still a little girl—her words, not mine. So I've determined that I'm always going to be honest with her. She is worried, of course, but it helps to know there's a whole group of us, including a U.S. Marshal."

Mitch stepped forward and took his mother's hands. "I've found a woman like you, Mama," he whispered. "Strong. Faithful. Courageous."

"Weepy," she added.

"Yes, that too," he chuckled.

"And there's something else, Mitch. Edie has a very special gift, you know."

"Oh?"

"Yes. I'm not sure how to describe it. Inspiration? Maybe revelation? But neither of those exactly captures it. So for now, I'm going to call it spiritual perceptiveness."

"Not sure what you mean."

"The night before she was to leave with Evelyn and Leona to go north, she came to say good-bye to us. And she was quite troubled. She had a bad feeling about it."

"Then why did she go?"

"That's what I asked her too. And she said that she also had a strong feeling that the Lord was going to do something to finally bring you two together."

"She said that?" he asked in astonishment.

"Yes. When you told us about her being caught in the blizzard and all that followed, I kept saying over and over to myself, 'Oh my word. Oh my word.'" Gwen went up on tiptoe and kissed her son's cheek. "It's a special gift, Mitch. Learn to trust it. Now, I'd better go get your father."

April 20, 1888, 5:25 a.m.—Upper Comb Wash, San Juan County

The posse consisted of eight men: Marshal Bush, Mitch, Arthur, Lem Redd, Kumen Jones, Joe Hammond, and the two Navajo trackers. Jim Jo, the older of the two Navajo, was about thirty. Though he wore buckskin moccasins, other than that he dressed in typical white man's clothes—Levi's, a thick leather belt with a silver buckle, a gun belt and revolver, a long-sleeved cotton shirt, and a straw cowboy hat. He was lean as a broomstick, with dark eyes that were always scanning the landscape around him. He spoke good English and seemed at ease with his companions, joining in their conversations and even joking with them.

The second Indian was younger, near twenty, and more muscular than his companion. Bush introduced him as one of the Manito brothers but always called him by his last name only. Manito spoke passable English but said little.

After almost twenty-four hours in the saddle, with only a few hour-long stops to rest and eat, they had reached the upper reaches of Comb Wash about an hour before dawn, leaving Mitch to marvel at Kumen's ability to guide them by the pale light of a half moon. They were on the east side of the wash, which ran basically north and south. Their positioning was deliberate. When the action started, the posse would have the sun at their backs and the cowboys would have it in their eyes.

They left their horses about a half mile above the wash and then moved silently into position above the side canyon, where a thick copse of cedar trees gave them good cover. It also allowed them to see the rustlers' camp down in the canyon about forty or fifty yards away.

Dawn was lighting the eastern sky, though the land itself was still dark. They had been in place for about half an hour now. All were sitting in a half circle behind Marshal Bush. He was seated too. His knees were up so he could rest his elbows on them and steady the field glasses he held up to his eyes. The rustler camp had been up now for about a quarter of an hour. They had dumped fresh wood on the coals of their campfire, hung a pot of coffee over it, and smoked cigarettes while one of them cooked up some johnnycake.

"I count only four men." Bush said as he lowered the glasses and turned to Kumen. "You sure there was five?"

"Positive," Kumen whispered back.

"I only count four saddle horses, too," Bush went on.

"Let's hope the fifth man was the boss," Lem responded softly, "and left these four to do the grunt work of branding them." Bush said nothing to that.

Mitch said, "It looks like their horses are still saddled. Are they going after more cows?"

Bush shook his head. "Rustlers keep their horses saddled when they're up to no good."

"No surprise there," Lem muttered.

"But I don't like having a fifth man out there we don't know about," Bush mused. Then he turned to Mitch's father. "Arthur, just to be sure, why don't you move downstream about a quarter mile and drop down into the wash. Find a good spot where you can make sure no one surprises us. If the shooting starts, come running."

Arthur nodded and immediately stood and backed silently away. Mitch watched him go with relief. Had Bush deliberately sent the oldest man in their group to the spot least likely to see action? Whatever the reason, Mitch was glad for it.

Bush was a big man, probably six feet four or so, and thick as a bull buffalo. He was somewhat of a hero to the Saints in San Juan County. Though he was not a Mormon or a native of Utah, he had none of the bias against the Mormons that so many nonmembers did. But he was most appreciated for bringing some semblance of law and order into the county, even if it was only infrequently. He carried a wicked-looking, sawed-off, double-barreled shotgun, which he wore in a scabbard on his belt wherever he went. There were numerous stories of him fearlessly taking on the most violent of men and bringing them to justice.

Bush removed his hat, swiped at the sweat on his forehead, and took out his canteen and drank deeply. The air was still cool, but he was clearly perspiring. When he finished drinking, he capped the canteen and lifted the glasses again. "Okay, good.

The man who seems to be their leader is laying wood on those two dead fire pits. That means they're gonna do some branding. Time to get into place. But remember, until we actually see them using a running iron on a cow that we know for sure isn't theirs, we don't have a case. So no one moves until my signal."

Everyone nodded. He turned to the two Navajo. "You two are my ghosts." He handed the glasses to Jim Jo. "Look on the opposite side of the wash, ten yards or so downstream from their camp. It looks like there's a rock shelf about ten feet above the floor of the wash. See it?"

Jim Jo grunted and handed back the glasses.

"Think you can get up there without being seen?"

"Does the puma see the scorpion before it stings him?" he scoffed, and then he disappeared.

"Manito," Bush went on. "I want you to work your way down into that middle corral. Get in among the cattle. When the action starts, those boys might try to turn those cows loose—cover their escape with a stampede. You make sure that doesn't happen, savvy?"

One brief nod and then he too left without a word.

Bush was speaking quietly but quickly now. "Lem, if those boys panic, their mostly likely escape route will be down the wash. Why don't you go down and hook up with Arthur? Make sure no one gets by you."

"Can do."

"Kumen," Bush went on. "I want you to do the same up the wash."

"Got it."

"Westland, you and Hammond stay with me. We'll be the ones getting these boys' attention. So let's see how close we can get without them seeing us."

6:49 a.m.

The first of the sun's rays were now throwing everything into sharp relief. Mitch and Marshal Bush were lying about five feet apart from each other behind a thick clump of sagebrush. Hammond was behind a boulder about sixty feet to their left. All had their weapons out but were patiently waiting. Now the cowboys were smoking one last cigarette while the irons got hot enough to burn hair.

By this point there was sufficient light for Mitch to see the rock shelf Bush had referred to with Jim Jo. He had been watching it closely now for several minutes but saw no sign of him. And now, with the sun up, it was too late. The shelf was no more than twenty yards from the cowboys' campsite. "Don't think Jim Jo's going to make it," he whispered to Bush.

Bush grinned lazily and handed Mitch the field glasses. "Look just to the left of that second shad scale bush. Look real good."

Mitch did, again, concentrating hard. Nothing. Then suddenly a tiny movement made him jump. It was as though the dirt itself had moved. And then something jumped into focus. There was a hump of dirt about the same length as a man, half hidden behind the shad scale. He hadn't seen that before.

He turned and gaped at Bush, who chuckled softly. "He's covered himself with dirt. Blends in pretty well, don't you think?" Suddenly, Bush motioned for the glasses again. "Look," he said. "The big guy's going to the corral. I think our little show is about to begin."

He was right. The cowboy who was the largest of the four was moving toward the nearest corral, a coiled lariat in his hand. The other two fell in behind him, leaving the leader waiting at the fire. Working together with practiced swiftness, in less than a minute the three men had dragged out a kicking and bawling calf on a rope. The big man scooped the animal up, lifted him an inch or two off the ground, and then dropped him on his side. One of the others dropped to one knee and secured the calf's thrashing feet with a short piece of rawhide.

Mitch held his breath as the leader withdrew a glowing iron from the fire and stepped swiftly over. A moment later the calf went crazy as blue smoke curled upward in the still air. Normally, two or three seconds from a red-hot branding iron was enough to make the brand permanent, but this guy was bent over the animal for ten or fifteen seconds while the big guy knelt on the calf's neck. Mitch guessed he had just witnessed his first application of the M-pole brand.

As they led the calf back into the corral, Bush spoke. "Steady. It's only a calf. Can't prove that it's not a legitimate sleeper calf."

Mitch gritted his teeth. Bush was right, but it was a Hereford calf, not a longhorn. Fuming and growing more frustrated while the men branded three more Hereford calves, Mitch could barely stay where he was and keep his mouth shut. Then finally, the three men lassoed a young heifer and brought her out.

Bush leaned forward, peering through the binoculars. "That one's branded. No question about it." He turned and signaled to Hammond that this was the one.

It took all three cowboys to take the bigger animal down and get her legs secured. As soon as they were, the leader grabbed another iron and went to work. "Let him finish," Bush hissed as Mitch got up to his knees. But the instant the heifer was on its feet again and put back in the corral, Bush leaped to his feet. His sawed-off shotgun was in his right hand, barrel pointing at the sky, his pistol was in his left. He stepped out from behind the bush and started striding down the hill.

BOOM! The blast of the shotgun shattered the silence and echoed off the surrounding cliffs. Startled at the sight of Bush standing up in full sight, Mitch jumped up, thumbing the hammer of his 30–30 back. CRACK! He too fired a shot into the air as Hammond came running.

"Hold it right there, boys!" Bush roared. "I am a United States Marshal, and you are under arrest."

What happened next came so fast that later Mitch would find it difficult to tell what came first. For a second or two the four rustlers froze in place, and then they erupted as one. The leader flung the running iron aside and whipped out his pistol. BLAM! He dropped to one knee, taking more careful aim. BLAM! Mitch flung himself to one side and dropped flat as a bullet ricocheted off a nearby rock. CRACK! He fired back as he dropped to the earth, knowing he was way off the mark. The big man jumped the corral fence and disappeared among the milling cattle. The leader, who was prone now, was scuttling for a nearby boulder. The one nearest the fire clawed out his pistol. BLAM! He fired wildly and then broke into a hard run and disappeared around the bend of the canyon. The fourth man raised his hands, screaming not to shoot. Then, seeing the confusion around him, he spun around and sprinted for the saddled horses. CRACK! CRACK! Mitch and Hammond fired at almost the same instant but only kicked up dust behind the running figure.

Suddenly across the wash, a reddish brown figure rose up from the rock shelf, clouds of dust billowing off of him like an apparition. Then Jim Jo's rifle came up. CRACK! Mitch saw that he was firing up the canyon, trying to stop the man who was getting away.

BOOM! This time Bush, who had dropped to his knees to provide a smaller target, fired his shotgun in the general direction of the camp. But the gun didn't have that kind of range, and it was more for effect than for any real damage. Pistol shots were still coming from somewhere.

Mitch saw Jim Jo lower his rifle. CRACK! There was a cry, and the leader of the bunch rolled into view, clutching his leg in agony.

That left two still in action. Mitch flicked his eyes to the left. The man who was running for the horses had disappeared, but the man who had tried to hide among the cattle was coming out of the corral, his hands held high. A moment later, Mitch saw why. Manito was about five steps behind him.

Mitch ran in a crouch toward Bush, who was reloading his shotgun. "There's still a man by the saddle horses."

"Yeah," Bush grunted as he snapped the shotgun shut. He holstered his pistol and slowly got to his feet, cursing like a Missouri mule-skinner. "Hey, you stupid Texan," he bellowed. "This is Deputy U.S. Marshal Joseph Bush. I've got seven other men surrounding you. Throw out your weapons and step out where I can see you."

Astounded that Bush could walk toward the horses so calmly while he provided a target as big as a barn, Mitch watched, tense and holding his breath. A head suddenly appeared behind the saddle horses, and Mitch saw the glint of sunlight on metal. "Stop!" shouted a voice.

Bush didn't slow his pace one iota.

CRACK! Sand kicked about five feet to Bush's right. Mitch dove for the ground again. "I've got you in my sights, Marshal," came the voice. "Stop or I'll drop you where you stand."

Bush took another step forward, though more slowly. "Now, you don't wanna do that, son," he called. "You kill a U.S. Marshal and your life will become a pure hell. There'll be a thousand-dollar reward put on your head. And you'll have three hundred deputy U.S. Marshals hunting you down. You'll also have every lousy bounty hunter in the West trying to get to you first."

"Stay where you are!" the voice screamed, his voice shrill with panic. "One more step, and I'll fire. I'll make you a deal. Let me go, and you'll never see me again."

Bush stopped but didn't cower in any way. "No deals. I ain't in the mood."

A movement caught Mitch's eye. He turned and saw two figures appear just above the camp. It was Kumen, and he had his rifle stuck in the back of the man who had fled. A moment later, Lem Redd and Mitch's father came around the bend to the south and dropped to their knees, weapons up. But Mitch also saw something else. Up on the rock shelf, Jim Jo was on his stomach and slithering in the direction of the saddle horses.

"You dumb ox," Bush roared. "Don't you know there ain't no place far enough or no hole deep enough for you to hide? You're done with, boy." And then, as Mitch suddenly realized that he was trying to keep the man's attention on him, Bush's voice grew more conversational. "Hey, boy. While you've been flapping your gums, my Indian friend, Ole Jimmy Jo, has disappeared." Bush cupped his hand to his mouth. "Jim Jo! Show yourself. Have you got a clear shot at that sidewinder?"

Jimmy Jo got to his feet. He was no more than twenty feet from the rifleman. "I do," he called back.

"If he so much as twitches an eyeball, you gut-shoot him. You hear me?"

"I hear you," Jim Jo called back without lowering the rifle.

A second later a rifle came sailing over the four horses and landed in the sand of the wash. The man's head appeared. He was waving his arms wildly. "I'm coming out, Marshal. Tell him not to shoot." A moment later the cowboy stepped into view, his holster and gun belt held high in the air.

"Sorry, Jim Jo," Marshal Bush called. "No shooting today, my friend. Get down there and put some handcuffs on that Texas trash."

"You got it, Marshal," Jim Jo called back. Mitch thought he could see him grinning like a boy who had just shot his first jackrabbit.

Notes

I chose to include this episode not only because it provides some exciting action based on actual events but also to serve as a reminder of how difficult those early years were for these San Juan pioneers. Morgan A. Barton, son of Joseph F. Barton, who came with the first Hole-in-the-Rock group, explained it this way:

"In settling this part of the country they [the Mormon pioneers] were an established outpost, detracting marauding Indians from interior southern settlements of Utah Territory as well as being a point of interception of bank robbers, horse thieves, cattle rustlers, jail breakers, train robbers, and general desperadic [sic] criminals. . . . Many times I have seen my father, with other men, rushing home and at times out of religious services, for their horses and guns to take up the chase of outlaws" (as cited in *Hole-in-the-Rock*, 8–9).

Albert R. Lyman gives us the most details about the ELKM Ranch and the nefarious activities of some of their cowhands. He tells us that Lemuel H. Redd, Kumen Jones, and Joseph Hammond were near the head of Comb Wash in the spring of 1888 rounding up their own cattle when they happened to see "an outfit" going down the wash with "the leading spirit of the M-pole gang." Kumen Jones rode back to Bluff to get Marshal Bush and his two Indian trackers and bring them back to set the trap that eventually snared them (see *Indians and Outlaws*, 102–103; see also *History*, 70–71).

Joseph Bush is a real person, and his description is accurate (see Robert S. McPherson, *A History of San Juan County: In the Palm of Time* [Salt Lake City: Utah State Historical Society, 1995], 325; see also Austin and McPherson, "Murder, Mayhem, and Mormons: The Evolution of Law Enforcement on the San Juan Frontier, 1880–1900," as cited in http://www.BlueMountainShadows.org/Vol1/mormons.PDF).

CHAPTER 7

June 2, 1888, 7:55 a.m.—Monticello, San Juan County

As Mitch rode down from his ranch site into the center of Monticello, he was struck with wonder once again. They had come up from Bluff to Verdure in mid-March, not quite three months ago. It took them about ten days to get a semipermanent settlement started on South Montezuma Creek, which they called Verdure, with George and Evelyn Adams and Parley and Ency Butt as the anchor families. Then the rest of the families had moved six miles farther, to North Montezuma Creek, now named Monticello. Though they had dug a ditch to bring water from the creek to the town site and put in a limited amount of fencing the previous summer, that was it. This spring they had come up to turn these beginnings into a real settlement.

Now there were almost a dozen cabins under some state of construction. Charles Walton almost had his cabin done, and Frederick Jones and Mons Peterson were not far behind him. Charles had surprised everyone when he brought in a load of shingles from Colorado and his cabin became the first to be permanently roofed. Shingles were so expensive this far away from civilization that the others would be settling for sod roofs. Though he was still finishing the roof, Mons was now operating a small dry goods store out of one room of his cabin. And, much to the joy of the whole community, he had also recently dug a well that was providing a limited supply of sweet, cold water.

The main roads in Monticello had been graded, and survey stakes now defined lot boundaries along both sides of every street. The site for the largest building in the town, which would serve as church, school, and community center, had been cleared, the foundations were laid, and four courses of logs were now in place. Shingles had been ordered from Colorado, and there was a growing confidence that they could have it ready in time for stake conference in late August.

Corrals were springing up everywhere. Many of the residents had started adding barns, lean-tos, and sheds to their properties. Splashes of green against the red soil marked gardens that were filled with vegetables. Mary Jones and Jane Walton had even planted flowers on the south sides of their homes. It was no longer a "site," Mitch thought. It was a town. A community. And it filled him with a deep sense of satisfaction to be part of it.

As he approached the Decker home site with its tent and wagon, Mitch felt a pang of loneliness. The wagon that served as Edie's bedroom was parked in its usual place, but she was not there. She was still in Bluff helping her parents prepare for their move back to Richfield.

As he swung down, he called out. "Anyone home? It's Mitch Westland."

He heard a sound of rustling and children's voices. Then a moment later, Sarah, the oldest of the Decker children, burst out of the tent. "Edie?" she cried, looking around eagerly.

Mitch moved over to join her. "Sorry, Sarah. Edie's not back yet. But she will be soon."

Emma Decker appeared, holding her baby in one arm. "Mitch! You're back so soon?"

"Yup. The spring rains were good in the high country, and

I was able to find good grazing lower than I thought. We won't move them up Elk Mountain for two or three more weeks." He looked around. "So how are things coming along with the Decker move?"

Emma pulled a face. "Much slower than I'd hoped. I swear that we now have twice as much stuff as we brought with us. Have you heard at all from Edie? When will she be coming up?"

"There was a letter waiting for me when I got home last night. Her parents are leaving Tuesday morning. They waited a couple of extra days so they can travel with two other families who are also going back. I'm taking a wagon down on Monday. Edie's parents have given her a bunch of their stuff to use in our home. We hope to be back by Wednesday. Will you and Alvin still be here?"

"Alvin's family has been urging him to come as soon as possible, but we're not ready. And my children are ready to mutiny if they don't get to see Auntie Edie before they leave. So we're now thinking we'll leave a week from Monday."

"Good," Mitch said. "She's been worried that she wouldn't get to say good-bye."

June 5, 1888, 11:50 a.m.—Zimmer Home—Bluff City

Mitch stood beside Frank Zimmer and together they watched as Edie and her mother fell into each other's arms, weeping so much that they could hardly speak. Finally, Frank leaned in and said, "Sorry, Mitch. I was really hoping to be on the road by nine this morning, but one of our other families had to repack their wagon, and. . . ." He shrugged. "I'm sorry to hold you and Edie up. Just go. We'll be all right."

Mitch waved that off. "The families we're going north with

aren't ready yet either. Nephi Bailey's at the blacksmith getting a new tire on his wagon wheel, and Willard Butt and his wife are trying to find a horse that wandered away last night. So you're not holding us up."

They watched the two women as they wiped at their eyes and whispered desperate promises to each other. Finally they came back to join the men. As they approached, Frank said in a low voice, "For all the tears being shed, I hope you know that Caroline wouldn't be making this move if she didn't know you'll be watching over our girl, Mitch. Words cannot express what it means to us to see her so happy."

"Edie is a marvel, and I plan to spend the rest of my life making her happy."

Tears started again as Caroline came up to Mitch. She threw her arms around him, hugged him fiercely, and kissed him on the cheek. "Promise me you'll take care of my baby."

"You have my word," he said. He put his arm around Edie's shoulders as she joined them.

Caroline looked at her husband. "I'm ready, Frank. Let's go. I don't care if the others are ready. We can wait for them outside of town. I can't bear this any longer."

Her husband nodded and helped her up into the wagon seat. Edie pressed her shoulder against Mitch's and grasped his hand so hard that it hurt. "Good-bye, Mama. Good-bye, Papa. Thank you again for all the beautiful things you've given us."

"Yes," Mitch blurted. "Thank you."

Caroline looked back as her husband climbed up beside her. "We'll see you next May for the wedding. Until then, you write me every week, Edna Rae."

Edie was too choked up to answer. Mitch lifted a hand in farewell. "She will. Good-bye and Godspeed."

As the wagon rolled away, Edie turned and buried her face

against Mitch's chest and didn't raise it again until the sound of the wagon was gone. Finally she stepped back, wiping at her eyes. "Are we all packed and ready?" she asked.

Mitch nodded. "I just need to get my horse from the corral. But the others are not—"

"I want to go now. I'm like Mama. Can we leave now? Please?"

"Of course. We'll go slowly. We're going to have to camp up on White Mesa anyway."

Concern suddenly filled her eyes. "Will people talk if we go off alone?"

He shook his head, touched that she would be concerned about that in the midst of her grief. "Maybe that will hurry them up a little. They won't be that far behind us."

He took her by the hand and started for their wagon, but suddenly Edie stopped and turned around. "This is farewell to Bluff too, isn't it?"

"I. . . ." Mitch's parents were still here, and there would be a lot of going back and forth between the two towns, but he knew what she meant. "Yes, the Blue Mountains are our home now."

"Then let's go home."

July 4, 1888, 8:30 a.m.—Monticello

As Mitch cinched up the girth on his saddle, Edie watched him chewing on a piece of rawhide and grimacing slightly as he did so.

"Is your mouth hurting you again?" she asked in alarm.

"No. Not in the way you mean. Ed Hyde says I've got more wisdom teeth pushing through the gums. So he gave me this piece of rawhide to chew on."

"Ah," she replied, deadpan. "Like a baby teething, right?"

"Make fun of me as you wish," he said, feigning deep hurt, "but chewing on rawhide is better than having him cut open my gums with a hunting knife again."

An involuntary shudder ran down Edie's spine and she was instantly contrite. "I'm sorry, Mitch. You're right. I shouldn't tease you about it. It makes my stomach turn over just thinking about it." She changed the subject. "Will you be gone all day?"

"Very likely. We're taking up two extra wagons so we can cut enough logs to completely finish the church house. Brother Jones would like to get the building finished in time to put in flooring before stake conference."

"You do remember what day it is today, don't you?"

"Of course. Independence Day."

"So there's no chance you'll be back for the parade?"

"Not unless you wait until sundown. And maybe not then."

Edie shook her head. "We'd have a revolt on our hands. The children are already dying with anticipation, and that's with the parade at noon. I hope Brother Jones isn't planning to go with you to Pole Canyon. He's supposed to give a speech when the parade ends."

"He's not. George Adams is taking his place on the crew."

"Oh, they're here already?"

"Yes, George and Evelyn arrived late last night with Parley and Ency. Ency's new little girl is so adorable. Huge dark eyes, jet black hair."

"What about Willard and Julia? Didn't they come?"

"They'll be here in time for the festivities."

Edie nodded. This was good. Ency Butt had given birth to a little girl in April but had been in her "woman's confinement" until recently. Parley Butt and Willard, his older brother, had been up several times to help their Monticello brethren, so their coming now was good news for Mitch. Since the Deckers had left, Edie had gone into what Mitch called a "baby blues" slump. There were other children in Monticello, but most were a little older. Now, with Evelyn's Nean, Ency's five-year-old, four-year-old, two-year-old, and a three-month-old baby, and Julia's two-year-old, she would have a whole gaggle of little ones to mother for the next couple of days. Mitch was glad for her.

"Better hurry, Mitch," Edie was saying, bringing him back from his thoughts. "Those men will be waiting for you."

8:48 p.m.—Pole Canyon Road

As the string of three wagons and several men on horseback wound its way down the two-track road toward the town site, Mitch sat low in the saddle, exhausted to the bone. But there was satisfaction as well. They had three wagonloads of logs, more than enough to finish the town's only public building.

But as they approached the lane that led over to Mitch's home site, they saw three figures approaching in a light buckboard. Straightening in his saddle, Mitch peered more closely. One of them was Edie. With her were the two Walton sisters.

Charles and Charlie Walton were driving the lead wagon, which was right alongside Mitch. Charlie nudged his father. "Pa, ain't that Maggie and Leona?"

The senior Walton nodded. "Whoa!" he called, as he pulled the team to a halt. His eyes narrowed. "Didn't expect a welcoming committee," he said. "Something's up."

Mitch saw that he was right. Maggie, who was driving, urged the horse into a trot as Leona and Edie started waving and shouting. As the buckboard reached the wagon, Maggie pulled it to a stop just in front of her father's team, handed the reins to Leona, jumped down, and strode over to her father. "Papa, there's more trouble with the Carlisle bunch."

There was a collective groan from all of the men. "What now?" her father asked.

"They've torn out the dam again, and both the creek and the ditch have only a trickle of water. And they left a threatening note."

Mitch started to rein his horse around. "We'll see about that," he growled.

"No, Mitch," Edie cried. "The brethren are meeting at the Jones house. They're waiting for you."

Maggie was nodding vigorously. "He wants you to tie up the wagons here at the Westland site and come as quickly as you can. Take the buckboard. Ride double if you have to. But hurry. We'll stay here with the wagons until you get back."

"Oh, no," Charlie said. "We're not leaving you up here alone."

Leona and Edie stood up in the buckboard. Both had rifles in their hands. "We'll be all right until you get back," Leona said.

Charles was shaking his head. He took his rifle from the scabbard beside him and handed it to his son. "Charlie, you stay here with the girls."

From the rear wagon, George Adams called out. "Fred will stay too."

In moments, the buckboard was filled with five men—one more than it normally held—and Mitch and Mons Peterson had men behind them on their saddles. With Charles in the lead driving the buckboard, they took off for town.

9:10 p.m.—Frederick I. Jones Home—Monticello

Brother Jones, who was the designated priesthood leader for their community, raised a hand and the buzz of angry conversation quickly died away. As the men turned to him he lowered his hand again, looking grim. They were gathered in the yard in front of his cabin, where the air was cooling rapidly. They all had mugs of water and sandwiches in their hands, thanks to several of the wives who were also there.

"Brethren," Jones said angrily, "this situation has become intolerable. Three times in the last two weeks, the Carlisle bunch has dammed up the creek. And now they've done it again. They probably saw all of you men headed up into the mountains for lumber and decided it was a good time. We've had the women and children carrying buckets of water from what little is left in the creek, but it's not enough for our stock and gardens."

"Maggie said they left a note this time," Charles Walton said.

Fred Jones's head bobbed angrily. "Yeah. Very simple. Very brief. 'Leave our water alone or be shot down like the scum you are.'" He shook his head in disgust. "They spelled 'leave' l-e-e-v-e and 'scum' s-k-u-m. They're a real educated bunch up there."

Parley Butt called out, "I say we saddle up and ride out to the Carlisle spread right now. Let them know they don't own the water rights. We do. We went to Durango and registered them with the land office."

"Yeah," Ed Hyde said. "And if it takes a few rifles in their faces to see that they can't push us around, then the sooner the better, I say."

That brought a roar of approval. A couple of men had rifles and shook them in the air.

Brother Jones nodded but said nothing until the men quieted

again. "Brethren, that is not as simple as it sounds. Carlisle now has two men patrolling the creek, which means they're expecting trouble from us." He let his eyes sweep across the group and continued softly. "We were not called over here to start a range war. If we start a fight with the Carlisle bunch, every cattle outfit within fifty miles will send men up here to stand with Carlisle against us." Those were sobering words, but every man there knew he was right.

No one in their little community questioned why Frederick Isaac Jones had been chosen by President Hammond to be the presiding elder there. In addition to being a tireless worker, he had a practical mind and managed to remain calm even in tense situations. He also had a knack for cutting through the clutter and getting to the heart of things.

Brother Jones raised his head. "Though we are in the right here, we cannot risk a war."

"So what do we do?" Charles Walton asked. "Two or three more days in this weather and there'll be no gardens left and our stock will be dying in the corrals."

Brother Jones didn't answer him but turned instead to Mitch. "Brother Westland, your ranch site is the closest to where they've been damming up the creek. I assume you're planning to be up there working all day tomorrow?"

"That's right. And Edie was going to be up there with me." He felt a little chill shoot through him as he thought about her and Maggie and Leona up there now. "But I think I'll have her stay down in town tomorrow."

"Good. And I'd like to suggest we get those sisters back down here now. Mean as some of those cowboys are, I don't think they'll go after the women, but I don't want them up there when it's full dark. Mitch, did I see you on a horse?"

When Mitch nodded, Brother Jones turned to George

Adams. "George, why don't you take the buckboard and ride back up there with Mitch and bring those sisters back to town? And Mitch, we'll leave Fred and Charlie Jr. up there with you tonight. Let's let that bunch see that we're back in town."

He turned to Mons Peterson. "Mons, the cowboys probably know you the best, 'cause they're coming into your store all the time."

Mons nodded.

"So here's what I'm thinking. At first light tomorrow morning, I want Mitch, Charlie, and Fred to go up to the dam. If someone's there, back off. But if not, tear it out. Let's leave *them* a note reminding them that we have legal right to the water. Once that's done, send Charlie and Fred back here."

He turned to Mons. "Then I want you to ride watch on the ditch tomorrow. Up and down between here and the dam. Let them know we're watching them."

"With or without a gun?" Mons asked, his face inscrutable.

"Without," he said. "We'll not be provoking them, and they won't shoot an unarmed man." Brother Jones turned to Mitch. "I want you to stay up on your ranch site all day. I want you close enough to back Mons up if things start to unravel. No one leaves town tomorrow. It'll be a workday on the schoolhouse." Back to Mitch. "If there's trouble, three shots will bring us running."

CHAPTER 8

July 5, 1888, 9:47 a.m.—Westland Home Site

When Mitch saw that the person coming up the lane toward the cabin was Edie, he immediately put down the drawing knife, brushed off the bark shavings from his shirt, and started down the lane to meet her. He was about to chide her for being up there, but the look on her face changed his mind. "Hi," he said as they came together. "What's up?"

To his surprise, there were no preliminaries.

"You know about Mons, right?"

He felt his stomach lurch. "No! What's happened?"

"Nothing yet. I mean, you know about him riding guard on the creek?"

"Yes, I knew that. And I saw Mons go by about an hour ago."

"And you know that he's unarmed?"

He sighed. "Edie, this is a very volatile situation. We have to stand up for our rights, but we cannot do anything that will provoke open war between us and the cattlemen."

She cut him off with an angry shake of her head. "And what about Eliza?"

Mitch reared back. "Eliza? What about her?"

Edie moved closer until she was almost nose to nose with Mitch. "I saw Eliza just now. That's why I'm here. She is nearly hysterical with worry. And she's not the only one. All of us sisters are worried about what's going to happen with these men. Remember how Carlisle threatened to annihilate us last summer when we took his water? He said he would kill men, women, and children. And he meant it."

So that was it. Mitch took a quick breath and touched her arm. "Of course, I remember, Edie. But. . . ." His mind was working quickly. "I can't speak for Brother Jones, but I'm guessing he chose Mons because he is not only known to the cowboys, but he is also a man of courage and is as steady as a rock in a windstorm. It takes a lot to rattle Mons, and Brother Jones knows that the last thing we need right now is a hothead on our side of the fence."

"I know all that, Mitch, but—"

"If you want, I'll go out there right now and relieve Mons. But I can only do that if Brother Jones agrees to it. He's the presiding elder, Edie, and I can't go behind his back."

She blanched at the thought of Mitch taking Mons's place, but that didn't end it for her. Her voice became pleading. "I believe that I understand why Brother Jones chose Mons for this. But it's not Mons that I'm worried about. Eliza has a four-year-old child and a nursing baby. She's in frail health right now, and she's emotionally very fragile. I'm not saying that Mons should be pulled off, just that Eliza needs help, too. Can't you do something for her?"

Mitch searched Edie's face for a long moment. He could see that she was on the verge of tears herself. "All right," he finally said. "Here's an idea. I'll take my rifle and pistol and I'll go over by the dam. There's plenty of oak brush and cedar trees there, so I can make sure no one sees me. If there's going to be trouble, it will be at the dam, and then I can back Mons up. If nothing happens, then neither the Carlisle boys nor Mons will even know that I am there."

Edie's face lit up with relief. "Oh, Mitch, that would be wonderful."

He held up a finger. "I'll do it under one condition."

"What? Anything!"

"You go straight back to Brother Jones. Tell him what we've talked about. If he agrees, you come outside his front door and wave to me. I can see you from here. If I see you waving, I will leave immediately. But if nothing happens, then I stay. Agreed?"

"Yes!" She threw her arms around him. "Thank you, Mitch." She pulled back and looked up at him. "Now I'll be the one who's worried sick, but can I tell Eliza?"

He buried his face in her hair, loving the smell of it and the feel of her in his arms. "Of course. But if nothing happens, Mons is not to know about this, okay?"

Edie nodded and then went up on tiptoes and kissed him hard. "I'll go right to Brother Jones."

12:15 p.m.—North Fork, Montezuma Creek

Mitch heard the horse before he could see anything. Staying low behind a thick clump of willows, he inched forward enough to get a clear line of sight. A few moments later Mons appeared. He was slouched in his saddle, both hands visible on the saddle horn as he held the reins. He was making sure anyone watching could see that he was not armed. That was Mons. Probably had kitty cats tiptoeing up and down his spine, but cool as a cactus in the moonlight.

Mons was about thirty yards downstream from Mitch's position but headed upstream toward the dam again. Mitch slithered backward until he was in the thick of the cedar forest and then started jogging up the hill, staying north of the creek. The question now—where was Bill Edwards? The last time Mitch had seen Carlisle's foreman, Edwards had been perched atop the rock dam, bare feet dangling in the water, eating bread and cheese from a leather pouch. He was a picture of confidence. His rifle was lying across his lap.

Earlier, Mitch had watched Edwards draw down on Mons as he rode by him going downstream. Edwards had the rifle up and trained on Mons's back, but Mitch hadn't really been too concerned. He knew Edwards pretty well and knew he wouldn't shoot unprovoked.

Edwards was a tall, lanky cowhand who looked as if he'd been born on a horse and suckled by a Texas Longhorn. He was an older man—rumor was that he had a wife and two kids back in Colorado somewhere—and one of the more level-headed of the cowboy bunch. He often came to Mons's store for bullets and other supplies, and he and Mons had an amiable relationship. And while Edwards had a reputation for being fearless and as tough as a horseshoe nail, he was a fair man with little of the brashness of the young bucks. Nevertheless, Mitch had kept his rifle trained on Edwards in case he did start shooting. He hadn't, and Mons had passed on, unaware that he was centered in someone's rifle sights. Nor did Edwards realize that he had been as well. Now Mitch's task was to spot Edwards before Mons reached the dam. It was a hot day, and nerves frayed in this kind of heat.

To Mitch's surprise, Edwards was still at the dam. Not on the dam, but nearby, once again well hidden in the brush. Mitch had not spotted him for almost two minutes, but then a flicker of movement gave him away. By then, Mitch could hear Mons approaching on his horse, even though he was still forty or fifty yards downstream. Mitch smiled. That was good. Mons knew better than to look like he was sneaking up on someone. But this time when Bill's rifle came up, Mitch took it seriously. Edwards was here to defend the dam, and defend the dam he would. There was no doubt of that.

Satisfied that he couldn't find a better place to watch what was about to happen without giving himself away, Mitch lined Edwards up in his sights and settled in to wait.

It didn't take long. Mons came into view a couple of minutes later, letting his horse push its way through the brush and the willows, making lots of noise. Mitch could tell that while Mons was trying to appear bold and confident, every nerve in his body was fully alert and ready for trouble. His head swung slowly back and forth as he searched the trees on both sides of the creek. When he stopped his horse next to the newly built dam, he didn't dismount but continued to search for any sign of trouble.

Finally, visibly relaxing, Mons got down and led his horse to where the water was backing up behind the dam. He dismounted, hung the reins loose over the saddle horn so his horse could drink, and went down flat on his belly to drink deeply himself. He lay there for a moment, listening intently, and then drank some more. Satisfied, he got up and tied his horse to the nearest tree. Once again he turned slowly in a full circle, searching the area around him. There was a look in his eye that sent a little shiver of worry through Mitch. It was one of pure determination. *No, Mons. Leave the dam be. You are not alone.*

Mitch's heart fell when Mons shook his head angrily, strode over to his horse, and untied a short-handled shovel from the back of his saddle. Edwards reacted instantly. With an explosion of noise, he leaped to his feet, cocking his rifle. Mons whirled and instinctively grabbed for his pistol, but there was nothing there. His hands shot up and he froze.

Spouting profanity, Edwards moved slowly forward, the

muzzle of his rifle never wavering. "Hey, Mormon! You touch that dam and I'll blow your ugly head clean off your body."

Mons said nothing but kept his hands held high. Mitch scooted a little to the right so he had a clear view of both men. A twig snapped as he did so. But the two men were so intently focused on each other that neither heard it.

Then, to Mitch's amazement, Mons slowly lowered his arms. "I'm unarmed, Bill," he called. "I don't have a gun."

"But you have a shovel, Peterson, and I know why you're here. I've a mind to kill you right here and leave your body to the crows and the coyotes. You can't steal our water!"

Mons kept his hands away from his body, but to Mitch's amazement, when he spoke his voice was quiet and without fear. "Don't you know this is our water?"

"Maybe it will be in heaven, but it's certainly not down here on earth. This is Carlisle water."

"We went to Durango last summer and checked at the land office," Mons went on. "Carlisle never officially filed for the rights. So we did. We have the paperwork to prove it."

"Don't lie to me!" Edwards barked, raising the muzzle of his rifle a fraction of an inch.

"Say what you want about us Mormons, Bill," Mons went on in that same even tone of voice, "but you know we don't lie. I can show you the paperwork if you want. All we want is what's rightfully ours."

For a long moment, Edwards stared at Mons as if he were mad. Mitch held his breath. Then the rifle lowered and Bill relaxed. "Well, durned if that doesn't beat all. Carlisle told us that you Mormons were a bunch of thieving squatters. Said you would shoot us in the back on sight."

Mons lifted both hands to show they were empty. He

managed a brief smile. "Maybe I could *poke* you in the back, but not much else."

For what seemed like a very long time, Edwards just stood there, mulling it all over in his mind. Muttering, he started to turn away, but then he whirled back around. "I've been riding this creek all day long, fearing I was gonna be ambushed. And now I find it's all a lie. Well, from now on, Carlisle can fight his own battles. Tear out the dam, if you like. I'm done with this damn-fool nonsense." And he turned and strode away.

1:03 p.m.

Ten minutes later, Mitch was standing on the creek bank when he heard the first gurgle of approaching water. Soon it was rushing past him in a steady stream.

He was still standing there, listening to the distant sounds of people celebrating in town, when he heard the sound of a horse behind him. He turned. It was Mons.

"Howdy, Mitch," he said, swinging down and coming over to join him.

"This your work?" Mitch asked, nodding toward the creek.

"Yup," Mons said with a grin.

"Any trouble?"

"None whatsoever," he said.

Grinning, Mitch said, "Mind if I saddle up and ride down with you? Maybe we can talk Edie and Eliza into fixing us some lunch."

"Sounds good to me. My stomach is as hollow as a kettle drum."

To the surprise of both men, while Mitch was still saddling

his horse, they heard a rider coming hard on the road up from the town. In a moment, they saw that it was Fred Adams.

"Uh-oh," Mons murmured.

Mitch finished cinching his saddle and swung up on his horse. They spurred their horses forward and met Fred on the road. "What's up?" Mons called as Fred arrived.

"Brother Jones wants you both down at his house," he blurted. "A marshal is there."

"Marshal Bush is back?" Mitch blurted in surprise.

"No," Fred said. "His name is Marshal Pratt. He's a U.S. Marshal, though. Don't know why he's here, but Brother Jones wants all the men at his home immediately."

When they arrived five minutes later, Mitch saw a crowd gathered outside of the Fred Jones home. Near as he could tell, about every person in the town was there, including young children. As they rode up, Eliza and Edie came running out to greet them. Eliza's face was radiant with joy as Mons dismounted and she threw herself into his arms. Edie was smiling as she ran up to Mitch and hugged him tightly. "Any problems?" she whispered.

"None. And thank the Lord for that."

Before she could answer, Brother Jones boomed out. "Brothers and sisters, quiet please. Gather in close." He was standing on the small porch in front of his cabin so he could be clearly seen. With him was a man in a large cowboy hat, a light blue, long-sleeved shirt open at the neck, and a leather vest with a silver star pinned to it. Brother Jones waited a moment until the people pushed in and then began without preamble.

"Brothers and sisters, I would like to introduce you to Marshal Arthur Pratt. He's come down from Salt Lake City, arriving just about an hour ago. He has an important announcement, so kindly give him your attention."

From the look on Brother Jones's face as he stepped back,

Mitch surmised that whatever the announcement was, it wasn't good.

Pratt thanked Brother Jones and then turned to the crowd.

"Ladies and gentlemen," the marshal began, his voice easily heard by everyone. "I am here by assignment from the Territorial Court in Salt Lake City, and I'm here about water rights."

That caused an instant stir among the crowd. Water rights and court used in the same sentence sounded ominous.

"I have been apprised of your situation here concerning who has the legal rights to the water of what you call North Montezuma Creek, which rights are currently claimed by both your community and Mr. John Carlisle's cattle company."

Someone near the front raised a hand, but the marshal ignored it.

"Mr. Jones here has shown me the papers you obtained from the land office in Durango, Colorado, last year, stating that they could find no record of Mr. Carlisle or his cattle company ever having filed an official claim for those rights."

"That's right," Ed Hyde called out. "They didn't, and we did."

Other voices were grumbling, but again Pratt ignored them. "After reviewing those papers, I am convinced that you have the greater legal standing in this case than does the Carlisle outfit."

"Yes!"

"Absolutely!"

"We sure do!" The crowd was pleased with his statement. And then the marshal raised one arm in the air and shouted over them, "But—"

Fred Jones, who seemed not at all surprised by what was happening, stepped forward and called out. "People, please! Let the marshal finish."

There were still whisperings among a few people, but the

marshal went on. "But, unfortunately for you, Mr. Carlisle has taken this case to the Territorial Court in Salt Lake City, and the judges have ruled in his favor." As shock rippled through the crowd, Pratt removed a folded paper from his inside vest pocket and waved it at them. "I have their ruling here, which gives all rights to the waters of North Montezuma Creek to Mr. John Carlisle. And I have been sent by the court to inform you of this ruling and to enforce the conditions of the court order."

Pandemonium erupted. Men were shouting and shaking their fists at him. Women gaped at each other in shocked silence. Bewildered children looked up at their parents, wondering why they were suddenly so upset. Pratt let it go on for almost a minute, calmly waiting for the noise to subside. Again, Brother Jones had to call for quiet. When they settled down, Pratt went on.

"I am sympathetic to your plight. And I believe that you are in the right, but—" There was that word again. "But I am not a judge, nor do I have the right to change this order in any way. I am charged to let you know that the courts have spoken and that unless you get a ruling from the courts in your favor, I have no choice but to enforce the terms they have set."

"But old man Carlisle pulled a fast one on us," Charles Walton called. "We didn't know he was taking this to court in Salt Lake."

Pratt frowned. "You should have received notification from the courts that you were a defendant in this matter."

"We did," Walton said bitterly, "two weeks after the date of the trial. We don't have regular mail service here, Marshal."

Pratt nodded, and his expression was sympathetic. "Another valid reason for an appeal to the courts. But again, that is beyond my jurisdiction."

Jane Walton, who was standing beside her husband, raised a

hand. Pratt nodded at her. "Knowing how the courts work, that could take years. What is our community supposed to do for water in the meantime?"

A deep frown crossed the marshal's face. "That is one of the things that troubles me most about this situation. Mr. Jones tells me that you have only one well in town."

Mons spoke up. "Yes, sir. My well. But that's not large enough to fill even the culinary water needs of all of our families. We've dug other wells, but so far with no success."

There was no question that the marshal was unhappy. He pulled on his mustache thoughtfully for a moment and then made up his mind. "I will do this much, and I think under the circumstances, I can convince the court to support my decision when I get back to Salt Lake. I am riding out to see Mr. Carlisle when I finish here. I will tell him that he has the right to the creek water, but that I'm going to allow the people of Monticello one exception." He turned to Brother Jones. "Here is my recommendation. For your culinary needs—drinking, cooking, medicinal needs—you will draw on the well that you have here in your community as much as possible. If that is not sufficient, which I am confident it will not be, then you have my permission to draw your additional culinary needs from the creek. But you will have to go up to where the creek will be dammed to do that. All other needs will have to be met from other uncontested sources."

Pratt turned to Brother Jones. "Mr. Jones, you may have heard that I am not a member of your Church, though I formerly was. But I am aware of your community's commitment to honesty and integrity. Therefore, I will put it in your hands to make sure this exception is not abused. Culinary water only, and then only after the well water is exhausted. If you take water for your laundry or to water your stock and Mr. Carlisle chooses to press charges, I will have no choice but to return, and some of you may be jailed."

Notes

It was Bill Edwards who confronted Mons Peterson that day over the water, and he did threaten to shoot Mons. His reaction when Mons explained the situation is as given in the historical sources (see *Saga*, 99–100).

Though no first name for the marshal is mentioned in the San Juan sources, it was likely Marshal Arthur Pratt, a Deputy U.S. Marshal from Salt Lake City. He was the son of Apostle Orson Pratt, but by this time was not a member of the Church. Though some accused him of bias against the Church, he had a strong reputation for integrity and fairness (see Richard S. and Mary van Wagoner, "Arthur Pratt, Utah Lawman," *Utah Historical Quarterly*, http://content.lib.utah.edu/utils/getfile/collection/USHSArchPub/id/7511/filename/7546.pdf).

Though the account of his coming is brief and has few details in it, it is based on that reputation for fairness that I have him sympathize with the Saints and come up with the compromise for water. But that is my assumption.

The Saints in San Juan did try to get the court order overturned, but the fight dragged on for many years and the injunction was not lifted. Finally, in 1896 or '97, after several years of severe drought, the big cattle outfits threw in the towel. They sold their herds to the Mormons and left San Juan County for good, thus relinquishing all claims to the waters of North Montezuma Creek and ending the decade-long conflict (see *History*, 118).

CHAPTER 9

July 11, 1888, 6:55 a.m.—Monticello, San Juan County

Mitch waved a hand. "That's good right there, Edie."

She nodded, yanked back on the handbrake of the wagon, tied the reins around the back rim of the wagon seat, and hopped down. She came over to stand beside Mitch, and together they looked out on the scene around them.

The first word that came to Mitch's mind was *pandemonium.* There were nine wagons in all, gathered in two rough lines. Six of those were for the women and children and their ten days' worth of laundry. Each of the other three wagons carried six empty, fifty-gallon water barrels. By tonight, they would be filled to the brim with semi-muddy water from South Montezuma Creek. That was supposed to last the community another three or four days. But with the heat of the last week, Mitch guessed that they would need to make another run in a couple of days.

Mitch watched now as the older girls and the women moved back and forth between their tents and cabins, bringing out their laundry in baskets or tied up in the sheets. Each wagon also carried one large heavy kettle, a box of homemade soap, jugs of drinking water, numerous picnic baskets, blankets to sit on, toys to keep the younger children occupied, and who knew what else.

Seeing the look on Mitch's face, Edie threw back her head

and laughed. "This is even more exciting for the children than Pioneer Day will be."

"Yeah," he sighed. "It's like watching a dog chasing a hundred little piglets."

She slapped his arm playfully. "Oh, come on, Grumpy. This is going to be fun."

He managed not to groan and then cupped both hands to his mouth. "All right, people," he yelled. "Let's load up. We're rolling out in five minutes."

8:25 a.m.—South Montezuma Creek, One Mile West of Verdure Township

"Mama! Mama! Mama!"

As the line of wagons pulled out single file and rolled one by one to a stop alongside each other, every head turned toward Mary Jones's wagon. Her oldest, Fred Jr., who was eight now, was standing up behind his mother, wiggling like he had ants in his pants. "Look, Mama! There's water in the ditch." His voice was filled with awe.

George Adams was just pulling his wagon alongside of Mitch's. He laughed. "I forget that you have nothing but a dry creek bed now."

Edie hopped down, tied the reins to a nearby cedar tree, and walked over to the Adams's wagon. Just as she reached it, Nean, who was seated on Evelyn's lap, launched herself out of the wagon. Catching her, Edie whirled her around as peals of giggles filled the air.

George watched, his eyes warm with pleasure. "The first thing she asked me this morning when she woke up was, 'Where's Auntie Edie?'"

"'Cause she's my girl," Edie said, laying her cheek against Nean's. "Aren't you, Cornelia?"

Nean looked up into Edie's eyes and laid a chubby little hand on her cheek. "I love you, Auntie Edie." It was so sweet that it almost made Edie cry.

But almost instantly, Nean's attention was pulled elsewhere. All up and down the line, children were bailing out of the wagons and running pell-mell for the creek, whooping like cowboys going to town for a Saturday night dance. Seeing that, Nean took off like a shot.

"Nean," Evelyn called after her, "don't get your dress wet."

Nean glanced back with an elfish smile on her face and then did a running jump into the water without taking off her shoes or worrying about her dress. Within seconds, she was seated in the water splashing wildly at anyone who ventured close.

Mitch couldn't help but laugh. "Well, it is wash day, Evelyn," he said.

8:55 a.m.

It was called wash "day" because it typically took from morning till evening. Even for women whose lives were one long string of labor-intensive and physically exhausting tasks, wash day was one of the *most* labor-intensive and physically exhausting things they did. And they did it every week. But to Mitch's amazement, not only did they seem to take it in stride, but they took great pride in having a brilliant white wash and in having everything starched and ironed just right so there was not a single wrinkle. In their eyes, it was a visible mark of their commitment to their families.

All along both sides of the creek at about ten-foot intervals, women had placed their baskets of dirty laundry alongside their wash tubs, scrubbing boards, and scrub brushes. Next to those were small boxes filled with the fresh chunks of the soap they had made a few days before, bottles of fresh potato starch, and smaller bottles of bluing.

Washing the laundry was a complicated process and would require a steady stream of buckets being passed up and down the line to keep the tubs fresh and to replenish the kettles of hot water. But all of that would come later. The first task was to fill the five kettles and wait the hour it would take for the water to get hot.

Once they had all five kettles filled and everything laid out in readiness, the women sent the children off to play. Evelyn Adams, whose cabin was just a few hundred yards downstream from where they were and who knew this area well, led them to a small clearing that had plenty of grass and was shaded by cedar trees. She gestured with a sweep of her hand. "Sisters," she called with a wide smile, "let's not waste this time we have. Let's talk."

9:25 a.m.

As Edie sat, her knees folded up and her head resting on them, she looked around at these "sisters" of hers and realized how fully content she was to be part of this community. They weren't discussing anything of great significance. It was just the natural day-to-day conversation that took place between women. Eliza Peterson reported that her stove cooked her bread unevenly in the oven. She quickly got lots of advice on how to fix the problem. "Turn the bread every twenty minutes."

"Make sure the fire is evenly distributed in the fire box."

"A low fire is better than a roaring flame."

Evelyn Adams triggered an enthusiastic response when she announced that she and George were now getting so much milk and cheese from their wild range cows that they thought they could make regular deliveries to Monticello and take things in trade instead of taking it all to Colorado for cash. She promised to bring wheels of cheese and bricks of butter to Monticello on a regular basis.

Mary Jones got everyone's attention when she mentioned that her husband had received a letter from President Hammond. Everyone immediately wanted to know if it contained any news that affected their little community.

Mary nodded. "He confirmed that stake conference is still on in August, and he said that he expects as many as a hundred people to come."

Jane Walton spoke up. "I got a letter too. He's asking the Relief Society to prepare meals for everyone and promises to bring flour, sugar, lard, and other things to help us out."

That created a buzz of conversation. Feeding a hundred people three meals a day for four days would be quite a task.

Eliza Peterson turned to Edie. President Hammond was her father. "I also got a letter," she said. "And some good news for you and Mitch, Edie. The Manti Temple was dedicated on May 21st and is now open for marriages and endowments."

Edie blushed slightly and nodded happily. "I'm glad that it wasn't delayed."

"Think about it," Sister Jones went on. "We now have three temples. One in St. George, one in Logan, and now one in Manti. Can you believe that? Almost anyone living in Utah Territory can now get to a temple in no more than a week."

Julia Butt smiled at Edie. "You'll probably be the first of any of us to be married there."

"Yes," Edie said softly. "Yes, I was just thinking that same thing, actually. Mitch and I are very fortunate."

"There's also some bad news," Mary Jones said. "Elder Erastus Snow passed away about month and a half ago."

"Oh, no!" Sarah Rogerson cried. Evelyn Adams whirled around. "He's the one who called our family to come to San Juan." Others said the same thing of themselves.

Jane Walton nodded. "Almost all of us in San Juan County are here because of him."

"I loved to hear him speak," Sarah Rogerson said. "He was so inspirational and yet so practical at the same time."

They talked about that for few more minutes and then fell quiet. Edie noticed that Eliza was looking somewhat depressed. She was staring at her hands, which were folded in her lap. When she looked up, Edie caught her eye and gave her a questioning look. That seemed to help her make up her mind about something. She looked around the group. "Papa shared some other bad news in my letter," she said softly.

Instantly every eye was on her.

Eliza took a quick breath and then plunged. "He received a letter from Salt Lake City saying that a committee in Congress back in Washington is recommending that all white settlers in San Juan County be removed and that this be made into a Ute Indian reservation."

CHAPTER 10

July 11, 1888, 1:25 p.m.—South Montezuma Creek

The wash site was a very different picture than it had been an hour or so ago. All up and down the creek banks, every bush, tree, or patch of grass was covered with drying laundry. The older children were downstream about a hundred yards playing games and hooting and hollering as they did. They had been given strict instructions not to trespass into the "clothing zone."

In the deep shade beneath the cottonwood, aspen, and cedar trees, three blankets were filled with sleeping babies or young ones. A few feet away, also on blankets, the women were seated in a loose circle talking quietly or taking an opportunity to rest. The sweat rings around the rims of their bonnets, their necklines, and their armpits were dried now. Their hair, which had been plastered to their heads, was now dry enough to be combed out with their fingers. As far as Edie was concerned, this was the best part of the whole day. She was exhausted, but she didn't want to sleep. This last week she had been overcome with what she guessed was a form of homesickness. She had received a letter from her parents saying they had arrived safely in Richfield. Their letter had been upbeat, chatty, and optimistic, but it still had hit her pretty hard as she realized how much she missed them and that it would be almost another full year before she saw them again.

But as Edie looked at the faces around her, she was surprised at the intensity of her feeling for these women. She was eighteen. Except for Maggie and Leona Walton, the rest of them were several years older than she was, and the oldest two were more than twice her age. But it didn't matter. The age difference was irrelevant up here. As Edie thought about it, she thought she understood why. For the first time in her life, she felt like a woman. Not just a grown-up girl, but a woman. One of them. Fully one of them.

Jane Jones sat up. Her eyes had been closed, but Edie didn't think she had gone to sleep. Now Jane looked around at the others—first at the babies, then at the women. "I think we're all pretty worn out," she observed. "And rightly so. We got a lot accomplished."

Emma Hyde also sat up and looked around. "Where are my girls?" she asked.

Edie pointed toward the older children. "They decided they'd rather play than rest," she said.

"That's my Louise," Emma said. "Not so much Winnifred, but Louise has boundless energy. She makes me tired just watching her sometimes."

Jane Walton had been sitting with her arms crossed on her knees watching the interchange but not participating. After a few moments of silence, she turned to Eliza, who was lying beside Edie but was fully awake. "Eliza?" she asked. "Did your father's letter say anything more about the Indian reservation issue?"

Eliza sat up. She looked over to make sure baby Mons was still sleeping and then shook her head. "Not much. Papa thinks it's just one more of those wild rumors that get started from time to time. He said that he's not worried about it."

Sister Walton's eyebrows lifted slightly, but she said nothing.

"I'd like to believe that," Sarah Rogerson spoke up, "but

knowing how much the U.S. government loves the Mormons right now, it wouldn't surprise me a bit."

Julia Butt was genuinely alarmed. "They can't do that, can they? Turn us out of our homes? Make us leave our farms and businesses?"

Sister Jones cleared her throat. "Actually, President Hammond did talk about it in his letter to Fred. He plans to share what he knows on Sunday with all of us."

"But we won't be with you Sunday," Evelyn Adams said. "Can't you tell us anything?"

Seeing that she wasn't going to be able to deflect this conversation, Sister Jones sighed. "All right, but it isn't much. So we have to be careful that we don't jump to conclusions based on very limited knowledge."

She looked around the circle, making sure they all got her meaning. They did. They were not to gossip about this. Several inched in closer as she began again. "This involves a Ute Indian reservation near Ignacio in Western Colorado—not far across the border from where we are, actually. It's called the Southern Ute Reservation, or the Ignacio Reservation. They say it is very fertile land and has some excellent cattle country. So the local ranchers have come forth with this idea that they give the Utes San Juan County as their reservation and—"

"The cattlemen?" Sarah Rogerson cried. "Oh, that's rich. These are the same men who steal our water and our cattle, and now they want the Indians' land, too?"

Mary nodded and went on. "The Ignacio Reservation would be given to the ranchers in exchange for San Juan County going to the Utes. The Indian agent—who is a white man and a far better friend to the ranchers than he is to the Utes—sent a letter to Congress making that recommendation. But we heard nothing more about it and assumed it was a dead issue. Now the rumor is that the government is going to appoint a commission. That's all we know."

"So it could happen," Ency Butt said. It was not asked as a question.

Edie had to smile. Sister Jones was a patient lady, but this topic had obviously hit some raw nerves, and now she could barely get a sentence finished before the women started venting their concerns. But she bored on anyway. "The commission is supposedly being sent out sometime in the fall to make a thorough study of the situation and then report back to Congress. Until then, nothing is going to happen." Her look clearly suggested, "So let's not fret about it yet."

It didn't seem to register. Ency Butt, who was a strong and self-sufficient woman, was still bothered. "And what if it does happen? Do we just walk away? Would they even pay us?"

"We have seen worse than this," Emma Hyde noted quietly, "and yet here we are. It's not been easy, but the Lord has not forgotten us. Nor will He if we strive to do His will faithfully."

Jane Walton, another one of the older and more steady of the women, was nodding. She also seemed unperturbed. "I know it is a worrisome situation and that it's hard not to fret about it, but nothing's happened yet. No one is asking us to move yet. We've not been evicted yet. And the more settled we become, the less likely it is that they will try to get us out. Surely when the commission comes, they will see how much we have done for this country. And," she added as an afterthought, "for the Indians, for that matter. We have not only been good *to* the Indians, we have been good *for* them. I believe they are better off because we are here."

Mary Jones was pleased with these last comments. "Sisters, we cannot say what the future holds, but we must remember that one of the reasons we were called by President Taylor to come here was to be a good influence on our Indian brothers and sisters. And Sister Jane is right. We are making significant progress in that regard. I don't think the Lord will ignore that."

"Yes," Evelyn said eagerly. "I totally agree. I can attest that the Indians *are* changing. I've already told this to a few of you, but let me tell you what happened to my little Nean earlier this summer." A little shudder ran through her as she went on. "It was on a wash day like this. Last year, George brought me one of those newfangled, hand-cranked wringer machines that are available now. Because George is so busy with our dairy, he hired a Ute squaw named Old Sally to help me around the house. We give her food and a little money in return. Anyway, one day I was out in the barn pressing some cheese while Sally finished the wash. I had left the clothes in a tub of water, and she was wringing them out for me."

Evelyn's eyes were shining now. "You know Nean. Her curiosity is boundless. We're not sure exactly how it happened, but we think the metal cogs in the wringer mechanism were so fascinating to her that she leaned in too close while Sally was wringing out a blouse. The sleeve of Nean's dress got caught in the wringer.

Edie was gaping at her in shock. She had not heard this.

Evelyn's voice was hushed and strained. "Suddenly, I heard Nean screaming at the top of her lungs. I dashed out of the barn and ran to where she was. Her hand and arm were covered with blood. I nearly fainted dead away. Old Sally was staring at her in horror, not sure what had just happened. And yet, she knew that somehow she was partly to blame. She started rocking back and forth and wailing. But then, as I gathered Nean in my arms, Old Sally took off like a shot for the creek. When she came back a few minutes later, she had made a poultice of herbs she had found along the creek bank. She also had a dish rag and a pan of water in her hands. With tears running down her face, she washed off the blood, ignoring Nean's screams. Fortunately, it wasn't as bad as it looked. When Sally got it all clean, she tied the poultice on with a string of buckskin from her dress. All that time, she was crying and crooning an Indian song to Nean. And it worked. Nean quieted down in a hurry. And Sally brought a new poultice every day for the next week."

Evelyn turned and looked at her sleeping daughter. "If you look closely at her arm, you can see where it's still a little red, but it's not going to scar. So I owe a great debt to Old Sally. I was so hysterical I didn't know what to do. But Sally could not have been sweeter with Nean than if she had been her own daughter. And I'll never forget it."

Leona Walton spoke up. "Remember when Jody Lyman was shot by those two rustlers down at Halls Crossing a few years back? His leg was so full of infection that Lem Redd said he was on the verge of death. Then that band of Utes came along. The old chief took one look at his leg and sent the women off to find a prickly pear cactus. They stripped off the cactus needles and wrapped the plant around his leg. Within a couple of hours, he was getting better." She looked at Evelyn. "So I agree, I think we can learn some things from them, too."

For a long time, there was silence. Then, Maggie Walton gave a little shudder and forced a smile. "I say we talk about something cheerful."

Leona's mother got to her feet. "Actually, I think it's time we go back to work. It looks like our wash is pretty much dry now."

"Well, let me share one more story before we stop," Sister Jones said. "It is a good illustration of both our challenges and our blessings in working with our Indian brothers. This happened last summer, when there were only a few of us here. One day, Old Wash," she smiled, "whom most of you know, came up to our wagon. It was just at sundown. I offered him something to eat, but he refused. He was very upset and asked Fred if he would give him a cartridge for his rifle."

"Just one bullet?" Julia Butt asked in surprise.

"Yes. That made Fred suspicious, of course, so he asked him why he needed it. Old Wash told him that his son, Manduton, whom he loved very much, had been thrown from his horse and broken his leg."

Edie gasped. "And he wanted to shoot him? Like you would a horse?"

"Yes! Not because he didn't love him, but because there was no other choice and they had to put him out of his misery. Fred, of course, was horrified," she went on, "and he tried to convince Old Wash that the boy could be healed with our medicine. Angry and frustrated that Fred wouldn't help him, Old Wash got up and walked away.

"Fred immediately called Parley and George, and they rode at top speed for the Ute camp. By the time Old Wash came in—he was on foot, of course—they had the boy's leg splinted and had given him something for the pain. Old Wash was shocked but deeply grateful. Now the boy is fine again. And anytime he sees Fred now, Old Wash says, 'You friend. You good friend. You save my boy. Old Wash good friend to you and Mormons.'"

Everyone was quiet. Edie found herself deeply affected by that simple story, as were the others. So what Sister Jones said next hit them all with great force. "That's why we're here," she said. "To help these people." She looked around the circle, meeting their eyes one by one. "And this is why we are going to stay here for as long as the Lord sees fit for us to do so."

Notes

The stories the women tell here about the Indians all come from various family histories.

The story of Nean's arm being caught in a wringer and the details of Old Sally's tender caring for it are factual, though no date is attached to the story (see *Anchored*, 135).

The story of Old Wash and his son's broken leg is also true and did involve Frederick I. Jones. However, no date is given for it either. The account concludes by saying, "The boy healed and grew up, forever grateful to the men who had saved his life" (*Anchored*, 108).

CHAPTER 11

August 16, 1888, 4:30 p.m.—Westland Home Site—Monticello

"Mitch?"

He turned to Edie, who was standing near the doorway. "Yeah?"

"Someone's coming."

"Who?"

"Can't tell yet. It's a wagon, though, and it looks like they're heading here."

"All right. Let me secure this bundle of shingles and I'll come see."

There was no response, and then Mitch heard what sounded like a low exclamation of astonishment. He looked over at the open doorway. Edie was gone. "Edie?"

No answer. Muttering to himself, Mitch hurriedly tied the rope around the shingles and slipped it over the hook of the block and tackle. Only then did he head for the door. "Edie?" he called again as he stepped outside. She wasn't there, either. Squinting against the brightness of the sunlight, Mitch looked around. A squeal of joy swung him around to the east.

Edie was running full tilt down the two-track road that led from their home site out to the main road. Her bonnet was around her neck, and her long, dark hair was streaming out behind her. A wagon was just turning into their lane, and she was waving and shouting ecstatically at it. "What the heck?" Mitch murmured. Then a figure on the wagon seat stood up and started waving. Mitch's jaw went slack. "Mama?" he exclaimed. "Papa?" And he too took off at a dead run.

4:35 p.m.

Mitch put an arm around his mother's waist and pulled her in so they were shoulder-to-shoulder. "I can't believe it," he said. "You're here."

Gwen Westland leaned into him. "I told you we were coming for stake conference."

"I know, but we didn't expect you for another couple of days."

His father, who was walking arm in arm with Edie toward the cabin, turned around. "I told you we'd be trying to come up and help you with the roof. Actually, we hoped to get here even earlier than this, but Bishop Nielson asked us to bring a load of stuff up here for Brother Jones."

Mitch looked around. "Where are Johnnie and Martha?"

"When they learned that their friends wouldn't be here until next Thursday, they wanted to wait. So Johnnie's coming up with Ben and Mary Ann Perkins, since their son Dan is Johnnie's best friend. Martha's coming up with the Lymans to help with their children."

Gwen let her eyes sweep over the partially completed cabin. "It's larger than I expected."

"I'll say," Arthur said.

"Well," Edie said, coming forward. "Mitch insists that my Oma Zimmer have a room of her own if she comes to live with us."

"I see," Gwen said, "but I thought she wasn't coming until next summer."

"That's right," Mitch said, "but it's easier to do it now than to try to add a room later."

"There's wisdom in that," his father said. He walked slowly along the length of the log wall, examining the log work carefully. "Very good," he called back over his shoulder. "I'm impressed. And it looks like you got your rafters on without me."

"Yeah, several of the brethren helped me get them up. That was the hardest part."

"Good. I'm sorry that we couldn't make it sooner."

"No problem, Dad. I'm just glad you're here."

Arthur was looking at the bundle of shingles twisting slowly at the end of the block and tackle. "So you're doing shingles? I thought you said you'd have to wait for that until next spring."

"That's what I thought too, but then I got to thinking. With Edie's grandmother coming, I couldn't risk her living under a sod roof. You know how they leak when it rains."

"Yeah, and how easily they can collapse."

"So I traded three cows to Mons Peterson before he went to Colorado, and he got me shingles."

"So you're definitely not coming down to Bluff for the winter?" his mother asked.

"I'm not," Mitch said, turning to Edie. "We're still debating whether Edie will or not."

Edie wrinkled her nose at him. "*He's* still debating. I've already decided. I'm staying. The Waltons have their cabin done and are letting me sleep in the bedroom with Maggie and Leona. I can stay there until we are married."

"We'll see," Mitch muttered under his breath.

Father and mother exchanged quick glances, but Arthur

changed the subject. “I’m pretty handy at laying down shingles if you’ve got an extra hammer.”

“I do, and I’d welcome the help.”

Mitch’s father turned to take in the view to the east. They were about a quarter of a mile above the town site, which was a beehive of activity at the moment. Beyond that was a patchwork of fields under cultivation—the dark green of alfalfa, the golden waves of nearly ripe wheat, barley, and oats, and then more green fields filled with meadow grass. Arthur shook his head in amazement. “How many acres have you fenced off now?”

“Three hundred and twenty. About a hundred of that is planted this year.”

“That’s impressive. President Hammond will be pleased.”

“I think so too. It’s going to be a rich harvest this year.”

“Yeah,” his father said, “and I heard that Charles Walton bought a threshing machine.”

“He did. And John Rogerson bought a grain cradle. Don’t know if you know the Rogersons. They arrived about six weeks ago from Mancos.”

“What’s a grain cradle?” Gwen asked. “Remember, I’m the girl from England.”

Mitch’s father answered. “It’s like a huge, mechanized scythe pulled by a team of horses. The cradle not only cuts the grain but lays it in neat rows so it is easier to tie into sheaves.”

Mitch was enthusiastic. “A really good man with a scythe can cut about an acre of grain a day. The cradle cuts that much in an hour.”

“So,” Arthur said. “We saw Fred and Mary Jones as we came in. Mary has invited Gwen to stay there. I’ll bring the wagon up and sleep here. Do you plan to start shingling tomorrow?”

“Well, I was going to, but the meetinghouse isn’t quite finished yet, so Brother Jones has asked all of the brethren to work on that this weekend. But I'd like to get the bundles of shingles up on the roof by tonight. Then tomorrow, we'll go down and help put in the pews."

"Actual pews?" Arthur asked in surprise.

"No, no. There's no way we can do that with the tools we have. No, we've set some short cedar posts upright in the dirt floor. But we still need to saw the lumber slabs that will provide the seating."

"And then they've got to tamp down the dirt floor until it's really hard packed," Edie added.

"Yeah," Mitch nodded. "Brother Jones was hoping to have wood flooring in, but we're not going to make that. Don't have the finished lumber for it yet."

"That's a problem," Arthur said. "But as we came through Verdure, we saw the Butts. Parley and Willard told us they'll have a sawmill here by next spring."

"Yes," Mitch said. "The Butt Brothers Lumber Company. And thank heaven for that."

Edie slipped an arm through Gwen's. "The sisters are meeting tonight at the Walton home. The Relief Society is responsible for all the meals, so Jane wants to get them all planned out in advance. On Saturday, all of the sisters are going to do a garden harvest. Then on Wednesday, the men will start butchering hogs and a few heifers."

"Good," Gwen said. "We saw a few people as we came through town, but I'm so excited to see everyone again. And everyone in Bluff is excited to see what you've done up here."

Gwen stepped away from Edie and held Mitch at arm's length, studying his face intently. He submitted to her scrutiny with a smile. When she nodded and seemed satisfied, he cocked his head and asked, "So? Do I pass muster?"

She laughed. "You're happy, Mitch. I can see that in you."

He reached out and took Edie's hand and pulled her close. "I'm happy because I have Edie and I know she's going to be mine forever."

"And I'm happy too," Edie said, "and for the same reason."

Gwen shook her head. "No, I wouldn't say you were happy, Edie."

"You wouldn't?" she cried in dismay.

"I think positively radiant is a better description. Don't you, Arthur?"

Arthur smiled and nodded. "Absolutely."

6:05 p.m.

Arthur Westland set another bundle of shingles on the roof and straightened slowly. Mitch was down below inside the cabin, securing the next bundle to the block and tackle. "Son?"

Mitch stepped into view. "Yes, Pa?"

"You've got company coming."

"From town?"

"No, from the north."

Immediately, the shingles were forgotten. Mitch looked out the opening that would eventually be his back window and saw four riders about a quarter of a mile away coming at a steady trot. He went to the corner where his canteen, tool box, and other belongings were and strapped on his six-shooter. His father had come over to the hole in the roof through which they were passing the shingles up. He sobered. "You expecting trouble?"

"No." Mitch smiled without mirth. "But we're always prepared. With the cowhands, you never know. Remind me to tell you their latest."

Mitch looked again. The riders were coming at a leisurely trot. "We've got time, tell me now."

"Okay, but come on down, Pa." As his father descended the ladder, Mitch began to talk. "George Adams, who has his dairy down on South Montezuma Creek, has been putting bells on his milk cows so they're easier to find when it's time to round them up for milking. Well, about a month or so ago the bells started to go missing. Turns out that some of the Carlisle hands decided they made nice souvenirs and so they were cutting them off. So, George and Fred tried something different. They used small lengths of chain instead of leather straps, padlocked them so they couldn't be opened, and cinched them tight enough that they couldn't be taken over the animal's head."

"And did that work?"

"No. Three days later George found one of his cows with its head cut off."

Arthur gasped. "They killed the animal for a bell?"

"That's right. Only it's four animals now. They were shot between the eyes, their heads were severed, and the bells were gone. They didn't take the hide or any meat, just those stupid cowbells. George went to Carlisle and confronted him, but he just laughed it off, saying that it was Indians, not his boys."

"They're real hell-raisers all right," his father agreed. "One of the favorite 'practical jokes' down our way has to do with the Mexican sheepherders."

"Oh?"

"Yeah. If the cowboys come across their camps while the herders are out with their sheep, they'll bury bullets in the cold ashes of their campfire. Then that night, as the herders get their fires going again, suddenly bullets start blasting off in every direction. So far, none of the herders have been hit, but someone's gonna get killed. The cowboys think it's hilarious."

Arthur watched the approaching riders, who were now just a couple hundred yards away. "Shall I get my pistol? It's in my valise."

"No, you're fine. It'll be fine."

As the riders approached, Mitch was relieved to see that Bill Edwards rode at their head. Without turning his head, he spoke quietly to his father. "This is good. The lead rider there is named Edwards. He's a little older and a pretty level-headed guy." He then told Arthur quickly about the run-in between Edwards and Mons Peterson. By the time he finished, they were pulling up in the yard. Mitch raised a hand in greeting. "Evening, Bill."

"Howdy, Mitch." He looked at the cabin. "You're making good progress."

"It's coming," Mitch acknowledged, then nodded to the other three. "Howdy." He gestured toward his father. "This is my father, Arthur Westland. He's up visiting from Bluff City."

Arthur raised his hand and let it drop but said nothing as the others murmured greetings.

Edwards didn't bother to introduce the men, but Mitch recognized a couple of them. They were all his age or younger. One of them was named Dave something or other—a French-sounding last name. The one next to him was William Gordon, but everyone called him Latigo. He was actually the son-in-law of old man Carlisle. And he was a hard case. Rumor was that he came there after shooting down his friend in a saloon brawl in Durango.

"Headed into town?" Mitch asked.

Edwards nodded. "Heard Mons got in some fresh supplies."

"Yup. Brought in a wagonload about a week ago."

"Does he have whiskey?" the one called Dave said.

"Not in this town," Mitch answered easily. "You'll have to go to Moab or Mancos for that."

"Bullets?" Latigo asked.

"Some. Mainly thirty-thirty shells and pistol cartridges for the Colt .45."

"Good. Them's what we're looking for."

"He's there. If he's not at the store, he'll be close by. Ask anyone."

"Know where it is." Edwards said. He leaned forward, both hands resting on his saddle horn. "Boys have another question, if you don't mind."

"Don't mind at all. What is it?" He looked to the other three.

Latigo spoke for them. "Understand you Mormons are partying this weekend. That true?"

"Not this weekend. Next one. We call it a conference, and we have members from all over the area coming in. We'll be having church meetings all day Saturday and Sunday, but—"

The young one, whose name Mitch didn't know, guffawed. "You go to church on Saturday, too? I heard you Mormons were fanatics, but two days? Man, that's just plumb crazy."

Mitch nodded soberly. "The hard part is not getting to eat for forty-eight hours and never being allowed a trip to the outhouse."

The men's eyes widened in shock. Edwards grunted. "He's jerking your tail, you log heads." Mitch turned back to Latigo. "But yes, Friday's a day of fun and games for the kids, some horse races for the men, a quilting bee for the ladies, and a dance that evening."

"Yeah," Latigo said eagerly. "That's what we heard. Are we invited?" He leered at Mitch. "You've got some purty-looking fillies down here."

"So you're not interested in the quilting bee?" Mitch said, straight-faced.

Edwards hooted. "Probably not, but I'd like to enter Latigo

in the gunny sack races with the kids. See if he can win something for once." As Latigo's face flushed, Edwards went on. "But seriously, we have some mounts we'd like to put up against your best horseflesh."

"The races are open to anyone. Just come early enough to get your animals registered. Twenty-five-cent fee per animal, which will be divided amongst the four winners. The races will start about five-thirty on Friday."

Edwards nodded, seemingly pleased, but Latigo wasn't smiling. He was smoldering at being made fun of. "You gonna turn us away if we come to the dance, Westland?"

Mitch shook his head. "Neighbors are welcome. But you know the dance rules, Latigo. No liquor or guns or cussing allowed. Our girls will be treated with courtesy and respect. If you come drunk, you'll be turned away. And no dancing with the same girl two dances in a row. That's the same for us, too. Remember, we only have a few single girls of dancing age in Monticello right now."

"And one of them is your fee-ance-say, right?" the one called Dave chortled.

"That's right."

"Only a few?" Latigo sneered. "I thought there was about a hundred people coming in this weekend."

"Ah," Mitch said. "I wasn't thinking about that. Yup. You're right. With the families coming in, we'll probably have fifteen or twenty single young ladies of age."

"Yee-haw!" the young one cried. "Real girls." Edwards took up the reins with a sardonic smile. "Much obliged, Mitch. We'll see you on Friday." And with that, they moved away.

Mitch called after them. "Hey, Latigo!"

He half turned in his saddle.

"If you've got a white shirt and can get the manure off your boots, you're welcome to come to church on Sunday, too."

Latigo jerked back around, saying something Mitch didn't catch but that he was sure was profane, and then put spurs to his horse.

To Mitch's surprise, Dave held his horse in check while the others rode off. He looked down at the two Westlands. "Just wanted you to know, we're not all like Latigo." He leaned in, lowering his voice, as if the others could still hear him. "You'll find this hard to believe, but I'm the son of a Baptist preacher back in Tennessee."

That did surprise Mitch, and it showed on his face.

"And there are three others who are sons of ministers too. So, we'll honor those rules, and we'll help you enforce them." He lifted a hand, spurred his horse into a lope, and quickly caught up with the others.

Notes

In some ways, the Mormon pioneer settlers, particularly around Monticello, had many more problems with the cattlemen and their hired hands than they did with the Native Americans in the area. The life of the American cowboy has been widely romanticized and fictionalized, but in reality they were a tough bunch of independent men, most without families or social ties. It was a hard life—spending days in the saddle, sleeping on the ground in bedrolls, cooking meager meals over open campfires, and often not seeing another living person for weeks at a time.

Many were decent young men who had left their families to gain independence and try life on their own. Sometimes they were forced to leave because the family's small farm wasn't large enough to support two families. But many were raucous men, given to violent practical jokes Then there was a significant number of cowhands who were not only men of low or no morals—crude, profane, hard-drinking, hard-fighting men who lived by the gun—but were also on the run from the law. The big cattle outfits willingly hired them because good cowhands were hard to find, especially in the isolated areas of the American West.

The two examples given here—putting live ammunition in the campfires of sheep herders as a "joke" and cutting off the heads of milk cows in order to steal a cowbell—are actual examples of some of the problems the Mormons had with the cattlemen (see *Saga*, 106, 228).

The policy of the Latter-day Saints in dealing with the cowboys was the same as it was with the Indians. Avoid open conflict if at all possible. However, it was more complicated than that. The Mormon settlements provided the only real social life of any kind for miles in every direction, which created a constant problem for the Saints. The pioneers were a happy and fun-loving people. Picnics, parades, plays, musical dramas, and dances were common in their isolated lives. Dances in particular were popular and were held regularly. The Mormons set strict standards at them, which only added to the tensions.

Albert R. Lyman describes it thus: "The rip-roaring men of the Texas outfit seemed to think that if he bought a clean shirt, and possibly a [clean] pair of trousers, and girded his neck with a red bandana handkerchief, he was fully eligible for all the honors and privileges of this country ball room. He generally removed his spurs, though he did not always venture to remove his revolver. Worse than his gun, was the bottle concealed on his person, or hidden outside in a nearby fence, for he must be well primed with whiskey to [have enough courage] to meet his lofty goals" (*History of San Juan County*, 64).

Knowing the standards of modesty, decency, language, and decorum that were generally held by the Latter-day Saints, one can only imagine the tensions that were created as they danced with these men who reeked of tobacco and whiskey, whose reputation for violence was well known, and whose social graces were lacking, to say the least.

CHAPTER 12

August 24, 1888, 7:15 p.m.—Walton Cabin—Monticello

Gwen Westland and Edie Zimmer answered the door together, their long skirts swishing softly as they stepped back to let the men into the house. But Arthur and Mitch didn't move. They just gaped at them. Then Mitch gave a low whistle of amazement. "You two are exquisitely lovely," he said.

Gwen tipped her head back and laughed. "Did you hear that, Edie? Exquisitely lovely."

"I mean it, Mama."

His mother's dress was a deep maroon color with white pearl buttons, spaced less than an inch apart, from her throat to her waist. Smaller but matching buttons fastened her sleeves at the wrist. The top of the dress was fitted so as to emphasize her tiny waist, but with the help of a small bustle, the skirt puffed out three or four inches and fell in pleasing folds to the floor.

Then he looked at Edie. Her dress, or rather blouse and skirt, were simpler in style, which made her seem all the more lovely. The blouse, which buttoned at the hollow of her throat and had long, puffed sleeves, was made of a pale green, starched linen. White lace trim around the neck and the wrists provided a lovely accent. All of that was set off by her skirt, which was of a slightly heavier material and dyed a deep forest green.

"When did you get that?" Mitch asked, realizing that he had never seen it before.

"Mons brought the cloth back from Mancos," Edie said, pleased by the approval she saw in his eyes. "Sister Rogerson helped me sew it." She twirled around once. "Do you like it?"

"I think it's . . . stunning."

"Ooh," she cooed, "exquisite and stunning. Keep it up, mister, and I may let you sign my dance card."

"Hey," he said. "I'm signing up for every dance."

"That's not allowed," Edie said demurely.

"I'll say not," Mitch's mother said, feigning a pout. "What about me? I certainly hope to dance with my son tonight."

"Of course, Mother. I meant every dance but the three or four I dance with you."

"And at least two with me," a voice cried out from off to their left. They turned to see Mitch's fourteen-year-old sister coming out of the bedroom.

Mitch fell back, pretending shock. "And who is this lovely young lady?"

Martha blushed. "It is I," she said airily, "Martha Gwendolyn Westland, your little sister."

"That's not possible," he retorted. And then he swept her up in his arms. "You look beautiful, Martha. I'm so glad you're here."

She pulled a card from her small purse along with a stub of a pencil and thrust it at Mitch. "Sign up for three dances at least." As he took it, she looked past him. "And Papa, three for you also. I do not want to be standing on the sidelines all night tonight."

"Oh, you won't be," Mitch said. "But I don't want you dancing with any of the cowboys." He swung around to face Edie. "And that goes for you too."

"Why not?" Edie said.

"Because I don't want you dancing with Latigo Gordon, and I know he's going to ask you."

Edie's smile faded quickly. "Much as I'd like not to, you know we can't do that. Brother Jones says we have to accommodate the cowhands as long as the dance master says that they've met the requirements to enter. And since he is the dance master, his word goes."

The bedroom door opened again, and Maggie and Leona Walton came out in their long dresses, one a pale blue, the other a deep gold. Maggie carried a matching parasol. A moment after that, Jane Walton appeared, followed by her husband, Charles, and their son, Charlie.

"My, my," Arthur said, feigning complete astonishment. "It looks like there might be a dance going on tonight somewhere." Then he turned to Brother Walton. "Are you playing fiddle tonight, Charles?"

"I am." He moved to the table and picked up the leather case there. "And Brother Jones has given his permission to bring our little organ out so that Charlie can chord along with me. And he will join me with his harmonica."

"And who's calling the square dancing?" Gwen asked.

"Brother Rogerson," Edie said. "He's the best."

Charles took his pocket watch out of his vest pocket and looked at it. "And since the dance is supposed to start in ten minutes, I suggest we get on our way."

Mitch looked at his mother. "What about Johnnie?"

"He'll come with the Hydes. In fact, knowing your brother, I'm guessing he's already there and right in the midst of things."

Mitch extended both elbows. "Sister Westland. Sister Zimmer. May I have the privilege of escorting you to the dance?"

Edie immediately put her arm through his, but Gwen demurred. "Sorry, son, but I've recently met this dashing man from

Bluff who has offered me his arm." And she took Arthur's arm and started toward the door.

7:30 p.m.

By the official starting time for the dance, the square in front of the meetinghouse was packed, and wagons, carriages, buckboards, and two-wheeled carts lined the street in both directions. It was an exciting moment for the fledgling little town. The air was filled with excitement and the mood was festive. Mitch was eyeing the crowd as they approached. People had seen their party approaching and were calling out and waving, but there were no cowboys that he could see.

Mons and Eliza Peterson came up and joined them and were warmly greeted. Mons turned to Brother Walton. "My wagon's right over there. We've got a chair up in it for you. And we've got the organ up there, too. People shouldn't have any trouble hearing you from that vantage point."

Maggie turned to her brother. "Do you already have pumpers for the organ, Charlie?"

"Yes. Already lined up. We'll be changing every fifteen minutes."

Just then a clatter of hooves off in the distance sounded over the noise of the crowd. Everyone turned to see who it was. The sight of a substantial band of mounted horsemen coming at a steady trot was enough to instantly squelch all conversation.

Mons let out a long breath. "Looks like we've got most of the bunch. Do you see Carlisle?"

Mitch shook his head. "No, but Bill Edwards is in the lead. That's good."

Brother Fred Jones came up and joined them. "Come on,"

he said to Mitch and Mons, grimacing as he spoke. "Let's go welcome our *guests*. And make sure they're not packing iron and don't have bellies full of whiskey."

As the riders dismounted and started looking around for a place to tie their horses, Mitch and Mons walked over to join them. "Feel free to tie your mounts to the wagon wheels, the corral fences, or any available hitching post that's not already full." He went right up to Edwards and stuck out his hand. "Welcome, Bill." He looked around. "And welcome to the rest of you as well."

"Evening, Westland. Mons." As they returned his greeting, Bill turned around and looked at his men. "All right, you guys. We appreciate the invitation to join in with the Mormons tonight. You know what the rules are. Leave your rifles in their scabbards and your pistols in your saddle bags. No strong drink of any kind." He looked at Latigo. "And the first time I hear one of you cussing, I'll personally toss you out on your ear."

"I ain't here to cuss," Latigo sneered. "I'm here to dance." He looked at Mitch. "Where's that fee-ance-say of yours?"

"When I told her you might be here, Latigo, she left for Richfield to stay with her parents."

The young cowboy's face darkened, but Mitch went right on. "She said she had heard you were so handsome that she might be tempted to break off our engagement once she saw you."

That brought guffaws and laughter from the men around him, and finally Latigo managed a smile too. "She got that right," he sneered.

Mitch saw the young cowboy named Dave and smiled up at him. "Who–ee!" he said, "and look at you. Clean shirt. Bolo tie. Freshly washed Levi's. No dirt under your fingernails."

Edwards chuckled. "I told them that these are nice girls and they ain't gonna want to dance with a man that smells like the corral. So they all took a turn in the creek this afternoon. The only problem is we had ten head of cattle die after drinking the water downstream."

Mitch hooted. This was good. The mood was light. These men were as nervous as a cat holed up in a barn with a pack of hounds. He turned and pointed toward the square. "The ladies are having their dance cards signed right now, so I suggest you dismount, tie up your horses, and get on down there."

Fred Jones came up just then. "Welcome. Glad to have you boys join us. Just so you know, I'm the dance master tonight. As in all dances, the dance master has the final say if there is a dispute about who gets to dance with whom. I'll also be checking everyone—including our people—to make sure that no guns or liquor of any kind are brought onto the dance floor."

"Liquor?" someone called out mournfully. "Not even sure what that word means anymore."

No one laughed. Edwards nodded at Brother Jones. "That's true. Your county is a little short on saloons."

"Good," Fred said. Then he went on. "There are twenty spaces on each dance card. No one can dance with the same girl twice in a row unless it's his wife."

"What about a fee-ance-say?" Dave called out. "They held to that rule too?"

Fred punched Mitch playfully. "Sorry, Mitch. Fiancees don't count as being married yet."

Just then the sound of a fiddle started up, and people began to clap. Edwards swung down off his horse. "You boys sit around and jaw all you like. Me? I'm gonna go down and sign me some dance cards."

"Hee-yaw!" someone shouted as a dozen men spurred their horses toward the nearest open hitching rails.

11:00 p.m.

Precisely at eleven o'clock, Fred Jones climbed up on the wagon beside Charles and Charlie Walton and called for attention. The people quickly quieted and moved in closer. He smiled. "Brothers and sisters, and gentlemen from the Carlisle spread, we are—"

One of the cowboys in the back broke in. "Thank you, sir. Ain't no one never called me a gentleman before. I'm going to write my ma and tell her."

Everyone laughed.

"Well," Brother Jones went on, "we have had a good time tonight. It is now eleven o'clock, so this will be the last dance. We have completed all twenty of the dances listed on the dance cards, which means that for this last dance you men are free to invite any woman of your choosing."

Pandemonium broke out as everyone rushed forward. Caught completely off guard by the announcement, Mitch immediately turned and made a beeline for Edie. But Latigo beat him there by four steps.

"Miss Zimmer," he said, bowing low and flourishing with his hand, "would you do me the honor of having the last dance with me?"

"Sorry, Latigo," Mitch said as he came up to them. "She's already spoken for."

For a moment, Edie looked back and forth between them, but then she shook her head. "And I'm sorry too, Mr. Westland, but Mr. Latigo did ask me first."

Mitch's jaw went slack as Latigo yelped in delight. As he did so, Edie held out her hand to him. Latigo took it as the fiddle began to play and he walked her away. As Mitch watched in obvious dismay, his mother came over to join him. "Well, well," she chuckled. "You'll learn to be a little faster next time."

"I can't believe she just did that," he grumbled. "She saw me coming."

"You're lucky to have her, son."

"Oh, really? I'm not seeing that right now, actually."

"Well, you ought to," she shot right back. "Of all the cowboys here tonight, Edie detests Latigo the very most. He's arrogant, conceited, brags incessantly about himself, and reeks of tobacco. But she also understands that he's the son-in-law of Mr. Carlisle, that he's got the hottest temper, and that the other cowboys look up to him. So she just made a very wise choice. Let him have something else to brag about now, and maybe he'll behave himself the next time he comes to town."

Mitch glared at his mother for several seconds and then blew out his breath in exasperation. "Mother, will there ever come a time in our married life when you side with me and not Edie?"

She slipped an arm around her son's waist. "I'm sure there will. But at the rate you're going, that's not in your foreseeable future."

August 25, 1888, 10:00 a.m.—Meetinghouse—Monticello

The meetinghouse was crammed to capacity as the first session of the San Juan Stake conference began on Saturday morning. Even then, there were close to a dozen men and older boys who stood outside the doors and the windows. Inside, women and children fanned themselves continuously, for the air was close and quite stuffy. But heat was something they had learned to endure with good humor. Precisely at ten o'clock, President Francis Hammond stood up. He welcomed the congregation warmly, joked about having sore feet after all of the dancing the previous night, and then announced the opening hymn and prayer. With Charlie Hammond at their small organ, they sang "High on the Mountain Top," which seemed particularly appropriate with the Blue Mountains towering over them just a mile to the west.

After the prayer, President Hammond came to the pulpit again. "Brothers and sisters, before we begin our gospel instruction, we have a matter of business to conduct, and then I should like to make two announcements. I hope you will find these edifying as well as instructive. Before leaving Colorado, I received authorization from Salt Lake City to formally organize the townships of Monticello and Verdure into a branch of the San Juan Stake of Zion and an established unit of The Church of Jesus Christ of Latter-day Saints. It will be known as the Monticello Branch. I am proposing that we do that now. All in favor?"

Hands shot into the air.

"Are there any opposed?" There were not.

"It is also proposed that we sustain Frederick I. Jones as branch president, Charles E. Walton as first counselor, and George Adams as second counselor. All in favor?"

Another enthusiastic response.

"Any opposed?" No hands came up.

"For your information—and this does not require a sustaining vote—though Verdure is part of the Monticello Branch, because it is somewhat removed from Monticello, I have designated Brother George Adams as the presiding elder at Verdure. He is authorized to make decisions and take action when it is not possible to get an immediate answer from the full presidency of the branch."

President Hammond paused for a moment and then continued, pleased with the response he was seeing. "I have also counseled the presidency to fully organize the branch as soon as possible. Though you are a small branch at the moment, more are coming all the time, and soon you shall be large enough to be a ward. But in the meantime, you should have all of the organizations that are found in other units of stakes in Zion. When the branch presidency have counseled together, they will present names to you for your sustaining vote in these matters as well."

His face was covered with a light sheen of perspiration. He withdrew a handkerchief from inside his jacket, removed his glasses, and wiped at his brow. When he was done, he went on.

"Now, two short announcements, and then we shall proceed with our conference. Unfortunately, the first is not good news, but you need to be informed."

That changed the mood in the hall almost instantly.

"I would speak of the rumors that have been flying back and forth now for some time about Congress creating a Ute Indian reservation here in San Juan County."

That brought a buzz of reaction, including downright anger. President Hammond raised his voice and went right on. "I believe that nothing is going to come of this and have expressed myself in that regard several times. But just before leaving Mancos to come here, I received a telegram from Salt Lake City. From President Wilford Woodruff."

That quieted the room almost instantly.

"I was informed that the U.S. House of Representatives has confirmed that it is sending a commission here to study the issue and to make a recommendation to Congress and the president in this matter. They will be arriving in Salt Lake City sometime in late September or early October. President Wilford Woodruff will meet with them. He has asked that I come to Salt Lake and meet with them as well. Then he has asked that I accompany the commission down here and escort them around the county so they can see for themselves what we have accomplished. Since I am not as familiar with the county as I should be, I have asked Brother Lemuel H. Redd to serve as our guide. The commission has indicated that they want to see all of the county, not just our three settlements."

Mitch leaned over and whispered to his father. "They couldn't do better than Lem Redd, that's for sure. No one knows this county better than him."

Arthur nodded.

President Hammond fell silent for several seconds, his face troubled. Finally, he looked up. "Brothers and sisters, I present this information to you to keep you informed. I know this is an issue of grave concern to you, but I feel impressed to say this much. I urge you to pray in behalf of your land here. I believe that our faith can influence the outcome."

He suddenly smacked the pulpit sharply with the flat of his hand, causing several in the room to jump. "You are here in answer to a call from the Lord. Do not forget that. Most of you have stayed here in spite of flood and drought, Indians and outlaws, and all of the combined forces of earth and hell that are trying to dislodge us from our place. But I say to you again, if we exercise faith and do what we have been called to do, we can have a powerful influence on what happens here."

As they watched, they could see him visibly relax, and then he actually smiled. "Now, on to something more pleasant. As you know, our beloved Prophet Joseph Smith clearly taught us the importance of education. I cite two statements he received by revelation before he was taken from us. The first one is quite simple, though very profound. It is that 'the glory of God is intelligence, or in other words, light and truth.' The second"—and now he looked down at a paper he had placed on the podium—"is this. 'Whatever principle of intelligence we attain unto in this life, it will rise with us in the resurrection. And if a person gains more knowledge and intelligence in this life through his diligence and obedience than another, he will have so much the advantage in the world to come.'"

He looked up. "I love that concept, brothers and sisters. I love the idea that learning has eternal consequences. Therefore, I am very pleased to announce to you this day that starting in a little less than a month from now, after you get in your gardens and row crops, Sister Sarah Rogerson, who recently arrived here with her husband and family, will be starting a formal school for the children of Monticello."

As cries of surprise and elation rang out, Edie gripped Mitch's arm. "Wonderful! Oh, Mitch, that's wonderful." She turned to Gwen. "This is wonderful news. Sarah taught school over in Mancos. She will be a marvelous teacher."

President Hammond went on. "Sister Rogerson is an experienced and accomplished schoolteacher and will hold classes for children between the ages of seven and sixteen. It shall be held in this building until the Rogersons complete their cabin, and thereafter will be held in their home. The branch presidency will be asking some of you brethren whose children will be attending school to help the Rogersons complete their home as rapidly as possible before the weather turns bad. Also, we'll ask participating families to contribute what they can to Sister Rogerson, either in cash or in kind."

This was greeted with much enthusiasm, and the hall was filled with noise now. President Hammond let it roll for a moment and then raised his hands for quiet. When he got it, there was a playful smile on his face. "And . . ." he said, clearly enjoying himself now, "you'll note that those revelations did not say that education was for children only. So, I would like to ask

President William Adams, my counselor in the stake presidency, whom you all know well, to stand for a moment."

Every head turned as an older man got to his feet, clearly not at all surprised by the invitation to do so. Edie gave Mitch a quizzical look, but he shook his head. William and Mary Adams, parents of George and Fred Adams, had come up from Bluff earlier in the summer to join their two boys in the Blue Mountain Mission. But they had chosen to live in Monticello rather than Verdure and were building a cabin not far from where they now sat.

"Before leaving Ireland to come to Zion," President Hammond continued, "Brother William received an excellent education from a Belfast academy. He also served as a schoolteacher prior to coming to San Juan. So we are very pleased to announce that he will be holding evening classes for the adults of this community once or twice a week in his home."

There was a cry of delight, followed by applause. The president, pleased with that response, raised his voice and spoke over it. "He will teach classes in mathematics, grammar, reading, history, and geology."

Edie glanced up at Mitch and was pleased to note that he was smiling. Then she leaned over to Gwen. "Do you think I can get Mitch to attend with me?"

"I think you will have a hard time keeping him away," she murmured happily.

Notes

The stake conference held in Monticello in August 1888 was a very important time for the Saints there. To have members come from all over the Four Corners area and see their little town in the wilderness was very significant to the Monticello and Verdure Saints. Here is how one source described it:

"Conference was the religious and social event of the year. The big event was anticipated and prepared for weeks in advance. More than a hundred people came in their wagons, buggies, and by horseback from the wards of the San Juan Stake—from New Mexico, Colorado, Moab and Bluff, with their bed rolls and food enough to sustain them on their trip. The Jones home and yard was the main center for the gathering of the travelers. . . . The visitors made their beds in wagon boxes, in the yard, and on the floor of the Jones cabin. Sister Jones and other women of the town had prepared their choicest recipes for a week or more" (*Anchored*, 90; see also *Saga*, 100–101).

It appears that the Monticello Branch was organized sometime that summer, so it seemed logical that would be done as a part of stake conference. No other details are given about speakers or the topics addressed in the conference.

CHAPTER 13

September 4, 1888, 9:40 a.m.—Peterson Store and Cabin —Monticello

Mons Peterson looked up as Edie came through the door and entered the Peterson Dry Goods Store. He smiled and lifted a hand. "Morning, Edie."

"Good morning, Mons."

She saw quickly that she was the only one in the store at the moment. The store was actually one of four rooms of the Petersons' recently completed cabin. One served as the bedroom for Mons and Eliza; a smaller bedroom was for the two children. The room that served as a combination kitchen, sitting room, and waiting room for store customers was separated from the store by three Navajo blankets hung on a rope strung across the opening. During the day, the blankets hung down but actually provided very little privacy. They neither shut out the noise nor stopped curious customers from pulling the blankets back and poking their heads in to see what else there was to be seen in the house. At night, Mons would lock the outside door and pin the blankets back with clothespins, and the store would become an expanded living area. The far corner of this larger room had an iron cook stove, a round table and four chairs, and a sideboard that held dishes and cutlery.

Suddenly, one of the blankets pulled back and a little head

with dark, curly hair and dancing brown eyes peered through the opening. "Hi, Aunt Edie."

Immediately Edie went over to the girl. She went down on one knee and held out her arms. "Good morning, Ellie. And how are you today?" Elna was the Petersons' oldest child. She had turned three in June.

She looked up, her dark eyes large and forlorn. "I sad."

"Oh, I'm sorry to hear that, Ellie. Why are you sad?"

"'Cause Mama's sick."

Edie whirled around and looked up at Mons. "Again?"

He nodded.

"But I just saw her yesterday afternoon."

Ellie tugged at her skirt. "Mama has a bad cough."

"That makes me sad too, Ellie." Edie stood up, turning to Mons. "Can I see her?"

"She's sleeping in the back bedroom. Little Mons fell asleep after she nursed him, so I told her to try to get some sleep too. She coughed most of the night."

"Is there anything I can do to help? Can I bring in supper tonight for you and Ellie?"

His face softened. "That's kind of you to ask, but Sister Walton has already offered. She was just here a few minutes ago."

Of course she was. That was Jane Walton. And it wasn't just because she was stake Relief Society president. Since Edie had moved in with the Waltons, she had learned that it was Jane's nature to always be reaching out to help others, to cheer them up, bake them bread, run an errand for them, or do anything else that was required. And since the Waltons lived just across the street from the store, she would certainly know something was amiss at the Petersons'. "Well," Edie said, "I'll talk to Maggie and

Leona, and we'll convince Jane to let us three make you dinner. That is, if you trust three single young women to cook for you."

"Of course," he laughed. "I've tasted all of your cooking. That would be wonderful."

"Will you make Lizzie some cookies, Aunt Edie?"

She turned. "Of course. But who is Lizzie?"

She held up the doll she was holding. "Lizzie."

"Oh," Edie said soberly. "Then yes indeed, I shall make cookies for you and Lizzie and for your papa too." Then she had another thought. "Do you have something you need to do, Mons? I'd be happy to stay here and play with Ellie and listen for the baby."

Mons hesitated but then nodded gratefully. "Actually, I do need to go down to Verdure and get my younger sister, Emma. She's from Mancos but came over to Bluff with Eliza's father, President Hammond. She's coming to stay with us for a while, to help Eliza with the children."

"Oh, good. And how old is she?"

"She's sixteen."

"And that's even nicer. Maggie and Leona and I shall put on a welcome party for her."

"She would like that very much. Anyway, I promised I'd come down to Verdure and pick her up this morning, but with Eliza sick, I didn't dare leave."

"Then go, Mons. I'll stay here."

"Are you sure?"

"I told Sarah Rogerson I'd come to their cabin and help her get things ready for school. But that's not until after two this afternoon, so I have plenty of time. And if you don't make it back, I'll just go down there when I can."

"That's very kind of you, Edie. Thank you. I'll hang out a sign saying the store is closed until later and lock the door. I hope nobody will bother you." He walked over and pinned the blanket back and then turned to his daughter. "Ellie, Lizzie looks tired. Why don't you lie down with her and see if she'll take a nap too, like Mommy and Baby Mons are doing?"

Ellie saw through that subterfuge instantly. "No, Papa, I not tired. Lizzie tired."

Edie went over to her, waving her hand behind her for Mons to go. "I've got an idea," she said, sitting down beside her. "If you lie down beside Lizzie, I'll tell you both a story."

"Yay!" Ellie went back into the main part of the house with Edie following her. There was a quilt spread out in one corner. Several of her toys were on it. Ellie walked over and carefully laid the doll down. She pulled a corner of the quilt over her and then lay down beside her doll.

Edie joined them. "What story would you like me to tell you?" she asked.

"Cinderella. That's my fav-oh-rite."

"Then Cinderella it is," Edie said.

As she started with "once upon a time," Mons quietly went about tidying up the store. Two minutes later, when he tiptoed past them to gather up his things, Ellie's eyes were already heavy. When he came out of the bedroom about three minutes after that, she was gone.

He smiled at Edie. "You're a wonder," he whispered. "I should only be about three hours."

Edie got to her feet. "Take what time you need, Mons. We'll be fine."

"Okay. I'll lock the store door behind me. And thanks again."

But as he moved to the door and opened it, he gave a low cry and fell back a step. Edie stiffened too. Standing just outside the door were three Indians, and behind them were two Indian ponies with only blankets for saddles.

Mons recovered quickly, turning to Edie. "It's all right. These are just some of our Indian brothers. Would you pull the blanket down?"

She did so, closing off Elna from their view, but stayed in the store with Mons so that he wasn't alone. The man standing nearest the door entered the room. He was a man of about thirty or thirty-five she guessed, and he was dressed in a combination of native clothing and western cowboy dress, which was becoming more and more the norm with both the Utes and the Navajo. He wore faded Levi's and a long-sleeved, red and white checkered shirt, which was buttoned at the neck. His hair, as black and shiny as a raven's feathers, was thick and worn loose. It was as long or was longer than Edie's. He wore a traditional beaded necklace that came down to mid-chest, but his Levi's were held up with a belt and belt buckle that could have come right off one of the Carlisle cowhands. On his feet he wore scuffed cowboy boots.

Mons raised his right hand, fingers up, palm toward them, in the traditional sign of greeting. "*Mique*," he said easily. It was Ute for hello. He motioned to them. "Come in, my brothers."

"*Mique*," the first Ute replied in a low, gravelly voice. "*Nuni Neeyah*—" He hesitated for a second or two, then said in English, "Me John Blackhorse."

"Yes," Mons said. "I know of you, John Blackhorse. Welcome." He pointed to himself. "My name is Mons Peterson." He pronounced it slowly.

"Yah. My people say you good man, Mons Peterson." He turned and looked at Edie. "This your squaw?"

Mons shook his head. "No. Squaw is sick. This is squaw's good friend." Edie smiled at the man as Mons explained her presence.

"Yah," the Ute said as he turned back to the door and motioned for his other two companions to come in. "We have sick man too," he said as a young Indian came in, heavily supporting an old man who was bent over and moaning in pain. The young one kicked the door shut with a bang. Here the contrast in dress was dramatic. The boy—for he looked no more than fifteen or sixteen—also wore Levi's and a white man's shirt, but over that he had a heavy woolen vest that was buttoned to the middle of his chest, and over that he wore a blue jacket with epaulets on each shoulder. It looked like it had once belonged to a U.S. cavalry man. Edie was astonished. It was already hot outside, and they had obviously come from some distance, yet the boy showed no signs of perspiration. His hair was braided in twin braids that were draped down the front of his shirt. They nearly reached his waist, and Edie wondered if his hair had ever been cut.

But the old man wore all native dress except for a light blue shirt. His jacket, which looked to be made of soft sheepskin, had stripes down the full length of the sleeves, with an intricate triangular design woven into them. That design continued down the legs of his trousers, also made of that same soft material. His ankle-length moccasins had bead work on them. It was really quite striking in its overall effect, and Edie wondered if they had dressed the old man in his ceremonial best before bringing him to the white man's store. The other thing that distinguished him from his two companions was that he had a scraggly mustache and a tuft of a beard on his chin. That, and the fact that on his forehead was a sheen of perspiration.

Edie took all that in while Mons studied the oldest of their three customers. "What is wrong with your friend?" he asked Blackhorse as he stepped up to the old man and looked into his eyes.

"He Little Whiskers," Blackhorse replied. "He big sick."

"I can see that." Mons put an arm around the man and motioned toward a stool in the corner. "Let's get him over there. Let him sit down while we talk."

Blackhorse nodded and spoke in low tones to the boy.

Together they walked the older man to the stool and helped him to sit down. In spite of his gritted teeth, the old man yelped with pain as they got him down. Mons reached out and put a hand on his forehead and then jerked back. "Whoa," he cried. "He's burning up."

"He very bad. Need white man medicine," Blackhorse responded.

"How long has he been this way?"

Blackhorse didn't understand. He glanced at the boy, who said two or three words. Then he turned back. He held up two fingers. "Two suns."

Mons glanced at Edie. "Not good. It looks like he might be on the verge of a heart attack."

Blackhorse moved forward to the counter. He was staring at the shelf with all the medicine. Then he looked at Mons. "You give Little Whiskers medicine. We pay."

Mons waved that off. "No pay. My gift to Little Whiskers." He moved over behind the counter and stopped before the medicine shelf.

"Papa?"

The tiny, plaintive voice jerked both Edie and Mons around. Standing at the gap between the blankets, clutching Lizzie tightly to her chest and clearly frightened, Elna was staring wide-eyed at the three Native Americans. Edie was to her in three strides. She bent down in front of her, partially blocking her view of the Indians, and took her in her arms. "It's all right, Ellie," she soothed. "They are our friends. They're not going to hurt us." Then she looked at Mons, whose eyes were anxious. "It's all right," she said. "I'll stay right here with her. You go ahead."

Mons gave Edie a grateful look and then grimly turned back to the medicine shelf. He picked up a bottle, read the label, and then replaced it. He did the same with two more. Finally, he turned back with a bottle in his hand and motioned for Blackhorse and the young man to come closer.

"Indian sick, like Mama," Elna whispered, peeking around Edie to look at the three men. It was a statement, not a question, which surprised Edie a little. It also surprised her that the little girl's eyes were wide as she stared at their visitors, but they were filled with curiosity more than fear.

"Yes, Ellie. His name is Little Whiskers. He is very sick."

That seemed to satisfy her. Her father turned back around and set the bottle on the counter. Blackhorse went to reach for it, but Mons held on to it. "John Blackhorse," he said, very sober now. "This is very strong medicine. Big, strong medicine. Do you understand?"

He nodded. "Is good, no?"

"Yes." Mons went on, speaking very slowly. "It is called sweet spirit of niter, and I think it will help his pain. But Little Whispers is a very sick man. Maybe medicine will help. Maybe not. You take it and try. But you must be careful with it."

Mons unscrewed the lid and sniffed at the opening and then held it out for Blackhorse and the young buck to smell. The boy broke out in smiles. "Mmm. Smell good."

"Yes," Mons said, clearly concerned, "and that's part of the problem. It's sweet, like sugar. Understand?"

"Yah. We like sugar."

Mons replaced the lid. "But this isn't sugar, John. It is very strong medicine. You give him a little bit only." He held the bottle up in front of him. With his finger he drew a line across the halfway point of the bottle, holding it out so that both Blackhorse and the young boy could see what he was doing. "You give only this much. No more than half. Yes?"

There was a curt nod. "John Blackhorse understand." The boy was nodding vigorously too.

"Only half. No more." Then Mons reluctantly handed the bottle across to the man.

"We thank you, Mons Peterson. You good friend to *Nuciu.*"

Mons looked over at Edie. "*Nuciu* is what they call themselves. It means 'the people.'" Then he had another idea. "John, would you like me to give him some medicine right now?"

Blackhorse considered that but shook his head. "No. Wickiup not far. We go there. He sleep."

"All right, but remember—" He held up his finger against the bottle. "That much. No more."

"Yah. No more." And with that, John Blackhorse and the young lad moved over to Little Whiskers, and supporting him on either side, they helped him outside and got him up on a horse. Then the boy swung up behind him and got a good grip on him before kicking his horse into a walk to follow after his leader. Little Whiskers was still moaning softly as they rode away.

Mons stared after them and then looked at Edie, his eyes troubled. "Let's hope that I didn't just make a big mistake," he said softly. Then he had another thought. He moved over to his daughter and took her in his arms. "Ellie, Papa has to go now, but Aunt Edie is going to stay with you. I'll be back in a little while, okay?"

"Okay, Papa," and she gave him a quick hug.

He took his daughter gently by the shoulders. "Ellie?"

"Yes, Papa?"

"Let's not tell Mama about the Indians, all right? Mama's sick, and we don't want her worrying about other things. It will be our secret, okay?"

She nodded solemnly and pressed her finger to her lips before turning to Edie. "You can't tell Mama either, Aunt Edie."

Edie took Ellie in her arms, trying not to smile. "I won't, Ellie. I promise."

CHAPTER 14

September 5, 1888, 8:35 a.m.—Walton Cabin—Monticello

Mitch swung down from his horse and tied the reins to the hitching post. Then he stepped onto the porch of Charles and Jane Walton and raised his hand to knock. But something caught his eye across the street. He had glanced at it before but hadn't given it much attention. Now that he was closer, he didn't like what he saw. There were several horses tied up in front of the Peterson store, and all of them were Indian ponies.

Just then the door opened, bringing him around again. "Good morning," Edie said, opening the door wider and stepping back. "I saw you coming. Come in. Breakfast is. . . ." Her voice trailed off when he didn't turn to look at her. She turned to see what he was looking at and then gave a low gasp of dismay. "Oh!"

"What's going on? Why all the Indians at Mons's store?"

Edie came out and shut the door softly behind her. "I was going to tell you what happened yesterday, but. . . ." Mitch had been working with John Rogerson and Charles Walton on the threshing crew and hadn't got back until too late to stop by and see her. She took his elbow and quickly told him about yesterday's visit from the three Utes.

"Why would they be back so soon?" she wondered. "Mons

told them they couldn't give him more than half a bottle, and—" One hand flew to her mouth. "Oh, no. What if—"

Mitch was there ahead of her. He quickly removed his gun belt and handed it to Edie. "Take this inside. Tell Charles and Charlie what's going on. Have them be ready to come quickly if it looks like we're in trouble. Send Maggie or Leona out the back to tell Brother Jones. Hurry!"

"I'm coming too."

"No!" Mitch barked. Then he gave her a gentle nudge toward the door. "Tell the others what's going on. I'll be okay. I'm just going to walk in like I've come to buy something." When he saw how pale her face was, he added, "Maybe they've come to thank him."

He didn't wait to see if she believed that. Obviously, he didn't. As Edie watched him stride into the street, she flung the door open, tossed the gun inside on a small table, called out something to those inside, and then shut it again. "Mitch, wait." She ran to catch up to him.

He stopped short. "No, Edie!"

"Mitch, listen to me. I was there yesterday. I saw the whole thing. If Little Whiskers has died, they'll blame Mons. But I was there. I can tell them that Mons warned them not to use too much. Maybe they'll listen to me. You know how they respect us white women."

Mitch was torn. She could see it in his face, so she didn't let him think about it anymore. She grabbed his arm and pulled. "Come on. Mons needs us."

When Mitch lifted the latch and started to push on the door, it was flung open and a tall, muscular Ute blocked his way. He wore a six-shooter around his waist but had nothing in his hands. "No come in!" he barked. "You stay out!"

Mitch pretended not to understand and tried to shoulder him aside. "I need to go in."

"No!" the man said, putting his hands on Mitch's chest. It was just the opening Edie needed. She ducked past them both and slipped inside, looking up at him as she passed. "I need to buy flour and sugar." The Ute went to reach for her, and that was all Mitch needed to push him aside and enter.

There were three more Indians in the room, all of them adult males. Edie saw that the boy was not with them today. She also saw that they were all armed and that it was John Blackhorse who stood directly in front of the counter. He had a rifle cradled in one arm. She quickly stepped to Mitch's side and slipped her arm through his. "Excuse us, please," she said, smiling warmly at them. "We need to buy some food."

Mitch was tempted to glare at her, but instead, understanding what she was doing, he looked around at the four braves. "Sorry. Didn't mean to interrupt." He turned to Mons. "Morning, Mons. Edie and I were wondering if we could get some supplies."

Mons seemed calm and unruffled, but Mitch saw that his face was pale and the corners of his eyes were pinched with concern. "Be with you in a moment," he said. "I need to help our Ute brothers first."

"No problem," Mitch said, and taking Edie's hand they moved over to the corner, where they could watch both Mons and his visitors.

For a moment, they thought that the leader was going to force them out. Mitch saw his fingers tighten on the rifle, but he must have changed his mind, because he turned back to face Mons.

"White man no good! You kill Little Whiskers, our brother. Now Utes kill Mons Peterson. Tribal council say you pay. Little Whiskers die. Mons Peterson die. It is our way."

Mons put his hands flat on the counter and leaned forward. "I am sorry that Little Whiskers died. I have much sadness. Little Whiskers was my brother, too."

"No!" Blackhorse exploded. "You give Little Whiskers bad medicine. You kill Little Whiskers." Mitch felt Edie's fingernails digging into the flesh of his arm, but he gave an imperceptible shake of his head without looking at her. The three Utes were moving their heads back and forth between Mitch and Mons, poised to react if Mitch so much as twitched.

Mons shook his head back and forth; then he very slowly and very calmly said, "Mons Peterson did not kill Little Whiskers. Medicine not bad." He turned and took down another bottle from the medicine shelf.

"That's the same medicine he gave them yesterday," Edie whispered.

Holding it up, he traced his finger across the center of the bottle, as he had done yesterday. "Mons Peterson tell John Blackhorse and his young brother. 'Do not give all medicine to Little Whiskers. Only half. Only little at a time. Strong medicine.' I told you that."

Then he did something that caught them all off guard. He unscrewed the lid and took a quick swig of the medicine. Maybe a teaspoonful. That had the desired impact. The Indians gaped at him, almost as if he had just worked some magic.

Mons shook the bottle at them. "You see. I drink medicine. No kill me. Medicine no kill Little Whiskers. Maybe Little Whiskers so sick, he die anyway. Maybe Little Whiskers like medicine too much. Maybe Little Whiskers took whole bottle. Then he die."

Edie found herself holding her breath. She could see that Mons's words were definitely having an effect. The Indians were muttering among themselves, still angry, but clearly not so sure of themselves now. Then Blackhorse went to the others, and they circled around him and conferred in low whispers. Over and over they kept shaking their heads, muttering angrily.

Just then, a movement out of the corner of his eye caught Mitch's attention. He half turned his head and felt his heart lurch. Behind the blanket that separated the store from the rest of the cabin, out of sight from all but Edie and Mitch, there was a figure. It was Eliza Peterson. And she held a baby in her arms. Her face was as pale as bleached muslin. Her eyes were wide with fear, and her mouth was pressed into a tight line. Glancing quickly at the four Indians to make sure they weren't watching them, Mitch motioned with his hand to stay back out of sight.

Edie gasped as she saw what Mitch was looking at. She wanted to yell at Eliza, shout at her not to come in, but she didn't dare move.

Finally, Blackhorse turned away from his council and stalked back over to Mons. His face was twisted with anger. "Tribal Council say Mons Peterson kill Little Whiskers, so Mons Peterson must die too."

Mitch saw Mons's Adam's apple jerk once, and then again, but his face still remained calm. He spoke slowly and distinctly. "Mons Peterson did nothing wrong. I am sad that Little Whiskers died. I give family of Little Whiskers one horse as a token of my sorrow."

Blackhorse's head moved back and forth in clear refusal. "No. Horse not die. Little Whiskers die."

"I give family one horse and five hundred dollars," Mons said calmly.

That clearly took them by surprise. There was another brief consultation. When they finished, Blackhorse turned back, and now his rifle came up to point at Mons's chest. Edie gasped, and Mitch took a step forward. Instantly, he had three six-shooters pointing at him. He was hoping that Eliza couldn't see into the room.

"Council say you die," Blackhorse growled, "so you die. You come. We take you to council. Then you die."

Mons didn't stir, except that he lifted the bottle of medicine again. "Ute Council is wise. Ute Council wants justice. That is good. But I did not kill Little Whiskers. When John Blackhorse came to store with Little Whiskers, Mons Peterson said Little Whiskers only need this much medicine—" He touched the half point on the bottle. "No more. Whole bottle is no good. Maybe that is why Little Whiskers die."

Edie let go of Mitch's arm and took one step forward. "John Blackhorse, may I speak?"

He whirled around, glaring at Mons. "Squaw no speak."

Sensing that Edie was going to speak anyway, Mitch said, "Squaw was here yesterday, yes?"

After a moment, Blackhorse gave a curt nod.

"So squaw knows Mons Peterson speaks truth." He motioned to the others. "She would speak with your brothers and tell them what she saw." He reached up and pointed at his eyes. "With her own eyes."

For a long moment, Blackhorse eyed Mitch up and down, but his eyes never once so much as glanced at Edie. And then Mitch remembered something that Kumen Jones had once taught him. It was one of Thales Haskell's "Rules for Dealing with Our Indian Brothers." It came to his mind now: deal with them by appealing to what they think is right. Kumen emphasized that point especially. "The Indians have a deep sense of justice, of what is fair. If you can appeal to that, then you can often win them over." He decided it was worth a try.

"You are right, John Blackhorse. The council has spoken. The council has ruled. But maybe the council didn't know all the—" He'd been about to say "facts" but knew that wouldn't mean much to them. He started over. "Maybe council thinks Mons Peterson lies about the medicine. But my squaw was here. She knows what happened. And she speaks only the truth."

John Blackhorse had also been here and knew exactly what had happened, but the others had not. He saw a couple of them nod their heads and murmur something to each other. Several more long and anxious moments passed, and then Blackhorse spoke to Mons. "Squaw may speak."

Edie bowed her head briefly in deference and didn't meet his eyes. Following Mons's example, she spoke slowly and calmly. "Mons Peterson was afraid Little Whiskers would take too much medicine. He said it was very strong medicine. He said it was very bad if whole bottle was taken. He did not want Little Whiskers to take too much. He said it over and over."

She hesitated, wondering if she was being too bold, but decided to risk it. "Did Little Whiskers take all of the medicine?"

Blackhorse's face was impassive, but she saw the others exchange glances. Did they know? Did Blackhorse know? There was no way to tell.

Finally, Blackhorse lowered his rifle. "We talk." He motioned for the others to follow and went outside. The instant the door shut, Eliza burst into the room and threw herself into her husband's arms. "Oh, Mons, Mons, Mons!" she sobbed. "I heard it all."

"It's all right, Eliza. It's going to be all right."

She straightened. "I'm going for help," she cried.

"I'll go with her," Edie said. "I'll alert the others."

Mitch shook his head. "No, Edie. You need to stay here, right where you were. And Eliza, you need to go back into the bedroom. If they think we're sending for help, this could explode in our faces. But it's not going to explode. It's going to be all right."

Mons glanced out the window, where he could see the men talking with great animation. "Mitch is right, Eliza. We can't do anything to make them think we're angry. Go back into the bedroom. They think you are sick. I'll be there in just a minute."

She had barely disappeared when the outside door opened. To their surprise, only Blackhorse entered. He ignored Mitch and Edie and spoke only to Mons. "Maybe Little Whiskers take all medicine. Maybe Little Whiskers die anyway." He shrugged. "But Mons Peterson not kill Little Whiskers."

It was all Mons could do not to sink back in relief, but he only nodded soberly. "Thank you, John Blackhorse. My Ute brothers are wise. My Ute brothers believe in justice. My Ute brothers are welcome in my store any time." He turned and took down a ten-pound sack of sugar. "You take my gift to family of Little Whiskers. Tell them I am very sad that Little Whiskers lives no more."

"This good," Blackhorse grunted as he took the sugar. He lifted his hand briefly in farewell and went out to rejoin his companions. A moment later they were trotting away, ignoring the several very curious settlers who stood on their porches and watched them go.

Notes

Strangely enough, a history of Mons Peterson, posted on Family Search in 2014 by a descendant, says that this incident involved the death of a sick horse, not an Indian. That is highly unlikely for two reasons. The Indians would be upset by the loss of a horse but would likely have accepted a horse or monetary reparation as just payment for their loss. Mons offered both and was flatly rejected. Second, the other sources name Little Whiskers by name and specifically say that the Utes were so upset by his death that their tribal council basically sentenced Mons Peterson to death for his part in it (see *Saga*, 223; *Anchored Lariats*, 107).

A comment on Indian names, which are a complex issue: Native Americans often had more than one name—an Indian name given at birth (e.g., *Denetsosie Bitsie* or *Nekai Nez*) and a second name derived from a personal trait or an incident in their life (e.g., Blackhorse, Little Wagon, Buckskin Charlie, Whitehair). Indian families had also lived around white men enough that some European names were also used (e.g., Archie Jones, John Hart Rockwell). All of these are Native American names of the era taken from cemeteries in San Juan County (see Toni Richard Turk, *Rooted in San Juan: A genealogical study of burials in San Juan County, Utah, 1879–1995* [1995], 1–3).

Sweet spirit of niter was a medicine of that time that contained about 90% alcohol and a small degree of ethyl nitrate. This was a colorless, sweet-tasting liquid that was highly toxic in large quantities. Somewhere around the 1860s it was discovered to be an effective and fast-acting treatment for angina—severe chest pains resulting from restricted blood flow to the heart. Taking a whole bottle of the medicine could have been fatal in and of itself, no matter what Little Whiskers's physical problems might have been.

CHAPTER 15

September 10, 1888, 8:27 a.m.—Walton Cabin—Monticello

"Mama?"

Jane Walton, who was at the stove preparing scrambled eggs and fried potatoes, turned her head. "Yes, Leona?"

"Do you have anything you need us to do today besides the ironing?"

"Not really, but that will take you at least half a day. Why do you ask?"

Edie spoke up. "Mitch left for Mancos early this morning, so I won't be going up to the ranch house to work with him. So I can help Maggie and Leona with the ironing. Then we were thinking of hiking up into the mountains to look for wild gooseberries."

Maggie spoke up. "Doesn't gooseberry pie with whipped cream sound delicious? You know how Papa loves it."

Charlie was seated at the table with his sisters. "Not just Papa. I love it too."

"Actually, we all do," Leona said.

Jane Walton's brow furrowed as she mixed the eggs and diced potatoes together and dumped them into a bowl. Setting the pan down, she brought the bowl over. "Charlie, get some bread, please. Leona, fetch some milk from the cellar." When they both returned, she sat down. "Edie, would you offer a prayer of thanks for our food, please?"

Edie did so, asking for a blessing on Mitch and the other men who were on their way to Mancos. When she was finished, Jane watched until everyone had a plate full of food and started to eat before picking up the conversation again. "I don't want you girls going up in the mountains alone," she said.

"Icungowiem," Charlie mumbled. His mother shot him a look, so he quickly grabbed his glass and took a swig of milk, swallowed, and tried again. "I can go with them, Mama."

"I thought your father asked you to clean out the stalls in the barn."

"He did, but I can do that while the girls are doing the ironing. Really. It would be fun. And I'll stay right with them."

Jane took a bite while she considered it. The four of them watched her closely. Suddenly she started, looking out the window. "My goodness. Was that Mitch?"

Edie almost dropped her fork. "What?"

Sister Walton got to her feet and walked to the window. "It *is* Mitch. And he's got Fred Jones's buckboard."

Leaping up, Edie started for the window, but a knock on the door sounded and she turned in mid-course and went to the door.

"Hi, hon," Mitch said, hat in hand and grinning foolishly.

"But. . . ."

He opened the screen door and came inside. He gave Edie a quick hug. "I had a change of plans. I'm not going until later today. I'll catch up with them because I'll go on horseback."

That won him some curious looks, especially from Edie, but Jane was the one who spoke. "We're just having some breakfast. Come join us."

"No thanks, Sister Walton. I ate about an hour ago when I thought I was leaving."

"Well, sit down and have a little something." She loaded up a plate and set it before him.

He grinned. "It does smell better than cold mush and stale bread." He set his hat on a chair and pulled up a chair between Edie and Leona as Jane brought him his plate. He took one bite and then laid his fork down, but Jane cut him off. "Whatever it is you want to talk about, Mitch, it can wait while you eat."

It was said in a way as to brook no objections, so Mitch fell to eating, as did the others. But that didn't stop the exchange of glances going on between him and Edie.

When the last of them finished, Jane looked at Mitch. "You and Edie are excused if you need to talk."

"Oh, no. It's not a secret, it's just that . . ." He turned to Edie. "As I was saddling up, I decided that you and I need to get this thing we've been talking about settled so I can stop fretting about it."

She stared at him. "What thing?"

"You know, about this winter."

"Oh, that," she said, her voice dull.

Jane had watched this interchange closely and saw much more than Mitch had intended for her to see. "Come, children," she said. "We'll give Edie and Mitch some time."

"Actually, Sister Walton," Mitch said, "I came to see if Edie could go for a ride with me up the canyon so we can talk some more about our plans. It's a beautiful day."

Leona gave a little cry of joy. "But we were just talking about going up in the mountains."

"You were?" Mitch said.

"Children," Jane cut in. "Mitch and Edie need some time alone."

Mitch shook his head. "But Sister Walton, I was going to ask if Maggie and Leona might go with us, so we wouldn't be without a chaperone."

"Ah," Sister Walton said. "And what about having some time to talk, just the two of you?"

Mitch blushed. "Edie and I could still talk while they do something close by."

"Like hunt for gooseberries!" Maggie exclaimed.

"That would be perfect," Mitch agreed quickly.

Jane let her eyes move back and forth between her children and her guests and then sighed. "Okay. The ironing can wait. You girls get ready, and I'll put together some lunch for you."

"What about me?" Charlie cried. "I want to go too."

"Sorry," his mother said. "I think two chaperones are quite enough. And your father wants those stables cleaned out." As Charlie started to protest, Sister Walton turned away. "Girls, Mitch is anxious to get going. Why are you still sitting there looking silly? Go get ready!"

8:55 a.m.

As they waved good-bye to Jane and a disgruntled Charlie, Mitch flicked the reins, and the horse started forward at a walk. Edie was on the front seat with Mitch, and Maggie and Leona were in the back seat with the picnic basket and a jug of water between their feet. Edie scooted closer to Mitch on the wagon seat and slipped her arm through his. "Where would you like to go?" he asked.

"I don't care," she exclaimed. "You're with me for a few more hours. Anywhere is fine with me."

"Where's the best place to find wild gooseberries?" Maggie asked, leaning forward.

They were just approaching Second South Street by this time, and Mitch turned the horse to the right so they were headed west directly toward the mountain. "Actually, I know of a little spring up in the pines on Horsehead Mountain. It's not too high up. There's lots of grass around it. It's only a couple of miles from here. And I think there are gooseberry bushes in the area."

Edie leaned her head against his shoulder. "Sounds wonderful to me."

"To us, too," Leona said.

Snapping the reins lightly, Mitch urged the horse into a steady trot that would eat up the distance quickly. About a minute later, Edie suddenly straightened. "Oh, my, look at Horsehead Mountain. The aspens are just starting to turn to gold. I hadn't noticed that before."

Mitch nodded. There was a dusting of snow on the upper peaks, the first of the season. The groves of aspen trees below the pines were starting to show the first signs of the liquid gold that would cover the mountainside in another week or ten days. And here and there on the mountainside, they could see the first isolated spots of red and orange. "These last few cool nights are getting things started. Soon it will be spectacular."

"It is right now," Edie retorted. "I love it. Who else can say that they have a giant horse watching over their town?"

"Not many," Leona agreed.

"Not any!" Maggie corrected.

It was true, Mitch thought. This had to be unique in all the world. Monticello was nestled in the eastern foothills of the Blue Mountains—or the Abajos, as the U.S. Geological Survey had chosen to call them. This was not an extensive range of mountains. The La Sals to the north of them and the Henrys to the west were both larger. But short as it was, the range formed an impressive frontal boundary on Monticello's back doorstep. South Peak, Abajo Peak, Twin Peaks, and Horsehead Peak were all above eleven thousand feet in elevation and towered four thousand feet above the site of Monticello. Dense cedar forests covered the lower flanks of the range, with numerous stands of aspen trees up a little higher. Above them, especially on the north-facing slopes, there was a deep carpet of lush pine forests. These were crowned with relatively barren tops, peaks rising above the tree line.

But it was the northernmost peak that was strikingly unusual. Before ever going there himself, Mitch had heard men who had been up around the Blue Mountains talk about the figure of a horse's head on the east flank of the mountain formed by an unusual configuration of pine tree groves. Out in this country, a lot of geographical features were given names because they somewhat resembled something familiar: Six-Shooter Peaks, The Bear's Ears, Woodenshoe Buttes, The Toe, The Beehives, Cheese Box Butte. *Somewhat* was the operative word in most cases. You had to use a lot of your own imagination to see why a particular formation was given the name it had. But Mitch remembered well that day a year ago when he and Alvin Decker had rode to the Blue Mountains from Verdure looking for springs and creeks. Alvin had stopped him somewhere in the vicinity of where they were now, pointed, and said, "There's Horsehead Peak."

When Mitch nodded but was obviously not impressed, Alvin asked, "You can't see it, can you?" Then he began describing it to Mitch, giving him reference points. And then something very strange happened. It was as though Mitch's vision suddenly snapped into place or something. Suddenly there it was, the massive head and neck of a horse with its ears cocked forward and a long, white blaze on its face, just looking down on them from the side of the mountain. It had stunned him. It wasn't absolutely perfect, but once he saw it, he wondered how he had not seen it before.

"What a remarkable accident of nature," Edie breathed, still entranced.

"The Indians don't think it was an accident," Mitch observed.

"They don't?" Leona asked.

"No. Haven't you heard about the legend of Bally?"

"No," Leona said slowly, looking suspicious. Mitch was a natural-born tease and was constantly telling them things to see how gullible they were.

Edie was also giving him one of her looks. "Are you just making this up?"

"Thanks for your confidence," he said as he pulled the reins back so the horse slowed to a walk. "I heard it from Old Wash himself."

"Really?" Maggie asked. "Tell us."

Mitch half turned in the seat so he could speak to all three of them. "Well," he began, "according to the Utes, many, many moons ago there was a tribal chief named Chico."

Edie harrumphed softly. "That sounds more Mexican than Ute," she said.

Mitch's look instantly chastened her. "Sorry," she said, suppressing a giggle.

He went on. "Well, each autumn, once the leaves had fallen from the trees, the tribe had a great deer hunt up here in the Blue Mountains. They did this so they could lay up enough meat to see them through the winter. So one frosty morning, Chico called in all the warriors of the tribe and told them it was time for the great hunt. The warriors got their horses and armed themselves with their spears and bows and arrows and set off for the hills. Chico, as always, chose his favorite horse, whose name was Bally. He was a beautiful, coal-black horse with a shapely head and a large, white blaze on his face."

The Walton girls were nodding. That was a good description of what lay before them.

"It was evening as they finished the hunt and the warriors began bringing in their deer. But Chico and Bally had gone up higher than most of the others. The chief had gone clear up on top of the mountain, so it was rapidly getting dark when he started down toward the camp again. As he approached the camp, one of the braves looked up when he heard the noise of an animal coming through the brush. In the half light, all he could see was a dark shape moving toward them through the trees. So he grabbed his bow and let an arrow fly. His aim was good, and it struck the animal in a fatal spot. Bally dropped to the ground, mortally wounded."

"Oh, no," Edie exclaimed softly.

"Chico was devastated, of course, but nothing could be done to save Bally. So Chico decided to leave Bally where he had fallen. But because he loved his horse so much, he refused to stay camped on the mountain where his horse had died. He feared that something bad might happen to the tribe just like it had happened to Bally. So they moved south and made a new camp somewhere down by where Bluff is today.

"For many years, they refused to go back. However, Chico eventually died and the tribe got a new chief. They decided to return to their old hunting grounds for deer. But when they came north and reached the base of the mountain, they were astonished to see the image of Bally, including his white forehead, filling the whole mountain. They decided that the Great Spirit had placed Bally's head on the mountain so that everyone could forever see what a beautiful horse he had been."

For several seconds Edie studied Mitch's face, still not sure whether he had made it up. Finally satisfied, she sighed. "I like it. That's better than thinking it was an accident. It's a memorial to a gallant horse." She leaned in against Mitch. "Will you tell that story to our children?" she asked.

"I will. Even if it's been embellished, it is a part of our heritage here. Maybe I'll even start watching for a horse that matches Old Bally's description, so we can have one just like him."

"Oh, I like that idea. And would you call him Bally?"

"No."

"Why not?"

"Because he—or she—won't be my horse, he will be yours."

"Oh!" Then as Maggie and Leona broke out laughing, Edie realized what he had said. "Really?"

"Would you like that?"

Her nod was immediate and vigorous. "Very much. Then we'll have two Ballys—one we see out the window, and one I can ride with you when we go up into the mountains."

"Sounds like a good plan to me," Mitch said. He flicked the reins and moved forward at a trot again.

"But," Edie said, as a sudden thought came to her. "Before I do that, you'll have to teach me how to ride a horse straddle."

Mitch's head jerked around. "Straddle?"

"Yes. You know. Not sidesaddle like a woman. Straddle on the saddle." She smiled at the unintended rhyme. "Like you men do."

"Edie Zimmer!" Maggie gasped. "What are you saying?"

She turned and faced her two friends. "Well, why not? Why should we be forced to sit perched up on one of those silly sidesaddles that don't allow you to hold on to the horse with anything but the saddle horns? Wouldn't you like to be able grip the horse with your legs and ride like the wind?"

Even Leona, who was not as strict as her older sister, fell back at the word "legs." "Edie! We don't call them . . . them. . . ." She shook her head, too shocked to put words to it. "We call them our lower limbs."

"Oh, pshaw," Edie snapped. "They're called legs on men. Why not on women?"

"But what about our maidenly modesty?" Maggie whispered, blushing furiously to even be speaking of such things in front of a male.

"Well, what if we made ourselves some kind of women's trousers?"

That did it. The Waltons looked so scandalized that Edie decided it was time to bite her tongue. She turned back to the front, folded her hands in her lap, and stared straight ahead. Her cheeks felt hot, and she guessed that she was blushing too. She thought she heard Mitch chuckling softly, but she didn't dare look at him. Then, smiling to herself, she snuggled in against him, not caring if her two friends thought this was shocking behavior as well.

Notes

There really is a Horsehead Peak in the mountains directly to the west of Monticello. While snow on the mountain accentuates the horse more dramatically, especially the blaze on its face, it is still clearly visible in summer. The picture on the dust jacket of this book shows Horsehead Peak with Bally's head clearly discernible.

Interestingly, I found the whimsical story of Chief Chico and his horse Bally on the cover of a menu in a local restaurant in Monticello. The front of the menu had a picture of Horsehead Mountain with the story of Chico and Bally below it, pretty much as I have told it here. I realize that a restaurant menu may not be one of the more reliable of historical sources, but I decided that if it was part of the folklore of San Juan County it was worthy of inclusion here.

At this point of very modest fashions (it was considered shocking for a woman to show her bare ankles), if women rode horses they rode them sidesaddle in their long skirts. But this was very awkward and made it much harder for a woman to feel secure atop a horse. The words "straddle," "lower extremities," and "maidenly modesty" are not my inventions but come from an account relating to feminine styles and practices.

CHAPTER 16

September 10, 1888, 10:20 a.m.—Horsehead Peak —the Blue Mountains, San Juan County

With the horse unhitched and hobbled, Mitch turned him loose to munch the grass along the track of the tiny stream. As the girls got out and looked for a place far enough away from the spring to be dry, Mitch carried the picnic basket and the jug of water over to where they were. "You want to eat lunch now or wait a little?" he asked.

The three of them exchanged glances, and Maggie spoke. "It's only been a couple of hours since breakfast. I'm not hungry yet."

"Agreed," Edie and Leona said together.

Maggie went back to the buckboard and got two small pails. "I think Leona and I shall leave immediately to go look for gooseberry bushes."

Chuckling, Mitch removed his hat and ran his fingers through his hair. "Ladies, Edie and I are going to talk about our plans for the winter. It's not some great secret. You don't have to run off like a pair of scared rabbits."

Leona vigorously shook her head. "You heard, Mama. *We* are here to find gooseberries. *You* are here to talk. And we shouldn't be interfering with each other while we do it."

"We'll stay close enough that we're in shouting distance," Maggie said.

Mitch, who was feeling awkward about the situation, looked at Edie, but she said nothing. Her face was inscrutable—which meant, "They're right. Stop arguing with them."

They watched the girls go and waved to them as they turned one last time before disappearing into the trees. Edie sighed, gave Mitch a probing look, and sat down on the blanket. After a moment Mitch sat down as well, facing her. Neither spoke for several moments. A sudden awkwardness hung between them. Both knew that there were strong feelings here, and neither of them was excited to start.

Finally, Mitch cleared his throat and began. "I have a suggestion. What if one of us starts and says everything that he or she is thinking without the other interrupting? Then the other does the same. And—"

Edie was frowning. "You know that never works. You can't stand not breaking in, and neither can I. Can't we just talk? Neither one of us is looking for a fight, right?"

"Right. Of course, you're right. Do you want to go first, then?"

A mischievous twinkle filled Edie's eyes. "No, you go first. I prefer having the last word." But she instantly became serious. "But can I ask you one question first?"

"Of course."

"I know this issue is an important one for us," she began, "but last night you said that it could wait until you got back from Mancos. What changed your mind?"

"Ah, yes. Good question." Mitch sighed. "First, may I tell you why I feel it's important for you to go south for the winter? Then I'll answer your question."

"Fair enough. Go ahead."

He leaned back, staring up into the aspen trees that surrounded them. With the coming of fall, the first of the leaves were starting to break free and flutter down all around them. They landed without a sound, not disturbing the deep hush of the mountains. Mitch took another breath and plunged. "First, you know that it goes without saying that I don't want to be separated from you for three or four months. That thought makes me ache inside."

"I know that," Edie said. "But, thank you. It's nice to hear you say it."

"And second, this is not a repeat of what happened last year down by the river."

"You mean when you hinted I was too young to care for myself?" she said sweetly.

Mitch winced. "Yeah. I'm not worried because you're not old enough or mature enough. That's not it at all. In fact, I realized something last night."

"What?"

He leaned forward, eager to make her understand. "Well, it struck me that I don't think of the other sisters in terms of how old they are. When I think of Eliza Peterson, for example, I don't think about how old she is. I don't say to myself, 'Oh, she's twenty-four or twenty-five.' Whatever she is."

"Actually, she turned twenty-two last month. She's just four years older than I am."

He nodded. "See, that's what I mean. And when I talk with Jane Walton or Mary Jones, I'm not thinking that they are older women in their thirties and forties. Evelyn Adams, Sarah Rogerson, Emma Decker. I just think of them as mature, confident, competent women, no matter what their age." He looked at her directly now. "And that's how I see you. I see you as a mature, confident, competent, independent, strong woman."

Her eyes were wide and glistening as she studied him.

"Thank you, Mitch," she murmured. "That means more to me than I can say."

He fell silent, staring at his hands now. Edie reached over and poked him. "Don't stop. That's a pretty good start. "

"All right. So here are my reasons. Reason number one: this is the first year that we are attempting to winter over. I say *attempting* because no one knows for sure if we can do it. We have only a rough idea of what to expect. How bad will the storms get here in the winter? How deep will the snow be? How cold will it get? Can cattle even survive up here in the winter? Those are questions that we are all asking ourselves. And because we can't answer them with any certainty, only six of our families are talking about staying. The rest are going south. Not just the women and children. The men, too."

"But six are not. And their wives are staying. Right?"

"Actually, Ency Butt has decided she's not staying. Parley is leaving in a couple of weeks to take her and the children over to Parowan. Then he'll come back to help George and Evelyn with the dairy. Willard and Julia are one of the families returning to Bluff."

That took Edie aback. She had not heard that news. Then an answer came to her. "Ency's baby is just five months old. I don't blame her for going. But, Mitch, Mary Jones is not leaving, and she has young children. Evelyn Adams and Eliza Peterson are not leaving, even though they both have young babies. Are their husbands telling them they have to go, too?"

"I don't know," Mitch said stubbornly. "That's not my affair." He rushed on before she could reply. "Reason two: the situation with Little Whiskers may not be over yet. Mons said he had a couple of Utes from the tribal council in the store the other day and they were giving him dark looks and muttering among themselves. He's afraid that there may be members of the tribal council who still want to make him pay for Little Whiskers's death. If that happens and we only have a few us here, then. . . ." He shrugged. He didn't want to finish that sentence.

Edie had no answer to that. Chills were running up and down her back as she considered what that might mean.

"Reason three: the Carlisle bunch will be here too. You know what those cowboys are like when they're bored or get their hands on some liquor. That's another big worry. Come winter, there'll be no sending for a sheriff to come bring them in line." Mitch's brow was deeply furrowed. "We're worried about staying, Edie. We're all worried."

"Fine, if everyone chooses to leave, then I'll leave too. But if you stay, then. . . ."

"But *someone* has to stay. Don't you remember? When we left Verdure last fall, we left only a barn, a couple of sheds, a corral, and some fencing. Oh, and several hundred pounds of seed wheat stored in a shed. We hired one of the cowboys we thought we could trust to guard it. When we came back this spring, guess how much was left, Edie? None! Indians or cowboys had stolen it all. Now look at us. We've got more than two dozen structures complete or nearly completed. Our homes are full of furniture, clothing, cooking utensils, and all of our other stuff. We can't take all that with us down to Bluff. Think of Mons. What will be left of his store if he leaves it for three or four months unprotected?"

Edie was sobered by his words, and yet it irritated her that he couldn't see the flaws in his reasoning. "All right, if the decision is to go, I'll not say another word. Or, if the decision is to send all of the wives and children down to Bluff for the winter, I'll go without protest."

"Edie, I—"

"But if Eliza, and Jane, and Mary, and Sarah, and Evelyn

stay, then I'm staying. If their husbands don't send them away like you're trying to send me away, then I'm staying, Mitch. I'm sorry, and I appreciate your concerns for my safety, but I have some strong feelings about this too."

"There is a fourth reason," he said wearily.

Edie's head came up. Something in the way he had said it sent another chill through her.

"For about a week now, as I have thought about this and prayed about it, I've kept getting this bad feeling about you staying."

Her mouth fell open and she reared back. Mitch hurried on. "No, calling it a bad feeling is too strong. But something is definitely wrong. I can't shake it, Edie. At first I thought it was just *me* being stubborn, me wanting *my* own way. I know it sounds crazy, but it's more than that. Is the Lord trying to tell me that I need to get you to a safer place for the winter?"

She stared at him for several seconds and then whispered, "You are scaring me, Mitch."

"I don't mean to, but I felt that you needed to know that. That's why I didn't leave with the others this morning. I wanted you to understand the whole situation so you can think about it while I'm gone."

Edie was biting her lip. Mitch had completely knocked her off guard. And yet. . . . Her head came up. "But why just me? Are you going to tell President Jones about this feeling? Tell him that he needs to get Mary out of here, too? And Mons? Brother Walton and Jane?"

Another weary sigh. "Of course not. I can't speak for them. Maybe they're not in danger. They have to make their own decisions. This is a highly personal decision for each couple to make as they counsel together. But I know what I'm feeling, Edie.

That's why I'm not on my way to Mancos right now. I'm here to talk it through with you."

Edie sat quietly for almost a minute, staring past him at the surrounding forest. Finally, she turned back to face him. "Believe it or not, Mitch, I'm not trying to be stubborn." A smile momentarily softened her expression. "Actually, I don't have to try. Papa says I was born stubborn and have greatly increased my birthright."

As Mitch laughed at that, Edie quickly sobered again. "I find it interesting that you speak of your feelings. And I need to think about that. I trust your feelings, Mitch. I really do. But here's my dilemma. How can you be having those kinds of feelings when I'm feeling just the opposite?"

His eyes widened.

"Yes," she exclaimed. "I've been thinking about this a lot too, and I can't deny my feelings either. To be honest, I guess I am a little surprised at how strong they are. That doesn't prove they're right. I know that. But they *feel* right, Mitch."

He lifted a hand to signal he had a question. She smiled. "You don't need my permission to break in."

"Can you be more specific?"

She was pleased to see the genuine concern in his eyes. He wanted to understand; she could see that. And that pushed down some of the feelings of frustration she was experiencing. "Well, here's one example. The other day, while you were up in the hills rounding up cattle, I went over to Sarah Rogerson's cabin. She is starting school as soon as the harvest and roundup are over. She wants me to help her. She had heard how I helped Ida Nielson at the school in Bluff, and she's hoping I can help her, too."

"You would like that, wouldn't you?"

Tears sprang to Edie's eyes. "No, Mitch. I would *love* it. So is this just me being selfish?"

"No. Not at all."

"Then, there's Eliza. I've been having some very strong feelings about her lately. She tires so quickly lately. But it's more than that. She has those two little ones, and the usual cooking and cleaning that we all have, but . . . well, having a store as part of their cabin really complicates things for her. She has very little privacy during the day. If Mons isn't there, she has to wait on the customers. So she can't just leave and take a nap whenever she wants. And her little Ellie is getting to be handful. She's constantly pulling stuff off the shelves." Edie stopped, blushing slightly. "Oh, this is going to sound so conceited of me to say, but—"

"Say it, Edie."

"I feel like she needs me. Not just that she needs help, but that she needs *me.* We have grown so close lately. She's like the big sister I never had. I love her dearly, and I love those children with all my heart. So in a way, I need her too. But this is stronger than that." The tears spilled over and rolled down her cheeks. "I feel very strongly that I need to be here for her."

She wiped at her cheeks angrily. "I'm sorry, Mitch. I'm not trying to be difficult. But tell me. Are these feelings of mine just me being a weepy woman, or are they from the Lord?"

"Not the former. You are not a weepy woman, Edie."

"But if it is from the Lord, doesn't that mean I am supposed to stay?" she cried.

Mitch stared at her for a long moment and then got to his feet and started to pace back and forth along the edge of the blanket. After a moment, she quietly asked it again. "Does that mean I need to stay? And if so, then why are you getting these bad feelings?"

He stopped, his expression pained. "We can't both be right, can we? I mean the Lord wouldn't give you one answer and me the opposite, would He?"

Edie shook her head, a sense of depression settling in on her. Mitch came over and sat down next to her again. He put his arm around her and pulled her close but said nothing.

"So what do we do?" she asked after a moment. "How do we resolve this?"

Mitch's nose wrinkled slightly in that peculiar way it did when he was concentrating hard. "Well, that's one reason I postponed going. I have been thinking that we have to decide so we can start making plans. But now I realize that we're not ready yet. So, for now, let's decide not to decide. I'll be gone about a week. Let's both think about it and pray about it while I'm gone, and we'll talk some more when I'm back."

"Thank you," Edie whispered. "That feels good. You're right. We are not ready to decide."

It was like he had lifted a burden off her shoulders. And then, as she looked into his eyes, those emerald green eyes that she so adored, she saw something that actually startled her. For a moment, she thought what she saw was love. And that, without question, was part of it. But it was more than that. In his steady gaze, she saw respect. For her. Not just for her as his future wife, but for her as a woman. As an individual. It was a moment that almost stunned her, because it came with such power and clarity.

And that realization gave her the courage to ask what had been on her mind for several days. "And if we can't decide then, Mitch, what do we do? What if we both feel as strongly then as we do now? We can't wait forever to decide. So then what?"

He stared at her forlornly for several seconds and shook his head. "I don't know." There was a long pause before he went on, not meeting her gaze. "I guess—" He stopped. "You're not going to like this."

"I'm a big girl, Mitch. Say it."

"Well, if we really can't resolve it, then I guess as head of the house—or soon-to-be head of the house—it will have to be my decision." At her look, he rushed on. "As the priesthood holder, I am the head of our family. It's my responsibility to make the hard decisions."

"Just like that? You command and I obey?"

Dismayed by the sharpness of her reaction, Mitch went on the defensive. "There can't be two heads, Edie. Someone has to lead if we can't agree."

"I see. And where's my agency in all of this? What happens to these feelings that I feel so strongly are from the Lord?"

"I'm not saying that's what we will do, Edie. You asked me a hypothetical question, and I gave you a hypothetical answer."

"No, Mitch. I don't think it's hypothetical at all. You've been asking yourself that same question, and that *is* your answer." She jumped to her feet and snapped off a salute. "All right, sir. I'll do it. Say the word, and I'll go away. And I'll even try to be pleasant about it, but that doesn't mean that you are right, Mitch. Not in any way."

She instantly regretted her words, for the hurt in his eyes cut through her like a knife. But she was too angry to take them back.

He got slowly to his feet, his eyes not meeting hers. "I think I'd better go, Edie."

"What? No, Mitch. We need to talk this through."

"We're not talking anymore, Edie. We're shouting."

That was the wrong thing to say. "You mean, *I'm* shouting."

He turned away. "I need to get on the road. I'll walk back. It's only a couple of miles. I'll see you when I get back."

"Now you're being ridiculous."

"Probably," he said, "but this isn't getting us anywhere."

"And what about Jane not wanting us girls up here alone?" She flung the words at him.

That stopped him for a moment, but then he shrugged. "If it will make you feel better, I'll send Charlie up."

Edie was a cauldron of emotions—anger, frustration, regret, hurt, shame at hurting him. *Please, Dear Lord, what can I do?* It was a cry of desperate anguish.

And just like that, it came to her.

"Mitch!" When he turned, she ran to him. He touched her briefly on the cheek. "I'm not just pouting, Edie," he said. "I really do need to get started if I'm going to catch up to the rest of them tonight."

"I have an idea," she blurted.

"Oh?"

"You said you have to go down to Bluff after you get back to talk to your father about what he wants you to do with his cows, right?"

"Yes?" He was clearly taken aback by that.

"Will you take me with you?"

Mitch's eyes widened in surprise. "You mean to stay for the winter?"

Edie actually laughed. "No, you don't get off that easy, mister." Then she was serious again. "What if we talk to your parents about all of this? Surely they've gone through times when they couldn't agree on some important things. So let's lay it out for them—my feelings, your feelings—and see what counsel they have for us."

He considered that and then nodded. "I like it. I agree."

"Then don't leave."

He leaned in and kissed her softly. "I think it's best if I do. I need to get on the road, and I think we both need some time to think about it."

"Just tell me that you don't hate me, Mitch," she pleaded.

His surprise was complete. "What?" Then he blew out his breath. "Don't you get it? The reason I am so frustrated is because I love you more right now than I thought was possible."

Edie moved in closer and put her head against his chest, not trusting herself to speak as tears burst out and trickled down her cheeks. "Really? How can that be when I'm such a—"

He took her face in his hands and kissed her gently. "Oh, Edie. So I'm not the only one who can't see some things clearly?"

Before Edie could answer, Leona's voice floated down to them from somewhere above them. "We can see you," she sang out.

They both jerked around and started to laugh. Then Edie threw her arms around Mitch's neck as she called over her shoulder. "Good. Then watch this." And she kissed him back long and hard, trying hard not to laugh as she did so.

CHAPTER 17

September 18, 1888, 5:10 p.m.—Westland Home—Bluff City

Mitch and Arthur Westland had spent part of the day down at the co-op store, reading the latest newspapers about beef prices and discussing with other ranchers the current market. They had also ridden out of town a short distance to assess other herds, trying to get a sense of how theirs would measure up on the selling block.

When they returned to the house, they were covered with dust and smelled strongly of what Gwen called "Perfume de Corral." By that point, Edie and Martha were helping Gwen prepare dinner, and Johnnie had a large kettle of water heating over a fire outside. Gwen went up on her toes and kissed her husband and then stepped back, waving her hand back and forth in front of her nose. "Whew! You smell of horse and smoke and . . . well, who knows what else? Why don't you take a bath? Dinner will be ready in about half an hour."

"That sounds great," Arthur said, stepping back.

Mitch came over and gave his mother a kiss on the cheek. "Hello, Mama."

She wrinkled her nose. "You too. No dinner until you've spent some time in the river."

Edie watched with amusement. When Mitch started toward

her, his arms extended, she waved him off. "I love you lots, but could you stand downwind of me right now?"

She squealed and darted away as he came at her, his hands forming claws. She wasn't quick enough. He wrestled her down onto the settee and tickled her until she was howling for mercy.

7:40 p.m.

Because it was a school day, Johnnie and Martha were sent to their bedrooms at 7:30 to do their homework, both of them vigorously protesting. When they were both settled, Gwen suggested that the adults move into the parlor where they could talk without interruption. Arthur lit one lamp, which filled the room with a soft glow that seemed to create just the right atmosphere.

As they sat down—Mitch and Edie on the settee, Arthur and Gwen on side chairs across from them—Gwen looked at her husband. "I think we are ready to begin."

He nodded. "I think it appropriate to begin with prayer. Mother, would you do that, please?"

As they all folded their arms and bowed their heads, Gwen began. "Dearest Father in Heaven, we bow our heads before Thee in prayer this night. We come seeking to know Thy will, especially for Mitchell and Edna Rae. We are so grateful to have Edie as part of our family, Father. We thank Thee for the richness of Thy blessings to us. Be with us, we pray, in the name of Jesus, amen."

There was an awkward moment, and then Arthur spoke. "Okay then. Your mother and I have some idea of the overall question, but we know very little of the details. So why don't you summarize it for us? And we'd like you both to explain why you feel as you do as best you can."

Mitch looked at Edie and nodded for her to begin. She shook her head and gave him a teasing smile. "You first, remember?"

"All right." He turned to his parents. "The question before us is this: should Edie stay up in Monticello for the winter? There are several reasons why the idea makes me nervous, but Edie has some pretty good counter arguments to those. So the primary thing for me is that whenever I think about her staying, I get this deep feeling of uneasiness. I'm not sure why. There are only about six families who are staying there. The rest are coming down here or going elsewhere to stay with their families."

"And do you still have those feelings now?" Edie asked quietly.

Mitch nodded but continued looking at his parents. "In fact, it's even stronger now than when Edie and I talked about it last week. There's nothing specific, just this sense that something's not right about it. But it's very strong." He shrugged. "That about sums it up for me."

Edie was a little surprised that he hadn't gone through his four reasons as he had with her, but it pleased her that he acknowledged that she had some pretty good responses to those concerns. So she decided to get to the key issue for her as well. "Unfortunately, I also have some very strong feelings that it's important for me to stay, and that's not just because I want to be with Mitch, which goes without saying. I feel like I'm needed there." She told them quickly about Sarah Rogerson's invitation and about Eliza Peterson.

"Those seem like pretty solid reasons for staying," Mitch's father said when she finished.

"That's what I told her too," Mitch said.

"On the surface, at least," Edie went on, "it seems like we're getting contradictory inspiration. But that can't be right, can it? I mean we both can't be right, can we?"

"Mons is definitely staying for the winter?" Arthur asked Mitch.

Mitch shook his head. "I don't think anything is absolutely definite yet. I told you about the problem with the Utes. That worries him a lot. It worries us all a lot. And Eliza's health really concerns him, too. But he doesn't see how he can leave the store, and there are far too many goods for him to haul away for the winter. Everyone up there agrees that barring some major catastrophe, some of us need to stay up there for the winter to look after things."

"So," Arthur mused, "what we have here does seem to be, in Edie's words, contradictory inspiration. And this is the real quandary, right? Neither of you is concerned that the other person is being selfish or just plain stubborn?"

Mitch shook his head, but, to his surprise, Edie hesitated. "I worry I may be," Edie said. "I know that Mitch's concerns are about my safety, but I—"

Mitch broke in. "You're not being selfish. Your desires are good, too. I've never disagreed with that. If it weren't for this feeling I have, I would be delighted to have you stay."

"Well then," Arthur said, sitting back, "that helps. So let me make a few observations, and I'll invite your mother to do the same. First of all, I'm sorry to say that Gwen and I are not going to tell you what to do." At Edie's look of disappointment, he hurried on. "This is your problem, and while we may give you counsel about it, we cannot make the decision for you." He smiled wryly. "Highly tempting though that is for parents."

As Gwen stirred, he nodded for her to speak. She was looking at Edie. "Why do you say that you both can't be right?"

"Because our feelings are opposite. They contradict one another," she said.

"No, they don't. Not as you just expressed them to us. Mitch didn't say that he had a strong feeling that you should go, only that he felt uneasy about you staying. That may not be the same thing." She went on quickly as Mitch started to respond to that. "And you, Edie—I also find it interesting that you didn't say you had strong feelings that you had to stay, only that you feel strongly about helping Eliza and Sarah."

"But, Mama," Mitch exclaimed, "aren't you just playing with words? Doesn't it come down to the same thing? I think she should go because I'm worried about her. She thinks she should stay because she's worried about Sarah and Eliza. So, does she stay or does she go?"

Gwen was nodding before he finished. "When you put it that way, of course you can't have it both ways. But I have learned that sometimes what we want is not a choice between good and bad, but between two good things that may exclude one another. For example, you once talked about opening a freighting business, Mitch. Then you decided to become a full-time rancher. Both are good things, but you can't have them both, not at the same time."

Edie was peering at her. "I understand, but help me understand how that applies here."

Gwen nodded. "I believe your feelings are from God, Edie. To help Sarah teach the children would not just be wonderful for them, but for you, too. And helping a dear sister in need? Who would question that? But I think you're assuming that those two things are incompatible with you leaving Monticello, and that may not be the case."

"Mama," Mitch said, truly exasperated now. "Sarah Rogerson's school is in Monticello. Eliza Peterson is in Monticello. They are incompatible if Edie leaves."

"I didn't say they *weren't* incompatible, only that they *might* not be. For example, let's suppose that when you return home tomorrow, President Jones calls everyone in and announces that the situation with the Utes is so untenable that no one will stay in Monticello for this winter. Suddenly, you two have no dilemma."

"Yeah, but—" Mitch started.

Arthur interrupted him. "I've found that's often the case. We want something badly, but the Lord doesn't answer us because the situation might be changing in ways that eliminate the problem. Here's another possibility. When you return, Mons announces that he's so concerned about Eliza's health that he wants her to come to a warmer climate, like down here in Bluff. So he stays but Eliza comes to Bluff, and Mons asks Edie to come with her to help care for her. *Voila!* No dilemma."

"I can see that," Edie said, "but Eliza feels as strongly about staying in Monticello with Mons as I do about staying with Mitch," Edie said.

Mitch's head came up slowly as he looked at Edie. "Actually, something might happen there. Just before we left to come down here, Mons told me that he's planning to go to Mancos about the same time that I leave for Thompson Springs with our cattle. He wants to get one more load of goods in before snow comes."

"So?" Edie asked, not sure why that was significant.

"So, Mancos is where President Hammond lives."

Now it was Gwen who was puzzled. "He wants to talk to President Hammond about this?"

But Edie had seen it immediately. "No, President Hammond is Eliza's father, remember? She's a Hammond."

"Ah." Gwen turned to Edie. "Suppose Eliza did go to stay with her parents for the winter, do you think Mons would ask you to go with her then?"

That was an easy question. "No. Not if she has her mother."

Mitch was eager now. "So let's suppose the question of Eliza is resolved. If it were only helping Sister Rogerson with the school, would you still feel compelled to stay?"

Edie studied Mitch for several moments and finally shook her head. "I really want to do that, but it's not as important to me as it is to help Eliza."

Mitch sat back. "I know all of this is conjecture, but I think that's what you're saying, Mama. Right? Other options may open up that will help us resolve the issue, and that is why we can't get an answer?"

"Yes," Gwen replied. "We're not saying these things will happen, only that they could."

Mitch's mind was racing. "Point well taken. But that is just speculation. So let me speculate in another direction. Let's assume things don't change. When I return from Thompson Springs, we will have to decide what Edie does. One of us has to give in to the other, right?"

"In other words," Edie said, suddenly looking quite glum, "does Mitch get to say, 'Because I hold the priesthood and am the head of our household, I get to be the one to decide'?"

Gwen cocked her head a little and gave them both a long look. "Ah. Now we're getting to the real issue."

"No," Mitch replied, "the real issue at that point will be, does Edie stay or go?"

"No, Mitch," Edie cried. "It's *how* we decide whether I stay or go." She turned back to Gwen, pleading now. "I really want to do what is right. I know that Mitch will be the head of our family, and I honor that. But does that mean I just set aside my feelings, my inspiration? Where is my choice in all of this?"

Both of the older Westlands were silent, keenly aware now of how much emotion was going on just under the surface here. After a moment, Arthur spoke. "Okay. So let's address this issue head on. Who gets the final say if a couple cannot agree on a major decision they have to make?" He chuckled. "Actually, your mother and I had this discussion some years ago."

Gwen laughed too. "It got pretty heated, actually." Then to Edie: "You're not the only stubborn woman in the room."

Arthur reached over to the lamp table and picked up a book bound in black leather. Mitch saw that it was the Doctrine and Covenants. He quickly thumbed some pages. Then, finding what he was looking for, he put his finger in the place and closed the book again. "So, let me put your question to your mother. Gwen, can Mitch, by virtue of the priesthood he holds and by virtue of him being the head of this new family they are going to create, say to Edie, 'Since we cannot agree, then I get to make the decision'?"

A smile slowly began to play around the corners of Gwen's mouth. "No."

Mitch jerked up. "No?"

With her smile broadening, she looked at her husband. "Arthur, does Edie get to say to Mitch, 'Since we cannot make a decision, and because we both agree that the Lord is prompting me to stay with Eliza Peterson, I get to make the decision'?"

He didn't hesitate at all. "No."

"Aw, come on!" Mitch exploded. "That's no answer."

"Explain yourself," Arthur said to his wife, totally ignoring Mitch.

Leaning forward, she spoke to her son. "Yes, you are the head of the household and you preside over this family. But that doesn't mean that you are somehow superior to Edie and that by default your wisdom and judgment are superior to hers. So no, you cannot force your will on her using the priesthood as your justification for doing it."

"I never said I was superior to Edie," Mitch cried, his face reddening.

"No," Edie said, quickly. "I've never felt that about Mitch."

"Sorry," his mother said. "I didn't mean to make it personal to you, Mitch. But some men do have that feeling. So let me rephrase it. The fact that the Lord has said that the man presides over the home doesn't mean that he's inherently superior to his wife. I believe strongly that in a marriage, though the husband and wife are very different, they are equal in the sight of the Lord as far as their place in the marriage goes. Do you agree?"

Mitch nodded, relaxing a little, but he was clearly still on the defensive. So his mother turned to her husband. "Arthur, I think you have something you wish to read to these two."

Arthur opened the book and began to read: "'No power or influence can or ought to be maintained by virtue of the priesthood.'" He stopped. "Did you hear that? A man cannot say to his wife or anyone else, 'Because I hold the priesthood, you have to do what I say.' The Lord makes that clear in another verse when he says—" He started reading again. "If we 'exercise control or dominion or compulsion upon the souls of the children of men in any degree of unrighteousness, behold, the heavens withdraw themselves and the Spirit of the Lord is grieved.'" He closed the book again but kept his finger in his place.

"The word *dominion* comes from the same root as domination. If a man uses his position to force, coerce, intimidate, demand, or compel his wife and children to comply with his will simply because he is the head of the house, he will lose the Spirit."

The room was quiet now. Mitch had his hands clasped together and was staring at the floor moodily. Edie was watching him anxiously out of the corner of her eye. Gwen and Arthur were exchanging glances with each other. Finally, Gwen turned back to her son. "Mitch, we still haven't answered the main question. So ask it again."

He shook his head without looking up. "Oh, you've answered it all right. I can't tell Edie that she has to go. It's that simple. I get it."

"That wasn't the question," his mother replied softly. "You asked *what you do* when you can't agree on who is right."

"All right," he said dully, "so what do I do when we can't agree? When I come back from Thompson Springs after selling our cattle, the other families will be leaving. We will have to decide. So what do we do at that point when we are no closer to unity than we are now?"

Arthur smiled that same kind of pleased smile that Gwen had smiled and opened the book again. "Let me read that first verse again, only this time I'll read what follows." His head tipped down. "'No power or influence can or ought to be maintained by virtue of the priesthood, *only*—" He looked up and raised his left hand high. His fingers and thumb were folded into the palm. His index finger came up as he continued. "'*Only* by persuasion.'" He extended a second index finger. "'By *long-suffering.*'" The other two fingers came up. "'By *gentleness* and *meekness.*'" His thumb extended. "'And by *love unfeigned.*'"

He closed the book, pleased to see that about halfway through that, Mitch's head had come up very slowly as he stared at the raised fingers.

"There's your answer, Mitch," his mother said. "Five simple words. Persuasion. Long-suffering. Gentleness. Meekness. Love." Before Mitch could respond, she turned to Edie. "So let me ask you a question, Edie, and I want you to be completely honest. Let's suppose Mitch is right. When he returns from the north, nothing has changed between you. You are still deadlocked. But instead of him saying, 'This is what I think is right, and so this is what we will do,' suppose Mitch takes you in his arms and, with love and gentleness, says something like this. 'Edie, my darling, I firmly believe that your way is not the best way to go. But I have so much love and trust and respect for your wisdom and your goodness that we'll do it your way and I won't say anything more about it.' How would that make you feel?"

Edie was staring at Mitch now, her eyes glistening in the lamplight. "I would love him—" Her voice caught, and she couldn't finish. No one moved. Mitch was watching her intently as the tears spilled over and ran down her cheeks. Finally, she got control and finished in a whisper. "I would love him more than I can put into words."

Arthur turned to his son, holding up his hand again. As he spoke each word, the fingers came up one at a time. "Persuasion, long-suffering, gentleness, meekness, and love. That's *how* you reconcile your irreconcilable differences."

"I understand," Mitch said in a hoarse whisper of his own.

But Gwen wasn't through quite yet. "Edie? That's one way to solve it. Can you think of another way that it could be resolved?"

For a moment Edie looked at Gwen blankly, but then her eyes slowly widened as understanding dawned. "Or, when he says that to me, I could say this to him." She turned to face him directly now. "'Even though I firmly believe that I am right in my feelings, I honor you as the head of our home. I know that you want only what is best for me. I know that you love me and are trying to follow the Lord's promptings. So, I will go away for the winter. Not because I want to, but because I choose to. I choose to let you choose for me.'"

Mitch didn't need to be asked. "And if you did that, I would love you more than I could put into words." He turned to his parents and with a choked voice said, "Thank you." And then a thought hit him, and wonder filled his face. "That's how you resolved whether you would go back to Beaver or not, isn't it?"

Now his mother was crying. "Yes, but in our case, it was your father who said those words, not me." She wiped at her eyes.

"And it was your mother who said," Arthur whispered in a husky voice, "'I want to stay.' And I love her more now than I can ever put into words."

Notes

At this time in history, some of the sections of the Doctrine and Covenants were numbered differently that they are now. Arthur Westland read or referred to what is now D&C 121:37, 41.

CHAPTER 18

September 30, 1888, 6:55 a.m.—Corrals near Westland Cabin —Monticello

When Edie Zimmer was walking up to their cabin site from town in the near darkness to say good-bye to Mitch, she vowed yet again that she wasn't going to cry. His last image of her would not be tear-stained cheeks, puffy eyes, and a red nose. Now as she watched him check the load in his wagon one last time and stow away the food that she had packed for him, she felt the tears starting. She decided she had to do something quickly in order to ward them off.

"Do you think you'll ferry the cattle across the Colorado River?"

Mitch looked up, a little surprised at the question. "No. They're asking a dollar a head for each head of stock, and four dollars for the wagon and team." He smiled, kissed two of his fingertips, and planted the kiss on her nose. "If it were spring and high water, then we'd have no choice, but this late in the year the current is so lazy that if we can get those cows running fast enough, they might just skip across and not even get their hooves wet."

Edie shook her head at him. "You're starting to sound like Latigo Gordon."

Laughing, he stepped back to the wagon, looked inside one more time to make sure everything was secure, and then helped

Edie up onto the wagon seat. As he walked around and climbed up beside her, she looked at the cabin and laid her hand on his. "It's wonderful, Mitch. I still can't believe this will be our home."

"I'll bring the window frames and glass back with me from Thompson Springs, and then it will be completely enclosed. Then I can work through the winter putting a floor in. We have to have a floor before we bring Grandma Zimmer here, assuming that she comes."

"I'm astonished at what you've been able to do."

They fell silent, but to Edie's surprise, Mitch still didn't reach for the reins. She decided to take advantage of whatever time he could give her. "Mons came over to the Waltons' and talked to me last night. He leaves tomorrow for Mancos. He asked me to stay with Eliza."

"I thought Eliza was going with him."

Edie looked away. "Her cough is worse. They both decided it would be too much for her."

"But she wasn't going to stay there with her family, right? Even if she did go."

"That's right. She's adamant. If Mons stays here, then she stays here." Suddenly Edie couldn't hold the tears back, and she started to cry. "I think she's afraid she's going to die, and she wants to be with Mons if she does."

Mitch's head came around. "Do you think it's come to that?"

"I don't know," Edie wailed. "She doesn't talk about it. It's just a guess." Then suddenly, her face was stricken. "Maybe this is our answer, Mitch. If Eliza dies, then. . . . It's been two weeks since we talked to your folks. Why can't we get an answer?"

He pulled her closer. "I'm ready to say that I'll do whatever you think is best, Edie."

"No, Mitch! Not yet. I think that is only a last resort. And, by the way, if it comes to that, we'll go the other way. I'll go to

Bluff and stay with your parents. And I'll be fine with that." But even as she said it, she was biting her lip to stop from completely falling apart. "Eliza is devastated that she won't get to say goodbye to her parents."

"Maybe Mons should bring them back with him."

"He can't. Her mother's been sick too. And no one knows where President Hammond is or how to contact him. Remember, he's out with Lem Redd and that party from Washington."

That hit Mitch pretty hard. He had forgotten that. And that made up his mind. "Edie, listen to me. Eliza is your first concern. You are right. She needs you. And you are going to stay with her as long as she does, even if it's clear through the winter."

Edie reared back, totally taken by surprise. "But what about your feelings?"

"I don't know. What I do know is that Eliza needs you. We'll work the rest out somehow."

October 5, 1888, 9:30 p.m.—Mons Peterson Cabin and Store —Monticello

Edie slowly pushed the door open and peeked inside. The lamp was set low, but she could see that Eliza was still sitting up in bed. She looked up and smiled. "Is everyone asleep?"

Edie sighed. "Yes. Finally. Evelyn and Nean were especially tired."

Evelyn Adams had come up from Verdure with George the previous afternoon. While George went out to round up his cattle, she and Cornelia would stay with Eliza for a couple of days. Which was good. Evelyn and Eliza were close friends, and their two girls were inseparable.

Eliza patted the bed beside her. "You look tired too, Edie. Come to bed."

Edie couldn't resist that, so she came in, moved around the bed, sat down beside her friend, and started unbuttoning her blouse as she removed her shoes.

"Was that lightning I saw a few minutes ago?" Eliza asked.

"Yes. It's raining. I'm guessing there will be snow on Horsehead Peak by morning."

"Oh, I hope that doesn't delay Mons. He hoped to be back by tomorrow or the next day."

Edie frowned as she removed her skirt and got her nightgown from off a chair. "It looks pretty widespread. I'm afraid it will slow down Mitch and Fred too."

Eliza sighed. "Why is it when our men are gone, the hours seems like days?"

"That's a woman's lot, I guess." Pulling on her nightgown, Edie quickly slipped under the covers beside Eliza. She turned on her side to face her, but neither spoke. After a moment, Eliza yawned, and yawned again. Edie touched her arm. "Go to sleep. I'm right here now."

Eliza reached across under the covers and took Edie's hand. "There's something I want to discuss with you, Edie."

Edie nodded. "All right."

To her surprise, her grip on Edie's hand tightened. Sensing that something was troubling her, Edie began to softly massage the back of Eliza's hand with her thumb.

"That feels nice," Eliza said after a moment.

"Your hands are cold."

"My hands are always cold." And again Eliza fell silent. A full minute went by. Edie turned so she could see her more clearly. Her eyes were closed, and Edie wondered if she might be falling asleep in spite of her protests. But then her eyes opened again. "I need you to do something for me."

"Anything, Eliza."

"I need you to help Mons and Elna when the time comes."

Edie stiffened, and her thumb stopped its movement. "When what time comes?" she asked, not knowing what else to say.

"My time. It's coming, Edie. I don't know how soon it will be, but I don't think it will be long now."

"No!" Edie tried to stifle a sob in her throat. "No, Eliza. Your cough is better. You're stronger. Even Jane Walton commented on how much better you're doing."

Turning onto her side so she could look up at Edie, Eliza went on. "It's all right. I'm at peace with it." The tears spilled over, running sideways out of the corners of her eyes. "It's different this time," she whispered. "I can feel it. But I'm not afraid." Then her shoulders began to tremble, and one hand came up to her mouth. "I just can't bear the thought of never getting to raise my Little Mons. And Ellie. Oh, how I will miss my Ellie."

Edie threw her arms around her friend, and together they clung to each other as the tears broke loose. After a long time, when the shudders gradually subsided, Edie sat up. "What do you want me to do?" she asked.

"I want you to be with me. As much as you can."

"I will." And her tears started again as she remembered the last thing that Mitch had said to her as he left: "Be with her, no matter what."

"And I need you to help Elna. She loves you so much, Edie. Help her understand why Heavenly Father is calling me home."

"But . . . *I* don't understand, Eliza. Why you? You're so young. You're so good. You have your little family to care for. I don't understand."

"You will know what to say," she said firmly. "And promise me that every day, you will tell Ellie how much I loved her."

"Yes. Of course I will."

"Will you help Mons find a wet nurse for Little Mons? It's too early for him to be weaned."

Edie hesitated. Right now it looked like there would be no more than six families staying during the winter. And none of those sisters was nursing right now. Annie Bailey had a little one of about fifteen months, but their family was leaving in the coming week.

Seeing the consternation on her face, Eliza reached out and touched her arm. "Just help Mons find a way to care for Mons Jr. He'll be at a loss on things like that once I'm gone."

"Does he know?"

"I think so. I tried to tell him the night before he left, but. . . ." Her voice broke, and her body began to shake again. "Before I could get it out, he broke down and just sobbed and sobbed." Eliza wiped at her nose with the handkerchief. "It's the first time I've ever even seen him cry."

Edie had to turn away. She was talking about dying, and all she could think of was how hard it was going to be for her husband and children. "How can you bear it?" she cried suddenly. "How can you be so strong?"

Eliza rose up on one elbow, her eyes locking with Edie's. "Because I know this is not the end of our story." Her voice dropped to a bare whisper. "Mons and I were sealed together in the Endowment House in Salt Lake. So I'm not losing him. I'm going away for a while. On a trip of my own." She squeezed Edie's hand. "It's not the end, Edie. It's not."

Eliza lay back down, her energy gone. "There's one more thing I need to ask of you."

"Anything," Edie said, blinded by her tears now.

"Will you say good-bye to Mama and Papa for me?" The tremor in her voice belied the calmness on her face. "I was going to write to them and send it with Mons to Mancos, but Papa's not there right now. He's with that commission somewhere. So I didn't do it. Now I wish I had."

"We'll write a letter in the morning. We'll send it off with the next mail rider."

"Thank you." Eliza let go of Edie's hand. Her whole body seemed to relax, and after a moment her eyes closed. "I'm so tired, Edie. I think I will sleep now."

"Yes. You need to sleep."

Her eyes fluttered open again. "Will you stay with me, Edie?"

"Of course."

October 9, 1888, 6:37 a.m.—Peterson Store and Cabin —Monticello

Edie groaned softly and turned over in the bed. When the knock sounded a second time, she raised her head. "Go away," she hissed. "We don't open until eight."

The sound came a third time. It was a soft but an insistent rapping. She turned and looked at Eliza. The first light of morning was visible beneath the shutters and gave enough light for her to see. Eliza was still sleeping deeply. Muttering to herself, Edie threw back the quilt and swung her legs off the bed. She didn't want whoever it was to wake up the whole house. Not at this hour of the morning.

Wrapping her bathrobe around her, she left the bedroom, careful not to bump into any of the buckets, tubs, pots, or pans that were scattered around the room to catch the water that had been coming through the sod roof for two days now. As she reached the door, she realized the sound of dripping water had stopped and remembered that sometime in the middle of the night she had awakened enough to notice that the rain had finally stopped.

Carefully pulling the bedroom door shut behind her, she moved quickly across the large room that was kitchen and store. Here the shutters on the two windows were open and the light was better. The rapping sounded again. To her surprise, it wasn't from the door that opened into the store, which was padlocked from the outside, but from the door that led into the backyard. Puzzled, she turned in that direction and lifted the bar that locked it from the inside.

"Edie?"

She gaped for a moment at the man standing before her in the soft light of morning and then gave a low cry of joy. "Mons?"

"Mornin', Edie."

Edie saw several things at the same time. Mons's face was lined with exhaustion and his eyes were dull. He was shivering noticeably, even though he wore a sheepskin jacket. His boots were caked with mud, and the bottom half of the legs of his Levi's looked much the same. Where in the world had he been to look like that?

"How is Eliza?" he asked softly.

"She's good, Mons. Having Evelyn and Nean here helps. That always cheers her up."

"And you."

Edie nodded. "I love being with her too." She stepped back. "Come in, you look half frozen. I'll go wake her."

"No," he blurted. "No, let her sleep."

"But. . . ."

He sighed. "I got my wagon stuck in a mudhole last night about eight or nine miles out of town. I've got to go back and get it before someone comes along and helps himself to my dry goods. I've got about a thousand dollars' worth under canvas out there."

Shocked, Edie exclaimed. "And you walked all that way?"

Mons rubbed his hand across the stubble on his face, and she saw now that his eyes were red. "No. Once I realized that my team was too tuckered out to pull me free, I walked over to the Carlisle Ranch headquarters because it was closer. They let me sleep in their barn. Got there about midnight and slept for a few hours, then came on the rest of the way this morning."

Edie was shocked. "Come in. You must be starving. Let me get you something to eat."

"No," he said, keeping his voice low. He gestured at his feet. "I'm a mess, as you can see. If you could get me some bread and some of that dried jerky, maybe a canteen of water. I stopped by the Waltons' a few minutes ago. Charles and Charlie Jr. are going to take me back out and help me get my wagon unstuck. They're hitching up now."

Edie couldn't argue with that. She went to the bread box and took out half a loaf of bread, got a sack full of dried jerky, and took some cheese from the cooling box. She found a flask with a stopper and filled it with water from their drinking bucket. Mons took it, smiled gratefully, and then said, "Tell Eliza what happened. Tell her not to worry. I should be back by noon or so." Then he raised a hand and was gone.

Notes

It is hard to say exactly when the government in Washington created a commission in Congress to study the issue of whether to make all of San Juan County a Ute Indian reservation. But they did arrive in Utah Territory sometime in the fall of 1888. Francis Hammond, president of the San Juan Stake, was asked by Salt Lake to accompany them. Lemuel Redd, who knew the county as well as anyone, was asked to guide them (see *Saga*, 214–15).

CHAPTER 19

October 9, 1888, 6:40 a.m.—Thompson Hotel
—Thompson Springs, Grand County, Utah Territory

Mitch cracked an eye open and turned his head toward the window. There was some light around the edges of the blind, but not much. Which meant that dawn was still maybe half an hour away. Good. To wake up in a real bed was a luxury that he needed to enjoy.

He turned his head the other way. Sleeping beside him was Fred Adams, his riding companion on their cattle drive. Joseph Frederick Adams was the youngest son of William Adams and his second wife, Mary. He was their fourth child and their third son. Soon to be nineteen years of age, he bore a strong family resemblance to both his father and his older brother, George A. Adams, with whom he lived down in Verdure. About a year younger than Mitch, he could work as hard as any man in their community. He had a thatch of thick, rough-cut hair that seemed to explode whenever he removed his hat. His light brown eyes were filled with good humor and a love for life. Fred and Mitch had worked together on many occasions, and not only had Fred earned Mitch's respect, but they had developed a close friendship.

Mitch lay back. They had a corral full of cattle to tend to, but there wasn't much sense in getting at it too soon. The buyers wouldn't get there until eight. His thoughts turned to Edie and their dilemma. He was a little surprised at how much he had missed her on this trip. Much more than usual, and he wondered if that was because of the struggle they were going through right now. And that, of course, turned his thoughts to their dilemma. He was thinking of their last time together. He had told her that she needed to stay with Eliza, especially if Eliza was right about what the future held for her. And that felt right to him. But that was all that felt right. If anything, he was more unsettled and more uncertain now than he had been before he left.

He was still wrestling with that contradiction when an idea came. It so startled him that he nearly sat up in bed. For a while he tried to discount it, but finally he accepted that this was not a whim. Once he did that, it wasn't long before his eyes closed and he drifted off to sleep again.

9:05 a.m.—Texas-Oklahoma Cattlemen's Association Office —Thompson Springs

Fred pulled his sheepskin jacket tighter around himself as he gloomily watched the wind whip the rain into sheets that swept past them going nearly sideways. He was sitting on the porch of the Texas-Oklahoma Cattlemen's Association building, near the west end of Main Street, just a block away from the stockyards that lined the railroad tracks. When he heard the door open and saw Mitch, he jumped to his feet. "How'd we do?" he asked.

Grinning like a bear cub who'd just stumbled across a fresh honeycomb, Mitch gave him a thumbs-up. "Thirty-five dollars a head."

"For every one of them?"

"Yeah. It was a package price. Even included those two scrawny heifers of yours."

"Wonderful. George will be delighted."

"Come on, let's go back to the hotel. I'm buying us the best breakfast in town."

"When do we get our money?"

"At ten. We meet them at the bank."

9:28 a.m.—Road to Mancos, a Few Miles East of Monticello

When Mons Peterson and the Waltons reached the top of the hill, Charles Walton pulled his team to a stop. All three men climbed down from the wagon, looking down at the road that stretched out before them. It curved out of sight thirty or forty yards ahead of them, but what they could see was mostly hard-packed gravel or stretches of rock pan. Mons grunted. "If I could have made it past that mud hole to this kind of road base, I'd have been all right."

"You aren't the first one to get stuck down there," Charles observed. "Someday we need to haul in a few loads of gravel and fill in that low spot." He and Charlie went to their team and began undoing the harnesses. "No sense risking getting our wagon stuck, especially when there's no good place to turn around down there. We'll just bring the team. You go on down and get your animals ready. Charlie, you go with Mons. I'll be right behind you."

Mons waved and started down. Charlie had to break into a trot to catch up with him.

Five minutes later, as Charles led his team of matched draft horses down the hill and came into view of the Peterson wagon, he stopped. He was a little surprised to see that Mons's team was still in hobbles and off in the trees away from his wagon. Mons was in deep mud at the back of his wagon, a look of consternation on his face.

Charles moved off the road and tied the reins of his team to a stout branch of scrub oak. "What's the matter?" he called. "Something wrong with your team?"

Mons shook his head, muttered something Charles didn't catch, and held up a corner of the canvas cover. "I've had company since I left this here last night."

"Somebody's cut the lashings on his canvas," Charlie called, coming out from behind the wagon. "They stole some of his goods."

"Indians or cowboys, can you tell?" Charles asked, increasing his pace.

"All the horse tracks we can see were shod," Mons answered. "No question; it's white men. Looks like maybe three or four horses. Two, maybe three hours old."

"That means they were here pretty early," Charles observed.

Mons was staring down at the muddy tracks around him. "I did something bone-headed stupid, Charles," he muttered. "When I finally got to the Carlisle place, I thought Bill Edwards was the only one that was up. As you know, he's a fair-minded man. When I told him my predicament, he made up a bed for me in the barn."

"But?"

"I wasn't thinking very straight by then. As we finished talking, I saw that several of the cowhands had come out to see what was going on and probably heard what I was saying."

Charles nodded very slowly. "Any that you recognized?"

His face said it all when he answered. "John Gibson. He's not a bad sort. But there was also Bob Kelly, Latigo Gordon, and Tom Roach." He muttered something under his breath and added, "Only three of the biggest drunks in the lot."

"And that Roach is meaner than a she-wolf with pups when he's drunk." Charles didn't try to hide his concern. "So they got up before dawn and rode down here to take a look. What did they get? Can you tell?"

Mons was looking pretty glum. "Can't tell for sure until I get the cover clear off, but two things for sure: two cartons of .45 shells." His eyes darkened. "And a case of brandy."

That Mons was hauling brandy was no surprise. Virtually every pioneer home had a bottle of brandy or whiskey up high on a shelf, which was used for medicinal purposes. It made a good sedative, pain killer, anesthetic, and antiseptic. Charles Walton was not a swearing man, but at that moment, he was sorely tempted to let loose with a long string. Finally, he just shook his head. "Let's get you out of here. Then we'll go pay Edwards and Old Man Carlisle a visit."

"Won't do no good," Charlie observed.

"I know that," his father snapped, "but it's gotta be done. Let's just hope that by now they're back at the ranch sleeping it off."

10:05 a.m.—Thompson Hotel—Thompson Springs

Mitch wet his thumb and continued counting. "Three hundred, three hundred and ten, three hundred and fifteen." He shoved it across the table at Fred and then thumbed off a ten-dollar bill and handed it to him. "And there's your wages for a week's work."

Fred's eyebrows shot up. "Wait. I was bringing up George's cattle. I don't get paid for this, because he gives me free room and board."

Mitch took out the pouch that he wore under his shirt and

started inserting the nearly six hundred dollars that was his share. "True," he admitted, "but George had only nine head, and I had seventeen. Take it. You earned it. I couldn't have done it without you."

Deeply pleased at this unexpected bonus, Fred extended his hand and shook Mitch's vigorously. "Always a pleasure working with you, Mitch. Thank you." He stood up. "So, are you thinking of starting back now, or waiting 'til morning?"

"Uh . . . sit down a minute, Fred. I've got something I need to tell you."

Fred did, giving Mitch a puzzled look.

"I'm not going back with you."

Fred shot to his feet. "*What?* Why not?"

"Not sure I have a good answer to that, to be honest."

"I don't understand."

"Not sure I do either. But this morning, I woke up real early. I couldn't sleep because I was worrying about things. Then I had this impression that I needed to go to Salt Lake City."

"*What?*" Fred was totally dumbfounded. "But why?"

"Dunno. It was a strong impression. But it makes no more sense to me than it does to you."

"What's in Salt Lake City?"

"Dunno."

"But—how long will you be gone?"

"Dunno."

"You gonna take the train?"

"Yes, definitely."

"Are you gonna leave today?"

"Yes. There's a six-twenty westbound this evening. It'll put me in Salt Lake by about three tomorrow morning. But first I need go to the lumber mill to buy those window frames and the glazier to get the glass I need for the cabin. Don't want to take a chance that they'll be sold out by the time I get back. Both places have agreed to hold the stuff for me."

"Gee willikers, Mitch. What's going on?"

"I don't know, Fred. I really don't. I just feel like it's what I need to do."

"So what do I do?"

"You go back home." Mitch sighed and reached inside his jacket to withdraw an envelope. He handed it to Fred. "Will you give this to Edie? I've tried to explains things to her, but if she has questions for you, just tell her that I didn't give you any details."

"Not even that you're going to Salt Lake?"

"No, you can tell her that. But that's all."

Fred shook his head in disgust. "That's all I know."

"I know, but I've tried to explain things in my letter. Be sure you get it to her first thing."

"Okay," Fred said, clearly not happy with what he had just heard.

Anxious to change the subject, Mitch asked him, "Will you be all right going back alone?"

"Yeah. If I push hard tonight, I can probably be back to Verdure by late tomorrow night."

"Not if it's raining as hard down south as it is here."

"Yeah," he said glumly.

"Look, why don't you just keep this room for tonight? It's close to forty miles to Moab, and you've only got a few hours left of daylight. And with all the rain, the river may be runnin' higher than when we came through. It'll be better not to cross it at night."

"Agreed. Okay, I will. Thanks. Want me to take your wagon and team to the livery stable?"

"That would be helpful. Thanks."

"What shall I tell people about when you'll be back?" Then Fred grinned. "Dunno, right?"

"Right," Mitch said, his expression one of perplexity and frustration as he handed Fred a five-dollar bill. "Tell them at the livery stable that if it's more than that, I'll pay them when I return."

CHAPTER 20

October 9, 1888, 11:13 a.m.—Peterson Store and Cabin —Monticello

Evelyn Adams gave a long, weary sigh and started to get up out of her chair. "I'd better check on the girls. In the last few weeks, Nean has been getting into everything. I can't turn my back on her for a minute."

Emma, Mons's sister, immediately got to her feet. She was sitting by the rug in front of the fire, where she had spent most of the morning. "I'll go."

Edie was at the stove, cutting carrots into the pot of stew. "They're all right," she called. "I can see them from here. She and Ellie are out by the tack shed playing with their dolls."

Eliza Peterson, who was holding Little Mons in her arms and sitting next to Evelyn, raised her head. "Is it muddy out there?"

"Not really," Edie said, checking to be sure. "They're in a spot where it's pretty sandy soil." Evelyn motioned for Emma to sit down again. "They're fine. We'll have lunch in a little bit. Then we'll put them down for a nap."

Eliza turned to the side window that looked out on the street. "Mons should be back before long with the wagon, but let's not wait lunch on him. It may take him longer than he thinks."

Watching Evelyn, Edie felt a sharp pang of envy. She was pretty sure that Evelyn had not planned to make an announcement today, but at breakfast they had watched her picking at her food and wrinkling her nose in disgust as she picked up a piece of bacon and put it down again. "Ugh!" was all she had said, but Eliza pounced on her like a dog on a gopher.

"Evelyn Adams, are you expecting?"

And so, with face flaming, Evelyn had shyly admitted that she and George were expecting a baby in early March. This was wonderful news. Nean was getting older. Evelyn had given birth to another girl the previous summer, but she had lived only a few hours. Evelyn had taken it particularly hard, so this was especially good news for her.

Edie spooned up some stew, sipped a little of it to test it, and replaced the lid. She moved over and took the chair next to Eliza. As she sat down, Emma turned to Evelyn. "Sister Adams, do you hope it's a boy this time?"

"Well, George would be delighted if it was a little boy, but Nean has already declared that it has to be a girl."

"Of course," Edie hooted. "That way she gets a doll that is even better than Elna's Lizzie."

Evelyn nodded and added, "She really wants a little sister."

Eliza laid a hand on that of her friend. "If it is a girl, will you call her Minnie, too?"

Evelyn sat back, thinking about that. She and George had named the girl that had lived only a few hours Minnie. "No," she finally said. "I think it might be too painful. George wants to name her Zola Evelyn."

"Oh, that's sweet." Emma said. "Will you call her Evelyn?"

"No. George really likes Zola. And so do I."

"And what if it's a boy?" Edie asked.

"It's not."

"Oh? How can you be so sure?"

"Because of the morning sickness."

Both Edie and Emma looked puzzled by that.

Evelyn smiled. "Not sure if it's true, but they say that if you don't have bad morning sickness, it will be a boy, and if you do, it's a girl. I had it real bad with Nean and Minnie, and it's bad this time, too."

"I think that's an old wives' tale," Eliza said, half teasing, half chiding.

"Well," Evelyn huffed, "sometimes old wives know more than young doctors."

It surprised Edie a little how quickly Emma Peterson had fit into the household. Now she spoke up as if she were one of the women. "My grandma says there's a sure way you can know if your baby is going to be a boy or a girl."

Evelyn chuckled. "Then I want to know what it is."

"You take your wedding ring and tie it to a strand of your hair. Then you lie on your back on the bed and dangle the ring over your belly. If it goes back and forth like a pendulum, then it's a boy. It if starts moving in circles, it's a girl."

"I tried that too," Evelyn said. "With Minnie. Guess what happened?"

"What?" Emma asked eagerly.

"Absolutely nothing. It just hung there, limp as a dishrag."

They all laughed. Then Eliza spoke up. "And my mother told me that you can tell what gender it will be by what you crave when you're first carrying the child. If you crave sour or salty foods, then it will be a boy. And if you crave sweets, like fruit and candy and cookies, then it's a girl."

"Really?" Edie said.

"That's what she said."

"And did it work? You have both a boy and a girl."

She nodded somberly. "Absolutely. When I was carrying Elna, I couldn't get enough salty and sour stuff. I made poor Mons buy every jar of pickles in Mancos. And when—"

"Wait!" Emma cried. "But you said that when you craved sour and salty foods it was going to be a boy."

A devilish smile stole slowly across Eliza's face. "Exactly. And with Mons Jr., guess what?"

"Sweets?" Evelyn asked.

She was trying very hard to keep a straight face. "No. Pickles and pork. I even put salt in my oatmeal."

They went on that way, each sharing some other "sure test" that had been passed down through expectant women for centuries, laughing harder and harder and getting sillier and sillier. Midway through that, Edie suddenly cocked her head. She thought she had heard something from the bedroom. But when she held up her hand for silence, they heard nothing.

"My goodness," Evelyn said, wiping at the tears in her eyes with the back of her hand, "I do believe we're getting a little rowdy, girls."

"Yes," Eliza agreed. "And it feels so good. I'm just glad that baby Mons is sleeping through it all. But maybe we should talk about something else."

Just then, Edie's head snapped up and she quickly raised her hand. "Shhh!" She turned and looked toward the bedrooms. "Did you hear that?"

"What?" Evelyn asked, but barely had she got it out when they all heard it distinctly. Hoofbeats. A lot of them.

Eliza clapped her hands. "Oh, good. Mons is back."

Edie shot to her feet. The sounds were not coming from the east but from the west, and there was no distinctive rattle of wagon wheels. Moving quickly, she went into the bedroom where the baby was sleeping and stepped to the window. What she saw turned her rigid. About fifty yards away, coming toward them at a steady lope, was a group of eight to ten horsemen. And the lead rider was Latigo Gordon.

Whirling around, Edie shouted at the others. "Cowboys from Carlisle's bunch! And they may be coming here."

Eliza had followed Edie into the room to see for herself. She gasped, going instantly white. Then, with a low cry, she bent down and snatched up little Mons from his bassinet and clutched him to her breast. He started to howl. She ignored him. "Edie! Hurry! Go lock the door to the store." Half turning, Eliza started for the main room. "Emma! Close the shutters. Pull the curtains." By this point, little Mons was screaming at the top of his lungs. Eliza continued to ignore him. "They can't know that we're here."

Emma leaped into action and began slamming the shutters on the windows shut. Edie raced past her into the store portion and went to the shelf where Mons always left the heavy padlock. It wasn't there. "Eliza! Where's the lock?"

Evelyn was just getting up from her chair. Eliza raced to her and shoved little Mons into her arms, pushing her down again. "No, Evelyn. You stay right where you are." Then she strode over to where Edie was feeling with her fingers along the next higher shelf. "It's not here, Eliza."

Only then did it hit her. "That's right! We never unlocked the store this morning. Remember? We decided people could wait until Mons got back. Good."

As Edie whirled to see what else was needed, two things happened at the same moment. Outside, the sharp crack of a pistol shot rang out, making all four of them jump. With the bedroom door open, they could see through the window to the street. The riders were now less than half a block away. Latigo was standing in the stirrups, the reins draped over his saddle horn. He had his hat in one hand, waving wildly above his head, and a pistol in the other. He blasted another shot into the air. Then he dropped back into his saddle. "Yee-haw!" he yelled. "Hey, Mormons! Here we come!"

And at that same instant, Evelyn gave a piercing shriek. "*Nean!* No! Oh, no! Eliza! Nean and Ellie are still outside."

Momentarily stunned that in their panic they had forgotten the two girls, the reaction was instantaneous. "Ellie!" Eliza screamed her daughter's name as she bolted for the nearest door. She grabbed the latch and threw her shoulder against it to open it. It knocked her back, jarring her violently.

"It's locked on the outside," Edie shouted as she raced into the hallway and started for the back door, Emma hard on her heels. Half dazed, Eliza started after them and then saw that Evelyn was struggling to get up even though she was holding the baby, who was kicking and screaming at the top of his lungs. Eliza snatched little Mons out of her arms and straight-armed Evelyn back down a second time. "No, Evelyn. You'll lose your baby." Not waiting to see whether she complied, Eliza darted into the bedroom and thrust Mons Jr. back into his bassinet, ignoring his screams. Then she raced after Edie and Emma.

The sound of pounding hooves was now coming from all around them. BLAM! They jumped as a pistol shot rang out just outside the cabin. BLAM! Another shot came from the front of the house.

As Eliza started down the short hallway, she saw that Edie and Emma were at the door. Emma was opening it slowly and peeking out. When Edie saw Eliza coming, she waved her to silence. Outside, the sound of hoofbeats was loud now.

"Do you have a gun here, Eliza?" Edie hissed. "A rifle, a pistol? Anything to scare them away?"

"No, I. . . . Wait, Mons keeps a pistol in the store." She whirled and ran back into the main room.

Mons's sister had the door open a good foot now, and Edie

saw two horses go past. A man's voice called out. "Hey! Look! There's a couple of Mormon brats over there."

"Hee-yaw!" Latigo yelled. BLAM! BLAM! That was followed by the piercing shriek of two little voices.

The horror was so instant and so intense that for a moment, neither Edie nor Emma could breathe. Then Emma exploded into action. She flung open the door and raced through it. Edie was hard on her heels. What Edie saw when she came through the door would forever be burned into the core of her memory. The two riders were just a few feet apart. Their backs were to the cabin. Latigo had his pistol up. The other one was leaning forward in the saddle, laughing uproariously. Beyond them, Edie saw Nean and Ellie crouched down in front of the back wall of the tack shed. They were desperately clinging to each other and screeching in terror.

BLAM! Latigo fired again. A plume of dust spurted up just ten feet away from the girls.

"Stop it!" Emma roared as she launched herself at the closer rider. Seeing her, he wheeled his horse around, trying to knock her down. She sidestepped quickly and went after Latigo. She grabbed his leg, screaming like a banshee, trying to pull him off his horse.

For a split second Edie thought about waiting for the pistol from Eliza, but she saw there was no time. She went after the nearest rider, who was moving forward, trying to trap Emma between their two horses. Reaching down as she darted forward, Edie scooped up a handful of sand and hurled it at the nearest man's face. "Stop it. Leave them alone. Stop!"

Startled by her sudden appearance, the man pulled back hard on the reins, causing the horse to rear. The rider almost toppled off backwards before he grabbed the saddle horn with one hand. Then his reaction was like that of a striking rattlesnake.

He whipped out his pistol and pointed it directly into Edie's face as she ran up to him. "Hold it right there, missie!" he barked.

"Ellie!"

Edie half turned. Eliza burst out of the cabin. She had nothing in her hand.

BLAM!

Not sure who fired, Edie saw a bullet tear away a piece of log just over Eliza's head. She slid to a halt, sobbing and yelling and waving her arms all at once. "Not our girls. Don't hurt them."

The man put the toe of his boot against Edie's shoulder and gave her a hard shove toward Eliza. "Get over there with your sister, missie." he snarled. "Or you'll be getting a bullet in your head." Then he turned, grinning maniacally. "Hey, Latigo. I'll keep the women back. Go ahead and make those little whelps dance."

"No!" Eliza started forward again, sobbing hysterically. "Ellie! Ellie!"

Edie threw her arms around Eliza and pulled her to a halt. One thing was clear in her mind. She could not let this frail woman get past her or something terrible would happen. Ducking under Eliza's flailing arms, Edie dragged her friend back into the house. Evelyn was still in her chair, her face buried in her hands and sobbing hysterically. Mons Jr. was howling from the bedroom. It was a nightmarish scene.

"Eliza!" Edie shouted into her ear. "You have to stay with little Mons. Evelyn, stay right where you are. Emma and I will get the girls." Hoping that her friends would heed her, she raced out the door again.

BLAM! BLAM! BLAM! "Dance, you little devils!" Latigo was yelling between every shot. Edie took in the scene in one glance. Nean and Elna were in each other's arms now, huddled into a small ball up against the wall of the tack shed, too terrified to do anything but whimper like frightened puppies. The second man, his pistol still out and waving at Emma, had moved in and cut her off from Latigo.

Bending down, Edie snatched up a rock about the size of her fist. There would be no warning this time. She cut to the left, moving in a half crouch, keeping herself directly behind his horse. When she was about six feet away from him, she straightened and threw the rock with all of her might. It caught him high on the left shoulder, knocking him forward. He screamed with pain and whirled his horse around.

Freed again, Emma launched herself at Latigo with a cry of rage. When she slammed into Latigo's horse, it snorted and jumped five feet sideways, nearly throwing Latigo off. Edie was backing up now, her hands high in the air. The second rider was coming at her, rubbing at his shoulder with one hand, his pistol in the other, his eyes almost black with fury. Then, from out of nowhere, there was a flash of movement across Edie's vision. It was Eliza, and she had their straw broom in her hands. Swinging it as if it were a club, she knocked the man's pistol aside and hit the man in the face.

Edie didn't wait to see what happened. Like Emma, she was focused was on one thing—getting Ellie and Nean to safety. She bored in on the other side of Latigo, who was fighting furiously to keep Emma off of him and his horse under control at the same time. Grabbing at his other leg, Edie yanked hard, nearly pulling him off the horse. He responded with a curse and kicked at her face. She wrapped her arms around his boot and hung on with all the strength she had. That made the horse jump away again, and she was jerked off her feet.

That was all Emma needed. She sprinted past Latigo, running full tilt for the two girls. With a howl, Latigo kicked free of

Edie, whirled his horse around to face Emma's racing form, and started to raise his pistol.

BLAM! Edie jerked around. The shot had come from a third rider who had appeared from nowhere coming at a full gallop. Latigo's reaction was quick. He started to swing the pistol around at the newcomer, but the man fired again. BLAM! Edie heard the snap of the bullet go over Latigo's head. She dove free as the third horseman charged Latigo. Latigo was cursing and shouting at him and raised his pistol again. But the new man was too quick for him. With a yell, he swung the butt of his pistol at Latigo's head. He missed, but it connected with Latigo's right arm, nearly knocking the pistol from his hand.

"Are you crazy?" the newcomer roared, swinging at him again, but missing. "You drunken fool! Those are little girls."

"So?" Latigo screamed at him, spittle spraying everywhere. "Nits make lice. We don't need any more Mormons around here. Get out of my way, Johnnie. We're just havin' some fun."

The newcomer jerked his pistol up, pointing it directly at Latigo's face. "I said that's enough."

Emma was now to the tack shed. She dropped to her knees, throwing her arms around the two sobbing girls. Latigo saw it too. "Leave 'em alone!" he screeched. "Get back." He raised his pistol and pointed it in their direction.

Edie recognized the newcomer now. He was John Gibson. She had danced with him at the dance that night before stake conference. Mitch had said he was one of the more level-headed hands of the Carlisle bunch. Quick as a cat, Gibson leaned forward in his saddle, thrusting his pistol not more than two inches from Latigo's face. He thumbed the hammer back. "I mean it, Latigo. You pull that trigger and I'll blow you right out of that saddle."

Now the other man came over. "Come on, John. He's not hurtin' them none. Just skeerin' 'em a little."

"Back off, Kelly," Gibson said. "The fun's over. You're done here." Then, without turning his head, he called to Emma. "Ma'am, take the girls and get them outta here."

With a strangled cry of relief, Emma snatched up Ellie under one arm and Nean under the other and took off at a lumbering run, half carrying them, half dragging them. Edie was to her in three great leaps and grabbed Nean from her. As she did so, Eliza ran up behind them, waving the broom and guarding their backs as they ran toward the cabin.

It was no longer necessary. Gibson was herding Kelly and Latigo out of the yard.

Evelyn was waiting at the door, sobbing and holding out her arms for Nean. Eliza took Ellie in her arms and was patting her back and crooning softly to her. Edie herded them back inside and then slammed the door behind them and leaned back against it. She felt as though her legs were going to collapse, but she reached out and threw her arms around Emma. "That was incredible, Emma. Absolutely incredible. Thank you. Thank you."

Emma, visibly shaken and white as a snowdrift, tried to say something, but all that came out was, "I'll get baby Mons. He doesn't sound too happy."

When she returned with the baby, the four of them started moving back into the main room, all talking at once. But suddenly there was a crash and the back door was flung open again. All four women screamed and whirled around. But it wasn't one of the cowboys. It was Jane Walton, followed by Maggie and Leona. Jane had her husband's shotgun cradled in her arms.

"Quickly," she shouted. "Over to our house. It's not safe to stay here."

There was no hesitation. They didn't wait to get anything. Jane stepped to the door, peered out in both directions, and waved them forward. Ducking low, they ran hard, staying low and zig-zagging back and forth, even though no one was firing at them. There were several men on horseback in the street, but they watched without reaction as the women and children crossed in front of them.

Less than thirty seconds later, all were safely in the Walton cabin with the door bolted behind them and Jane standing guard at the door. As they sank into chairs or onto the divan, from across the street came the cackle of a chilling voice. It was Latigo Gordon. "Hey! Lookie here."

Edie peeked out the window in time to see him draw his pistol and blast the lock on the door off. He tipped back his head and roared. "The Peterson Store is open. Help yourselves, boys!"

Notes

Of the three great challenges faced by the Mormon pioneers when they came to San Juan County—taming the harsh land, living peacefully among the Native American tribes, and getting along with the lawless element that populated the various cattle ranches—the last one was probably the most intense and caused them the greatest grief.

The story described in this chapter is based on a real event that occurred in Monticello early in their settlement experience. Here is one account of what happened:

"Another cowboy raid was staged March 13, 1890. Most homes kept a bottle of brandy on hand in case of sickness. Mons Peterson, returning . . . with a load of merchandise, left his wagon at Peter's Hill because of the deep snow and walked to the Double Cabins [the local name for the Carlisle ranch]. While he was sleeping, a case of brandy was taken from the load by the cowhands. The next morning, two small girls, Cornelia [Nean] Adams and Elna Peterson were playing in back of the Peterson store when the drunken men galloped up, firing shots at the children's feet as they came. Darting from the house Emma Peterson half carried, half dragged the frightened children across the street to the safety of the Walton home. Some of the men stopped firing when they saw the children, but not so with Bill [Latigo] Johnson. 'Nits breed lice,' he yelled between each shot" (see *Saga*, 107).

Note that this source calls him Latigo Johnson, but other sources say his name was Gordon, and that seems the more likely.

The flight of the women and children to safety did not end the drunken rampage, however. A short time later, Mons Peterson returned with his wagon and walked into a hornet's nest. By this time, the inebriated cowboys had shot the lock off of the door and were ransacking the store. They made him watch as they scattered candy, flour, oatmeal, sugar, and whatever else was loose inside the store and across the yard. They looted his wagon as well. One source says they dumped some goods down his well. One of the drunks tried to set fire to the store, but some of his companions managed to stop him by striking him with a pistol and dislocating his shoulder.

The cowhands eventually fled but added one last insult to their day's work. They tied bolts of calico to their horses' tails then raced off with the bolts of cloth unwinding and billowing in the wind behind them (see *Saga*, 107–08; *Anchored Lariats*, 101–2).

Evelyn Adams was pregnant at this time. She gave birth to Zola Evelyn Adams on March 8, 1889 (see Adams family group sheet).

CHAPTER 21

October 11, 1888, 9:45 p.m.—Charles E. Walton Cabin —Monticello

Edie awoke with a start and for a moment looked wildly around her, not sure where she was. Then, in the light of a kerosene lantern at its lowest flame, she recognized the face of Jane Walton. She was in her night clothes, with a robe around her shoulders. And it was then that Edie remembered that she was not in the bedroom where she normally slept with Maggie and Leona. At Jane Walton's insistence, Eliza and Mons Peterson and their two children had taken over that bedroom until the major cleanup effort on their home and store was finished. So Edie, Maggie, Leona, and Mons's sister, Emma, were sleeping on makeshift mattresses in the kitchen.

"Edie." Jane spoke in a low whisper. "I'm sorry to awaken you, but someone is at the door."

She came instantly awake and jerked to an upright position. "Mitch?"

Jane shook her head. "No. It's Fred Adams."

"But he's with Mitch, right?"

She shook her head again and handed Edie a robe. "He's waiting on the front porch."

10:05 p.m.

Edie watched Fred as he mounted up and rode off into the darkness. With her mind whirling, she went back inside and shut the door quietly behind her. Jane had put the lamp on the kitchen table and left it burning at the same low level as before.

Moving quietly so as not to waken the others, Edie quietly got a knife from the dish cupboard drawer and slit the envelope open. With a grave sense of foreboding she moved to the table and sat down. For a long moment she stared at the front of the envelope with two words printed on the front. "Edna Rae." She frowned. *Why Edna Rae? He never calls me that unless it's something really serious. What weren't you telling me, Fred?* But she shook that off. Fred had clearly known very little about what was going on. After a moment, she pulled the letter from the envelope and leaned in closer to the lantern.

October 9th

My dearest and cherished Edie,

If you are reading this letter, then I have to assume you have seen Fred. And therefore, you know I'm not coming back to Monticello right away. I am sure this comes as a big shock to you.

Her head raised. *That's putting it mildly.*

All I can say is that it was a big surprise to me, too. No, I did not have the slightest inkling that this was coming when I left you. None whatsoever. All went well on the cattle drive, except for the several days of hard rain. Fred and I were glad we had the wagon to sleep in, but it was still pretty cold.

Anyway, we did arrive in T.S. safely without losing a

single animal. And we were able to get $35 a head, which was a couple of dollars more than I expected. So that is good. Even after I buy the window frames and the window glass, I think we will still have about $450 to $500 in cash. We didn't get the cattle in until late, so Fred and I took a dollar-a-night room at the hotel. It felt good to sleep in a real bed again. But for some reason, I woke up early the next morning. Even though I was still tired, I couldn't go back to sleep for a while. And that was when it came. The thought actually startled me. "Go to Salt Lake City."

"Salt Lake City?" Edie blurted it out without thinking, staring at the letter in astonishment. Fred had not told her that, though he surely must have known. A sound to her left brought her around in time to see Maggie get up on one elbow. "Edie?" she mumbled. "Is that you?"

"Sorry, Maggie," she whispered. "Go back to sleep. I'll be there in a minute."

Maggie looked around, obviously not comprehending much, and lay back down again.

I'm sure you've got many, many questions about now . . .

"Not more than a thousand," she muttered.

. . . but I'm afraid I don't have many answers at this point, which is only going to frustrate you more. But I'll share what I have.

Q. What is in Salt Lake City that takes me up there?

A. I have no idea. I just felt very strongly that I needed to go there.

Q. Do I feel like this is from the Lord?

A. Yes, but I'm not positive of that. It wasn't like a blinding light or a voice speaking to me. Just a feeling.

Maybe it was that steak with a spicy sauce for dinner the night before. (Sorry, that was meant to be a joke, but I can see it's not funny.)

"No, it is not funny. Not in any way." But even as she said it, she was smiling a little.

Q. Am I taking the train?

A. Yes. I am leaving my horse, the team, and the wagon at the livery stable until I get back.

Q. How long will I be gone?

A. I cannot answer that because I don't know why I am going or what I am looking for. If it is more than a few days, I'll write you from there and let you know what is going on. If it's not that long, I will be back before a letter can reach you.

Q. Does this have anything to do with the "spiritual contradiction" we talked about earlier?

A. I don't think so. I still feel strongly that you need to stay with Eliza for however long it takes. So I thought that kind of answered our question. But I have to say that even though I still feel strongly about you staying for Eliza, that decision hasn't made me feel more settled about you staying. I still feel uneasy about you not going for the winter, like there's something wrong or something more that we're missing. So who knows what is right? I certainly don't.

Q. Do I still love you?

A. Does the sunrise light the mountains? Is moonlight beautiful? Do the stars burn on forever? Does Bally live on Horsehead Mountain?

Edie stopped, her vision suddenly blurred, though she was smiling. "All right, Brother Westland, that buys you back a few points."

Q. Can I explain to you what is going on with this whole Salt Lake City thing?

A. Not really. Here is the only thing I can think of that might help. Please read what Nephi said when the Lord told him to go back to Jerusalem to get the brass plates. See 1 Nephi 4:6.

All my love to my Edna Rae,
Mitch

She read through the letter a second time, very slowly, and then read the last question and his answer to it yet again. Moving very quietly, she stood up and tiptoed over to the small set of shelves by the fireplace. Each morning before breakfast, Charles Walton gathered his family to read a chapter from the Book of Mormon together before they had family prayer. He always left his book there.

A moment later, Edie had the book in her hand. Returning to the table, she set the book near the lamp and thumbed through the first few pages until she found the place. Only then did she sit down and read it.

It was surprisingly short, but as she read the words, she felt the frustration and the uncertainty and the questions slowly melt away.

And I was led by the Spirit, not knowing beforehand the things which I should do.

She read it twice more and then closed the book, blew out the lamp, and carefully made her way back to her bed. There she knelt down and began to pray.

October 17, 1888, 11:10 a.m.—Peterson Store and Cabin —Monticello

Eliza's eyes fluttered for a moment before opening. Her head turned and looked around the bedroom, and she tried to raise up. Instantly Edie was to her side. "I'm right here, Eliza."

"Where . . . where's Mons?"

"He's out back with Emma and Elna. They're patching up some of the bullet holes in the tack shed."

"And the baby?"

"He's asleep." Edie pointed to the bassinet, which was on the other side of her bed. "Right here beside you."

Nodding weakly, Eliza fell back. Even that little effort was too much for her. And that started the coughing again. She rolled onto her side, wrapping her arms around herself and clutching tightly at her chest to ease the pain. It was all Edie could do not to look away. "Mons has some mint tea on the stove. And he said I could give you some more laudanum for the pain when you woke up."

Eliza shook her head as the coughing gradually died away. "The tea, yes. Laudanum, no. Not yet. I want to be awake when Ellie comes in."

"All right. I'll be right back." Edie closed the door behind her as she went into the small kitchen attached to the cabin. As she approached the stove, she suddenly dropped to her knees beside the table. "Oh, beloved Heavenly Father. Help her! She is in so much pain." Her throat constricted as a sob welled up within her. "Father, if it is her time, please ease her passing. Please ease her pain so she can rest. She is such a good woman, Father. Please don't prolong her suffering." She sniffed back the tears. "But . . . I know of Thy love for her. I know of Thy power and goodness. So in all things, I pray that Thy will may be done. In the name of Jesus, amen."

Edie remained on her knees for several moments, one word going through her mind over and over. *Why? Why? Why? Why Eliza? Why does she have to suffer so?* And then, *Oh, Mitch! Where are you? Why have you left me alone?*

But when she reentered the bedroom, she put on a bright smile. "Here. This should help with the cough."

"Thank you, dear Edie."

"Let me help you sit up a little. That will help with the cough too."

Eliza didn't protest, so Edie helped her sit up and put both pillows behind her. Once Eliza was settled, Edie got the cup of herbal tea and helped her slowly sip at it. "Are you sure Ellie is with Mons?" she asked after a moment.

"Yes. I watched them from the window just a moment ago. She and Emma are drawing pictures in the dirt with sticks while Mons works."

"That's my Ellie," Eliza said. Then concern wrinkled her brow. "Mons is such a good father. She's going to be all right, isn't she." She didn't state it as a question.

"Yes, Eliza. She's going to be fine. And you'll be watching over her too."

To Edie's surprise, a weak smile came. "So you've finally accepted that I'm going to die?"

Tears came in an instant. "Yes," she whispered.

"Good. So have I. It's time, Edie."

"Why won't the Lord just let you go, then?"

Eliza managed a weak shrug. "I don't know. Maybe it's because I'm too stubborn."

When Edie went to put the cup to her friend's lips again, she turned her head aside. "That's enough," she said. "Thank you."

Putting the cup aside, Edie helped Eliza lie back down again and then sat down on the chair beside her. "Would you like me to read to you?"

She shook her head. "No. Just be here with me. Even if I sleep."

"I will."

It was only a few minutes later that Elna suddenly started shrieking outside. Eliza's head jerked up. Her eyes were wide and filled with terror. Ellie's shriek sounded so much like her shrieks from that day when the cowboys came that it sent cold chills all through Edie's body. In three strides she reached the door and flung it open. Ellie streaked across her vision, pigtails flying, arms outstretched. Mons was striding across the yard after her, his face wreathed in smiles. And then Edie understood what she was yelling. "Grampa! Grampa! Grampa!"

Bewildered, Edie stepped outside. Three men were coming around the corner of the cabin. She gasped as she recognized who it was. President Frederick Jones was in the lead. Brother Lemuel H. Redd was beside him, and Francis A. Hammond, president of the San Juan Stake and Eliza's father, was right behind them.

Ellie hurled herself at President Hammond with a cry of joy. He swung her up in his arms, twirling her around and around as they laughed together.

Barely able to believe it, Edie ran back into the bedroom. Eliza was up on one elbow, her face like chalk. "What's wrong, Edie?"

Edie sat down beside her and took her hand. "Oh, Eliza," she cried. "Wonderful news. Your father's here."

"What? Where?"

She squeezed Eliza's hand. "Just outside the door. That's what Ellie was shouting about."

"Of a truth?" Eliza cried, falling back against her pillow. Then she smiled up at Edie. "That's why," she breathed.

"What's why?"

"That's why the Lord hasn't let me go yet."

10:55 p.m.—Woodhouse Hotel—300 South Main Street, Salt Lake City, Utah Territory

Mitch groaned as he straightened in his chair. Though he hadn't been sleeping, it was the first time he had moved for over an hour, and his whole body was stiff. He leaned forward in the hotel room's only chair and stared out the window into the moonlit night. Scattered clouds were scudding slowly across the sky, alternately revealing and concealing a silver moon that was slightly more than half full. It was a beautiful sight, but it did nothing to lift his spirits.

One hour. Without moving. Thinking of nothing except what he so desperately wanted to know. And he got nothing! This was his seventh day in the city. Seventh! And he had come thinking he'd be here a day or two at the most. Now it seemed like he'd been here forever. And if it felt that way to him, what was Edie feeling about now?

When he had arrived in Salt Lake on the tenth, he wasn't sure where to start or how to proceed. Like Nephi, he was wandering around not knowing beforehand what to do. After two days of that, he had decided that he was wrong about it being a prompting from the Lord and decided to go home. By that point, he had already been gone for almost two weeks—two weeks that he could ill afford to be away from the ranch.

But when he got up on that third morning, he remembered the night when he had rescued Edie and Evelyn and Leona when they were lost in a blizzard and the impression that had come to him that he needed to keep going straight rather than turning down the road toward home. He had fought his feelings back then too, telling himself that he'd go one more mile. If nothing happened, he'd turn back. And then he'd gone that mile, and then another, and another. It was somewhere around mile four that he had finally found them.

So on his third day here, he vowed not to give in so quickly. He would stay one full week. If nothing happened in that time, then that would be his answer, and he'd go back. He had walked the streets for hours at a time, hoping and praying that something would click for him. He had spent a whole day on Temple Square, watching the cranes lift more of the grey granite blocks onto the topmost tiers of the temple. He had tried to picture what this magnificent building would look like when it was done. He went inside the world-famous Tabernacle with its egg-shaped dome and marveled at the craftsmanship, but there were no answers there, either. He went to church on Sunday, fully expecting that one of the speakers might say something that would be the "bolt of lightning" he was looking for. It was an enjoyable service, and he received three invitations for supper afterwards, but no lightning struck.

Yesterday, he had mostly just sat on a bench on the temple grounds all day waiting for some kind of inspiration. Nothing. He had fasted. He had prayed. He had walked the streets late into the night and early in the morning. Nothing made any difference. There was no answer to his questions, no solace for his turmoil.

Mitch got to his feet and went to the window. Well, tomorrow the week was up. The train for Denver left at 9:20 in the morning. If no answer came before then, he would be on it.

Notes

At this time, the Salt Lake Temple was still about four and a half years from its completion. It would be dedicated on April 6, 1893, forty years after its construction had begun. The Woodhouse Hotel mentioned here is a fictional entity.

CHAPTER 22

October 18, 1888, 7:25 a.m.—Walton Cabin—Monticello

Maggie and Charlie were clearing the breakfast table and bringing the dishes to where Leona Walton and Edie had a kettle full of steaming, soapy water, and a smaller pan to rinse the dishes in.

As Maggie approached with another batch, she stopped, turning to look out the window. Edie's back was to her, and she didn't notice anything until she heard a sharp intake of breath. "No!"

Spinning around, Edie saw Maggie's face and felt her heart drop. She moved forward and looked out the window. Through the glass she saw Emma Peterson just coming out of the store. She was partially hunched over and her whole body was trembling. She turned, looked in their direction, and then, crying hysterically, came toward them in a stumbling half-walk, half-run.

"No!" Edie cried. She had to clutch for the table. Jane Walton was putting away the last of the food. She set it down and joined them at the window, as did Leona and Charlie. A moment later, Emma burst through the door. Sobbing so hard that she could barely get the words out, she fell into Edie's arms. "Eliza's gone. Eliza's gone," she cried. Edie hugged her tightly, rocking back and forth, her vision so blurred she couldn't see. She stroked Emma's hair over and over. "It's all right," she sobbed. "It's all right. Eliza's at peace now. She's at rest."

7:30 a.m.—Union Pacific Train Terminal—Salt Lake City

Mitch groaned a little as he got up from the wooden bench and stretched. It felt as though every joint in his body was in need of a little axle grease. He rubbed at the stubble on his chin and decided to move around. As he passed the ticket window where a bored railway clerk sat reading a magazine, the man glanced up. "Working some of the kinks out?" he asked.

"Yeah," Mitch replied. "Didn't want to miss the Denver train, so I've been here since six."

The man chuckled. "Well, since you've got another two hours to go, I'd suggest you walk around a bit. You've got a long sit on the train before you reach Thompson Springs."

Mitch walked on, and the man went back to his reading. It felt good to walk, and Mitch decided he would take several laps around the cavernous train station. He was not happy at how things had turned out, but he was at peace with himself. He still wasn't sure whether it was the Lord who had told him to come or his own emotions, but he had stuck it out. Now he was going home.

Mitch made two laps around the hall, stopping for a moment to retrieve the ball of a little boy who had kicked it a little too hard. He was about to retake his seat on the bench where his bag was waiting when something caught his eye. He had seen it before. It was a large-scale map of Utah Territory titled "Railway Lines in Utah." It was framed with narrow strips of lath and nailed to the wall next to where doors led out to the boarding platforms.

Curious, he moved back over to it. All kinds of dark lines with cross-hatching to signify railroad tracks converged on Salt Lake City and Ogden, the two major rail hubs in the territory.

But he was surprised to see lines snaking out in every direction from those hubs. Some were only short lines that dead-ended where nothing else showed on the map. He assumed those were spurs to mine sites or something like that. His eyes followed the line he would take. It ran south from Salt Lake to Spanish Fork and then cut east through the mountains to Price, turned south to Green River, and turned east again to Thompson Springs.

Mitch's thoughts turned to Edie and their coming marriage. Next May they would be crossing the territory to be married in the Manti Temple. He searched quickly, found Sanpete County, and spotted Manti in the lower half of it. There were no railroad lines leading there. But he knew that already. So he focused on the roads, especially the ones coming from Green River and the east. He found them easily and saw that the main east-west road from Green River crossed a couple of high passes, so it was a good thing it would be May by the time they traveled them.

And then he had a thought that he hadn't considered before. Would traveling to Manti be faster if part of the journey were made by train? It would be much farther, no question about that, but a train averaged somewhere around twenty to twenty-five miles per hour, while a wagon was more like fifteen or twenty miles per day. He found the idea intriguing. After his week in Salt Lake, Mitch had promised himself that someday he would take Edie there to see their territorial capital. If they went to Manti by train, they could honeymoon in Salt Lake on the way back home.

The questions kept coming at him. So how far from Manti was Richfield, where the Zimmers now lived? He found Richfield on the map, checked the scale of miles, and was surprised to find that it was less than fifty miles from Manti. Could they take the train to Richfield? That was an easy one. There were no rail lines going into either town. But there was a line that ran through

Deseret down to Milford. Deseret was west of Richfield, and not terribly far away.

Intrigued, Mitch glanced over at the ticket window. An older woman was buying tickets. He waited until she was done and then moved over to the window. "Hi."

"Hello, again," the man said pleasantly. "Can I help you?"

"Yeah, I have a couple of questions. If I wanted to go by train to Richfield, would—"

"Ain't no trains into Richfield," the man cut in.

"I know, but where would be the closest train station? Deseret, maybe?"

"Yeah, that's right. As I remember, Deseret is about eighty miles from Richfield."

"Hmm." That was pretty far. "Okay, thanks."

Mitch started away but then stopped short. Another idea had come, but this one slammed into his brain like a runaway coal car. He turned back. "Uh . . . one more question. What if I. . . . ?" He had to stop. The thought was staggering to him. "Would it be possible to change my ticket to Thompson Springs for a ticket to Deseret?"

The man's eyes narrowed. "Those are a long ways apart, son. You sure you wanna do that?"

"I . . . no, I'm not sure. But is it possible?"

The man glanced up at the clock on the wall. "Yup. Still got time to make that change."

"Let me think about it for a minute."

"All right, son, but don't take too long. Can't be changing tickets once the Denver train arrives."

"Uh, what time does the train for Deseret leave?"

"Twenty-five minutes after Denver does."

Mitch's mind was whirling as he turned and walked toward

where he had left his bag. This was crazy. Go to Richfield? Just like that? Why?

In four more steps he stopped again. This was it. This was his answer. Why Richfield? It didn't matter. He strode back to the counter. "All right. I'm going to make the change."

The man shook his head in wonder. "Ain't never had that happen before."

Mitch chuckled. "That makes two of us."

"You want a round trip, or one way?"

"Oh." That option hadn't occurred to him. This was insane. Mitch felt his heart pounding in his chest. And then there popped into his head those words again: "*And I was led by the Spirit, not knowing beforehand the things which I should do.*"

"Well, young man," the ticket man said impatiently. "One way or round trip?"

Mitch actually laughed aloud. "One way. I think that's all I can handle at the moment."

October 19, 1888, 7:10 p.m.—Zimmer Home
—Richfield, Utah Territory

As Mitch stepped up on the porch and removed his hat, the sheer craziness of it all hit him hard. *What are you doing here?*

It was a question he had asked himself a hundred times or more since boarding the train in Salt Lake City, and he was no closer to an answer now than he had been when he left Salt Lake. Tired, perplexed, and highly frustrated, he took a deep breath, muttered something in disgust, and raised his fist and knocked sharply on the door.

He heard the murmur of voices, then footsteps. When the

door opened, Frank Zimmer appeared. "Yes," he started to say. Then he gasped and fell back a step. "*Mitch?*"

"Hello, Brother Zimmer."

"But. . . ." He was gaping at him as though he were some kind of a specter.

"Who is it, dear?" a woman's voice called from another room.

"It's—" He shook his head, still not believing. "It's Mitch, dear. Mitch Westland."

"*What?*" There was the sound of a chair pushing back.

Another woman's voice, this one deeper, cried out, "Who?"

Caroline Zimmer burst into the entryway, followed closely by an elderly woman with white hair. "Mitch? But what are you—" She stopped and looked around. "Edie's not with you?"

"No, Sister Zimmer. I came alone."

To his astonishment, the elderly woman gave a low cry. "No! Not my Edie! O Lord, not my Edie." Her legs started to buckle and Sister Zimmer grabbed her before she fell.

Too shocked to react, Mitch stared at the stricken woman. Suddenly he was aware that Brother Zimmer had a hand on his shoulder and was shaking him. "Mitch, where is Edna Rae?"

"She . . . she's back in Monticello." Then it hit him. "Oh, no. Edie's fine. There's nothing wrong. That's not why I'm here."

Now it was Edie's mother who looked like she needed to sit down. "Are you sure?"

"Positive. Everything's fine. Oh, dear. I'm sorry that I frightened you."

Slowly the gnarled and twisted hands of the old woman dropped away from her face. She pulled free of Sister Zimmer and took a step closer. "Svear it!" she said. "Tell me dat my Edie is all right." Her German accent was distinct, but not overly intrusive.

"I swear it." Mitch tossed his hat on a stool and took both of her hands. "You must be Oma Zimmer," he said, smiling. "I am Mitch. I'm the man who's going to marry Edie."

"And she is all right?" she asked again.

As he nodded, Sister Zimmer came up and put an arm around her. "Edie is fine, Oma. She's fine. Mitch has just come to see us." Then to Mitch, she said, "Last night, Oma Zimmer had a bad dream. About Edie. She's been troubled by it all day." She started to turn her around. "Come, Oma, let's sit down and you can tell Mitch about it."

But Oma Zimmer didn't move. She was gazing into Mitch's face. He submitted to her scrutiny. Her head was tipped back because she wasn't much more than five feet tall, a good foot shorter than he was. Part of that was because her shoulders were stooped a little, but mostly it was because she was a tiny little wisp of a woman. Her hair, pulled back severely from her face and fastened in a bun at the nape of her neck, was pure white. Her face was crisscrossed with deep wrinkles, especially around the corners of her mouth and eyes. It looked almost leathery in texture. Wide, intelligent, brown eyes peered up at Mitch from beneath thick eyebrows. He started a moment. They were Edie's eyes. And he also saw a small dimple beside her mouth. Like Edie's. He squeezed her hands. "I can see where Edie gets her beauty from," he said.

Her eyes were momentarily startled, and then she openly scoffed at him and looked over at her son. "Now I see vhy my Edie says dat he talks a good talk." And with that, she turned and went into a small sitting room off the entryway.

Smiling, Mitch submitted to a warm hug from Edie's mother. "It is *so* good to see you again," she said. "How is Edie? Why are you here?"

Frank Zimmer came up to them. "There's no denying this is a shock to us, Mitch," he said. "So what brings you down this way?"

"Franz!" Oma Zimmer had reappeared at the entrance to the room. She wagged a finger at him. "You let that boy come in here. I vant to tell him about my dream."

"Yes, Mama," Brother Zimmer said with a smile. And the three of them followed her into the sitting room. When they were settled, Mitch spoke first. "May I call you Oma Zimmer?" he asked.

"Of course. Vee already have one *Schwester* Zimmer here. Oma vill do."

"Then, Oma, please tell me about your dream, and then I will tell you why I have come. I have a feeling that the two may be related."

She sat back, folding her hands in her lap. "I do not dream much anymore," she explained. "This is vhy it upset me so."

"She hasn't been able to get it out of her mind all day long," Edie's mother said.

"No," Oma agreed. "It vasn't just a bad dream. It vas like it vas actually happening. I can still picture little Edie's face. She was crying and crying, like her heart vas breaking."

"And she was calling for help," Frank said. "You said she was calling for help."

"Not out loud, Franz. Vit her eyes. She looked up at me. And I could see it in her eyes."

"Did she say why she needed help?" Mitch asked. He was reeling a little bit from this.

"*Nein.* She vas in a large open field that stretched avay as far as I could see. I remember there vas nothing else. No grass. No flowers. No trees. Just dirt everywhere. And she vas very sad. Like something bad vas going to happen."

Mitch visibly started. "Did she actually say that? Something bad?"

"*Nein,* but I knew. She vas crying very much. She vas on her knees and her head vas bowed. But she vasn't praying. She vas crying. Her cheeks vere covered vit tears. And she vas very sad."

She looked at Mitch, her eyes boring into his. "And she is all right? You svear it?"

"Yes, Oma. When I left, she was a little sad because I was leaving her to take some cattle to market, but she has lots of people with her. She is happy there."

"Then vhy vas she so sad? And do not tell me it vas just a dream."

"I don't know," Mitch said slowly. And then, to his complete astonishment, he added, "But I know how to make her happy again."

All three of them were staring at him, but his eyes were only for Oma. "How will you make her happy?" she asked.

"Not me, Oma. *You.* You are the one who will make her happy."

Notes

Eliza Dilworth Hammond Peterson, wife of Mons Peterson, died on October 18th, 1888 (see *Saga*, 104; *Anchored*, 94; *History*, 69). She turned twenty-two years old just two months before her death. The cause of death is listed as pneumonia in two of the sources, but a family history written by a descendant states: "Mons said that life was too hard for Eliza, which contributed to her death in 1888" ("A History of Mons Peterson," by Leanne Marie Peterson, 1).

Since this was the first death in Monticello, there was no cemetery yet, so Eliza was buried behind the Peterson cabin and store. Today, one can see her grave behind the Community Church, which is on the corner of Second South and Second East in Monticello.

Her father, President Francis Hammond, arrived in Monticello after touring San Juan County with delegates from Washington for about ten days. He arrived on the day before her death (see *History*, 69).

Mons eventually remarried, but not until 1905, seventeen years after Eliza's death. Their daughter Elna would have been twenty years old by then.

The town *Deseret* that Mitch refers to is in the vicinity of the town now known as Delta in west-central Utah.

CHAPTER 23

October 24, 1888, 6:35 p.m.—Peterson Store and Cabin

As Edie walked quietly around to the back of the Peterson cabin, she looked through the windows into their bedroom. The curtains were drawn back, and no light was visible. Through the next window she could see into the room that served as kitchen, living room, and dry goods store. There were no lights on there, either. No movement. Good. She really didn't want to be seen or to have to talk to anyone. She went on around to the back of the cabin.

Her step slowed as she saw the rough-hewn wooden grave marker and the mound of dirt that was behind the cabin. The red dirt looked as fresh as if it had been dug that morning, and the sight of it sent a wave of pain coursing through her. In the fading light she could still read the inscription that Mons had chiseled into the wooden grave marker: *Eliza Hammond Peterson. 27 August 1866–18 October 1888. She has gone to be with the angels.*

Edie moved forward, paused for a moment, and then laid the oak branches at the base of the plaque. Then she sat down beside it. "I brought you something, Eliza. I'm sorry that it's not flowers. I know how much you loved flowers, but the hard frosts are here now, and all the flowers are gone. But you also loved the autumn colors. They're fading fast too, but I found these. With all the rain we had this fall, the reds and oranges are especially brilliant this year."

She glanced again at the house. "Mons isn't home right now. I'm guessing he and Emma and the children are having supper with another one of our wonderful families. He's been invited somewhere every night since the funeral. And people keep bringing him food. And it's not just for him and Emma and Elna. It's their way of honoring you, too." Edie's voice caught in her throat. "You are so missed."

She had to look away, and one hand came up to wipe away the tears. "If I didn't know that you were in a happier place, I don't think I could stand it. But I do weep for Mons. For all he's putting on a brave face, he reminds me of a lost little boy. I walked in the store yesterday morning and caught him by the stove, just standing there and weeping.

"Elna is doing fine, though. I take her every day. She knows that you've gone to heaven, but she thinks you'll come back to her in a few days. I'm not sure how long it will be before she understands. Emma, though, is the one who has been hit the hardest by your going. If anyone even mentions your name, she just falls apart and leaves the room. I think you were—"

Footsteps crunched on the gravel behind her. Startled, Edie jerked around and then jumped to her feet. She whirled in time to see a figure coming from around the front of the cabin, approaching her in the semi-darkness.

"Edie?"

She gasped. "Mitch?"

"Yes, it's me."

With a cry of joy, she flung herself at him. He caught her and swung her up off her feet, hugging her so tightly it took her breath away. Or was that just because he was here? He set her down, took her face in both hands, and kissed her long and gently. When he finished, he pulled back. "Hi," he whispered.

"Oh, Mitch!" Edie cried breathlessly. "Is it really you?"

"Yes, my dear. I'm back." He kissed her again. "Finally."

To her utter surprise, that last word hit her hard. In one instant, it unleashed all of the pent-up frustration, loneliness, sorrow, fear, anxiety, worry, and pain that she had been holding in for the last three weeks. She stepped back, pushing away from him. "I'll say, 'finally.' Where were you? Where have you been? I've been worried sick about you."

"I know," he said, crestfallen now. "Jane told me that you didn't get my letter."

"Jane?"

"Yes, Sister Walton. My wagon is over behind their house. I stopped there assuming that's where you'd be."

"How long have you been here?" *He stopped and visited with Sister Walton?*

"About three minutes. She told me you were up at our cabin. I was just headed up there to find you when I saw you over here." He turned, taking her by the hand, and faced the grave. "I saw Fred Jones as we drove into town," he said quietly. "He told me about Eliza. I am so sorry, Edie. So sorry."

She sniffed back the tears. "I still can't believe she's gone. But she was ready. Her health was getting worse and worse."

"She is a loss to all of us," he said. "I'm glad you were here for her until the end."

"It was awful. We had all of that rain. The sod roofs all over town were leaking, including the Petersons'. She had water dripping on the bed when I went in one day. She was too weak to get up. And then. . . ." She was fighting hard for control. "We had that horrible day with those animals from the Carlisle spread. And . . . and. . . ."

"What about Carlisle?"

Edie hugged herself, staring at the ground. "It was horrible, Mitch. Horrible beyond belief. After that happened, Eliza just seemed to give up." Then her head jerked up. "Where were you?" she cried. "I thought something had happened to you. I was sure you were never coming back."

"I . . . Edie, I wrote you after I'd been in Salt Lake for a couple of days to say I would be longer, but the postmaster warned me that with the limited mail service to San Juan, it might take a month or more for you to get it." He reached for her to hold her again, but she stepped away from him.

"And what did your letter say?" she snapped. "Did it explain what was so important in Salt Lake that you stayed up there for three weeks? Did you have a wonderful time?"

Stop it, Edie! she thought to herself. *What are you doing? Mitch is home. He's home.*

But the floodgates were open, the dam had burst, and it was all pouring out. Looking hurt and confused, Mitch finally managed, "I wasn't in Salt Lake all that time, Edie. It took us ten days to get the cattle to—"

Her look cut him off. "You left here twenty-four days ago. You told me you'd be back in no more than ten days. And here it is almost a month. "

"I was trying to find answers. That's why I went to Salt Lake in the first place."

"Why Salt Lake City?" she asked incredulously. "Do you think they have more revelation up there than we can get down here?"

He thought she was half joking and smiled. "Supposedly they do, I mean, that's where the prophet is," he said.

She slugged him hard on the arm. "It's not funny, Mitch. I missed you. I *needed* you. Things have been horrible here."

"Tell me what happened."

"It doesn't matter. I can't believe you'd leave me for that long without telling me."

Stunned at her anger, he stared at her for a long moment. She could see the hurt and the confusion in his eyes.

Fine. And can he see how much he hurt me?

"Edie, I. . . ." He reached out and took both of her hands. She didn't resist. "I have an explanation, but it's complicated. Would it help if I told you I brought you back something special?"

She jerked away. "I'm sorry. I know I ought to be so happy that you're back, but right now all I'm feeling is anger. You think buying some trinket makes everything all right?"

To her surprise, there was a sudden twinkle in his eyes. "This trinket might."

That brought her up short. "What? What did you—" Then she guessed what it was. She shook her head. "I hope you didn't buy me some fancy wedding ring. I'm happy with the one you bought before."

He was trying hard not to chuckle. "It's not a ring."

"Oh, then the windows and doors for the cabin, right? And I appreciate that, but. . . ." She was near tears again. It was like she was two different people right now. One was so happy to have him back that she wanted to cling to him and smother him with kisses. But the other part of her, the one that had waited for over three weeks without knowing whether he was dead or alive, was finally giving voice to her frustration.

He pulled her to him and peered into her eyes. "Edie, you have every right to be angry."

"I'm not angry," she snapped. "I'm just upset. I was so worried about you."

"You have every right to be upset. But if you'll give me one more minute, I can explain everything. Come on. One minute, all right?"

"All right. But do it here. I don't want to have the Waltons seeing me like this."

He pulled her gently forward and started across the street. "Sorry, but the gift I brought you is already in the house."

"You showed it to the Waltons before you showed it to me?" she cried.

"Trust me," he soothed, "Just once more. Please." And then he got this strange look on his face, looked in her eyes again, and said, "*Würdest du mir bitte vergeben, mein Liebchen?*"

He might as well have punched her in the stomach. She couldn't have been more stunned. "What did you say?"

"*Würdest du mir bitte vergeben, mein Liebchen?*" He gave her a sheepish look. "My pronunciation is atrocious, but I was trying to say, 'Please forgive me, my love."

"But . . . you said it in German."

He grinned. "I'm glad it was recognizable."

"Where did you learn German?"

His grin broadened, and he laughed softly. "I've just started. While I was gone, I decided that if we're going to have your Oma Zimmer come stay with us, then I ought to start learning German."

Thoroughly confused, Edie let him lead her forward again. But as they crossed the road and approached the Walton home, she stopped again. "You are up to something, Mitchell Westland, and I want to know what it is. Right now. Before we go in. As you might have guessed, I'm in no mood to be teased right now."

He leaned in, put a finger to her lips, and slowly shook his head. "I kind of guessed that," he said with a smile.

Just then, the Waltons' front door flew open and a

white-haired, diminutive figure came flying out of the house. She was waving her arms wildly and crying out. "Edie! Edie! Edie!"

Edie was dumbstruck. Mitch put one hand on her back and gave her a gentle shove. "Edie, I'd like to introduce you to someone you might—"

He didn't get to finish. "Oma?" she cried. "Oma Zimmer?" Then with a cry of pure joy, Edie started slowly forward, too dazed to accept what her eyes were seeing.

As Edie and her grandmother fell into each other's arms, tears streaming down their faces, one by one the Waltons stepped out onto the porch. Mitch walked over and joined them. It was Charlie Walton who started it. As they watched the joyous reunion taking place before them, he started to clap his hands. In a moment, all the rest of them joined in, applauding with great gusto.

Whether Edie and Oma Zimmer were aware of the noise wasn't clear at that moment.

CHAPTER 24

December 8, 1888, 9:45 a.m.—EDW Ranch—Monticello

When Mitch came into the main room of their cabin with an armload of firewood, Rena Zimmer was standing by the large window of the cabin. "Any sign of Edie yet?" he asked.

"*Nein.* And I am vorried for her now."

He went over to stand beside her. "Oma, she's down helping the Hydes and the Rogersons get ready for the baptism of their children. She won't be back until ten thirty or eleven."

"I know dat," she grumbled before turning away. "And vhy do they think dis old Oma cannot be helping?"

Ah. So that was it? Edie had slipped out this morning while Oma was still in her bedroom because she didn't want her to be out in the bitter cold any longer than necessary. This afternoon at one o'clock, the Monticello Branch was having its first baptism service. Louise Hyde, whom everyone called Lou or Louie, was nine. Edward Rogerson, son of John and Sarah Rogerson, was ten today, and both were going to be baptized.

Since their creek had no water thanks to the Carlisle Ranch, and since there was no baptismal font within several hundred miles, they would all be driving down to a small spring some distance from town. Yesterday, Mitch, the two fathers, and a few other men had gone to the site and dug out a hole below the spring deep enough to accommodate two people. Then Mitch and John Rogerson had spent the afternoon using a crude snowplow to clear the road of about eight inches of snow, the first serious storm of the season.

The temperature was hovering around twenty degrees. Edie had decided that Oma didn't need to spend any longer than was absolutely necessary outside in the cold, so she had sneaked out of the house before Oma came out for breakfast. And Oma was still miffed about it.

"She didn't want you getting cold, Oma. She knows it makes your arthritis worse."

Oma Zimmer sniffed in disgust. "Does my granddaughter think I am puff of powder?"

Mitch smiled. "Do you mean a powder puff?"

"*Ja*. Is dat not vat I said? She thinks I am puff of powder. She just does not vant me there to show her how to make the *Pfeffernüsse*. She thinks dat she can do it fine alone."

Mitch reached for the poker and stirred at the coals, deciding not to argue the point with her. "By the way, what does *Pfeffernüsse* mean? Cookies?"

"*Nein*. That is *Plätzchen*. *Pfeffernüsse* means pepper nut."

"Ah, because they have a touch of black pepper in them?"

"*Ja*, but not just pepper. Sometimes vee use other spices instead, like ginger or cloves. They are also called spice cookies. And there must be just the right amount of spice."

He gave up. "Oma, if you want, I'll take you down there."

She cocked her head at him, her brown eyes very somber, and came over to him. She reached up and patted his cheek with one of her gnarled hands. "You are good boy, Mitchell. You are good to my Edna Rae. Vee vill just have to trust that she does not poison all of the people, *ja?*"

He laughed right out loud. "That would be—how do you say it?—*Shrecklisch?*"

"*Ja, ja.* Terrible. That vood be very terrible." Her eyes were suddenly twinkling. "It vood likely ruin the day of baptism, no?"

He hooted. How delightful she was. And he now better understood where Edie got some of her spunk. That night in Richfield when he had asked if he could take Oma Zimmer back with him to Monticello immediately, he had been stunned at how quickly she had said yes. Much more quickly than Frank and Caroline Zimmer had. He guessed that was partly because of her bad dream about Edie, but now he was coming to realize that she, like Edie, had a sensitivity to spiritual feelings and was quick to act on them.

Mitch had worried about how he would get along with her, but by the time they had spent eighteen hours on the train together and then driven two more days in his wagon, she had made up her mind about him. He was going to be good for her Edie. She made that clear when they caught their first sight of Monticello. He had stopped for a moment so she could see their little town. After a moment, she had laid a hand on his arm and said, "I vood like to have you learn *Deutsche,* Mitchell. Vood you do dat for me?"

It had startled him, but his response, which had come quite spontaneously, pleased her immensely. "I would like that very much, Oma Zimmer," he said. "Edna Rae has told me about the promise in your patriarchal blessing, that your posterity will take the gospel to your family in Germany. And how am I going to do that if I don't speak German?"

"*Ja,* this is exactly right," she had exclaimed, "But is not Edna Rae teaching you already?"

"Uh. . . ." She had caught him completely off guard, and he had no choice but to reluctantly admit that while Edie had often used German words when he first met her, now it was very rare.

"Vell den," she had responded tartly, "vee shall see to dat, no?"

Since then, the three of them had spent at least one hour a day with Oma tutoring them. Fortunately, Edie's facility with the language was quickly returning, and she and Oma often conversed in German, especially when they were talking about Mitch.

1:05 p.m.

Mitch and Edie sat together in their wagon with its back facing toward the baptism pool and the canvas flaps pulled back. All of the wagons were facing the same way so that people could stay out of the biting wind while the men took turns chopping through the two inches of ice that had formed overnight. The thermometer on Mons Peterson's store had shown eighteen degrees when they left, and now President Jones and two other brethren were using axes to break up the ice and shovels to get the chunks of ice out of the water. Everyone else waited in their wagons while they did so.

"Are you sure Oma is all right?" Mitch asked. "Shall I go check on her?"

"All right?" Edie exclaimed. "She is having the time of her life."

"Who is she with? And what are they doing?"

"She's with Mary Adams and Mary Jones, and the three of them are chattering away in three different languages like they were little girls."

"Three? I know that Sister Adams was born in Germany and those two speak in German all the time to each other, but what else besides English?"

"Danish."

"Ah, yes. Of course." Mitch had forgotten that Mary Jones, wife of their branch president, had been born in Denmark. From what she had told them, because Denmark and Germany shared a common border, the two languages were close enough that one could mostly understand the other. "And what are they talking about?"

"Christmas. They've already told Sarah Rogerson that the three of them are going to provide all of the desserts. Sister Jones will bring her famous white-frosted cake. Sister Adams is equally famous for her grape tarts and has already had requests that she bring those. And Oma will make her *Prinzregententorte.*"

"Oooh. With a name like that, it has to be delicious."

"Oh, yes," Edie chuckled. "It's a Bavarian recipe that consists of at least six thin layers of sponge cake, with chocolate buttercream between each layer, all covered with a dark chocolate glaze. And just so you know, Oma says that she's going to have to practice on us before Christmas, to make sure the oven works right."

"I think I can handle that," Mitch said somberly.

"I thought you could. Anyway, I'm happy that she has made friends so quickly here. I went to make sure she was wrapped up in her quilt, but I didn't have the heart to interrupt them."

"I'm glad. She was a little put out at you this morning for leaving her. Said she was worrying about you poisoning everyone with those spice cookies."

She slapped his arm. "She did not."

"She did. And then she said that—"

But right then, President Jones and the other two men at the pool tossed their shovels aside and waved toward the wagons. "All right," President Jones called. "It's time. Gather around and let's get this done before we all turn into icicles."

The response was immediate. Everyone climbed quickly out of their wagons, gathering in a circle around the water. Oma Zimmer came over and joined Mitch and Edie, and they sat her between them, making sure the quilt was wrapped tightly around her. She made no objection.

A moment later, Eddie Rogerson and Lou Hyde appeared, accompanied by their parents. Both children had on white clothes and were wrapped in woolen blankets. Both wore men's heavy grey woolen socks without shoes. Eddie was looking at the water with some apprehension, but Lou, who had her hair pulled into a ponytail and looked as pert as a prairie dog popping out of its hole, seemed ready to run and dive right into the water. It surprised Edie, however, to see that only Brother Rogerson was wearing a white shirt and had his boots off.

Seeing her look, Mitch leaned in. "Because it's so cold, John is going to baptize both kids." As the two families took their places near where a little ramp had been dug out to provide access to the pool, President Jones raised a hand and everyone quickly quieted. "Brothers and sisters, we have a short baptismal service prepared, but due to our ever-present, Blue Mountain balmy breeze, we shall have only an opening prayer here. Then after the baptism, we shall return to our home, where we will have the service, and then our good sisters have made us some wonderful sweetmeats and pots of hot chocolate. We have asked Brother Edward Hyde, father of one of our candidates, to give us an opening prayer, and then we shall proceed." He looked at Lou Hyde. "We shall baptize Louise first, and then Eddie second."

The prayer was short. As soon as it was finished, John Rogerson took a deep breath, clenched his teeth, and waded into the water. He gasped and bit his lip as he moved until it was nearly to his waist. "Whoo-ee!" was all he said. Then he held out his hand. Emma Hyde removed the blanket from her daughter's shoulders, and everyone smiled as Lou strode into the water without a moment's hesitation. Shock registered on her face, and instantly her teeth began to chatter as she moved up beside Brother Rogerson. "It ain't so cold as I thought," she called up to her parents. That delighted everyone.

When she came up out of the water a moment later, she was actually laughing. "I'm baptized, Mama. I'm baptized now." The people clapped as her mother moved in and wrapped her in the blanket and hugged her tightly.

Eddie Rogerson was not quite so eager. As he reached the water's edge, he stopped, hugging himself tightly against the wind. "Come on, son," John said. "It'll only take a minute."

He took a deep breath and waded in and then yelped as though he had been hit with a board. "Holy jiminy!" he yelled. "That is cold!"

His father took one hand and pulled him in closer. He showed him how to stand and how to hold his hand and arm so that John could pull him up easily. Eddie barely heard him. He was shivering like an aspen leaf in a windstorm.

After the short baptismal prayer, John Rogerson dunked his son, pushing him down as he began to fight back. He held him just long enough to make sure he was totally immersed and then pulled him up again. "Jumpin' Jehoshaphat!" Eddie hollered. "That is dang cold water!"

Sarah Rogerson went beet red. "Edward Rogerson! What did you just say?"

John's face went hard. He grabbed his boy again. "Can't have you talking like that when you're being baptized," he snapped. "Let's do it again." And not waiting for him to get positioned, he pushed his son under a second time.

"Criminy sakes!" Eddie gasped as he shot up out of the water for a second time. "That's enough!"

"Again," his father growled, red-faced now. "And no more cussin' this time." And down he went. Everyone held their breath as Eddie came up for the third time. His teeth were chattering so violently that everyone could hear them, but he clamped his mouth shut and said not a word.

President Jones nodded at his father. "That will do," he said, trying very hard not to laugh.

Notes

On December 8, 1888, Monticello had its first baptism. Albert R. Lyman is the source for that information, but he mentions it only briefly (see *History*, 69). He does say that they had to break off ice from the water and that John Rogerson performed both baptisms, along with listing the names of the two children baptized.

Louise Hyde was nine. The 8th of December was Eddie's tenth birthday. Whether that is why that date was chosen or not is not indicated. In those days, it was not unusual for families to wait several months or more after their children turned eight to baptize them.

The "cussing," including Eddie's actual words, comes from an account that involved a young boy named Tom Perkins from Moab (see Norma Palmer Blanknagel, *Portrait of Our Past: A History of the Monticello Utah Stake of The Church of Jesus Christ of Latter-day Saints* [1988], 266). I found it so delightful that I worked it in here, attributing it to Eddie. I hope the Rogerson descendants will forgive me for taking that much literary license with one of their ancestors.

CHAPTER 25

December 24, 1888, 12:40 p.m.—John Rogerson Cabin —Monticello

When all was said and done, only six families besides Edie, Mitch, and Oma decided to winter over at the Blue Mountains, and one of those families was Parley Butt, who was alone down in Verdure. He and his wife, Ency, had a nine-month-old baby, so Parley took Ency and the children back to Parowan to be with her family and then returned to take care of things in Verdure. He would go back for her sometime in the spring.

Edie wondered how much the death of Eliza Peterson had influenced Ency's decision. She didn't know, but the death of someone so young had shaken a lot of people, especially the women, and maybe Ency was one of those.

"What are you thinking about so deeply?" Mitch asked as he came over to Edie. He reached out and with his thumb gently smoothed out the wrinkles that had formed between her eyes.

Momentarily startled, she forced a quick smile. "I was just trying to get a count of how many of us there are."

"And?"

"Let's add them up. We've got Fred and Mary Jones and their five kids."

"That's seven."

"William and Mary Adams."

"Nine."

"And the Hydes have seven, and the Rogersons and their three children make five more."

"Umm . . . so that makes twelve more. Twenty-one."

"And Parley and the three of us make twenty-five."

"And Mons."

"Oh, yeah. I forgot Mons. We don't need to count the baby, just Mons and his sister, Emma, and Elna. So twenty-eight in all." Edie sighed as she looked around at the bustle going on around them. "I miss the Waltons. Especially Maggie and Leona. They would have loved all of this."

She shrugged off the sudden melancholy. She also missed Evelyn and George Adams and Nean, and Nephi and Annie Bailey, and. . . . Another sigh. "Will you give Sarah the count and tell her that we're probably going to need four tables?"

"Sure, but where's Oma?"

"She and Louise and Winnie are down in the cellar, using the school desks to help the younger children string the firethorn berries for the Yule tree."

Mitch frowned. "Does she know that those berries are poisonous?"

She laid a hand on his arm, amused. "Yes, dear. Oma has been doing this longer than you and I have lived. And besides, the berries are only mildly poisonous. If a child were to eat a few of them, it might give them a bellyache, but that's all."

"Okay, so I'm not much help here. When do you want us to go get the Yule tree?"

"How long will it take you?"

"Well, we're taking Parley's sleigh. We'd like to go high enough that we can find a real pine tree and not just a cedar, but with yesterday's snow, I'm not sure how high we'll get. Two- to two-and-a-half hours, I'd guess."

"Oh, then I think Sarah will want you to go immediately."

"Okay." He bent down and kissed her on the cheek. "I'll go talk to Sarah, and then I think Parley and I will head out."

"Okay. Will you peek down in the cellar and ask Oma how soon she wants us to start cooking the popcorn?"

That also surprised him. "You've got popcorn?"

"Yes. Mons brought some back from Durango just for Christmas."

He shrugged. Another witness of how useful he was here. He waved and went to the cellar stairs. After checking with Oma, he came back and moved into the kitchen. Sarah Rogerson and Brother and Sister Adams were hovering over a large kettle on the stove. To his surprise, it was William who held the long wooden spoon and was in the process of tasting the brew. "Smells good," Mitch said as he joined them. "Wassail?"

"Aye, laddie," William said with a twinkle in his eye, "but unlike that watered-down wassail your parents made in England, this is Irish wassail. This is the real thing."

Mitch nodded soberly. "So you added a fifth of whiskey to it, did you?"

The two women looked up, clearly shocked. Mitch feigned surprise. "But I've always heard that's how the Irish put some kick into their wassail. At least, that's what my parents say."

"Don't be cheeky," William said solemnly. "It was you Brits that started the wassail tradition, and the basic ingredient was originally ale." Then he spooned out more of the golden brown liquid and held it out toward Mitch. "In the Adams family, we don't need whiskey to give our wassail flavor. See what you think."

It was steaming as Mitch carefully took the spoon, blew on it, and then sipped the golden brown liquid. "Oh," he said, licking his lips. "Now that is good."

The twinkle in Brother Adams's eyes deepened. "I'll be expecting a wee apology, ya bloomin' Yank."

"You'll have it," Mitch said. "And if you save me an extra cup, I'll get down on my knees to offer it." He turned to Sarah as both William and Mary laughed. "How soon are you going to be wanting the tree? Assume it's going to take us two to three hours to find one, bring it down, and get it into the house and standing up straight in a tub."

"Then go," Sarah answered. "When Oma Zimmer finishes with the popcorn, all that will be left for the decorations will be tying strings on the lollipops so the children can hang them on the tree."

December 25, 1888, 9:05 p.m.—EDW Ranch

Moving quietly, Edie came up behind Oma Zimmer's chair, wondering if her grandmother might have dozed off while she and Mitch were talking. But as she bent down to look, Oma turned her head, looked up, and smiled at her. "*Frohe Weihnachten, Liebchen.*"

Edie kissed her wrinkled cheeks. "Merry Christmas, Oma. It's been a wonderful day. Thank you so much for being here with us." She glanced up at Mitch for a moment. "And giving me the perfect excuse to stay in Monticello."

"It has been a very good day. You have vunderful people here. So good to me. I am already making many friends. And I am very glad to be vit you and Mitchell, *mein Liebchen.*" She turned to Mitch. "*Danke*, Mitchell. Thank you so much for listening to your heart and coming to Richfield to find me."

Mitch was sitting across from her. He nodded soberly. "And

Danke Schön to you for leaving your home and coming with us. It was an answer to our prayers."

Edie moved around and sat down beside her grandmother and then took a hand in hers. "I have been thinking about Mama and Papa today, Oma. How they must be missing you tonight."

Her grandmother's shoulders lifted and fell and she looked away. "*Ja*," she murmured. "And you. I think vee both are very lonely for our Franz and Caroline."

Mitch said nothing but decided to try to lift their spirits a little. "And, Oma, that *Prinzregententorte*—is that how you say it?—was divine. Will you teach Edie how to make that?"

"Yes," Edie agreed. "There are so many things I want you to teach me how to cook. I plan on making Mitchell as plump and round as Saint Nicholas himself."

Mitch decided to change the subject. "Wasn't Brother Adams a delight today? Dancing that Irish jig with his shillelagh? He's as spry as a twenty-year-old."

"Vat is dat stick called?" Oma asked.

"A walking stick," Mitch said.

"But vat is its name?"

Edie turned to face her so Oma could watch her mouth. "It's pronounced shi-LAY-leh. It is an Irish walking stick, but Brother Adams told me that in Ireland it's often used as a weapon, too."

"Yes," Mitch said. "And speaking of dancing, how about Sister Hyde when she wrapped that lace curtain around herself and did the Highland Fling while President Jones played 'Scotland the Brave' on his mouth harp?"

Edie clapped her hands together. "That was wonderful."

"Yeah," Mitch said, "and then ol' Ed, not to be outdone by his wife, gets up and sings, 'I'm Not as Young as I Used to Be.' I thought I was going to bust my belt buckle, I was laughing so hard."

"I especially liked the Christmas songs. Vhat do you call them again?"

"Carols," they both answered together.

Oma Zimmer's eyes were a little misty now. "Dat vas the very best part for me," she whispered. "To sing the songs and to read the Christmas story from the Bible. Dat is vhat my *Mutti* and *Vati* did vhen I vas a little girl." She sniffed back some tears. "I think in years to come, vee vill not forget this Christmas day. Not ever. I am glad I vas here."

And that seemed to be the moment Mitch was waiting for. He got to his feet. "Perhaps, before we all start crying, we should open one last Christmas present." He winked at Rena. "What do you think, Oma. Is it time?"

"*Ja, ja*," she said, instantly perking up.

"Okay, Edie," Mitch commanded. "Eyes closed."

Her head came up with a snap. "It's for me? But you've already given me a present. And, to be honest," she adding, teasing him a little, "I am quite astonished that you got the size right."

"Ah, but Oma gets the credit for that," he explained. "She helped me pick it out while we were in Salt Lake. We had a three-hour stopover. She's the one with a good eye."

"Well, it's a wonderful dress and I love it. And I don't need anything else."

Oma nudged her. "*Liebchen*, just close your eyes. Vee are all vaiting."

So she did. She heard Mitch's footsteps move across the room and go out the back door. "It's outside?" she blurted.

Oma sighed. "*Sei geduldig, mein Kind*."

Edie burst out laughing. "Have you ever known me to be patient, Oma?"

"*Nein!* Not ever," she agreed.

They heard the door open again, and something bumped

against wood. "Keep your eyes closed," Mitch called out from the other room. "Oma, are her eyes still closed?"

"*Ja.* And I will spank her behind if she opens them before you say."

"Oh, this is wonderful," Edie groused, "now my fiancé and my grandmother are conspiring against me." But she clamped her eyes more tightly shut as she heard Mitch come into the room.

There was a solid clunk directly in front of her, and then Mitch spoke. "*Frohe Weihnachten, Schatzi.*"

Slowly Edie cracked one eye. Then both eyes flew open and she gave a low cry as she shot to her feet. "A rocking chair?" she squealed. She whirled around and threw herself at him. "You remembered?"

"Of course I remembered. I told you that someday you'd have a rocking chair to sit in front of our window so you could enjoy the view."

"But . . . when did you get it? You didn't bring it home with you from Richfield."

"Yes, I did. Before Grandma and I met you, we left the chair in President Jones's barn."

She turned to her grandmother just in time to see her wink at Mitch. "Vee are good sneakers, *ja?*"

Still reeling a little, Edie came around and sat down in the chair. She was motionless for a moment and then began to rock back and forth. She looked up at Mitch as she did so. Her eyes were filled with tears again. "It's beautiful," she whispered. "But I feel awful."

"Why?"

"Because all I got you was a new shaving mug."

Mitch laughed. "And that was more than I wanted." He

went to her and pulled her up. As he kissed her, Oma spoke again. "Der is vun problem wit the chair, Edna Rae," she said.

Edie turned in surprise. "What?"

"Vee vill be fighting over who gets to sit in it all the time, no?"

Notes

The two most detailed sources that I used in my research both agree that six families stayed in Monticello for the winter of 1888–89. They do not list who they were, but from the descriptions of what happened and who participated (William Adams dancing with his shillelagh, Emma Hyde doing the Highland Fling, etc.) we can identify five families for certain: Fred and Mary Jones and their children; William and Mary Adams, the oldest couple in the group; Ed and Emma Hyde and their children; John and Sarah Rogerson and their children; and Parley Butt, who was without his wife and children (see *Saga*, 102–3; *Anchored*, 93; E. Lenora Jones, *Life of Parley Butt*, 13).

One source says that the Christmas dinner and party were held at the Rogerson home, while another says the Joneses hosted it. The one thing that everyone agrees on is that it was a Christmas filled with tender memories that they never forgot and that have now been shared through several generations.

CHAPTER 26

January 1, 1889, 12:30 p.m.—Frederick Jones Cabin —Monticello

Though the foothills of the Blue Mountains received another eight to ten inches of snow between the holidays, on New Year's Day the residents of Monticello awoke to a brilliantly beautiful day. There wasn't a cloud to be seen, not even over the mountains. There wasn't even a whisper of breeze. It was still cold, but Mons's thermometer showed it was near thirty degrees now.

The adults and oldest children worked together to prepare dinner, set the tables, stoke up the fires, and get things ready for their next holiday feast. While this was going on, John Rogerson took the younger children and got them out of the way. To everyone's delight, he had taken an old cowhide that was stiff as a board, tied two ropes to it, and turned it into a makeshift toboggan, which he pulled behind his horse out in the open fields above the town.

Lou and Winnie Hyde were given the first turn. Cautioning them to hold on tightly to the ropes, John coaxed his horse into a walk. The cowhide jerked forward and then skimmed across the top of the snow with a soft hissing sound.

"Faster!" Lou shouted.

"Yes, faster!" Minnie cried.

"Whoo-hoo!" Lou shouted as the horse started into a brisk trot. She let go with one hand and waved to the other kids as they whizzed by. Then John pushed the animal into a lumbering gallop. The children on the sidelines nearly went crazy as the horse, rider, and two passengers went flying past them.

"I wanna be next!"

"I'm next!"

"Brother Rogerson, can I be next?"

All the while, Louise and Winnifred were urging him to go faster. "Hold on!" John shouted over his shoulder, and then he jerked the reins hard to the left. At that moment, Lou was reaching out with one hand and scooping up snow with her mitten. With the sudden turn, the cowhide whipped sharply right. She yelped and grabbed blindly for the rope with her other hand, missed, and went flying into Minnie. An instant later, the cowhide was empty.

A gasp went up. Were they hurt? But a moment later, two figures sat up. Both were totally covered with snow and unrecognizable, and both of them were laughing hysterically. Lou made one swipe across her face to clear away the snow, and then both hands shot into the air. "Whoo-ee!" she shouted at the top of her lungs.

Inside the Jones house, the adults had gathered at the window to watch. Parley Butt nudged Mitch with his elbow. "What are we doing in here? Let's go."

"Oh, no you don't," Mary Jones cried. "No men get to play until after supper."

Edie turned in dismay. "Why only the men? I want a turn too."

2:15 p.m.

When the dinner was over and the dishes done, the children were divided into groups. The older children went outside again where Will Hyde, Ed and Emma's oldest son, took over the duty of pulling the cowhide. He was only twelve, but the horse was a gentle one, and Will was a good horseman. Lou and Winnie Hyde had already had their turn, so they were assigned to take the younger children into the back bedroom and keep them happy. Judging from the squeals and laughter coming from the bedroom, they were doing a good job of it. The babies were put in the other bedroom on the floor or in cribs their parents had brought with them.

This meant that the adults were enjoying what was a rarity for them—time to sit around and relax and talk without interruption from demanding children. They had naturally gravitated into three groups. Oma Zimmer, Mary Adams, and Mary Jones were off in one corner, their chairs facing each other, talking animatedly in German and Danish. The younger women had pulled their chairs around the kitchen table and were talking quietly. The men were in a circle near the window, where they could keep an eye on the activity outside.

Edie and Mitch were the exception. They had kept their chairs together near the fireplace, content to listen and watch for now. But then Mitch heard the word *sawmill* from the men's circle and went over and joined them. Edie joined the group at the table.

"Did you just say something about a sawmill?" Mitch asked as he plunked his chair down.

"Yeah," John Rogerson said. "Parley and Willard are planning on building a sawmill this summer. Willard's going to Colorado in the spring to order some of the machinery."

"So will this be down on South Montezuma Creek somewhere?" Ed Hyde asked.

"Yes. We've found a good place a couple of miles upstream from Verdure," Parley replied.

John Rogerson said, "What a blessing. I'm tired of paying those outrageous prices in Mancos."

Ed Hyde snorted. "And I'm tired of working in the saw pit, especially when I'm down in the pit, with sawdust raining down my back, sweating like a jaded horse, and getting blisters big as gumdrops on my hands."

President Jones leaned in. "So how many saws are you planning on having, Parley?"

At the women's table, Edie joined in the middle of a conversation directed at Sarah. Edie quickly gathered that it was about her baby, who was due near the end of March.

"What about the school?" Emma Hyde asked. "When the baby comes, will you just stop school for a time?"

Sarah glanced at Edie, who nodded, knowing what she was going to say. Then Sarah answered the question. "As you know, dear Edie here has been such a help to me since we started school. I've already talked to President Jones, and he agrees with my recommendation. Edie will take over as schoolteacher until summer break, and then I'll start again in the fall."

That wasn't a big surprise to anyone, but they all congratulated her anyway. Edie tried hard not to show how absolutely delighted she was to be given this responsibility.

"And it will continue in our cellar," Sarah said. "It's all set up for it. Hopefully, by the time fall comes, we'll have flooring in the church house so we can hold it there."

Mary Jones glanced out the window at the children being pulled behind the horse. She frowned briefly but then turned back as the conversation went on about school. Curious at that brief reaction, Edie turned to look too. She, too, was taken aback. Outside, it seemed a bit darker than it had been before. She bent lower to look for clouds but couldn't see any. Then

Mary asked her a question about the school, and Edie forgot the sky and turned back to the women.

Ten minutes later, Edie and Sarah were still discussing the virtues of the new mathematics books Sarah had brought in from Colorado when the door banged open and children started streaming in. "Mama," someone bellowed, "I'm hungry!"

2:47 p.m.

The next quarter of an hour was wild as all the children, young and old, were given sandwiches, slices of cheese, cookies, and milk or hot chocolate. When the last one finally went to play with the others, Edie sank down in her chair, grateful to be off her feet again.

As she did so, she absently turned and looked out the Joneses' big window. To her surprise, the day was noticeably darker than it had been before. Her brow wrinkled. That was odd. Was there a storm starting to form? As she searched the sky, she could see no clouds from where she was, but then her window faced to the northeast. When clouds started to form, they were usually over the Blue Mountains to their west. She started to get up to look, but she felt a tug on her dress.

"Aunt Edie?"

She looked around. Elna Peterson was standing just in front of her with an empty cup. "Can I have some more coco-late?"

Edie bent down, smiling at the winsome four-year-old. "Ellie, we call it cocoa or we call it hot chocolate, but not coco-late."

That won her a look of disgust. She ran to Mons. "Papa, can I have some more coco-late?"

"Sorry," Edie said, getting to her feet. "Come, Ellie. I'll do it."

Before she had filled Ellie's cup, a lineup was forming for

refills. Mary Adams came over to help. As they refilled the cups, Edie kept glancing out the window, and a touch of uneasiness crept in. The day was definitely darker, but in a weird sort of way. Having clouds scud across the sky casting their gliding shadows along the ground was commonplace, but this was different. It was not shadows. It was as though the very light itself was diffused.

She saw that Mary Adams was staring out the window too. "Does that look normal to you?"

"No," Mary replied. "It does not. Is there a storm coming?"

Others were turning to look at what they were seeing. Sarah's hand came up to her mouth. "What in the world . . . ?"

With her uneasiness growing with every passing second, Edie wiped her hands on her apron and walked over toward Mitch. The men were all bent forward, listening as President Jones put forth the benefits of dry farming. He had some skeptics in the group, so there was a vigorous discussion underway. Mitch glanced up and saw her. She motioned that she wanted to talk to him. He got up immediately and came over to her. "Do you need something?"

"Have you looked outside?"

"Yes."

"It's getting darker, Mitch."

"Probably some high clouds moving in from the west."

"No!" She said it more sharply than she had intended, and the men stopped talking. Several heads turned to look at her. She spoke to all of them. "Look outside. That's not just clouds. It's—" She was groping for the right word. "It's like the light is muted or something."

"Uh . . . I don't think so, hon, but I'll—"

Parley got up and came over, his head turned toward the window. "She's right, Mitch," Parley said. "That's not normal.

Look at the snow on the windowsill. It's almost a grey color, but a few minutes ago it was brilliant white."

"Vhat is it?" Oma Zimmer asked Edie.

One of the older children made a crack about the sun going down early.

No one laughed. It was still only mid-afternoon, and the subdued light was eerie. "What's happening?" Sarah asked her husband.

He shook his head. Lou Hyde came over and stood beside her father. She took his arm, a deep frown creasing her brow. "Papa, what's wrong? What's happening?"

"I don't know," he said in a low voice, stepping right up to the glass and peering outside. "We can't see the sun from here."

Parley hooted. "Come on folks, it's just some weird cloud formation."

"There are no clouds in the sky," Edie shot back. "Look. The sky is perfectly clear."

He shook his head, and then a look of mock horror filled his face. The Butt brothers were well known for their sense of humor and for being practical jokers. Parley threw up his hands and shrank back. "Oooh! Maybe the world is coming to an end," he said in a ghostly voice.

That sent a shiver of fear up and down Edie's back. Seeing the look on her face, Parley laughed. "Come on, Edie. I was only kidding."

The smaller children, sensing the changed mood in the room, went to their mothers and clung to their skirts. "But," Mary Jones cried, "what if it is? We're so far from civilization out here, the whole world could collapse and we wouldn't even know it. Not for weeks."

All the color washed out of Edie's face. She felt as if

something was caught in her throat, and she was having a hard time breathing. Her eyes were wide with shock. Fear. Blind panic.

Stunned, Parley looked at the surrounding faces. "Aw, come on!" he cried. "It's only a joke."

"Who's joking?" one of the women asked. "Don't the scriptures prophesy that the sun will be darkened and the moon turned to blood? I remember reading that somewhere."

The whole group erupted, everyone talking at once. To his surprise, Mitch saw that Edie was visibly trembling. And then he understood. This was how she had been the day after he had rescued her from the blizzard. What had Sister Jones said that day? *Be gentle with her.* He put his arm around her and pulled her close. "It's all right, Edie. I'm right here."

"Hold it!" Parley bellowed, waving his hands for people to quiet down. As they did so, he spoke loudly, but calmly. "Okay, okay. Let's not panic here. Something's going on out there, but let's not fall to pieces until we take a look." He looked over at Mitch. "Come on. Let's go find out what is going on."

"Take a gun," someone called out from the back."

"Be careful," someone else said.

"Maybe we should pray," Winnie Hyde said to someone.

Mitch looked Edie in the eye. "We'll go see what it is," he said softly. "I'll be right back."

Her fingers dug into the palms of his hands. "No, Mitch," she cried, almost sobbing. "Don't leave me." She clung to him with all of her strength.

In an instant, Oma was beside them. She put an arm around Edie's shoulder and drew her close. "Edna Rae," she said softly. "It's all right, dear. I'm here. Nothing vill happen."

Edie heard the words, but they barely registered. She felt lightheaded, nauseated. She sat down quickly on the nearest chair, afraid that her knees were going to give out on her. It was all she could do not to bolt and run.

"You go," Mitch called to Parley.

Seeing what was happening, Parley nodded and strode for the door. Edie dropped her head in her hands, her face burning as she realized everyone was staring at her.

Mitch knelt down beside her and took her in his arms. "It's all right, Edie. I'm right here."

But what if the world IS ending? She wanted to scream it at him but choked back the words and just clung to him.

A moment later there was a collective cry. "He's coming back," someone exclaimed.

The front door burst open, and Parley came back into the house, stomping the snow off of his shoes. Every head jerked around. Mitch pulled Edie to her feet. Her gaze jerked to Parley's face. She was relieved to see that he seemed calm. In fact, he was smiling a little.

He raised his hands. Instantly the room went quiet. "Guess what, folks," he called, grinning like a man who had just found a gold nugget. "I can tell you right now, what you are seeing out there is definitely *not* the end of the world."

"Then what is it?" Winnie Hyde called out. "What's happening?"

His grin broadened even more, if that was possible. "I think the astronomers call it a full eclipse of the sun. Come out and see, folks. This is a once-in-a-lifetime sight to behold."

10:10 p.m.

"Mitch?" Edie looked at him out of the corner of her eye, wondering if he had dozed off.

He hadn't. He turned immediately. "Yes?"

"I'm sorry for today. I'm—"

His hand reached out and gently pressed over her mouth, cutting her off. "No, Edie. You did nothing wrong. It was a frightening thing for everyone today. I had chills going up and down my spine, I'll tell you that."

But I was the only one who fell completely apart.

He went on, his voice soft, soothing. "What you went through before when you were—"

Now it was Edie who put her hand over Mitch's mouth. "I know, but I don't want to talk about that." She turned now to fully face him. "I want to talk about something else."

"All right." They were alone in the living room. Oma had gone to bed more than an hour ago, leaving them to talk. But mostly they had just sat quietly together.

She moved a little closer. "I want to get married. Right away. I don't want to wait until May."

Mitch rocked back, his mouth agape. "But—"

"I know. It sounds crazy. But this isn't because of what happened today." She immediately shook her head. "Well, it partly is, but not why you think."

"Then tell me."

"I was frightened, I admit that. And some of the same panic I felt before came back. But I never really thought that the world was going to end. So that's not why I've changed my mind."

"Then why?" He touched the tip of her nose with the tip of his finger, a gesture that she had come to love. It was his special way of saying *I love you.* "Tell me."

"Because ever since it happened, I've been asking myself, 'What if it had been the end of the world? Or what if it was some kind of horrible disaster or something and we were both killed?' I pictured us both waking up in the spirit world. And do you know what the first thing I said to you was, in this imaginary experience of mine?"

"No."

"'Why didn't we get married before this happened?' So will you marry me, Mitch? Please?"

Seeing the bewilderment in his eyes, she rushed on. "I know I'm the one who said we needed to wait until we could get married in the temple. But we can go to the temple in May like we planned. I want to be married now. Before something happens. No more waiting."

Mitch sat motionless for almost a full minute, obviously trying to take it all in. She felt her heart quicken. He was so sober, so grave. She could only imagine how this must all sound to him. *Oh dear, Edie's falling apart emotionally. Again.*

But when he finally spoke, he said only one word. And in her mind, he couldn't have said it better with a thousand.

He reached out and caressed her cheek, and then asked, "When?"

Notes

The story of the solar eclipse on New Year's Day 1889 and the reactions of the six families who stayed in Monticello comes from the historical account (see *Saga*, 103–4; *Anchored*, 93–4). Many years later, Cornelia (Nean) Adams Perkins wrote a letter of inquiry to the Utah State Agricultural College (now Utah State University) to confirm what they had seen. The letter she received in reply confirmed that there had been a solar eclipse in California and Nevada, which would have been visible in Southern Utah (see *Saga*, 103).

CHAPTER 27

January 4, 1889, 10:20 a.m.—EDW Ranch—Monticello

On the morning after New Year's Day, Edie and Mitch went from home to home announcing that they had decided to be married immediately and that they had set the date for Tuesday, January 8th. The effect on the community was electrifying. They had just celebrated two joyous holidays, but as far as the women were concerned, the first marriage in their little settlement would be an even greater celebration than Christmas or New Year's Day. Consequently, while the men went back to their normal workday activities, the women trekked up to the Westland cabin and began to plan a wedding.

The first question was where to hold it. That was quickly resolved. Though the Westland cabin was large enough to hold everyone, if they held it there, it meant that everyone in town had to trek a quarter of a mile up and back. It could be a problem if it happened to snow on that day or the night before, so it was determined that the wedding itself would be performed in the John Rogerson cabin. The Christmas tree was still up in their main room along with all the Christmas decorations the children had made. Though the tree might be a little droopy in another week, Edie enthusiastically endorsed the idea having the wedding there. The banquet and reception afterwards would be held in the home of President and Sister Jones, for they had the most room.

Under the direction of Mary Jones, inventories of the various root cellars were taken, menus were drawn up, and food assignments were made. Mitch volunteered to butcher one of his young heifers to provide plenty of roast beef. Parley offered a young pig too, so they could have ham as well. Mons Peterson donated a fifty-pound sack of flour and twenty-five pounds of sugar to Mary Adams and Renate Zimmer, who were assigned to make the wedding cake and other tasty sweets. William Adams was tasked with making another kettle of Irish wassail.

The children were not left out of the preparations either. They were ecstatic when Sarah announced that in lieu of school classes, her nine students would, for the next week, be helping to make the wedding decorations. Under the direction of Emma Hyde and her two oldest daughters, they set to work making papier-mâché wedding bells and hearts or cutting out small flowers, hearts, and diamonds to string up on the Christmas tree or around the room.

Edie felt as though a cyclone had swept down and snatched her up, twirling her around and around in a dizzying spiral, and yet she reveled in it. It was the perfect antidote for the guilt and shame she was feeling after her panic attack during the eclipse. It also assuaged her fears that people would criticize her for rushing into a wedding because of it.

On this morning, Sarah had left things at her house in the charge of Emma, Winnie, and Louise Hyde and taken a buggy up to the Westland homestead. Their task, still unresolved, was to settle the most pressing question of them all. What would Edie wear for the wedding? At the moment, she stood on a three-legged stool in the center of their living room feeling very awkward and embarrassed, even though only Sarah Rogerson and

Oma Zimmer were in the room with her. But, at Sarah's insistence, Edie had removed her dress and now stood only in her chemise and bloomers. She was also barefoot.

"Oma," she said nervously, "will you make sure that no one can peek through the curtains and see in here?"

Oma Zimmer had already done that once, but she got up without protest and went to the window. She pulled the two curtains together, making sure that not even a crack of light was visible. Then, guessing what Edie's next request was going to be, she went and made sure the door was locked and barred. "No vun can see in here," she affirmed. "No vun can come in here. Not even Mitchell, who is gone now."

Sarah looked up, sympathetic to Edie's feelings. "You still have a strong urge to grab a sheet or a blanket and cover yourself, right?"

"Very much so," Edie said.

Sarah turned to where a white blouse was hanging on the back of a chair. She went over and fetched it. She held it up in front of Edie. It buttoned all the way down the front, had long sleeves that ended just above her wrists, and a round, soft collar. "Is this your choice, then?"

"Yes. If you think it's all right. It's the best one I have."

"I think it's wonderful. Since we don't have enough material to make a wedding dress—"

"Or enough money," Edie broke in.

"Yes, that too. This is perfect for what we need. Go ahead and put it on."

As Edie did so, Sarah went to her large cloth bag and fished around in it. When she turned back, she held up a small bolt of lace. "Look what I found at Mons's store. Some bridal lace."

"He had bridal lace?" Edie exclaimed.

Sarah nodded gravely. "He said that it was Eliza's idea. Clear back last summer she asked him to find some while he was in Mancos and Durango."

"For me?" she cried, tears instantly welling up.

"Yes. And Mons said there is no charge for it. This is their wedding present for you."

Edie wiped at her eyes with the back of her hand, unable to respond to that.

Sarah unwound about six inches of the lace and held it up for Edie and Oma to see. Edie gave a low cry and clapped her hands. "Oh, Sarah. I love it."

The lace was white, about three inches wide, and had tiny rosebuds woven into an intricate but delicate design that repeated itself throughout.

"If we were to trim the collar and the cuffs of your sleeves with it, I think I could transform your blouse into something quite lovely."

Sarah held it out so Oma Zimmer could see it. She moved forward and examined it more closely, fingering it gently. She looked up and spoke to Edie. "*Es ist sehr schön.*"

Sarah looked up at Edie. Edie smiled. "Oma says it is very beautiful." Then her face fell. "But Sarah, what do I wear with it?" she asked forlornly. "I was hoping to be all in white, but I don't have anything like that."

Sarah and Oma exchanged knowing glances, and then Oma walked swiftly back into her bedroom. A moment later she reappeared carrying something white across her arms. "And vhat if vee used dis?" she asked, barely able to contain her excitement.

"What is it, Oma?"

Sarah walked over to Edie's grandmother, took the item from her, and then held it up for Edie to see. It was a long white skirt of cotton brocade.

Edie almost gasped. "Is that your wedding dress, Oma?"

"*Nein*. It is my vedding skirt. Like you, Edna Rae, my family vass poor. Vee could not afford a vedding dress, but my *Mutti* saved up her money and bought me this material."

"And you've saved it all this time?"

"I saved it for my Edna Rae, because I hoped someday you vood vear it on your vedding day."

Edie rushed to her grandmother and threw her arms around her. "Oh, Oma. Thank you."

Sarah watched for a moment and then cleared her throat. "Let's see if it's going to fit before we get too excited." She motioned for Edie to get back up on the stool and held the skirt up to her. "Hold this up to your waist." When she did so, Sarah stepped back and let her eyes move up and down the material. Then she grunted in soft satisfaction. "Well, Miss Edie, we may have to take it out just a little, but I would say that you were fortunate enough to inherit your grandmother's waistline."

"*Ja, ja*," Oma Zimmer said with a broad smile. "It vill verk, I think."

Sarah moved back in. "I like how it puffs out a little at the waist and then smooths down over your hips." She turned to Oma. "When were you married?"

"My Dietrich and I vere married in eighteen forty-eight, forty years ago last July."

Sarah looked up at Edie. "I don't know what the styles were then, but this inverted tulip shape in the skirt is very fashionable right now. I think it will be very flattering on you."

Edie was looking down as she held the skirt to her. "But it's too short. I did not inherit Oma's tiny height, unfortunately."

Taking the skirt again, Sarah examined the bottom of it. "Ah." She held it up. "A three-inch hem. That should be more than enough if I let it out." She reached over and picked up the lace from a chair and held it up against the brocade. "We want to be careful that we don't use too much and make it look gaudy, but I think with just a touch of lace on the skirt, like around the hem, we can make it look like the blouse and the skirt were actually made for each other. Do you have white shoes?"

Edie's expression fell. "No."

"I'd like to hem it so that it comes just below the ankle, but not have it touch the ground. So you'll have to have white shoes because people will be able to see them beneath your skirt. But don't worry—I talked with Mons about that too. He has two pairs, both the same size. Don't ask me why. Your feet are so tiny that they're probably a little big for you, but we can stuff some paper in them. Mons will let you wear them at the wedding without buying them if you're careful with them."

Edie reached out and touched Sarah's shoulder. "Oh, Sarah. You are a godsend. My mother was sick at heart when she left knowing that she couldn't be here to help me with my trousseau. But when I told her that you had said you would help me, she was greatly relieved."

"I am delighted that you would ask, Edie. This is my way of saying thank you for all the help you have given me at the school."

At that moment, Edie was so happy she wanted to cry. For a second she wished that Mitch was here to see all of this, but then she had another idea. She looked at her grandmother. "Oma, when Mitch gets back, I want this to be a surprise for him."

"*Das* is a good idea."

"That won't be a problem," Sarah noted. "Mitch told me yesterday just as he was leaving that he probably wouldn't get back until late Monday night, the night before the wedding."

That spun Edie around. "What? He never told me that. He said he'd maybe be gone only three or four days."

She smiled. "Well, dear, he left yesterday. So if he's gone four days, that *is* the day before the wedding."

"Oh." Edie sighed painfully. "Why did he have to go right now?"

Sarah and Oma exchanged quick glances but said nothing. Sarah went right on smoothing the fabric around Edie's hips and measuring how much to let the skirt out.

January 7, 1889, 4:00 p.m.—John Rogerson Home

Eddie Rogerson burst into the back room of the cabin, slamming the door behind him. "Mama! Mama!"

Sarah was placing three papier-mâché bells along the mantle of the fireplace. She whirled around. "John Edward Rogerson, don't you dare come in here if your boots are muddy." The footsteps stopped and retreated. There were two soft clunks as his galoshes dropped on the floor. Watching this, Edie marveled at Sarah's mother instincts. Eddie had not been playing where Sarah could see him, but she knew his boots would be muddy.

A moment later, Eddie, who was ten and Sarah's oldest child, appeared at the door from the kitchen. "Sister Edie," he cried. "Mitch is back."

Edie was in the middle of hanging the wedding garlands—paper hearts and wedding bells hung on a length of string—on the Christmas tree. She finished and hopped down from the stool. "Really? Wonderful." She started toward the door, wiping her hands on her apron. Eddie leaped forward and blocked her way. "No, Edie. You can't go out."

She started to push past him. "Of course I can go out. I want to see Mitch."

He planted his feet. "No. He wants you to wait in here. He

has a surprise for you." She took Eddie by the shoulders and gently pushed him to one side. "I'm going, Eddie, but I'll tell him you tried."

Again he jumped in front of her, but this time he looked at his mother. "Mama, Mitch made me promise to keep Edie in the house. And I promised."

Sarah came over and joined them. "Sounds to me like you'd better stay in here so my boy doesn't have to break his word."

Exasperated, Edie finally nodded. She started for the window to see if she could see Mitch from inside instead. Again Eddie blocked her way. "You can't look out the window, either."

"Oh, for heaven's sake," Edie exclaimed. "I just want to see him."

Just then Oma Zimmer came out of the bedroom. "Vhat is all the noise about?" she asked.

"Mitch is back," Edie said waspishly. "But he doesn't want me coming outside. He supposedly has a surprise for me."

"He does have a surprise," Eddie said. A grin split his freckled face. "And it's really neat."

"Another vedding present?" Oma wondered. "This boy must really love you."

"It better not be another present. I told him that the rocking chair is my wedding present, too. I have nothing for him."

"Ain't no rockin' chair," Eddie sang out.

His mother shot him a dirty look. "Where did you learn to say *ain't?* Not in my school."

Suddenly the front door opened and Mitch stepped inside, sparing Eddie the need to answer. "Hi," he said, shutting the door behind him.

Edie ran to him. He opened his arms and scooped her up, giving her a solid kiss before putting her down again. "How are you?" he asked.

"Better now," she said, forcing a smile. "Did checking on your cattle really take this long?"

He looked puzzled. "Who said I was checking on my cattle?"

"You did!"

"No, before I left I told you that I *needed* to check on my cattle, which I do. But that's not what I've been doing. It's still too early. There's too much snow in the high country."

"Then what?" she cried. "You've been gone for four days!"

"Yeah, I know." Mitch tried to appear crestfallen. "You must think I'm a real lout, taking off like that and not getting back until the day before the wedding."

"Well, I am a little annoyed that you lied to me."

"Edna Rae," Oma chided. "He vass not lying to you. He did not say he vass after cows."

Edie's mouth opened but then shut again as Mitch took her hand and turned her into the room. "Come over here. I want you to sit down and close your eyes."

Edie groaned. "Not again, Mitch. We agreed that the rocking chair would be our wedding gift. I don't have anything for you."

He smiled patiently. "I know. Just close your eyes for one minute."

She folded her arms and planted her feet. "No! I want to see what you've done this time."

Mitch shrugged. "Okay, have it your way." He went back to the door, paused for a moment, and opened it with a flourish. For a moment there was nothing, but then a shadow appeared. A moment later, Gwendolyn and Arthur Westland came through the door. Mitch's brother Johnnie came in right behind them. He was followed by his sister, Martha.

9:55 p.m.—EDW Ranch

"Why didn't you tell me what you were doing?" Edie said quietly. She and Mitch were sitting in the living room before the fire, which was mostly glowing coals now. The house was quiet. Oma Zimmer had gone to bed at nine. The Westlands, who were exhausted from their trip, followed shortly thereafter. This was their first chance to be alone since Mitch's return.

"There are two reasons. First, I did want to surprise you. But also, I was afraid that if you knew we were traveling across the same road where you and Evelyn and Leona got trapped in a blizzard, it would really worry you."

"It would have!" Edie exclaimed. "How could you do that in the dead of winter?"

"Because Parley and I checked the road the day before I left. The snow was only about two feet deep in the deepest parts. So we took his sleigh to break trail through the deep stuff and my wagon to bring my family back. Once the snow petered out, Parley came back home."

"And what happens if we get a big snowstorm? How will your parents get back?"

Mitch laughed softly. "Actually, we talked about that. It would take a pretty big storm to make the road impassable again, but they have come prepared to stay for a while."

That took her aback. "Even until spring? Because that could happen."

"Yes. They plan to return sooner, but if something does happen, I'd love to have Pa's and Johnnie's help building some more stock sheds. I knew that Mama and Papa would be devastated if we didn't bring them up for the wedding when they're only fifty miles away." He frowned. "Actually, I thought about doing the same for your parents. I know how disappointed they will be when they hear, but that's over two hundred miles away and crosses several high mountain passes."

"I know," Edie said dejectedly. "There's no way you could have gotten them. Mama will be especially sad. Her only child, her only daughter, and she won't even know about the wedding for weeks." She brightened a little. "But I am so happy that your family is here."

"Even if it means that we might have company for a while?" Mitch flashed her a mischievous grin. "With my folks taking our bedroom, I'll have to stay out in the barn with Johnnie. Some honeymoon."

Mitch chuckled as Edie's cheeks colored. "But anyway, Mama and Papa plan to stay for church on Sunday, and then I'll take them back down on Monday. Would you like to come with me?"

"No!" She barked it out but then felt instantly stupid. "I . . . I'm not sure that would be wise. Too many memories, I guess." She looked away.

"I understand. Assuming it doesn't snow, where we've already broken a trail, I think I can make it down and back in three days instead of four. And I'll bring back the rest of the furniture your parents left for you."

When Edie merely nodded, Mitch stood up. "Well, I think we need to get to bed too. Big day tomorrow."

She was still staring at her hands. "Mitch?"

"Yes?"

"I'm sorry to be such a baby about all of this."

"About crossing over that road again, you mean? I understand. I think it's only natural that it's going to take a while—months, maybe even years—for you to get over that. It was a horrible experience for you."

"If that was the only thing, then—" She looked away.

"What else?"

"I'm sorry for throwing such a fit when you were gone for so long to Salt Lake. And I'm sorry for falling to pieces when that eclipse was going on."

"You know that neither one of those things bothers me, Edie. But are you sorry that we moved up the wedding?"

She reared back, clearly surprised by his directness. "Are you?"

"Can I be really honest?" When she nodded, he said, "At supper, as I watched you with my family, I had this crazy thought. First, the Lord had to send a blizzard to bring us back together. Now, He's sent an eclipse of the sun to kind of move things along a little faster. And do you know what thought came into my mind?"

"No, what?"

He laughed softly. "My first thought was, 'I thank Thee, Lord.'"

That finally got a laugh out of her. "Really?"

"Yes, really. But, Edie, if you're having second thoughts about getting married tomorrow, then you just say the word. There's nothing done that can't be undone."

She reacted to that vehemently. "No! No! I am sad that Mama and Papa can't be here. And I do have some regrets that we're not getting married in the temple first, but I am so glad we're getting married tomorrow. Ecstatic, actually. But—"

He put a finger to her lips. "No buts. I have only one word to say about this whole thing."

"What?"

He grinned as he pulled her in close. "I say, 'Hallelujah!'"

CHAPTER 28

January 8, 1889, 9:00 a.m.—John Rogerson Cabin—Monticello

President Jones raised one hand high and called for attention. People immediately ceased their conversations. Children turned to watch. Parents took the littlest ones on their laps.

As far as Mitch could tell, every single person in Monticello and Verdure was here. The Rogersons had set up six chairs in a slight half circle facing their fireplace. Oma Zimmer and Mitch's mother and brother occupied three of them. Sarah Rogerson, who was now six months along in her pregnancy, occupied another, and William and Mary Adams, the oldest couple in the community, had been given the other two. The rest of the room was packed with people who were standing.

Facing President Jones were the five members of the wedding line. Arthur Westland stood on Mitch's right. He was the best man. Edie had two people standing to her left. In a move that startled—and yet pleased—the community, Edie had chosen Emma Peterson, Mons Peterson's sister, to be her matron of honor. Since she was just sixteen, technically she should have been called the maid of honor, but Emma was standing in for her deceased sister-in-law. Shortly after they had announced the wedding, as Edie was making her wedding plans, it came to her very strongly that if Eliza Peterson were still alive she would have been her matron of honor. Why not choose her anyway, she thought, letting Emma—who loved Eliza as much as Edie did—stand in as her representative? Mitch had instantly agreed, and the invitation was extended. Mitch's sister Martha stood beside Emma, because Edie had asked her to be the one bridesmaid.

When the room had settled down, President Jones began. "Brothers and sisters," he called in his deep, sonorous voice. "The time has come for us to begin." He looked at Mitch and Edie and smiled warmly at them. "How grateful we are to be here today to witness one of the most joyous and significant things that can happen in this mortal life of ours—the creation of a new family unit that will continue on into the eternities, if they are faithful. It is my privilege, as president of the Monticello Branch of the San Juan Stake of Zion, to perform this sacred ordinance of matrimony. We shall ask Sister Renate Zimmer, grandmother of the bride, to open these services with prayer. Sister Zimmer."

Just seeing her grandmother stand and move up beside President Jones almost sent the tears cascading down Edie's cheeks. A rush of gratitude filled her heart. Because Mitch had felt impressed to go to Salt Lake and then down to Richfield, she had one of her family members here today.

Renate spoke in a low, reverent voice. The prayer was simple and somehow quite touching in her distinct German accent. When she sat down again, President Jones stepped forward once more. He was smiling at the couple before him.

A hush of expectation swept across the room. President Jones chuckled softly. "Brother Mitch Westland and Sister Edie Zimmer, I fully understand why you are looking at each other so deeply in this happy moment, but I would like both of you to face me now. And I would ask that you not hold hands at this point, for reasons I shall make clear in a moment."

They turned toward him and let go of each other's hands,

both of them blushing a little. "You will have the rest of your lives to gaze into each other's eyes," he added wryly, "so see if you can bear to look at this old face of mine for a few moments. Then you can look at each other for the rest of eternity if you wish."

A soft ripple of amusement swept through the crowd.

When it quieted, President Jones moved a step closer to them. "While it is tempting to give you some practical advice about how to create a happy marriage, I feel instead to talk about the very first marriage on this earth. That was performed by God Himself. I should like to talk about Adam and Eve, our first parents, for there is much we can learn from their experience."

Turning his head slightly so he was looking at Mitch, he continued. "Brother Westland, as you will remember, God created Adam first, and for a time he was alone in the Garden of Eden. Then the Father asked this question: 'Is it good for man to be alone?' We all know the answer to that. No, it is not good for man to be alone."

His eyes softened. "You've learned that already, haven't you, Brother Mitch? You have learned that what you have now with Sister Edie is profoundly better than what you had before she came into your life."

Mitch nodded, glancing at Edie and smiling. Then he turned back.

"That holds true for the woman as well," President Jones went on. "It is not good for her to be alone either, but I think she instinctively understands that, whereas the man sometimes has to be reminded of it."

More chuckles. Edie was listening intently. This was not at all what she had expected.

President Jones turned and began speaking to her. "And because it was not good for man to be alone, our Heavenly Father created a helpmeet for Adam. That is the word that is used. It is not help*mate,* as some people think. It is help*meet.* I am told that in the original language, the word conveys sameness. It literally means 'a mirror image.' The idea is that in Eve, Adam meets the only one of all of God's creations who was like himself. In my mind, that word conveys equality. Though we are so very different in many ways, in the sight of God, man and woman are equal partners in the marriage relationship. One does not hold a position inferior to the other."

He paused. He was speaking to everyone now. "What happened next, after Adam and Eve were both created? Well, God the Father said to Adam, 'Therefore shall a man leave his father and his mother and shall cleave unto his wife, and they shall be one flesh.'"

He was speaking to the couple again now. "Think about that. That is your charge, you two wonderful young people. You are to be as though you were one entity. You are to be one in purpose, one in faith, one in devotion. You are to be one in the way that a lock and a key are two separate things but one functioning unit. Neither can fulfill its purpose without the other." He chuckled as a thought hit him. "I will not be so presumptuous as to suggest which of you is the lock and which is the key."

More laughter filled the room. Even the younger children had understood that analogy.

President Jones turned and reached for a book on the table behind him and then turned back as he opened it to a place where he had a marker. "That commandment to cleave together was given to Adam and Eve about six thousand years ago. But in modern revelation, the commandment is repeated and given even greater emphasis. I shall read from Doctrine and Covenants, section forty-two, verse twenty-two."

He took a quick breath, raised the book, and read slowly,

raising his voice so that all could hear. "'Thou shalt love thy wife with all thy heart, and shalt cleave unto her and none else.'" He lowered the book and glanced over at his wife, who was watching him raptly. "I am happy to say that this is one of the easier commandments to keep when you marry the right person."

She nodded, her eyes glistening, as murmurs of approval and agreement sounded from the adults in the room. Then suddenly, Brother Jones was shaking his finger at Mitch. "Do you understand what I just read to you? There is only one other thing in all of scripture that a man is commanded to love with all of his heart, and that is God."

Now he glanced at Edie as he continued talking to Mitch. "In other words, your wife stands second only to God in your loyalty, your love, your faithfulness, your affections, your dedication, and your consecration."

He sighed thoughtfully and turned to Edie. "To be honest, I have wondered why the Lord doesn't say to the woman, 'Love your husband with all your heart.' I'm sure that the commandment applies to women, too, but I have come to a conclusion that answers that question for me. I speak not as if this were doctrine. This is only my opinion. But I believe that if a man truly loves his wife with all of his heart—no, *when* he loves his wife with all of his heart—then you don't have to tell the woman to love him back. That is her nature, her gift, her wonder. She will love him back in the same way. I think there are few exceptions to that."

He set the book down again. When he turned back he was even more solemn than before. As he looked at the young couple before him, he nodded in satisfaction and smiled. "All right, then. Brother Westland and Sister Zimmer, will you now turn and face each other? And feel free to gaze as deeply into one another's eyes as you wish. I say this because you are about to make a covenant with each other—not with me—and I want you looking at each other as you make that covenant."

They did so, smiling shyly now. "Mitch, please take both of Edie's hands in yours and hold them until I have concluded." He waited a moment while they did so and then continued. "This joining of your hands symbolizes that you are no longer two separate individuals, but one in the sight of God."

He let them stand there for ten or fifteen seconds, motionless as statues as they looked at each other. Then, in a voice that was noticeably lower in pitch and heavy with emotion, he continued. "Mitchell Arthur Westland, do you take this woman, Edna Rae Zimmer, to be your wife, lawfully wedded to you in holy matrimony, and do you most solemnly covenant with her that you promise to love and cherish her above all other people and all other things through all of time?"

"Yes." Mitch said it loud and clear, his eyes never leaving Edie's.

"Edna Rae Zimmer, do you take this man, Mitchell Arthur Westland, to be your husband, lawfully wedded to him in holy matrimony? And do you most solemnly covenant with him that you will love and cherish him above all other people and above all other things for all time?"

The tears were there, tears of radiant joy. "Yes."

"Then, with the authority given me as a minister in The Church of Jesus Christ of Latter-day Saints, I hereby pronounce you, Mitchell Arthur Westland, and you, Edna Rae Zimmer, husband and wife, married in this sacred union for the rest of your natural lives together. May your love for each other be as bright and as true and as pure as it is today."

He paused, smiled, and nodded. "You may now kiss each other as husband and wife."

CHAPTER 29

March 24, 1889, 5:42 p.m.—EDW Ranch—Monticello

"Edie! Oma!"

"We're in here, Mitch." Edie's voice came from Oma's bedroom, so Mitch turned and went into the hall. When he reached the door, which was open about halfway, he stopped as Oma Zimmer's voice sounded in a commanding tone.

"Again!"

He heard Edie sigh. "Okay. The *A* is pronounced like the *ah* in *father.* The *E* is like the *A* in *say.* The *I* takes the long *E* sound, as in *tree.* The *O* is the same as we say it, like *oh.*"

"*Gut! Gut!*"

"The *U* becomes like the *oo* in *moon.*"

"Very good," Oma declared. "Now the umlauts."

Mitch moved forward enough so he could see into the room. Grandmother and granddaughter were lying side by side on the bed. Oma was on her side, watching Edie. Edie was on her back staring up at the ceiling. She moaned. "Not the umlauts, Oma. Mitch is here. We need to start supper."

He stuck his head in. "Oh, no you don't. Don't use me for your excuse."

Edie jumped up, came over, and wrung his hand in desperation. "Please, Mitch," she whispered. "Tell her you're hungry."

"I heard that," Oma said tartly, sitting up as well. "Mitch, I vant you to help Edie on how to pronounce the umlauts." Then to Edie, "Mitch is very good in his pronunciation. Very good."

"I know. You tell me that every day."

Deciding it was time for some intervention, Mitch spoke to Edie. "Guess who just arrived at the Hydes'."

"Umm, let's see. Evelyn Adams? I heard they were coming up from Verdure soon."

"No, not Evelyn," he said, his smile broadening, "but she had her baby girl about three weeks ago."

Edie nodded. "I know. And she and George named her Zola, just like she said she was going to. So who is here?"

"Aunt Jodie," Mitch said happily.

Edie gave a low cry. "That's wonderful. Does Sarah know?"

Aunt Jodie was what everyone called Sister Josephine Wood. She and her husband, Samuel Wood, had come with five children to Bluff with the first pioneer company in 1880. She was considered to be the most proficient and experienced midwife in all of San Juan County and was much beloved for her tenderness and gentleness, even in times of great stress. And she had agreed to come up for when Sarah had her baby.

"Of course," Mitch was saying. "Sister Wood stopped at the Rogersons' very first. Now they're all over at Emma Hyde's house making plans for when the Rogerson baby comes. She also brought someone else with her."

"Who?"

"Think about it. Considering you wrote a letter to her and told her our good news, this shouldn't come as too much of a surprise."

Edie's mouth fell open a little. "Gwen? Your mother's here?"

"She is. And Martha and Johnnie are with her."

"Wonderful! How long are they here for?" Edie asked.

"Well, that's the other part of the good news. Mama and

Martha will stay with you and Oma, and Johnnie will help me with the spring roundup and branding. Pa may come up a little later to help too. They'll be here in about an hour, or you can go down to the Hydes' and help them get things ready for Sarah."

"Then vhat are vee vaiting for?" Oma asked, coming over. "Let's go meet this *Tante* Jodie that everyone is talking about. Let us see vhat she has to say about this little one in your tummy."

March 31, 1889, 11:30 a.m.—John Rogerson Cabin

It was a beautiful, early spring day, so the sisters of Monticello gathered around the John Rogerson cabin but stayed out in the sunshine. They had brought stools, small benches, and even a few chairs to sit on. Most wore bonnets. Several had brought parasols even though the temperature was a pleasant seventy-six degrees.

Children were playing where they could be seen by their parents. The children were in a high state of excitement because with a baby coming soon to the Rogerson home, the decision had been made that it wouldn't be wise to have schoolchildren going in and out of the home. This was especially wise since the number of students had quickly doubled with the return of the families who had left for the winter. Edie could have taken over the teaching for Sarah, but the only other place big enough to hold that many students was the church house. However, because it didn't yet have windows, it had filled up with drifting snow during winter storms. That was all gone now, but the floor was still a sea of mud.

Edie looked around, counting quickly. The number of women in Monticello had doubled now that the first of those who had left for the winter were back. Others were coming in almost every week. In addition, new families were starting to arrive as well. Nephi and Annie Bailey had come up early, and Nephi was hard at work on their cabin. In the meantime they were staying with Mary Jones, who was Annie's sister. Each had five children, including two two-year-old "handfuls," which made for a household "busting at the seams," as President Jones described it. The nice thing was that Annie, like Mary, had also been born in Copenhagen, and she joined Oma's little circle of German and Danish speakers.

Edie was especially glad that the Waltons were back. Maggie and Leona had not been home for more than an hour when they came racing up to the ranch house to see Edie, eager to hear every detail of the wedding. Right then, Jane Walton was inside the home helping Aunt Jodie with Sarah, fulfilling her role as stake Relief Society president as usual. There was something else they brought that was good news. Charles had brought back a small forge with them, along with a wagon full of coal and a sack of tools. He immediately opened a small blacksmith's shop behind his barn. It was more of a community contribution than a business venture, for he let anyone come in and use it without cost except for materials.

Edie leaned over to Mitch's mother. "Can you see Brother Rogerson out there by the corral?" Gwen nodded and chuckled softly. "In spite of his efforts to look busy, I don't think he's getting much done out there. A perfect picture of the nervous father." Then she grew more serious. "Have you had a chance to talk to Aunt Jodie yet?"

"Yes and no. We talked briefly yesterday. She had already heard that I was expecting. But assuming that Sarah's baby comes today and that everything goes all right, she plans to come up to the house tomorrow. She's not going back until Monday."

"Yes, that's what she told me, too."

"Will you be going back with her?" Edie asked.

Gwen frowned a little. "I don't think so," she said.

"I'm fine, Gwen. Really. I'm still having morning sickness, but I'm feeling good."

"It's not just that," Gwen said, though in truth it was mostly that. "I was thinking that Martha and I could help you put a garden in. I know it's still too early to plant, but we could have it all ready for when it's warm enough."

"I would like that very much. Oma and I were talking about that just a few days ago. She always had one of the best vegetable gardens in all of Richfield."

"Well, let's see what Aunt Jodie has to say tomorrow, and then—"

Suddenly a buzz of excitement cut them off. Aunt Jodie was standing in the doorway. Jane Walton was right behind her. "Where's Brother John?" Aunt Jodie asked.

But John Rogerson had already seen what was happening and was coming at a dead run. Just then, a baby's wailing cry sounded. Everyone started calling out. "What is it?"

"Is the baby okay?"

"Is it a boy or a girl?"

Seeing John coming, Aunt Jodie merely smiled. "The baby's fine, as you can hear, but we'll let the father tell you what it is after he's had a chance to go in and congratulate his wife."

Jane Walton appeared and called over her shoulder. "Someone go get the children. We'll let John have what time he wants, and then we'll bring them in."

Fifteen minutes later, John Rogerson appeared at the door again, a tiny bundle cradled in one arm. Instantly the crowd hushed. His grin was as wide as a barn door. "It's a boy!" he crowed.

There was spontaneous applause scattered with calls of

congratulation. "Aunt Jodie guesses he's about seven and a half pounds," he called over the noise. "He's as healthy as a horse. And we're going to name him George Halls Rogerson."

"How's Sarah?" a woman's voice called.

His smile grew even wider, if that was possible. "Sarah is fine. Exhausted, but fine. She's sleeping now. Gotta go. I've got three very anxious kids clamoring to see who gets to be the first one to hold their little brother."

April 1, 1889, 9:10 a.m.—EDW Ranch

Mitch paced back and forth in the main room of the cabin, stopping every few seconds to listen, but all he could hear from the bedroom was the murmur of female voices.

After another ten minutes, Aunt Jodie's voice sounded more clearly, closer to the bedroom door. He hurried over and plopped down in one of their overstuffed chairs and grabbed a book from the table. A moment later the door opened and Aunt Jodie appeared, followed by Oma Zimmer, then Edie, and then his mother. Aunt Jodie immediately came over and sat down in a chair beside Mitch. Oma took the rocking chair by the window, Mitch's mother took the other overstuffed chair, and Edie sat on the divan. When Mitch saw that, he immediately got up, went over, and sat down beside his wife. She reached out and took his hand, smiling briefly at him. "Aunt Jodie would like to talk to us."

"Good." He squeezed her hand and turned back to face Aunt Jodie.

Josephine Wood was a woman in her mid-thirties. She was broad of shoulder and somewhat stout through the body, but her features were pleasant and finely formed. She was a little taller than Edie's five feet three or four inches. She parted her dark hair down the middle of her head and pulled both sides back, where she fastened it in a bun. Her eyes were as dark as her hair and highly expressive. One moment they would be filled with merriment, the next with soft compassion. Everything about her radiated kindness, gentleness, and understanding.

Since her arrival in Monticello, Edie had learned more about Aunt Jodie and shared it with Mitch. She had been born and raised in Cedar City of pioneer stock. Her father had died three days before she was born, and her mother followed him in death when Jodie was three. She was raised by a half sister from that point on. When she was eighteen years old, she had married Samuel Wood, an English convert ten years her senior. They were among the Saints who left all when they were called to the San Juan Mission. They brought five children with them when they came across the Hole-in-the-Rock trail in 1880. Shortly after their arrival, Bishop Jens Nielson set her apart as a midwife and doctor. She was now starting her ninth year in that service.

She leaned forward, "Brother Mitch, I—"

"Please, Sister Wood," he interrupted. "Just Mitch is fine."

"Good," she said with a playful smile, "and just Aunt Jodie is fine for me." She went on. "I am happy to confirm what you already know—that Edie is definitely with child. I am guessing she is not quite three months along."

He felt Edie squeeze his hand hard. They had been pretty certain of that, but to have it confirmed by Aunt Jodie was exactly what Edie needed.

"Edie is a strong young woman in excellent health, and you don't need to be overprotective of her." She smiled and winked at him. "As Edie says you are prone to be."

"I—" Then he shrugged.

She was looking at both of them now. "However, in light of

Edie's family history, with both her mother and her maternal grandmother, I want both of you to be wise. Normal activity is good for her, but nothing that is really strenuous."

Edie raised a hand. "Stake conference is the last of May, and it's going to be held in Mancos. We were planning on going."

Aunt Jodie's brow knitted as she considered that for a moment, and then she shook her head quite firmly. "Uh-uh. Seventy miles in a wagon over rough roads is not a good idea. She would probably be all right, but—"

"We don't like the word 'probably,'" Mitch finished for her.

"Right," she said, pleased with his response. "Neither do I."

"What about food?" Mitch asked. "Is there anything she can't eat?"

Gwen laughed. "Be prepared for a wild ride."

"Yeah," Mitch said ruefully. "I've already been out begging pickles from all the sisters. And I can't even cook bacon in the house now."

"Ugh!" Edie said, pulling a face. "Don't even talk about bacon."

"There is a lot going on in her body right now," Aunt Jodie explained, "and she's eating for two now. That will get much more pronounced as the baby grows. On my third baby, at about three months, the smell of venison cooking was so repulsive to me it made me throw up. And it didn't go away. To this day, if someone's cooking venison, I have to leave the house."

Gwen spoke up. "I craved smoked pork for three or four months but then couldn't stand it after that. But finally, my taste for it came back again."

Oma laughed. "Mine vas bratwurst—German sausage—which I normally vasn't that vild about before. But I couldn't get enough of it. The spiciness was vhat I craved."

"Mitch is already seeing that," Edie said.

Aunt Jodie nodded and then grew serious. She slid forward on her chair as she looked directly at Edie. "Now, Edie my dear, I have one more thing I need to say, and then I must go and see to Sarah."

"I'm listening."

"I know that saying what I am about to say is fruitless in a way, but I'm going to say it anyway. You can't be worrying overly much about this."

"But . . . how can I not worry? I've been praying about this every night and morning since I was fourteen years old and got my patriarchal blessing. It's all I think about."

"I know," Aunt Jodie replied. "And we all do, to some extent. It's natural for a woman to fret about every little hiccough, every little twinge, every little bump when she's expecting, especially for the first time. But you have to fight it. There is some evidence that an excess of worry or stress can actually affect a woman's ability to conceive or to carry a baby to full term."

As Edie's eyes widened, Aunt Jodie looked at Mitch. "And your role in this is very important. Let me tell you two things that are *not* helpful if Edie seems anxious about things. One is to say things like, 'Oh, Edie, everything's fine. Don't worry.' That is *not* helpful."

"I can see that."

"But I don't want you being nervous, either, hovering over her every minute, coddling her, fussing over her and asking her every ten or fifteen seconds if everything is all right or if you can get her a drink."

"Got it," he answered gravely. "Any suggestions on how I can be more helpful?"

"Let her know you care. Be encouraging but don't fawn over her. Talk about the baby, what he or she will be like. That always works. But don't let her dwell on fretting about how the baby's doing."

"Just be there for me," Edie added. She smiled. "Like you always are."

Aunt Jodie was watching Edie thoughtfully. "Do you happen to have a diary or a journal?"

Surprised, Edie shook her head. "I used to keep one, but then I filled it up, and. . . ." She shrugged. "I've never gotten a new one."

Aunt Jodie turned to Mitch. "Do you happen to know if Brother Peterson has any in the store?"

Mitch slowly shook his head. "I'll ask him, but I don't think so."

Gwen spoke up. "The co-op store in Bluff may have them. I can send a letter back with you, Aunt Jodie, and have Arthur buy Edie one. There are people coming up to Monticello now all the time. It wouldn't take long to get it here."

"Good." She turned back to Edie. "I've found that writing in a journal can be one of the best ways of beating the blues. But in addition to that, I want you to keep a record of what's going on with this baby—what you're eating, what you're not eating, your mood swings, morning sickness, when you first feel movement. And put dates on them. All of these are very helpful for me as I work with you. You think you will remember when these things happen, but they slip away from you if you don't write them down right away."

"I will. I like that idea," Edie said.

Sitting back, Aunt Jodie concluded, "I will be coming up this way again in a couple of weeks to check on Sarah and little George. I will look in on you as well, if you'd like."

"Oh, yes!" Edie cried. "That would mean so much to me."

"Okay. Until then, you two try to enjoy this little miracle of life that you are now experiencing. This is what you have been waiting for since you and Mitch fell in love, right? So enjoy it. And may you have peace in your heart as you move forward."

Notes

Sarah Jane Rogerson gave birth to a baby boy on March 31, 1889. It was her fourth child, and she was twenty-eight years old. They named him George Halls Rogerson.

The physical description of Josephine (Aunt Jodie) Wood is my own, based on a photograph of her, but her personality is based on two comments in one of the sources: "Josephine had a vivacious personality and a keen sense of humor, which made her the center of every crowd," and "everyone adored her because of her love and tenderness in all kinds of trouble" (*Saga*, 340–41).

The other details of her life, including the loss of her parents at an early age and being set apart to be a midwife and doctor are all part of her life story. At about the same time she was called to be a midwife she was also called as Primary president for the Bluff Ward. She held both positions for twenty-five years. Eventually, she had ten children. She died in Monticello in 1909 at the age of forty-eight. She is buried in the Bluff Cemetery (see *Saga*, 341).

CHAPTER 30

April 7, 1889, 3:55 p.m.—EDW Ranch—Monticello

Mitch leaped down from his horse as Johnnie cracked his lariat and drove the last of the cows into the corral. Swinging the gate shut, Mitch secured it with the loop of rope that hung there. Then he looked up at his brother through the swirling clouds of dust. "Go around and make sure that gate on the other side is secure."

Wheeling his horse around, Johnnie trotted away. Mitch watched him go, keenly aware that every wrinkle and crease in his body felt as though it were filled with sandpaper. Riding behind a herd of cattle on a hot, dry day did that to you. As the dust began to settle, he pulled the bandanna down from the lower half of his face and took off his hat and flapped it against his shirt. Little clouds of red dust exploded outward. He knew that his face was streaked with dust and perspiration just like Johnnie's was. In spite of all that, he was deeply satisfied. Forty-two head, including nine new calves. Not bad for less than a week's work.

With the temperature rising every day, he didn't look forward to standing over a branding fire, but he figured that with one more two- to three-day sweep he'd have all but a few of his herd done. There were always those that wandered too far away to be found. Or maybe the Carlisle bunch had rounded them up for him and would bring them over later.

Yeah, right. More like rounded them up and put their brand on them.

But this was better than he had expected. Taking the reins, he rubbed Pinter's nose. "You're a hardworking cayuse," he said affectionately, "so let's get you unsaddled and wiped down, my friend. There's a stable with fresh hay and half a bucket of oats waiting for you. And then, my brother and I are each going to heat up a full reservoir of water and take a very long bath."

Five minutes later, just as Mitch was forking a pitchfork full of hay into Pinter's manger, the side door to the barn opened. He looked and saw a woman silhouetted in the doorway. He waved. "Edie, is that you?" he called. But as the woman turned, he saw immediately that it was his mother, not his wife. "Oh, hi, Mama."

"Hello, Mitch." She came inside and shut the door behind her.

Johnnie poked his head out from the stall where he was wiping down his horse. "Hi, Mama."

"Hello, John. How did you do?"

"Great!" he called.

Mitch nodded as he disappeared back into the stable. "He's a good hand. If he wants a job for the summer, you know where to send him."

"That will depend on whether his father needs him with us."

"That's what he said. But thanks for letting him help with the roundup. He probably saved me three or four days. So, where's Edie? Getting supper, I hope. We're starved."

"Actually, she's resting right now. But Martha's got supper on the stove."

"Okay. I'm going to wipe Pinter down, and then I'll. . . ." His voice trailed off as Gwen looked up at him. Something in her expression sounded an alarm bell in his mind. "What?" And then it hit him. "Edie? Is Edie all right, Mama?"

"Yes, she's all right. But. . . ."

He grabbed her arm. "What? Tell me."

Her eyes couldn't bear to meet his. "Fortunately, Aunt Jodie was here."

"Aunt Jodie? Mama, what's wrong?"

"She lost the baby, Mitch."

"*No!*" It came out as a strangled whisper.

"Two days ago. She's sleeping now, but Oma Zimmer is sitting with her. Aunt Jodie will be back tomorrow. But you need to go to her. "

He whirled and started away, but she called to him. He turned back.

Her face was stricken. "She may not tell you this, but I think you should know."

"What?"

"She thinks this happened because you didn't wait to be married in the temple first."

11:18 p.m.

Edie hadn't stirred for ten minutes or more, and Mitch wondered if she'd finally fallen asleep in his arms. There had been no tears, just this deep, pervasive sorrow. He lifted his head a little to see if he could see her eyes.

Edie's head lifted too, and she started to pull away from him. Mitch said, "You must be exhausted. I'm sorry to keep you up so late."

"I don't want to go to sleep. I'm so glad you're home again."

"I feel awful that I wasn't here for you. If I had known, I would have come home."

She reached out and found his hand and interlocked her fingers with his. "I know you would, but I. . . ." But she didn't finish, and he didn't push her to.

He remembered Mary Jones's counsel that morning after the rescue. "Be gentle, Mitch. Let her take it at her own pace." He reached out and gently stroked her cheek with his fingertip. "I love you, Edie," he whispered.

There was an almost imperceptible bob of her head. After another few moments she spoke, her voice very low but surprisingly steady. "There was no warning. Well, except that I wasn't sick when I got up that morning. Which I thought was wonderful. But I didn't fall, and I hadn't done anything strenuous."

She buried her head against his chest. "I woke up in the night, and . . . and. . . ." She was trembling slightly now, but to Mitch's surprise, she still did not cry. She finally got control again. "I am so glad your mother was here, Mitch. She got out of bed and ran all the way to town to get Aunt Jodie. Oma couldn't have done that." A long sigh. "Aunt Jodie came right away, but by then it was over."

"And what does Aunt Jodie think?"

"She is wonderful. So caring. So . . . so steady." Edie drew in a slow breath. "She said that sometimes it just happens. Something's wrong with the baby, and this is my body's way of dealing with it. But it doesn't mean it will always happen."

"She said that?"

"Yes."

"That's good, right?"

She nodded and then pulled out of his grasp and turned over on her back, still staying right up against him. "There is one bright spot in all of this."

"What's that?"

"We can go to stake conference now."

And then the dam burst and Edie began to sob—long, shuddering, heart-wrenching sobs. And all Mitch could think of to do was take her in his arms again and stroke her hair as he held her close.

April 8, 1889, 1:46 a.m.

They lay quietly together, side by side, shoulder to shoulder, hip to hip, holding hands. It was like the coming of the sun after a cloudburst. The tears had had a cathartic effect on Edie, and she seemed content. She was holding Mitch's hand and kept rubbing the back of it with her thumb in soft, gentle circles.

"Edie?"

"Yes?"

"I've been thinking."

"About stake conference?" She turned her head. "I want to go. It's still a month away. I'll be fine."

"I know. We're going. But I've been thinking that . . . what if after conference, instead of coming back to Monticello, you and me, and Mama and Papa, and Oma Zimmer, and Martha and Johnnie all went north instead?"

Her head jerked around. "North?"

"Yes. There's a road that goes north from Mancos and comes out around the south side of the La Sals and joins the road to Moab."

"You need to go to Moab?"

"No. To Thompson Springs."

"With your family? Whatever for?"

"To catch the train to Salt Lake City, and from there down

to Deseret. We could write your folks, and they could meet us at Deseret and bring a wagon and take us down to Richfield. And we'd write my brothers and their families in Beaver and they'd come to Richfield too."

Edie sat up and turned so she was facing him. The moon was just starting to wane from being full, and it shone through their window enough that she could see him clearly. "And then go to Manti?" she asked, finally understanding.

"Yes."

There was a long, long pause, and then, "Your mother told you what I said?"

Mitch wanted to say no, but knew she would see through that. "Yes."

"Mitch, that was right after all this happened. I was really, really upset. And—" She shook her head. "You can't be gone for that long in the spring. With conference too, that would take a month at least."

"Or better yet, what if we went to Richfield first? We could be sealed on your birthday, just as we planned. Then we'd go to conference on the way back, or if Oma was too tired we would bring her home and then go."

Edie smiled, and it was filled with love and sadness. She bent down and kissed him softly. "My dear, dear Mitch. How I love you."

"I'm serious."

"I know you are. Which makes it even more tender for me. But I'm all right now. The tears are gone. Life goes on."

"I'm not saying that because I think you're falling apart, Edie. We both want to get sealed as soon as possible. Why not on your birthday?"

"Because it's spring," she burst out. "It's roundup time, and branding time, and planting time, and fencing time, and logging time and—"

"None of which is more important than us being sealed together forever," he retorted.

Her jaw set. "We called this ranch the EDW Ranch. You do remember what the E D stands for, right?"

"Uh . . . yeah, of course. It is your name."

"Well, then," she said with fierce determination, "it isn't just your ranch anymore. It's our ranch. I want it to succeed as much as you do. If not more. So don't ask me to put that in jeopardy just because I'm going through a hard time emotionally." Edie shook her head. "Maybe in the fall, after harvest. Before the first snows."

Taken aback by the passion in her, Mitch nodded. "Okay, I understand."

Edie lay back down and snuggled up against him. "Sorry. Just wanted to clear the air about that. But thank you for even thinking about it." She touched his cheek for just a moment. "Now, I've got to let you sleep. Aunt Jodie is going back to Bluff tomorrow, and your family, too, now that you're back. We've got a lot to do to get ready. Go to sleep."

"Will you sleep?"

"Yes, now that you're home again."

Again he went up on one elbow and kissed her. "Then good night. I love you more than tongue can tell."

To his utter surprise, Edie giggled softly and poked him in the ribs. "Who's Tuncantel?"

Mitch sighed, feigning great weariness, but he was actually delighted to hear her laugh. He pulled the covers up over her shoulders and lay back down again. "Good night, Edie."

"Good night, Mitch."

It was no more than five minutes later, just as his eyes were getting heavy, that she spoke again. "Mitch? Do *you* think I lost the baby because we didn't wait to marry in the temple?"

He was instantly awake and sat up. "No, Edie. Absolutely not. Though I kid about the Lord sending an eclipse to prod us into marrying, I do strongly believe He wanted us to marry when we did."

"It felt right, but—"

"The Lord wouldn't punish you in that way."

"I know that. But maybe if we had been sealed first, I would have had more faith, or—"

"No! I don't believe that. I do not believe the Lord is displeased with you in any way, Edna Rae Westland. And I say that with all the power of persuasion that I possess."

She was silent for almost a full minute. She surprised him then when she laughed softly. "It seems like I'm always saying thank you, but thank you for that."

"I think we do need to go to Manti as soon as it is reasonably possible," he said, "but not as some kind of penance. We'll do it because it's the right thing to do."

"I agree. But not in the spring. I don't care about my birthday. In the fall."

"We'll see," he growled.

This time her laugh was genuine and full of mirth. "You old grump," she said as she lay down and curled up against him. "Go to sleep. We'll talk in the morning."

CHAPTER 31

June 2, 1889—EDW Ranch—Monticello

Sunday, June 2nd, 1889

This entry is the first in my new journal. We are having a quiet Sabbath afternoon and this is a good time to begin. Oma Zimmer is resting after going to church this morning. Mitch is in a meeting with President Frederick Jones and some of the brethren to discuss implementing recommendations Pres. Hammond made for our branch.

A brief catch-up on my life since I wrote in my last journal a couple of years ago. On May 13th, I celebrated my 19th birthday. I came up to the Blue Mountains for the first time two years ago but came up to stay in April 1888. Most significantly, after working through some difficulties, Mitch asked me to marry him in early April of last year. Wisdom dictated that we wait a year, and we planned to marry on my birthday, May 13th, 1889. Due to a most unusual event involving an eclipse of the sun, we decided not to wait any longer, and I became Mrs. Mitchell Arthur Westland on January 8th of this year. The happiest day of my life.

By that time, Mitch had completed enough of our ranch house to allow us to move into it as husband and wife. As mentioned above, my grandmother, Renate Zimmer, is living with us. Mitch brought her over from Richfield last October. This has been a source of great joy to me. She has been a second mother to me since I was little and it is a delight to have her with us. She is tutoring me and Mitch in German. Her patriarchal blessing promised her that her posterity would take the gospel to her family back in the Fatherland, and she believes that our family will be the fulfillment of that promise.

Mitch is taking to the language more naturally than I, even though Oma has spoken German to me much of my life. I would be less than candid if I did not say how much that frustrates me.

One reason Aunt Jodie recommended that I keep a journal was to keep a record of things related to my health, though I decided to keep that separately so I can mail it to her from time to time. This is because I lost a baby in early April, when I was just a few months along. She hopes that by monitoring my health we can prevent that from happening again. (I cannot speak more of that here or I shall blot out the ink with my tears.)

So let me speak of stake conference. Though the seventy-five mile journey to Mancos was long and tedious and we had rain some of the way, we traveled as a group, including the families from Verdure. I spent much of the time with Evelyn Adams and her darling Nean and their new baby, Zola, which helped pass the time pleasantly for me.

Conference is always a joyous occasion. Mitch's family was there, of course, and it was determined that his brother, John, or Johnnie as we all call him, would return with us and work with Mitch on the ranch this summer. Which he did. I am delighted with that. There is so much to do, and even though he is only twelve, he is already proving to be a great help to Mitch. He is such a happy boy. He brightens up the whole town with his presence. Winnie and Louise Hyde are both deeply smitten. Johnnie, of course, is oblivious to that.

It was especially wonderful to see Alvin and Emma

Decker and their children again. We all had a good cry (of happy tears) as we were reunited again, if only for a short time. Emma says Alvin's decision to join the family business was a wise one, and she seems happy. There were so many other dear friends there. We had a wonderful three days of social activities, games for the children, and spiritual uplift, which I badly needed.

I had a chance to visit with Aunt Jodie. I am very happy to announce that I am with child again. This is very encouraging because it means I conceived not long after losing the first baby. We also think I conceived just a few days after Mitch and I were married, which means that conceiving is not the problem. I just have to be careful that I take care of myself and the baby. The other good news is that two of the women whose families are coming to join us in Monticello are midwives. Marion Bronson, wife of Wilmer Bronson, and Cedenia (Deena) Foy, second wife of William Foy, are both experienced midwives. That will be a blessing to us all.

However, I told Aunt Jodie that if it was all right, I would still like to work with her, since she knows my situation and I am so comfortable with her. She agreed without hesitation. She warned me again not to get discouraged or stressed out about this. I am determined to follow her counsel, difficult as that is.

Well, I can see Mitch coming up the road from town. And Johnnie just poked his head in wondering how soon we would be eating. He is in a growth spurt and has a voracious appetite. So I must stop for now. But it does feel so good to be writing again.

Monday, June 3rd

I shall continue where I left off yesterday. As I mentioned, conference was a spiritual feast and very uplifting for all there. There were two or three disturbing items, however. President Hammond said that he has received official word from SLC. The U.S. Senate has created a committee to study the question of whether San Juan County is to be made into a Ute Indian reservation. This announcement naturally creates much consternation among us, but President Hammond believes that it is a tempest in a teapot and nothing will come of it. The committee has asked that Utah send a representative to Washington to represent our cause, and SLC will be sending President Hammond. This is good, since he went around the county with the commission that was here last fall.

The week before we left for conference, while Mitch and Johnnie were in the high country checking on our cattle, we had more cowboy trouble. Drunk cowboys coming into town is not unusual for us, but this time they had brought sufficient liquor to share with several of the young Utes. Indians seem to have a low tolerance for whiskey, and soon all the men were very drunk. About ten of them came riding into town yelling and hollering and firing off their guns and bows and arrows. Women were screaming for their children and racing for cover. Several children were playing in the yard outside the meetinghouse and dove inside. Thankfully, no one was hurt, but it gave us all a great fright. The meetinghouse and several homes now have bullet holes in them. Part of our legacy, I suppose.

The cowboys far outnumber us, and so this is a constant source of trouble to us. It concerns President Hammond for another reason. He says that Monticello now has a reputation in both Utah and Colorado as being a "rough little cow town." This is causing some of those who were planning to move here to change their minds. That is not good. He recommended that we have at least ten men stay in town at all times to protect the women and children from these drunken escapades. This is a wonderful idea but is simply not practical. There are too many things that take the men away from town—logging, cattle, farming, mending fences, making freight runs to Thompson Springs or Mancos, etc. We are lucky to have one or two men with us at any one time. Mary Jones said that we will just have to depend on our faith in the Lord.

Friday, June 28th

In spite of the challenges of restricted water rights, blistering heat, drunken cowboys, Indians who help themselves to whatever they see that they want, our men being gone so much, and the sheer overall challenge of establishing a fertile oasis in this barren and desolate desert, our community continues to grow. All of the families who left for the winter have now returned, and we have new ones as well. We now have about fifteen families.

Monticello is a wonderful location for our settlement. The town is a constant beehive of activity. There is no school now, but come fall, school will be held in the meetinghouse because we have more than doubled the number of children. The men are putting in the windows and flooring now. Mons P. has brought in two pot-bellied stoves, one for each end, to keep the building warm in the winter. The men are also making rough desks. It will be a real school, and I will be helping Sarah R. again this fall.

The adult classes taught once or twice a week in the evenings by Brother William Adams continue, and Mitch and I attend them together, unless he is out on the range. I have especially enjoyed the mathematics class and have progressed enough that Mitch now lets me keep the ranch books for him. He is fascinated by astronomy and often has long talks with Brother Adams about it after class.

Life is very hard in some ways. But it is also good. I am happy. I love Mitch more each day. He is so good to me. I have dear sister friends all about me and rejoice in our association. Being with child again has made it much easier for me to follow Aunt Jodie's counsel not to worry too much.

Saturday, July 20th

Hoorah! Received a long letter from Mama in the mail today, which made me laugh and cry. I miss them so much. But things are good in Richfield. Papa and his brothers are finding great success in the freighting business and are prospering. It was good to catch up on all the news of the extended family. Being Mama, she asked about having babies without ever coming right out and saying the word. She obviously hadn't received my latest letter. A double hoorah. Mitch has confirmed that we are going to Manti as soon as the harvest is ended—toward the end of August—where we will be sealed for time and all eternity. This is a sacrifice in terms of things that need to be done, but he is adamant. And I am grateful. It will depend, of course, on how the baby is doing, but we won't go by wagon all the way, only to Thompson Springs, and then we'll go by train. Because I am doing so well now—I am past my third month without any problems—Aunt Jodie says she thinks I'll be okay by then, since I'll be approaching my fifth month.

Oh, one worrisome thing. Brother Walton received a Denver newspaper in the mail in the pouch. The headlines were about a gang of robbers who call themselves "The Wild Bunch." In March they robbed a bank in Denver and got twenty thousand dollars! Last month they hit a bank in Telluride and got another twenty thousand. Telluride is only about a hundred miles from here. They have killed people who tried to resist. They are led by a man that Mitch knows somewhat. His name is LeRoy Parker, and he's from Beaver, where the Westlands come from. However, he calls himself Butch Cassidy. Mitch tells me that I have no need to worry about them because we don't have a bank in Monticello, and no one here is rich enough to rob.

Sunday, August 11th

I am writing this while Oma and Mitch are in church, leaving me here to rest. I am now well into my fourth month. I am still feeling well, but I do tire more easily. Aunt Jodie says I am past the time when I am likely to miscarry, which was wonderful to hear. She wants to see me again before we leave for Manti but is still saying I can go if I am careful. I think she knows how strongly I feel about having our marriage be sealed for eternity.

Wednesday, August 14th

Am too exhausted to write much, even though I haven't done so for a while. Somehow every day is filled from dawn to dusk, especially now when I'm harvesting all of my vegetable garden. Mitch is gone right now helping with the grain harvest. John Rogerson's cutting machine and William Walton's thresher are both in constant demand, but most of the other men have to be out there to help get the grain bagged and hauled to storage sheds.

By now I should be used to Mitch being gone at night, but I miss him greatly, even when it's only for a night or two. How grateful I am that we have Oma living with us. She grows dearer to me with every passing day.

But here is some wonderful news. Mitch and Johnnie will be back Saturday night. By then, Mitch's parents should be here with Martha to accompany us on Monday when we leave for Thompson Springs. There we will go by train to Salt Lake and then on to Deseret, and then by wagon to Richfield. My family will be waiting, as will Mitch's extended family, who will come up from Beaver. We will then all travel together to Manti, where Mitch and I will be married for time and all eternity.

Thursday, August 29th

Great rejoicing! On this day, Mitch and I were sealed together in the Manti Temple. What a beautiful and sacred experience that was. The Manti Temple is stunning. It sits majestically on a hill overlooking the town of Manti and the vast valley around it. You can see it for miles. The grounds around it are breathtaking, with flowers and shrubbery everywhere. Inside, everything is of such exquisite workmanship. The temple matron—wife of the temple president—took me and Mitch in to see the twin spiral staircases, which are found in each tower. They were amazing. Mitch said that in all his life he has never seen such remarkable craftsmanship, proof that when we build a house to the Lord, nothing but the very best is acceptable.

I was so touched to think that God was allowing us to be married in His house. The celestial room was so beautiful and seemed to be a fitting representation of where we hope our marriage will someday take us. In a sealing room, which is right off of the celestial room, Mitch and I were sealed together. This is the happiest day of my life!

Monday, September 9th

Today we started school. What an exciting day. The children were almost as excited as Sarah and I were, despite how much they moan and groan about it to their parents. The meetinghouse is so much better than the little room in Sarah's cellar. It is light and roomy and each child has a desk. Sarah has asked me to teach them mathematics for an hour or two each day so she can spend time with baby George, and I taught my first class today. I do much of it while sitting down, but I can tell I am going to love it.

I am lonely as I write this. Mitch is out bringing in the cattle. Mitch's parents begged Oma Zimmer to come to Bluff and spend some time with them, so she is not here. They will bring her back home in time for Mitch to take our cows to market, but that will probably not be for another month. I miss her almost as much as I miss Mitch. Almost! Johnnie is gone too. He went back to Bluff with his parents so that he can start school down there. His sunny disposition is also missed.

I am now into my fifth month and have had to have Sarah R. sew panels in my dresses and skirts to accommodate the life within me. I have been feeling movement for some time now, which never ceases to amaze me. Last time I never got that far. Mitch is likewise thrilled when he feels it. It means so much to me that he is looking forward to this baby as much as I am. I have a little more than three months to go. My life is so blessed.

Tuesday, September 24th

I took a bad fall today and lost the baby, a perfectly formed little girl. For a time I was bleeding badly and feared for my own life, but I was spared. I have written the details in a letter to Aunt Jodie and cannot bear to write them again here.

Friday, October 4th

Mitch returned this afternoon with my parents. Physically I am all right, but emotionally I'm pretty fragile. Mitch should have taken our cows to the cattle sale in Thompson Springs two weeks ago, but he was delayed when several cows broke down a corral fence and got out. That proved to be a tender mercy from Heavenly Father, because he would have been gone when I lost the baby. As soon as he was sure I was all right, Mitch rode north to Thompson Springs with the cattle and then went by train over to Richfield to tell Mama and Papa what had happened. He left me with Oma and his parents, who had come to be with us as soon as they heard.

When Mitch arrived in Richfield, Mama and Papa immediately decided to return with him, bringing sufficient clothes to stay with us through Christmas. This is a wonderful thing for me, especially since Mitch is gone some nights with the fall roundup. The worst thing for me right now is to be alone with my sorrow.

I still find myself crying without any warning. But there are a few times in the day that I am able to put it from my mind. But time heals all things. At least, I keep telling myself that.

Sunday, November 3rd

Today was a good day. Before we left for church, Mitch took me aside and told me that both of our families and all of the branch had fasted for me. This was my first time going back to church, so he and Papa and Arthur and President Jones gave me a blessing afterwards. Dear Mitch, my rock and my strength through all of this. He tries to blame himself for what happened, but I have accepted that it was no one's fault.

Mitch was voice in the blessing, and it was sweet and deeply touching to me. As he spoke, a great sense of peace came over me. He told me later that he blessed me to have a child and carry it to full term at some point in the future, but I guess I was crying too hard to remember.

I received a long letter yesterday from Aunt Jodie. She chastised me for still staying in bed during part of the day. She says it is imperative that I fill my days with activities that keep me occupied and focused on positive things. I know she is right, but that is not as easy to do as it sounds. Mama brought several books with her, and we read together with Oma often. That is good, but Mitch is gone most days preparing for winter, and each day seems like an eternity.

CHAPTER 32

November 10, 1889, 9:15 p.m.—EDW Ranch—Monticello

Sunday, November 10th

A wonderful thing happened this week. I decided to take Aunt Jodie's counsel and stop feeling sorry for myself. I determined to try to find things to occupy my mind and cheer me up, but what is there to do in a small town like this, especially with winter coming on? At least, that's what I kept asking myself, so the Lord decided to chastise me a little too.

This morning, Mitch was leaving quite early to go with some of the brethren to the sawmill for some more lumber. Though he told me to sleep in, I got up early to fix his breakfast and tell him good-bye. When he left, the house was still quiet, so instead of going back to bed, I got out the Book of Mormon (with all that has happened, I have neglected my reading of late). However, I found myself distracted and feeling blue once again. How was I going to endure a long winter, especially when my folks return home after Christmas? Oma and mother have started to teach me to knit, which is good, but I can only do that for about an hour, and then I'm ready to hurl the needles at the wall and scream at someone.

So I was reading along, only half concentrating, once again feeling sorry for myself, wondering how I could ever do what Aunt Jodie wants me to do. It was then that I came across this passage in the Book of Alma. It is Alma talking to his son Helaman.

"Behold I say unto you, that by small and simple things are great things brought to pass; and small means in many instances doth confound the wise. And the Lord God doth work by means to bring about his great and eternal purposes; and by very small means the Lord doth confound the wise and bringeth about the salvation of many souls."

That hit me with great force. Was that my problem? Was I expecting some grand and glorious thing to come into my life to bring me out of this black cloud I'm under? Have I just been sitting back, waiting for the Lord to plop something into my lap to make it all better? I knew the answer to both of those questions was yes. Well, I read on, still only half concentrating, and a few verses later I came to this passage:

"Cry unto God for all thy support; yea, let all thy doings be unto the Lord, and whithersoever thou goest let it be in the Lord."

That last part hit me hard. "Withersoever thou goest let it be in the Lord"? Even if where I went was into the valley of the shadow of death? Even if I lost two children on that journey? I realized that I had cried unto God again and again in these last months, but it was not to ask Him to help me accept His will for me. It was to beg Him to let my will take precedence—to let my desperate desires for a child be granted. I'm not saying that was wrong; it was just that I realized that Alma was telling his son that something more was required. That wherever life takes us, we must try to keep the Lord with us.

As that realization hit me, I closed the book and got down on my knees and poured out my heart to the Lord. I asked for His forgiveness. I asked Him to help me trust in Him, knowing that all that He does for me is for my benefit, my growth, and yes, even my happiness. I remembered how calmly Eliza Peterson accepted God's will that she be taken home, leaving her two precious children behind. She understood that principle, and I did not.

I can't remember which prophet talked about watering his pillow with his tears as he prayed to the Lord, but that's what happened to me this morning. I literally soaked a little spot on the sofa with tears of shame. Finally, when there were no more tears left, I asked the Lord if He perhaps could spare one "small and simple thing" to help me get past this very difficult time in my life. When I finished and got to my feet, I got out the knitting needles and set to work until Oma and Mama and Papa woke up.

Somewhere around ten o'clock this morning, to our great surprise, Nephi and Annie Bailey came to visit us. They are recent newcomers to our town, having come this last summer. Annie is a sister of Mary Jones. We quickly learned what a remarkable addition they are to our town. Nephi is English, having been born in Lancashire. Annie is Danish and is one of those in what Oma is now calling their "German Group." She is quite remarkable.

They have six children, and their seventh is due in January. Their oldest is fifteen, so Annie's had a baby about every two years. She has been helping Nephi build their cabin as well as working on the farm alongside him. She makes her own butter and cheese from their two milk cows. To amplify their income, she bought a knitting machine before coming, and the leggings and stockings she makes with it are in high demand by both our people and the Utes now that winter is almost upon us. She also has a handloom on which she weaves rag rugs and carpets.

Nephi is no less remarkable. As a boy in England he served an apprenticeship in a leather shop, and so, in addition to farming, he has a small boot shop in their cabin and makes very good cowboy boots. I bought Mitch a pair this fall. He is also a very talented musician. He played in a brass band before coming here and brought several musical instruments with him, including the first piano in our little village. What a wonderful thing this has been. He is teaching others to play various instruments, and often on Sunday evenings the older youth crowd into the Bailey home and stand around the piano and sing songs together. He has dozens of them memorized or can play them by ear.

Anyway, they are a wonderful couple and a great addition to our town, but having them come to the house was a great surprise. Why they came was an even bigger shock. Brother Bailey wants to start a branch choir, and President Jones wants it to perform at the Christmas program on the Sunday before Christmas. And guess what he wants us to sing? Two songs from George Frideric Handel's *Messiah*. Along with all of his musical instruments, Nephi brought with him about a dozen copies of the full score of the *Messiah*. We will only sing two songs—"For unto Us a Child Is Born" and, of course, "The Hallelujah Chorus." He's talking about performing more than half of the oratorio next year, when we have more time.

Nephi said that he had heard that I played the piano and asked if I might be their accompanist. It saddened me greatly to say no. I told him that I took piano lessons from my mother when I was growing up, but when we came to Bluff in 1884, Papa sold our piano. I haven't played it since. His face fell until I happily told him that Mama was a wonderful pianist and planned to stay through Christmas. And the problem was solved. Mama was delighted. Brother Bailey left her a copy of the score and invited her to come tomorrow or anytime to their home to start practicing.

All of this is just to explain what happened next. I had asked the Lord for some small and simple thing to help me, and then I got up and started knitting. And I decided that Oma's idea to teach me how to knit was the Lord's "small and simple" thing He had given me to do. Oh, how shortsighted we mortals are.

As I write, it is now past nine o'clock. Mitch is not home yet, so I am waiting up for him to share all of this with him. Mama and Papa have gone to bed, although I can still hear them talking. I think Oma is asleep. So while I have been waiting, I decided to look at the score to get a feeling for the music. And then it happened. I was looking at "For unto Us." I know the music somewhat, so I was softly singing along with it as I went through it. Suddenly, it was if the words were printed on the page in glowing fire.

For unto us a Child is born.
Unto us, a Son is given.
And the government shall be upon His shoulder;
And His name shall be called
Wonderful! Counsellor! The Mighty God,
The Everlasting Father
The Prince of Peace.

And suddenly there came into my heart this thought—and it came with great power. "Yes, my beloved daughter, you have two lost children now. But remember, My Child is not lost. My Child came to make all thing right. My Child came with healing in His wings. And My Child says unto you, 'Come unto me, all ye . . . heavy laden, and I will give you rest.'"

I was so overcome that I dropped to my knees and wept. Once again the sofa was wet with my tears, but this time they were tears of hope, tears of joy. And it was then that I realized that the small and simple thing the Lord had chosen to send me was not knitting needles. It was Nephi Bailey with the copy of the musical score of the *Messiah*.

December 22, 1889, 10:43 a.m.

When the choir came forward and occupied the stage behind the pulpit, it pretty well emptied the hall. There were a few adults who said their contribution to the choir was to *not* sing, and the rest of the audience was mostly young children. Brother Bailey had invited anyone ten or older to join the choir, and most had.

Edie turned and exchanged a quick look with Mitch as Nephi raised his baton, smiled at his choir, and opened his mouth wide, reminding them of his constant charge to them: "When you sing to the Lord, open your mouths so He can hear you." Then he gave four quick beats with the baton, and Edie's mother began to play.

For unto us a Child is born.

Instantly, Edie was transported back to that evening when the Lord had spoken to her through these inspired words of Isaiah and the feeling of joy and elation that had come to her then.

Unto us, a Son is given.

When Mitch had arrived home not long after Edie's experience that night, her cheeks were still wet. When she told him what had happened and asked him if he would sing in the choir with her, he had given her a long look and then said yes, even though he had always maintained that he couldn't sing and couldn't read music. Now he was four people to her left, sharing music with Mons Peterson and Ed Hyde, and she could pick out his clear tenor voice. Though still somewhat hesitant, it was remarkably sweet. What was more, she could see that he loved it almost as much as she did.

When they finished, they stood in place. President William Adams, the senior member of the extended Adams family and counselor in the San Juan Stake presidency, came to the pulpit. The Bible was already opened to the book of Luke, chapter 2. He stopped for a moment, clearly moved by the choir's singing, and then began to read slowly and distinctly in his rich Irish brogue:

"'And it came to pass in those days, that there went out a decree from Caesar Augustus, that all the world should be taxed. And all went to be taxed, every one into his own city. And Joseph also went up from Galilee, out of the city of Nazareth, into Judaea, unto the city of David, which is called Bethlehem; (because he was of the house and lineage of David:) To be taxed with Mary his espoused wife, being great with child.'"

Edie had steeled herself against those last four words, knowing they were coming. Had she not lost the baby, she too would be great with child right now. She and Mitch and Oma and her parents had read the second chapter of Luke together before leaving for Church this morning, at her request, specifically to help her get through that passage. And though a lump was suddenly constricting her throat, she managed to keep control as she followed along with Brother Adams in her mind.

When President Adams finished reading and sat down again, Brother Bailey stepped forward. Up came the baton. Caroline Zimmer's fingers poised over the keys. And a moment later they burst out, full throat, with that magnificent song of praise and adoration.

Hallelujah! Hallelujah!

Edie's head came up and she sang joyously, not needing to look at the words or the music. Which was good, because tears were streaming down her cheeks now and all she could see was a blur. She made no attempt to stop them or to wipe them away. Nor did any of the many others who were weeping along with her. It was part of their way of praising God in that Christmas season.

And Edna Rae Zimmer Westland felt a great desire to praise God on this day.

Notes

The passage Edie wrote in her journal is Alma 37:6–7, 36.

It is not clear exactly when Nephi and Annie Mackleprang Bailey came to Monticello. One source says not until 1894, but that almost certainly is too late. There is some evidence it was in 1889 or 1890. The personal information about this talented couple comes from the history of Monticello (see *Saga*, 117–18, 298). That source states: "Mr. Bailey found time, along with his choir duties, to organize a brass band and a mandolin and a guitar club. Soon most of the men were 'blowing a horn,' or beating a drum while the young folks strummed the strings" (Ibid.). During the winter, George Adams often made the six-mile trek up from Verdure on snowshoes so that he could sing with them.

The Baileys did bring the first piano to Monticello, though it is likely that was a little later than shown here.

CHAPTER 33

June 4, 1890, 4:45 p.m.—EDW Ranch—Monticello

"Hey, Edie?"

"What?"

"*Kommen Sie hier, bitte.*"

There was no answer, but then a moment later Edie appeared at the door of their bedroom. She had a towel in her hand and was rubbing at her wet hair. "What did you say?"

"I want you to come see something."

Oma Zimmer shook her head. "Mitch, if that was supposed to be, 'Come here, please,' in Deutsch, you'd better try that accent again."

Edie looked puzzled. "I was rinsing out my hair in the wash basin and didn't hear what you said." Then she looked at her grandmother. "Wait! Did you just correct your grandson-in-law's German? Your perfect grandson-in-law? Whom you've been teaching for over a year now?"

"Never mind," Mitch cut in quickly. "Come over here, there's something I want to read to you." He had a small piece of paper and waved it at her.

Edie went over and sat down beside him at the table. "What's this?"

"Mother sent it in her letter that just came today. It's a clipping from a recent *Deseret News* edition. It's a summary of an interview President Hammond had with the paper concerning what's happening with the Ute Indian reservation question. When Mama saw it, she knew it would be of interest to us."

Edie frowned. "Good or bad?"

Mitch's frown deepened. "Let me read it to you."

As he lifted the paper, Oma got up and came over. "Vhich means dat it is bad news," she said to Edie as she sat down beside her.

Mitch began. "'President Francis A. Hammond of San Juan Stake said that he particularly desired to be understood in the matter of the Ute Indian reservation proposed for San Juan County. He said that contrary to rumors circulating both in Salt Lake and in Washington, the people of San Juan never wanted to give up their land at all, but—'"

Edie jerked forward. "What? Who ever said that we wanted to give up our land?"

"Not sure," he answered, "but I think it was when that commission that was here last fall asked us if we would be willing to accept one half of what our land was worth if the government did decide to move in the Indians."

"But dis is not the same as saying vee want to move."

"Exactly, and I think that's why President Hammond is stressing that point." Mitch started to read again. "'But as the government had expressed a wish to have it pass into the hands of the Indians, the settlers did not want to place any obstacle in the way of the transfer. Seeing that they had no title, they were willing—'"

"Vhat is title?"

"It means we have no deed for the land we own. That's because we didn't buy it from someone when we came here. Nor was it surveyed by the government. We came in and did our own survey and assigned property accordingly."

"*Ja, ja*. I understand. *Danke*."

Mitch started again. "'Seeing that they had no title, they were willing to yield up to the government on receiving proper compensation. But it must be made clear. The settlers have no wish whatsoever to vacate the land. I made that position clear to the Senate and House committee when I was in Washington. But I emphasized to them that the government should act promptly in this matter one way or another and relieve the settlers of San Juan from the suspense in which they have so long been kept.'"

"He can say that again," Edie groused. "This has been dragging on now for over a year, leaving us wondering if all that we have worked for is for naught."

"Amen," Mitch said. "And I like what he says next particularly. 'If the land is not required for the Indians, then let the Secretary of the Interior reopen it for use and survey it so that we receive titles for it. Like us, the Ute Indians cannot understand the slothful way in which the government is acting in this matter.'"

Grandma Zimmer clapped her hands. "*Das ist sehr gut, ja?*"

"Yes, very good," Mitch agreed. "All the government is doing is mucking things up." He laid the paper on the table. Edie picked it up and glanced at. After a moment she leaned forward. "Wait. You skipped his last statement."

"Oh, yeah. Read it. This is prophetic, in my opinion."

She did so with great solemnity. "'The settlers of San Juan fully expect that unless speedy action is taken, much trouble will arise with the Indians.' Boy! He can say that again. We've already had Indians coming into town telling us this will all soon be theirs." Edie sat back, a sense of grey despair settling on her. "One day it's the Indians. The next day it's the cowboys. No wonder people don't want to come out here and join us."

"Vell, if you ask me," Oma said tartly, "if I have to choose, then I choose the Indians."

Notes

In June 1890, President Hammond, who had gone to Washington to testify before the Congressional subcommittee, did give an interview with the *Deseret News* about the situation with the Ute Indian reservation. I made a few slight modifications in the text to make it flow more smoothly, but the words are almost all President Hammond's (see *Saga*, 214–5).

CHAPTER 34

June 6, 1890, 6:08 p.m.—EDW Ranch—Monticello

Edie, Mitch, Oma Zimmer, and Johnnie Westland were seated in the living room of the Westland ranch house. They had finished supper and cleaned up the dishes and were now having a relaxing moment together. Oma was in the rocking chair talking quietly with Edie, who sat beside her. Mitch and Johnnie had their heads together, deciding whether they needed to get their boots, coats, and rain slickers on before they went out and checked on the first of the cows they had brought in on the spring roundup and that were now out in the corrals.

Outside, the vicious spring storm that had thundered in earlier in the day had lightened, but it was still coming down steadily. And the temperature was cold enough that the rain was now half sleet. After a hot supper and relaxing for a few minutes by a toasty fire, the thought of going out again didn't have much appeal to either of them, but there were several calves out there. If the storm continued all night, some of the younger ones might be at risk.

With a weary sigh, Mitch got to his feet. Seeing that, Johnnie stirred as well, but Mitch pushed him down again. "No sense in two of us getting chilled to the bone. If I need you, I'll call you."

"Are you sure?" Johnnie asked guiltily, clearly wanting to be told to stay where he was.

"Yeah, I'm sure. It shouldn't take that long. Keep the fire warm for me."

Edie got up and came to him. "I'll have some hot chocolate for you when you come back in." Mitch kissed her on the cheek. "That would be nice."

A few minutes later they heard the door open and shut. Johnnie got up and went to the window, watching as Mitch darted across the yard toward the corral and the barns. To Johnnie's surprise, his brother suddenly slid to a halt, lifted one hand to shield his face from the blowing sleet, and peered out toward the main road. Johnnie turned his head, looking to see what it was that had attracted Mitch's attention, because now he had changed directions and was moving out toward the lane.

Johnnie went quickly to the front door and stepped out onto the front porch. He cupped his hand. "What is it, Mitch?"

Mitch turned for a moment and pointed out toward the main road. "Got a rider coming down from the mountains," he called back. "Gonna check to make sure he's not in trouble."

Johnnie turned as Edie came onto the porch to join him, shutting the door behind her. "What did he say?" she asked. The wind was not howling as it had been earlier in the afternoon, but it was still blowing hard enough that it was whistling around the eaves and making it hard to hear.

"Someone's coming." Johnnie pointed. He could make out a dark shape on horseback out near where their land joined the road. "Probably Wilmer Bronson, I'm guessing. Mitch and I saw him go by just before the storm hit. One of his horses got loose and was last seen headed for the mountains."

Edie had her hand up, shielding her eyes from the wind. "Well, he must not have found it, because there's only one horse." She cupped her hands to her mouth and called out, "Mitch, bring Wilmer in to get warm for a few minutes."

But Mitch was already walking down the lane and didn't hear her. Edie opened the door and called inside. "It's all right, Oma. We've got a rider passing by. We'll come back inside in a minute." Then she shut the door again.

By this time, Mitch and the rider had met where the lane met the road. The man on the horse turned and pointed back toward the mountain. Mitch beckoned toward the house, and a moment later, the horse and rider were following Mitch as he started at a trot back for the house.

When they were about thirty yards away, Johnnie said, "Yup, that's Wilmer all right." Then his head jerked forward. "Whoa! There's somebody else on the horse with him."

"I don't think so," Edie said, stepping up beside him. But she could see now what Johnnie had seen. There was something on the saddle in front of him. Like a sack of grain or something.

Johnnie yelped in surprise. "Look, it's a child!"

Edie's hands flew to her mouth and she gave a low cry as she fell back a step. It was a child. A little girl, maybe three or four years old. An *Indian* girl. Edie could see now that she was wearing a simple buckskin dress and no shoes. Two braids of hair fell down the front of the dress. In an instant, Edie was off the porch, darting through the sleet and the muck toward Mitch and Wilmer. Seeing her coming, Wilmer pulled his horse to a stop. One hand came up with a jerk. "No, Sister Edie. Stay back. She's very frightened right now."

Mitch came over and took Edie's arm, speaking softly. "She's terrified. Almost jumped off the horse when I approached."

"But where did she come from?"

"Let's get her inside. Then Wilmer can tell us what's going on."

6:35 p.m.

Terrified was barely an adequate word for the emotional state the child was in when they brought her into the house. Her head jerked back and forth wildly as she looked at her captors. Her entire body was as tense as a steel rod, and she looked as though she were poised to break and run like a frightened fawn. Her eyes were wide, the black pupils dilated—both signs of panic—and her whole body trembled violently. How much of that was from fear and how much from being soaking wet and very cold, Edie couldn't decide.

To the surprise of all of them, it was Oma that she best responded to. Once they got her sitting in a chair with a blanket wrapped around her, Oma waved the others back and stepped in closer. The girl shrunk back, but Oma began talking to her in German, her voice low and soothing. Perhaps it was her white hair. Perhaps Oma reminded her of a grandmother whom she trusted. Perhaps it was because she wasn't speaking English. Whatever it was, within five minutes, Oma had persuaded the child to take a sip of hot chocolate, accept a sugar cookie, and let Oma sit down beside her and stroke her hair.

With that, Wilmer motioned to the others and they moved across the room to the far corner.

"So what's the story?" Mitch asked. "Where did you find her?"

"About two miles up the canyon. I had left the road looking for my horse. By that time it had started to rain and I couldn't track him anymore, so I was moving very slowly, listening for any sounds, hoping that if the lost horse heard or smelled my horse he might whinny. Suddenly, my horse was startled by something right in front of us and shied to one side, nearly knocking me off the saddle. At first I thought it might be a bear or a mountain lion and grabbed for my rifle, but imagine my shock when I looked more closely and I saw that it was this little papoose coming out from beneath a bush."

"Was she crying?" Edie asked softly.

"No. She'd not made a sound. I'm assuming she's Ute. I know a few Ute words and tried them on her, but she was far too frightened to respond. Seeing my rifle may have been part of that. She did finally let me put my arms around her to keep her warm."

Oma came over to join them, and they all turned to look at the girl. She had her back to them and was solemnly munching on another cookie. "I think she is finally getting warm," she said. "And she is not so frightened anymore."

"That's wonderful, Sister Zimmer," Wilmer said. "Thank you."

"So what are you going to do with her?" Mitch asked.

"Good question. I've asked myself that for the last two hours."

"We'll take her," Edie said eagerly. "If she's comfortable with Oma, we can let her sleep in with her."

Wilmer exchanged looks with Mitch and then nodded. "I think it is a good thing to not take her any farther tonight. But—" Again he looked to Mitch, obviously looking for help.

Mitch thought he understood why. "I agree. We'll keep her tonight." He turned and searched Edie's face. She was still looking at the girl, and there was so much longing in her eyes that he hesitated to say what needed to be said. So he began very slowly. "We're going to have to talk about what we do with her, Edie. There are some serious implications we have to consider."

She jerked around. "Like what?"

"This is someone's child. If she wandered away, then her parents will be looking for her."

"And then we'll give her back," Edie said tersely. "But what if she was abandoned? Did you see her dress? It's in tatters. She's been neglected. Maybe her parents are dead. You can see there's a haunted look in her eyes."

"I wondered that too," Wilmer reluctantly admitted.

"And if she is, then what?" Edie asked Mitch. Her eyes were pleading with him, but her voice was tight.

Mitch took her hand. "I think that has to be decided in counsel. The last thing we need right now is to offend the Utes in some way and have them turn against us."

She searched his eyes for a long time. "All right," she finally said. "But I want to put our name forth as one who would like to take her in and care for her if no one comes to claim her." Her chin lifted. "Do you object to that, Mitch?"

"Not at all. I would love that too. But this could affect our whole community, so it's got to be a community decision." He looked at Wilmer. "Why don't you stop by President Jones's house and tell him what's happened? See if he wants to call a meeting of families together. We'll bring her down tomorrow at nine."

June 7, 1890, 9:23 a.m.—Frederick Jones Home

Edie gripped Mitch's hand so tightly when President Jones and his two counselors came back out into the main room that her knuckles were white. He squeezed back and moved in until their shoulders were touching. Immediately the room quieted. It was nearly full, but it had surprised Mitch how many families didn't seemed overly concerned about the effect that keeping the foundling might have on their town. They had already told him that whatever the presidency decided was fine with them, but several had volunteered to take her in.

Little Bird was not here, of course. A setting like this would have traumatized her. Little Bird was what Edie and Oma had started calling her after she fell asleep in Oma's bed. She was a timid, fragile creature on the verge of flight when anyone approached. Oma suggested it, and Edie agreed instantly. At the moment, the girl was over at the home of Ed and Emma Hyde, where Oma was with her. She was being helped by the Hydes' two oldest daughters, Winnie and Lou. President Jones had come out to meet Mitch and Edie as they brought Little Bird into town and suggested taking her to the Hydes, thinking that two younger girls would be less threatening to her.

"Brethren and sisters," he began. "Thank you for coming. We all know the issue at hand, and we have given you a chance to express yourselves on what we believe is a very delicate situation. Thank you for your insights and your wisdom. As a presidency, we feel that we have more than one issue that needs to be considered. First, and most important, are the needs of this little girl who has come into our midst. She is frightened. She is lonely. She does not speak our language. And we do not know what circumstance—tragic or terrible—may have led to her coming here. But that must be our first concern."

"Yes," Edie said under her breath.

"The second issue is that since this girl is not one of our own, but a child of our Native American brothers and sisters, how we treat her and what we do with her could have enormous implications—or complications—for our community. As I think most of you know, the Indian people who live around us have great concern for their families. They care for their children with great affection and tenderness. Typically, if both parents of a child are lost, then the extended family takes the child in as one of their own."

Edie was staring at the ground now.

"So we must be very careful that we don't appear to be taking this child as one of our own unless we are sure that no one will claim her and care for her. I need not remind you of the negotiations going on in Washington right now about San Juan County. It would not help our cause if the Indians reported to Washington that the Mormons are stealing their children, even when there is no truth to that accusation."

President Jones was frowning deeply as he considered what to say next. "As a presidency, we discussed the idea of sending word out to the various Ute camps that we have one of their lost children—"

Edie's grip on Mitch's hand tightened. She shook her head vigorously. "No," she whispered to Mitch.

"But we feel that course of action is not without its own complications, and therefore feel to do all we can to care for the girl here and see what develops."

Mitch heard the breath go out of Edie as relief flooded over her.

"If the parents or family of this girl come forth and claim her, then we must give her up without hesitation. But if a year goes by and no claim is made, then we feel that one of our families can legally adopt her as their own. If there is more than one family who wishes to do so, which I'm sure there are, then we shall have to work that out at that time."

Edie looked up at Mitch, and her eyes were shining with tears. This was less than she had hoped for, but more than she had expected. "Can we be one of those who applies?" she murmured.

"Of course."

"But the question we have before us today is where to place this young girl in the meantime. Several have volunteered their homes, but obviously we can choose only one."

A murmur started through the group, so President Jones quickly raised his hand and it quieted again. To Mitch's surprise, Edie went up on tiptoe and whispered in his ear. "Thank you for putting our name forth."

"How did you know that?"

She just smiled. Then what she said next almost knocked him off his feet. "But we won't be chosen, and that's all right."

"But . . . how do you know?"

President Jones continued, cutting him off. "Our recommendation is that this young girl, whose name we do not know, will—"

Edie's hand shot up. Surprised, he nodded in her direction. "Yes, Edie?"

"My grandmother and I call her Little Bird." She shrugged. "Not that it matters, but we decided we couldn't keep calling her 'that girl' or 'the Indian girl.'"

He smiled. "I like it. Thank you. Until we learn her real name, she shall be called Little Bird." There were nods and murmurs of approval all around.

"So, our recommendation for Little Bird is that she immediately move into the home of Brother Ed and Sister Emma Hyde and be cared for by their family."

He stopped and let the reaction sweep through the room. It was one of approval. Then he spoke loudly and firmly. "Several good homes were considered, but as you know, with the exception of William Jr., the Hydes have a household of girls, including Angeline, who is three and about the same age as Little Bird. We hope this will prove to be very therapeutic for this child who has been through so much."

Mitch looked down. "Good choice, don't you agree?"

"Very much so. Wholeheartedly."

Mitch gave Edie a strange look and started to ask what was going on with her, but President Jones was not finished. "In addition, we as a presidency feel to make a special assignment. We would ask that Sister Rena Zimmer, who is with Little Bird as we speak and who has already established an unusual bond of trust with her, be assigned to spend as much time with the Indian girl as possible to help her adjust to her new home." He rushed on as the pleased reaction erupted. "And we are asking Sister Edie Westland to join with her grandmother in that assignment."

Mitch swung around. "That's wonderful, Edie," he cried.

"Yes," she said with a smug look. "I told him that too."

He rocked back. "Told who that?"

"This morning, while you were getting Oma and Little Bird settled at the Hydes', Brother Rogerson called me aside. He said he was speaking as a counselor in the branch presidency and by assignment from President Jones."

"Go on."

"Well, first he told me that you had turned in our name as caregivers, but the presidency was going to reject it. That was a blow to me, but he quickly went on and explained why."

"And what did he say?"

He said it had nothing to do with our not being capable. And in fact, the way Oma has bonded with Little Bird, they were strongly tempted to place her with us. But we live a quarter of a mile out of town and our homestead is completely isolated in terms of other houses being close by. They felt that if the Indians do cause problems, we were too vulnerable."

Mitch was slowly nodding. A wise insight.

"And then he told me what they had in mind for me and Oma, and I was at peace."

"That's wonderful." His own voice was suddenly husky. "As I have watched you with Little Bird, I've seen again what a remarkable gift you have with children. I'm glad others see it too."

"Well, the Lord hasn't seen fit to give us children of our own, so—"

"Yet," he cut in. "Children of our own *yet*."

Edie pulled him away from the milling crowd, who were all talking excitedly now. "Mitch, it's been almost a year and a half since we were married, and seven months since I lost the baby." She put a finger to his lips when he started to protest. "I'm not going to argue this with you. I'm just saying that I see this thing with Little Bird as the Lord's way of answering my prayers. At least for now. So I am content." She removed her finger. "Now, take me over to the Hydes'. I want to see how Little Bird is doing."

Notes

Though no year is given in the sources, they do specify that it was a stormy day in spring when Wilmer Bronson was out looking for a lost horse and stumbled across an unnamed Indian child who appeared to have been abandoned. The account says only that the girl was left with the Hydes with no explanation as to how or why their family was chosen. The idea that a community meeting was held to determine where she should be placed and that the Hydes were chosen because they had a houseful of girls (which they did) is mine. There are hints that the settlers knew this might turn into an explosive situation, and so it seemed logical that they would make it a community decision rather than have it be Wilmer Bronson's choice alone (see *Saga*, 223; *Anchored*, 107).

CHAPTER 35

July 16, 1890, 11:05 a.m.—Edward Hyde Home—Monticello

Edie Westland looked around the small circle of women and felt a warm glow of affection fill her soul. Here were her closest friends and sisters in the gospel. In many ways they were like the real sisters she had never had. They had wept with her over the loss of her two babies, rejoiced with her when she was married, and sent their children to her to be taught at Sister Rogerson's school. She had cooked with them, quilted with them, nursed sick children with them, done laundry with them, tanned hides with them, and planted flowers and vegetables with them. How rich was her life because of them.

At the moment, she was sitting in the shade of the Hyde cabin with several of them, talking quietly as their children played a short distance away. Emma Hyde had learned that the four families from Verdure were coming up with their husbands to deliver three wagonloads of lumber from the Butt brothers' sawmill. This was an exciting day for the Blue Mountain Mission because now the people could start building homes, stores, and other buildings that required more than pine and aspen logs as their walls. It also meant that the sod roofs that covered all but two or three of the cabins could be replaced with shingles that protected from the rain. That was cause for a celebration indeed, and so this evening, when the lumber was unloaded, there would be a potluck supper followed by square dancing in the street outside the log meetinghouse.

When Emma Hyde realized that all but one of the eight Verdure children were girls and that all of them were under eight years old, close to the age of her Angeline and Little Bird, she had invited them all over for lunch and playtime. This was an opportunity to expand Little Bird's social circle without it being threatening to her. Since Edie and Oma spent some part of almost every day at the Hyde home to be with Little Bird, they were invited too.

Now, as the women talked quietly in the shade, Edie watched those little girls with fascination. They were seated on the ground playing some kind of game together that seemed to have been made up by Nean Adams and quickly embraced by all the others. As always, Edie paid the most attention to Little Bird. She no longer wore buckskin—Emma had burned the ragged dress that she was wearing when they found her. Now she wore one of Angeline's dresses and looked every bit like the rest of them except for her golden brown skin and the long, braided black hair.

Little Bird was fully participating in the game at the moment, but her face was as stoic and inscrutable as ever. Her eyes moved back and forth between the girls as they spoke, but there was no expression of happiness, humor, sadness, loneliness, anxiety, anger, or any other emotion. It was as though her face were carved from stone.

Seeing that Emma was watching the little girl as well, Edie asked, "Have you ever seen her smile?"

"Not with her face," Emma said, her look softening as she looked at Little Bird. "But just this last week I've started to see a touch of a smile in her eyes." She blinked quickly to stop the tears. "And it fills me with such joy. I believe that she is actually starting to be happy here."

"Thanks to Angeline," Jane Walton said. "She is so patient with her."

Emma laughed. "I'm not sure that it's patience. With six older brothers and sisters always bossing her around, I think Angeline is delighted to have someone who does whatever she asks of her without question, who doesn't tell her what to do, who never disagrees with her, and who follows her around like a puppy dog."

Evelyn chortled. "Oh, my Nean would love that too. She's the one who's always bossing people around, including me and George."

"How do they communicate?" Julia Butt asked. "As far as you know, Little Bird doesn't speak any English, does she?"

"I don't think so," Emma replied. "But somehow they manage to make each other understand what they want. I've watched her and Angeline chatter away at each other, one in English, one in Ute, as if both of them perfectly understood the other."

Jane Walton was nodding. "It was a miracle that Wilmer found her. In that whole vastness of the mountains, he almost stumbled right over the top of her. That's remarkable."

"A miracle for her and a blessing for us," Emma agreed.

Ency leaned in. "Speaking of miracles, we had one of our own the other day."

Everyone perked up at that. "Vhat kind of a miracle?" Oma asked.

"Yes, tell us," Edie said.

"Well, with the sawmill up and running, one of the first things Parley wanted to do was get a roof on our cabin—cover up the old sod roof with a shingled one."

"There are a lot of us planning to do that," Emma said.

"So, the first thing he did was cut a bunch of two-by-fours and build a framework over the existing roof. But then, he and Willard decided they had to fill all of the orders they were getting from all of you up here. So that's as far as he got.

"Well," she went on, "about a week ago, Julia and Evelyn and I had gotten together at our house to work on a quilt we're making for Parley's mother. We, of course, had all of our kids with us. It was a nice day, so we were inside and the kids were outside making mud pies near the creek. About two o'clock, I looked out to check on the children and noticed that a small breeze had sprung up. It wasn't much, so I forgot about it, but about ten minutes later one of my shutters started banging back and forth. When we looked up, the breeze had turned into a brisk little windstorm. I checked the sky to see if there was a storm coming, but there was nothing."

She looked at her sister-in-law. "Julia, tell them what happened next."

Julia Butt was a quiet woman, often content to sit and listen to conversations rather than participate in them. Willard was four years older than Parley, and Julia was two years older than Ency, but she and Willard had married later and to this point they had been blessed with only one child. She smiled briefly and began. "It wasn't a terrible wind, but you know how fast the wind can change up here, so we decided to bring the kids inside."

"Nean was already wet and muddy from the mud pies," Evelyn broke in, "so I didn't want her out in a dust storm. We brought them inside, stripped off their wet outer clothes, and let them play in the bedroom."

"To our surprise," Ency said, picking up the story from them, "in the next few minutes, the wind got worse and worse.

Surprised that it had come up so fast, I went to the window and looked out to the north. What I saw turned my blood cold."

"What?" several of the women exclaimed.

"There was a huge dust devil bearing down on us."

"It was more than a dust devil," Julia said quietly.

"It was a small tornado, a real cyclone," Evelyn agreed. "It must have been two hundred feet high, and it was coming straight at us."

"It was really scary," Ency said. "We could see all kinds of stuff going round and round up in it—tree branches, full sage-brush bushes, trash, sticks. We hurried and brought all the children into the main room in case the windows blew in. When it came over the house, it sounded like a train going right by us. The kids were hollering and screaming." She smiled a thin smile. "And so were we. Then suddenly there was this huge crash. The whole house shook."

"I thought the house was caving in," Evelyn said.

"What was it?" Edie asked.

"We looked out to see," Julia answered, "but there was so much dust by that time, we couldn't see five feet away from us."

Ency went on. "When it finally blew over and the dust cleared, Julia and I went out on the porch to see what had happened." Her voice suddenly caught, and she looked at Julia and nodded for her to finish.

"I couldn't believe my eyes. There was a whole pile of smashed two-by-fours in the front yard, all twisted and broken. It looked like some giant had been playing jackstraws."

Jane's eyes had grown very big. "It was the framework for the roof?"

"Yes," Julia exclaimed. "The wind had ripped the whole thing loose and then picked it up like it was made of straw and dumped it right in the middle of Ency's yard."

"Wow!" Edie breathed, trying to picture what force that must have taken.

Ency looked around the circle, her eyes shining. "Care to guess where the cyclone dropped that framework? Exactly where the children had been making mud pies half an hour before."

1:20 p.m.

With lunch over and the youngest of the children down for their naps, the ladies took their chairs outside again where they could watch the children as they played. They talked quietly, sometimes content to say nothing. Angeline had found a ball of bright red yarn and a pair of scissors and begged her mother to let the children play with them. Emma had agreed when Edie offered to show them how to braid necklaces and wrist bracelets.

Once each girl was wearing something of her own, Edie returned to rejoin the sisters. "Thank you," Emma said. "Look how delighted they are."

"Now," Edie said huskily, "I understand what you meant when you said that Little Bird smiles with her eyes. I saw that when I put her necklace on her."

Evelyn spoke up. "What's amazing to me is how much the other girls love her, even if she can't speak to them. Nean asked me the other day if she could change her name to Little Chickadee so she could be like Little Bird."

Julia laughed. "My Elsie wants me to braid her hair. When I asked her why, she said, 'Because Little Bird is my best friend.'"

"In her prayers the other night," Emma said with some difficulty, "Angeline asked Heavenly Father if He would turn her blue eyes to brown, like her sister's. Those were her words. 'Like my sister.'"

"All of that in just a few weeks," Jane said, clearly moved. She turned to Emma. "Your family has worked miracles. President Jones was inspired to put her with you."

"Absolutely," the others agreed.

A few minutes later, as the women talked quietly, Angeline came trotting over. She was trailed by Little Bird and the others. Emma straightened as her daughter stopped in front of her.

"Mama." She rubbed her stomach with a circular motion of her hand. "Little Bird is hungry for a cookie."

"Oh?" Emma said, stifling a smile. "Just Little Bird?"

"Well," Angeline said, as if the thought had just occurred to her, "Lenora is hungry too."

"And me too," Nean sang out. Immediately all the others chimed in as well.

Smiling, Emma got to her feet. "Then I guess we'd better go inside and get you girls something to eat. I've got some biscuits and gravy I could warm up."

There was a momentary exchange of panicked looks, and then Lenora shook her head. "We're not *that* hungry. I think cookies will suffice."

Julia laughed aloud. "Suffice? My goodness, Ency. Who is teaching your daughter language like that?"

Ency just shook her head. As a group they all trooped into the house.

Seven or eight minutes later, as the girls sat at the table with their cookies and milk and the ladies stood around talking, the sound of footsteps on the porch sounded. A moment later the door burst open and Ed Hyde appeared. He was momentarily startled by the scene before him, but then his eyes found Emma and he walked swiftly to her. "We've got company," he said in a low voice.

Even as he spoke, other figures appeared at the door. One

of them stepped inside. Edie fell back a little. It was Old Wash, the Ute who often came to Monticello to visit the whites and ask for food. He had a brightly colored blanket wrapped around his shoulders, even though it was probably eighty-five or ninety degrees outside. On the porch behind him, Edie could see that he had brought five or six other men with him. They crowded around the doorway, peering in and speaking rapidly among themselves. At the table, the children had gone quiet at the sight of Indians at the door. To Edie's surprise, Little Bird had moved over behind two of the other girls and ducked her head down.

Old Wash, who spoke passable English, was clearly acting as the spokesman. He looked around at the women in the room and recognized Emma. He stepped closer. "You Hyde's squaw, no?"

"Yes," Emma said calmly. "I am his wife."

"We much hungry. You give biscuits."

"I do have some biscuits," she said. "Have your brothers come in. I will fix you biscuits and gravy." Before he could respond, she turned to Ency, Julia, and Evelyn and quietly said, "Why don't you take the children outside to play?"

Julia was looking very nervous. "Will you be okay?"

Ed nodded. "We're fine. They're just hungry."

As the three women went to the children and began speaking to them softly, Emma spoke to Edie and Jane Walton. "Can you help me get out some dishes?" Then to her husband, "Why don't you get some of that cider from the ice house?"

He turned, but just then Wash muttered something. As Edie looked up, he stepped over and blocked Ency, Julia, and Evelyn from taking the children out. He was staring at Little Bird, who was in the middle of the pack, her head still down. Wash was staring at her, a look of horror on his face. "What she doing here?" he barked at Ed. Without waiting for an answer, he shouted something to the men on the porch. Instantly they were pushing through the door, blocking any chance for the children to get out.

Edie was stunned. They were all too shocked to react. Old Wash was shouting at one of the younger men, who gave a curt nod and turned and ran back outside.

Frightened now, the children huddled together, whimpering nervously. Ed, momentarily startled, reacted swiftly. He took three steps and stood before Wash. "The children are going to go outside. Then you eat."

"No!" Wash yelled, his face a mottled mask of fury. He reached around and grabbed for Little Bird. She fell back as the other children screamed, but he was too fast. He caught a fistful of her dress and yanked her forward.

Ed's reaction was instantaneous. He chopped one hand hard on Wash's arm, who howled and let go of Little Bird. "Leave the children alone!" he bellowed. Old Wash gasped and leaped backwards. His face was a mask of shock and rage. Then to the women Ed hissed, "Get them out of here." There was no way they could push through the Indians at the door, so the women did the next best thing. They herded the children the other way, moving them toward the bedroom.

"What she doing here?" Wash cried again. "She not your daughter."

Ed, clearly stunned by this sudden eruption, turned to Wash. "We found her in the mountains. Your people abandoned her."

"No!" Wash screamed into his face. "This girl is witch. This girl must die."

Those words hit Edie as though he had thrown a tomahawk at her. She was standing where she could look past Ed and the old Ute through the door and into the yard. What she saw there turned her cold. The young Ute who had raced away was at his horse. He yanked a rifle from a scabbard, levered a shell into the chamber, and started on a run back for the house.

"Ed!" Edie shrieked. "He's got a gun!"

But Ed had seen it too. In one leap he was to his fireplace. He reached up and grabbed the shotgun he kept there. He whirled back around, breaking it open to see whether it was loaded. In one smooth movement he snapped it shut again and thrust the muzzle into Wash's face as the young buck leaped up onto the porch, his face murderous. "Tell him to stop!" Ed thundered.

Wash said something in Ute and the young man stopped in the doorway. All of the Indians now were in a fury, shouting and shaking their fists at the white people.

Ed leaned in so that his face was right up beside the muzzle of his shotgun and only an inch or two from Wash's face. "Wash," he hissed, "I don't know what's going on here, but let's talk. Tell your people to wait outside. Then we talk. But no shooting. Yes?"

Wash was still livid, but he was wise enough to see that he didn't really have much choice. There was a quick nod, and then he started rattling away at his companions, obviously telling them to back away. They didn't. They were in a fury. One had a knife out. Wash roared at them, drowning them all out, and after a moment they started backing out of the door, still muttering angrily.

When the last one was on the porch, Emma started for the door, wanting to shut it. "No," Ed said quickly. "Let them watch. The children are safe now. We need to find out what in the heck is going on here." As Emma stepped back, he lowered the shotgun and backed up a step. "All right, Wash. We talk. What is wrong? Why do you come into my house and make trouble?"

Wash drew himself up to his full height, which was about six inches shorter than Ed Hyde. Edie could see spittle on his lips. His eyes were black pools of fire. He spun around to Emma, quivering with anger. "Where you get Indian papoose?"

"Little Bird?" Emma said, still too shocked to understand what was happening.

"No. Her name Tuwa. Her very bad. Her must die."

Edie's knees almost buckled. "No!" she cried.

Ed cut in sharply. "No one is going to die here, Wash." He looked at Emma. "Fill a sack with biscuits. Give them everything we have. Hurry." Then back to Wash. "You tell your braves, little papoose stays here. You go. Take biscuits."

The other Indians were all shouting at them through the door. Oma stood off to one side, looking like she was going to faint. Emma was frantically pulling out sacks of biscuits. Edie leaped to a drawer and found a flour sack and started stuffing them inside.

Ed was perfectly calm now. He still had the shotgun cradled in one arm. "Wash, I don't know what's going on, but you tell your brothers to go now. We will talk. We will decide what is the right thing to do. But they must go."

Wash was shaking his head, but he didn't verbally respond. Edie moved quickly to the old Indian and handed him the sack that was now bulging with biscuits. He refused to take it for a moment but then grabbed it and strode to the door. He tossed it to the nearest man and started shouting at the other Indians. There was an angry torrent of words exchanged, but evidently Wash had some authority in the tribe, because they started moving off the porch even as they objected. Finally, they mounted up, shook their fists at Ed and called out some ugly invectives, and spurred their horses away, leaving one horse behind for Wash.

Edie had to sit down. She was trembling so violently she

couldn't stand any longer. Jane Walton leaned back against a wall to steady herself.

Ed watched until the Indians disappeared up the street and then turned to his wife. His voice was calm, but Edie could see that he was pretty shaken too. "Shut the door, Emma. I'm going to see if I can find out what is going on here." He stepped forward and handed her the shotgun.

"No, Ed," Emma exclaimed. Her face was a chalky white.

"It's all right," he soothed. "Just keep the children in the bedroom. Keep them quiet. It's all right." Then he shut the door and turned to Wash.

Wash was slumped on the small bench they kept on the porch, but as Ed shut the door he leaped to his feet. Ed went over to face him. "All right, Wash. Tell me why you are upset."

"This not good, Hyde. This very bad. Tuwa must die."

Ed spoke calmly. "That little girl is not going to die, Wash. Tell me why you and your brothers are so angry."

"Tuwa is child of witch. Very bad woman. Evil woman. Curse whole tribe with evil spirit. So she die. We stone her. Toss her body off cliff."

Trying not to look shocked, Ed nodded. "But that doesn't make the girl a witch, Wash. You know that."

Wash's lined face hardened. "Ute law say child of witch must die so she not curse tribe too." He was trembling with outrage. "Hyde is good man but must not try to change tribal laws, tribal customs. Girl must die."

"I'm sorry," Ed said, quietly but very firmly. "The girl will not die. We will keep her here so that she cannot curse your tribe."

Wash pulled the blanket around him and stuck his face right up next to Ed's. "White man not tell Ute people what to do," he said angrily. "Old Wash tell you. This is very bad mistake. I take girl with me now."

"I'm sorry, Wash, but that's not going to happen. Not today. Not ever."

7:35 p.m.—Frederick Jones Cabin

The group seated in the main room of the Jones cabin was pretty grim. Not everyone had been invited, but word of what happened had spread through the town quickly, and in addition to those inside, many had gathered outside to await the decision.

Edie, pale and withdrawn, sat in the corner with Mitch. He held her hand, but she was barely aware of it. Just before they had entered the house, she had looked up at him and said one thing. "They can't send her back, Mitch. I won't let them." Since then she had not said another word.

President Jones was standing beside his fireplace looking from face to face thoughtfully. He caught Mitch's eye and gave him a questioning look. Mitch shrugged and shook his head.

That seemed to make up his mind. "All right, brothers and sisters, here is my recommendation."

Every head came up; every eye was on him.

"No one questions the idea that our first and foremost concern is the safety of that sweet little Indian girl. In spite of the risk of alienating our Indian brothers, we cannot, we must not, give her back to them. I think we all know what will happen."

Mitch was gratified to see Edie's head come up and bob up and down almost imperceptibly. The relief in her was palpable. She had been convinced that the community was going to make Little Bird the sacrificial lamb so as not to bring down the wrath of the tribe upon themselves. Mitch had tried to convince her that wasn't going to happen, but she was far too upset to listen to reason.

"On the other hand, I think that we must face the fact that she is no longer safe here in town. We constantly have Indians coming and going, and considering how passionately they feel about this, it would be too easy to have her snatched away.

"Several have volunteered their homes as refuge for our Little Bird, but that doesn't solve the problem of her being discovered sooner or later. So I think we have come up with a good alternative. As you know, Parley and Willard Butt have recently completed their sawmill. While in Cortez, Colorado, earlier this summer, Parley met a man with experience in sawmills. His name is James Baker. Parley hired him, and he and his wife, Isabelle, have now moved to Verdure to work in the mill. When Brother Bronson found Little Bird, several families volunteered to take her in. The Bakers were one of those. Their home is near the sawmill, which is out away from any main roads and any Indian trails used by the Utes."

This was a new development, and Mitch saw that Edie was listening intently.

"Taking Little Bird out of the Hyde home will be difficult for the Hydes, as well as for the girl. But the Bakers have a little girl who is the same age as Little Bird. Sarah, I think her name is. Also, the other three families in Verdure have several little girls who are already friends with her. We therefore recommend that Little Bird become the ward of the Bakers."

"She won't have Oma anymore," Edie whispered. "That will be hard."

Mitch nodded. He was encouraged to see that she saw this as an acceptable solution. "But you and Oma can go to Verdure to visit her," he whispered.

President Jones looked around. No one spoke. No one raised a hand. His head bobbed once in acknowledgment and then he said, "We would ask for a vote. All of those in favor of this proposal, please raise your hands."

When Edie's was one of the first hands to shoot up, Mitch felt a huge sense of relief. She was going to be all right with this, as difficult as it was. He raised his hand and looked around the room. It looked like every hand was in the air.

"Then it's settled," President Jones said. "Today is Wednesday. We feel it wise to not make this transition for a day or two so that Little Bird can have a chance to have things return to normal for a while. On Saturday, Parley and Ency Butt will transport her back to Verdure in their wagon. They will leave before first light with her concealed inside. In Verdure, once it is ascertained that there are no Utes about, she will be taken to her new home."

He let his eyes roam around the room. "I need not say this, but feel compelled to do so. It is imperative that the Indians do not learn her whereabouts. Please do not discuss this with your children, and be especially careful when Indians come to town. If the Utes make inquiry of you, all you have to say is that she is no longer with us."

Notes

The story of the tornado dropping the framework for the roof of Parley and Ency Butt's house in the yard where the children had been playing comes from Parley's life story (see *Life of Parley Butt*, 16). It is not clear if the other two families were present at that time, but because there were only three families in Verdure then, it seemed likely that they could have been.

It was a few weeks after Wilmer Bronson found the little girl that some Utes came to town looking for food. When they stopped at the Hyde home, they saw the little girl there and grew very angry. One of them had a rifle and would have shot the girl if Ed Hyde had not intervened. Old Wash stayed behind after the others left and explained why the Utes were so angry. He sternly warned Ed against thwarting the tribal customs (see *Saga*, 223–24). The possibility of retaliation almost certainly would have caused some angst among the settlers. The record states that Isabelle Baker did take the girl into her home, but no explanation is given as to why. Other records, however, show that James Baker was hired by Parley for the sawmill (see *Life of Parley Butt*, 15). It is my guess that he would have lived in Verdure rather than Monticello, which provided a possible reason why the Bakers' home was chosen to hide the girl. However, some of those details are my assumptions.

CHAPTER 36

September 10, 1890, 11:30 p.m.—George Adams Cabin —Verdure, San Juan County

Wednesday, September 10th

It is late at night and I am the only one up at the moment. George and Evelyn put their two girls down at 7:45, and we had some quiet time to talk afterwards. Well, Evelyn and I did. Oma called it a night at about 9:00, claiming that was her right now that she's turned 60. George gave it up at 10:15, begging off because he has to be up at 4:30 each morning to milk about 65 or 70 milk cows (pretty good reason, I told him). Evelyn gets up at that same hour to help him but said she didn't care. She'd rather talk. She finally went to bed about ten minutes ago.

As usual I am still awake because I do not sleep well when Mitch is gone. Once again, he, took a herd of about fifty cows to Thompson Springs with Fred Adams, Mitch's father, and Johnnie. They left on the 6th and promised to be back no later than this coming Friday. I made him promise no more trips to Salt Lake City and coming back with this sorry excuse that he had to go get Oma Zimmer for me. I do miss him very much, especially on these trips when he is gone longer than a week.

It did help that Evelyn invited us down for a week. Spending time with her and Julia and Ency and their children has been wonderful, but best of all is getting to know the Bakers and spend time with Little Bird.

As I wrote previously, I was devastated when we had

to move her out of Monticello and put her somewhere the Indians could not find her, even though I fully supported the decision. Now, three months later, I not only see that it was the best way to keep her safe (the Utes have come to Monticello several times now, supposedly begging for food, but clearly also looking for Little Bird), but it has also been a good thing for Little Bird. Isabelle is so loving and so patient with her. And their Sarah, who will be six in December, is every bit as close to her as Angeline was. I truly believe she is as happy here as she once was at the Hydes'.

Oma and I were delighted—even ecstatic—when we went to the Bakers' home the day after we arrived with Evelyn, Ency, Julia, and their kids. Little Bird was very happy to see the kids, but when she saw that Oma and I were in the wagon, she actually gave a little squeal of joy and came running pell-mell toward us. And it wasn't just Oma. After she had given her huge hugs, she came over and shyly hugged me as well. Talk about melting my heart!

It is such a delight to watch her. She is now talking a bit. It's a curious mixture of English and Ute, but it is so good to hear her actually speaking. And yesterday, while the children were playing London Bridge, she actually started giggling so hard when they trapped her that she almost fell down. Oh, how precious she is. Whenever I think of what nearly happened to her, I am moved to tears.

Little Bird has been a godsend for me. I am still not with child, even though it was a year ago that I lost the last one. So much for my assumption that conceiving a child was not the problem. I am resigned to the fact that being a mother may not be in Heavenly Father's plan for me. Mitch fiercely corrects me when I say that to him, so I don't say it anymore. Except to myself. We just don't talk about it anymore.

Little Bird has been a wonderful antidote for my sorrow, however. Mitch has brought me here several times to see her. I am much encouraged that in spite of the fact that they deeply love her, the Bakers are not talking about adopting her if the time comes that it's safe to do so. Emma Hyde would take her in a heartbeat, but knowing that she has six children of her own and I have none, she has told me that she would support our bid to adopt her. But President Jones says that we have to wait at least one year before we dare move ahead on that.

Well, that's the third time I've yawned in the last minute, so I will finish. We leave early tomorrow. Parley and Willard are taking two more loads of lumber to Monticello, so Oma and I will travel back home with them. It is only six miles, but it is a comfort not to be out on the roads alone, especially knowing that the Utes are still not happy with us.

September 12, 1890, 6:40 p.m.—EDW Ranch.

"Edie?"

She looked up from the book she was reading. "Yes?"

"You'll vant to come out here," Oma called. "I think there's a wagon turning into the lane."

With a squeal of joy, Edie tossed the book aside, leaped off the bed, and tore out of the bedroom. "Is it him?"

"It is hard to tell in the moonlight," Oma said, "but who else vould be coming to our door at this time of night?" Then as Edie raced for the front door, Oma called, "Edie! You need some shoes! It's cold outside."

The door slammed behind her without her answering. Oma sat back and smiled in contentment. "Ah, love. Who needs shoes vhen you are in love?"

7:35 p.m.

When Mitch opened the bedroom door and came into the kitchen, Edie was there waiting for him. She threw her arms around him and kissed him joyously. "Mmm. You smell good now."

"I feel good," he replied. But that bath water has ten days of trail dirt in it. You may need a shovel to empty the tub."

Edie took him by the hand. "Come. Oma and I are anxious to hear how everything went."

As they sat down, Oma in the overstuffed chair and Edie on the divan, Mitch put another log on the fire. Then he came and sat beside Edie, putting his arm around her. "It's pretty nippy outside. We had ice this morning out by Peter's Springs."

"Yes. It's been quite cold. Almost all the autumn leaves are already gone." She took a quick breath. "So, did you get what you hoped for?"

"Not quite. Only thirty-two dollars per head. But that's better than I'd feared. Cattle prices are falling fast. But it's enough to pay off what we owe Parley for the lumber and the balance of what I owe Pa for the rest of his herd."

"And you're home. That's the very best part."

"Yes. So did you two go down to Verdure?" When they both nodded, he added, "And?"

"Vee had a *wunderbar* time," Oma said. "Vee just got back yesterday."

"And how is Little Bird?"

"Wonderful," Edie cried. "She's talking. She laughs out loud." Tears welled up unbidden. "She even came and hugged me when we first got there."

Mitch touched her cheek. "That *is* wonderful."

She wiped quickly at her eyes. "So anything else new from your trip?"

"Actually, yes there is. While we were in Thompson Springs we saw a newspaper. It is expected that in general conference next month, President Wilford Woodruff will issue a manifesto."

"Manifesto?" Oma said, repeating it slowly with a puzzled look.

"Yes, it's an official declaration."

Edie's face contorted. "On plural marriage?" she whispered.

"Yes. Then it will be official. No more plural marriages in the Church. Once the Supreme Court upheld the Edmunds-Tucker Act, there was really no choice. President Woodruff said that we would have lost everything, including the Salt Lake Temple, which isn't even completed yet." Mitch glanced at Edie. Her hands were in her lap, fingers twisting together. "I guess there's quite a few people who are quite upset," he continued. "They think we're caving in to the government. But President Woodruff received a revelation that it was to end. And I'm glad. I mean that, Edie. I'm really glad."

She was staring at her hands and said nothing, so Oma spoke for her. "And Edie is too," she said. "Even if she von't admit it."

Her head snapped up. "Of course one part of me is glad. I don't want to share you with another woman, but—" She looked away.

"But she is afraid that you vill never have children together."

"But I'm not," Mitch said, taking Edie's hands. "I'm not, Edie. Clearly, it's not going to be as easy for us as for some couples, but two years is nothing. You're barely twenty, Edie. You have twenty more childbearing years. We can't give up hope yet."

She was silent, still staring at her hands. "If we adopt Little Bird when the time is right, that will help."

"Yes it will. And we will do that. And I saw another article in the newspaper. It said that eighty percent of married couples who adopt go on to have children of their own."

Her eyes widened. "Really? You're not just saying that?"

"That's what it said. They think it might be because once the wife has a child to take care of, she stops worrying about conceiving and that helps. Remember? Aunt Jodie said something about that once, about how worry can create problems."

"Then we must adopt Little Bird as soon as President Jones thinks it is safe."

"Yes!" Mitch said firmly. "In fact, if you want, we'll go and tell him that."

"Tomorrow?"

"We can go down tonight, if you wish," he responded gravely.

"Tomorrow will be fine." Edie looked away, and he guessed that tears were starting again, but she reached out and clasped his hand, squeezing it very hard. "Thank you," she murmured.

September 17, 1890, 3:55 p.m.—Barn, EDW Ranch

Pinter's ears pricked up as he turned his head and looked toward the barn door. A moment later he whinnied softly, still looking in that direction. Mitch, who was filling the manger with hay, stopped, listening intently. He could hear nothing. But Pinter whinnied again, this time more loudly.

He set down the pitchfork and moved to the door. He saw immediately what it was. About midway between their lane and the town, a buckboard was coming up the road at full speed. There was a single driver in the seat and he was pushing his horse hard. Surprised, Mitch walked outside. Judging from the fact that the horse was a sorrel, he guessed it was either Ed Hyde or Mons Peterson. He started forward, walking swiftly now. When someone was coming that fast, it was either because he had very good news or. . . .

As Mitch passed the corral, the front door to the house opened and Edie stepped out. She lifted both hands up and shaded her eyes. Then she saw Mitch. "Who is it?" she called.

He peered to the east again. "Ed Hyde, I think."

Oma Zimmer came out too. She and Edie came down off the porch and joined Mitch as he stopped near the hitching post. By now there was no question about it. It was Ed, and he was still keeping the horse at a hard run.

The buckboard skidded some as he turned into the lane. A minute later he was there. He pulled the horse to a hard stop, spraying gravel as the buckboard swung partly around. "Mitch, we've got a problem. We're forming a search party. We need every man we can get."

"Who's missing?"

Ed glanced at Edie, then Oma, then back to Mitch. He swallowed hard. "Parley just rode in from Verdure. Little Bird has disappeared."

Edie gave a low cry, blindly grabbed for Mitch's arm, and almost went down to her knees. Mitch grabbed her and put his arm around her waist, steadying her against him.

Ed shook his head. "She and Sarah, the Baker girl, were outside playing in the yard. Sister Baker was in the kitchen keeping watch on them through the window. But then Sarah fell down and cut her knee. She ran into the house for a bandage to put on it. When she came back out, Little Bird was gone."

"No!" Edie sobbed.

"Could she have wandered off?" Mitch asked Ed.

"They found moccasin tracks," he said grimly. "And horse

tracks in the trees. Three unshod ponies. We're pretty sure the Utes took her."

Edie's shoulders began to shake as she sagged against Mitch. "Noooo!" It was the cry of a wounded animal.

Mitch straightened her and turned her around toward her grandmother. "Oma, take her into the house." Then to Ed, "I'll grab my stuff and saddle up. I'll be there in ten minutes."

Ed nodded, snapped the reins, and wheeled his horse around. "We're at Mons's store." Mitch turned and strode to catch up with Oma and Edie. Oma was heavily supporting her. "Here," Mitch said, taking Edie by the arm. "Let me help you get her inside."

Edie straightened, jerking her arm away from his grip. "No!" she cried. "You go. Go find her, Mitch. Go! Go!"

September 18, 1890, 2:22 p.m.

The moment she heard the sound of a buckboard, Edie was up and out the door. Oma quickly followed. It was Ed Hyde, and he was alone.

"Did you find her?" Edie cried, running up to him before he even got the horse stopped.

He shook his head, not able to meet her gaze.

Looking around wildly, Edie grabbed the side of the buckboard. "Where's Mitch?"

He took a quick breath. "Mitch went to the Ute camp looking for Old Wash."

She gasped. "Why?"

"We figure Old Wash is the only one who will tell us where she is."

"You have to keep looking!" Edie exclaimed. "They'll

abandon her in the mountains again. And it's so cold at night now."

"We don't know where to look," Ed said quietly. "We tracked them for a couple of miles until they got up into the red rock country. We lost their tracks. This is the only way. Mitch is authorized to pay the Utes handsomely to get her back."

Oma moved closer. "Vas Mitch alone vhen he went to the camp?"

"Yes. We didn't want the Utes thinking we were coming in to retaliate."

Edie visibly winced and then asked, "Was he armed?"

"No. But he'll be all right. The Utes are not looking for a fight over this, Edie, and they're hoping that we aren't either." He picked up the reins. "I have to go. I'll let you know when I hear anything. We could use your prayers."

"That's all we've been doing since you came yesterday," was her reply.

9:08 p.m.

Mitch looked up as Pinter suddenly lifted his head and cocked his ears forward. He had given the horse his head, and they were plodding slowly up the road, too tired to go any faster. Even though the barn was less than a hundred yards away now, Pinter was too exhausted to hasten his gait. In the light of the half moon, Mitch saw a dark figure at the gate that turned into the lane. "Edie?"

There was a sob of relief and the figure darted toward him. He swung down in time to enfold her in his arms as she ran up to him. "Are you all right?" she asked.

"Yes." He felt her shivering beneath her jacket. "How long have you been out here?"

"It doesn't matter. Tell me what happened."

"Let me get Pinter unsaddled and cared for. But you go inside. I mean it. I'll hurry as fast as I can." He gave her a gentle shove before she could protest and led Pinter away.

9:17 p.m.

"Did you find Old Wash, then?"

Mitch nodded, his face lined with pain and weariness.

They were seated on the divan together. Oma was in the rocking chair, watching both of them closely. Edie was leaning forward, elbows on her knees, her face down, eyes on the floor. "Is she alive?" she asked in a very low voice.

He shook his head.

Her head sank lower and her hands came up and covered her eyes. "Did she suffer?" she whispered. "Be honest with me, Mitch. I have to know. Did she suffer?"

"No, she did not."

Edie's whole body began to tremble. "So they didn't just abandon her, like they did before? Swear it."

"No, Edie. She did not suffer." When she said nothing, he went on, his own voice barely audible. "Old Wash told us where she is. Ed and I are going up there in the morning. We'll retrieve her body and bring it back here for burial."

Edie was weeping silently now, bent over all the way so her head rested on her knees.

"We don't dare bury her in the cemetery lest the Indians dig up her body again," he went on. "So I asked President Jones if we could bury her here, in that little spot you love so much out back in the cedar trees."

Edie's head came up and her body straightened. She sniffed back the tears and wiped at her eyes. "Thank you," she whispered. And then, what Mitch dreaded most happened. "Tell me how she died."

He moved closer and put his arm around her. "I don't think that's a good idea."

Her head snapped up. "But you said she didn't suffer."

"She didn't. But it's better that you don't know the details,. Please trust me on this."

"No!" she exploded. "Tell me. I have a right to know."

Mitch turned to Oma, his eyes beseeching, but he spoke to Edie. "I give you my word. She was not tortured. She was not left out in the open to die."

Edie erupted then, fists clenched as she started hammering at his chest and arms. "I'm not a child, Mitch! Tell me! Tell me right now!"

Oma got up, came over, and gently took her hands and held them against her. Edie was sobbing hysterically, still trying to flail at him. Oma looked at Mitch, her eyes wet now too. "Tell her," she said. "It is better that she know."

So Mitch gently took Edie into his arms, pulled her close to him, and laid his cheek against her hair. All resistance instantly stopped. She leaned against him and wept deeply, silently, as he began to speak.

"Wash said that the Tribal Council debated what to do with her. Some suggested that they take her farther into the forest and leave her as they had done before. But some of the young braves said that if she was as powerful a witch as her mother, she could hurl curses at them from the mountains before she died. So die she must, that was the ruling."

He took a deep breath, knowing full well what this was going to do to Edie, because he had been numb ever since Wash had told him.

"Don't stop," she whispered. "Please."

"So eight braves escorted her up to the mountains to the south of us. They didn't want to take any chance that we would see them and try to stop them. They had drugged her so that she was unconscious." His voice caught. "They found a steep precipice and threw her over the edge."

Edie stiffened as though she had been shot. "No!" she gasped.

Mitch hesitated, not wanting to say the rest, but knowing that he had to—that she had a right to know. "And then, to be sure that her spirit could not come back to haunt the tribe, they filled her dead body with bullets."

Notes

The end of the young Ute girl, whom I call Little Bird in this book, is accurately described here with the exception of her being drugged before she was tossed over the cliff (see *Saga*, 224). The sources do not indicate whether the settlers retrieved the body for burial or not, but knowing the affection they had for her, it seems unlikely that they would have left the body to the elements.

CHAPTER 37

September 19, 1890, 5:15 a.m.—EDW Ranch

Mitch jerked around when he heard a soft noise behind him. He was not surprised to see Edie and Oma. What did surprise him was that Edie was wearing one of his woolen shirts, a pair of his Levi's, and her cowboy boots. The Levi's were taken in at least three inches around the waist and were pinned in place with safety pins. The cuffs on each pant leg had been rolled up at least six inches. Under different circumstances Mitch might have laughed, but not this morning.

Edie's eyes were red, her face gaunt. "Would you saddle my horse for me, Mitch?"

Beside her, Oma, who looked as though she hadn't slept at all, said nothing, and Mitch guessed that she had unsuccessfully tried to prevent this from happening. He gave the flank strap on Pinter's saddle one last tug, took a quick breath, and turned. Before he could speak, Edie cut him off. "I'm going, and that's final. I don't care what the others say or think."

Their eyes met and held, and then Mitch shook his head. "Not today. Not for this."

Edie tried to step around him. He quickly blocked her way. "Listen to me," he said slowly. "This is an image that you do not want in your mind for the rest of your life."

"It is my choice. I'm going."

"No," he said evenly. "I understand why you want to, but I'll bring Little Bird back to the Hydes. There the other sisters will prepare the body for burial and then you can—"

"Get out of my way," she cried, plowing into him, trying to shove him away.

"No, Edie," Oma cried. "Mitch is right. Diss is not good for you to see."

Mitch stood his ground, letting Edie pound on his chest. He bent forward until he was looking straight into her eyes. "If I have to, I'll tie you to the corral railing. I mean it. I know how upset you are, but this is not what you want to do."

Her right hand flew up and drew back, palm open ready to strike him. "*Get out of my way!*"

He didn't flinch. "If that makes you feel better, then slap me. But you are not going."

For ten full seconds she stood there, eyes like two glowing coals, chest heaving, hand poised in the air. He watched her steadily, his eyes determined, but also filled with pain. And love.

Then her face crumpled. Her shoulders slumped and she lowered her hand. Great shuddering sobs rolled through her body and she began to weep. Mitch stepped forward to hold her, but with a cry she spun away from him. Then, lowering her head, she ran for the house. He watched her go and then looked at Oma. "We should be back before dark," he said.

"You have done the right thing, Mitchell. Thank you for being strong."

September 20, 1890, 11:00 a.m.—Cedar Trees near EDW Ranch

Numb. That was the only word Edie could think of to describe what she was feeling. *Or not feeling!* The pain, the ache, the emptiness, the sense of horror that had engulfed her these past few days had receded into emptiness, a strange detachment where another person named Edna Rae Westland stood off to one side of her, a distant spectator to what was happening here.

Even as Mitch took her by one elbow and Oma by the other and led her forward to where the small wooden coffin waited beside the gaping hole in the red earth, it was as if she were in a dream. When she saw that the coffin was open, a distant part of her recoiled. But now the numbness was her ally, her protection, her courage.

You have to apologize to Mitch, an inner voice chided. *How wise he was to spare you the awful realities of Little Bird's death.* Now Edie could look down on the figure lying there in quiet repose and feel at least some sliver of peace. The simple white dress Sarah Rogerson had sewn for her contrasted with her olive skin and black hair and made her look like a sleeping angel.

Holding tightly onto Mitch's hand, Edie bent down and touched the angel's cheek with her other hand. *Good-bye, my Little Bird. May you finally rest without fear.* As she stepped back, she was grateful that she had no more tears to give.

One by one parents brought her closest playmates forward—Angeline Hyde, Nean Adams, Elsie Butt, Bridgette Butt, Sarah Baker—and they wept tears for their lost friend. The rest of the community filed by silently. Many more tears were shed. Everyone was there except for the few men who had been left down below to make sure no Ute Indians came into town and got an inkling of what was happening. Mitch's family had somehow learned of the tragedy and all of them had come up to be with them. Aunt Jodie Wood had accompanied them from Bluff, even though Edie had long ago stopped sending her the reports on her health that she had requested.

The rest was a blur. Ed Hyde and James Baker, Little Bird's

two foster fathers, placed the lid on the coffin and tamped it shut. A double quartet of sisters sang "O My Father." President Jones spoke, but whether briefly or at length, Edie would not later remember. Ed Hyde dedicated the grave, praying that the grave site would be protected from any desecration. And finally the casket was lowered into the grave there beneath the cedar trees, and Little Bird was gone.

7:25 p.m.

"It's Sunday tomorrow, Mama. Can't you wait until Monday to go back?"

Mitch's father answered. "We had three wagonloads of freight from Durango come in at the co-op store before we left. We can't put it on the shelves until it's inventoried and priced. Now that I'm a member of the co-op board, that's my responsibility."

Edie leaned over and touched Gwen's arm. "It means a lot that you would come."

"When we heard of your loss, we knew we had to."

Edie turned to Aunt Jodie. "And you. It means more than I can say that you are here."

"I had to see this Little Bird for myself," she said softly, "after all the things you had written about her to Gwen. She was a special little girl."

Tears immediately filled Edie's eyes and she had to look away. "Then why didn't Heavenly Father save her?" she whispered in a choked voice. Taking a handkerchief from her pocket, she wiped her eyes. It did not stop the flow of tears. She turned to Aunt Jodie, beseeching her, begging her to help her understand. "Did you hear about the miracle of the cyclone that happened down at Verdure?" Edie finally asked.

Aunt Jodie's eyes were soft with understanding. "Yes, I did. Evelyn told us about it when we stopped there to rest the horses on our way up."

"He saved seven children that day. Couldn't He have saved one small Indian girl?"

Aunt Jodie nodded thoughtfully. "Of course He could have. The question is, why did He choose not to?" She reached down and picked up her purse from off the floor. She opened it and withdrew a folded paper. Then she turned to Edie. "One of the hardest things about my calling as a midwife is when mothers lose an infant or a small child. Like you, they struggle to understand why such tragedies happen.

"Some years ago, I found something the Prophet Joseph Smith said while preaching at the funeral of a young child." She opened the paper. "He too wondered why little children had to die. It is a source of great solace for me. I made a copy of it for you and will leave it with you, but I would like to read it to you now, if that's all right."

Edie was watching her intently. "Yes, read it."

Aunt Jodie's eyes lowered and she began. "'In my leisure moments, I have meditated upon the subject, and asked the question, why it is that infants, innocent children, are taken away from us, especially those that seem to be the most intelligent and interesting?'"

"Wait!" Edie cried. "Read that again."

Aunt Jodie did, and then said, "Even the Prophet was troubled by this kind of loss." She continued reading. "'This world is a very wicked world; and the world grows more wicked and corrupt. In the earlier ages of the world a righteous man, and a man of God, had a better chance to do good, to be believed and received than at the present day. But in these days such a man is much opposed and persecuted by most of the inhabitants of the earth, and he has much sorrow to pass through here. Because of this, I believe that the Lord takes many away, even in infancy, that they may escape the envy of man, and the sorrows and evils of this present world.'"

She stopped and looked up. "Let me read that again too. I love this concept. 'I believe that the Lord takes many away, even in infancy, that they may escape the envy of man, and the sorrows and evils of this present world.' And then he goes on. 'They were too pure, too lovely, to live on earth.'"

Aunt Jodie extended the paper to Edie, her eyes shining. "Today, we placed Little Bird's fragile little body in the earth. But we know that we did not bury *her.* That which made her so precious lives on. Her personality. Her sweet solemnity. Her purity and innocence. And someday I firmly believe it will be our privilege to meet her again. Your privilege especially."

Edie looked up as she took the sheet.

Aunt Jodie smiled. "And she's happy, Edie. At peace. At rest. No more sorrow, no more pain, no more loneliness. No more fear. And she will have met her mother, too."

Edie took the paper. "Thank you, Aunt Jodie. This is a great comfort. More than you can ever know," she added softly.

10:05 p.m.

As they knelt beside their bed, hands clasped together, Edie turned and looked at Mitch. "I want to say something before we pray."

He nodded and squeezed her hand. "All right."

"I want to tell you how sorry I am for the other morning. I—"

"I don't want you to apologize," he said. "You were justifiably distraught."

"But I almost hit you, Mitch." She lowered her head in shame. "I *wanted* to hit you."

"But you didn't."

"I am so glad that you made me stay. I am so glad that the image I have in my mind is of Little Bird lying there, so beautiful and peaceful in the coffin."

"You're always the one doing the right thing for us, Edie. I'm glad I did something for you."

She nodded and closed her eyes. "Your turn to pray or mine?"

"I would also like to say something before we do," Mitch said.

Surprised, Edie bobbed her head. "Say on."

"I'm going to leave before breakfast tomorrow."

"Oh. Okay. I'll fix you something to take."

He shook his head. "I'm not going to be eating for the next couple of days."

Edie cocked her head to one side. "Oh?" And then she guessed. "Are you fasting for me?"

Mitch shook his head, quite serious now. "No. I'm fasting for me. I want to give you another priesthood blessing, and I want to be sure I'm in tune with the Spirit when I do. I'll fast until Sunday night and then ask Brother Jones to help me give the blessing."

She gave him a long, appraising look and then nodded, her eyes glistening. "I would like that very much right now. I'll fast with you."

"No. If you do, then Oma Zimmer will too, and that's not good. Not for two days. Just pray for me and—"

Edie reached across and put her hand over his mouth. "Sorry, but just so you know, this is one of those times when you are not right. I'll encourage Oma to be wise, but knowing Oma, she'll fast with us too. Don't take that privilege away from us." She removed her hand and smiled sweetly at him. "I'll pray tonight."

CHAPTER 38

October 8, 1890, 8:40 a.m.—Edward Hyde Cabin—Monticello

Mitch dismounted in front of the Hyde cabin and tied the reins to the hitching post. He turned to help Edie down, but she was riding sidesaddle and slipped off easily before he could reach her. As he took her horse's reins and tied them next to her, she said, "Have I ever told you how much I dislike riding sidesaddle?"

That brought his head up. "Yes, as a matter of fact, you have. More than once, actually."

"Oh, I know what you're thinking, Mitch. It isn't ladylike for a woman to ride astride a horse, or straddle as I call it. But there's nothing ladylike about being up there with both legs draped on the same side of the horse, either. I feel like I'm a rock teetering on the edge of a precipice."

"Uh. . . ."

"You men get a full saddle with a high back, a saddle horn, and two stirrups. Ours has a very low back, is mostly flat, and has one stupid little place for my foot."

"Well," Mitch drawled, trying to appear serious, "part of the reason your saddles are flatter than ours is because when you sit on it sideways, your hips are too big to fit into a normal saddle."

She shot him a dark look. "Leave my hips out of it, if you please."

"Besides, our saddle horn is for a lot more than holding on. When I'm roping a calf or a horse, I need a pretty strong saddle horn because I cinch my lariat around it."

Edie snorted in disgust. "Come over here. I want you to get up there and see what it's like."

Mitch held up both hands to ward her off. "I'm not getting up on no girl's saddle."

"See?" she snapped. "See what I mean? You even talk about my saddle with contempt."

It was time to change the subject. "Well, I guess I could take your mare back to the house and put her out to pasture and then bring the buckboard back for you tonight. That way you wouldn't have to ride back sidesaddle."

"No. If you were going that way, I'd say yes. But you're headed east. It's not worth it. I'll suffer through the humiliation and the discomfort. I'm used to it."

"Or," he leaned back, as though an idea had just occurred to him. "We could borrow a pair of Ed's old Levi's for you. Then you could ride my horse back and I'll ride yours."

"Aside from the Levi's idea, which is ridiculous, would you really ride sidesaddle?"

"Of course not. I'd take your saddle off, throw it in a ditch, and ride home bareback."

"Very droll, Mister Westland," Edie sniffed, sticking her nose into the air. "You think you are so funny, but I see no humor in this at all. None whatsoever."

Mitch's smile was brief, and then he came to her. "I'm glad you're going to spend some time with Winnie and Louise. It will be good for you."

Edie gave him a long look. "Though it's going to be painful being in the house where Little Bird lived for a while, it does sound good to get out. And it's such a beautiful fall day."

"I'm sure Lou and Winnie are still mourning for her as well, but knowing them, I think they'll have you laughing by the end of the day."

Edie nodded and smiled briefly. "Especially Lou. She is such a free spirit."

"Like someone else I know," he said, kissing her forehead. "Do something fun with them."

"I will. Thanks for bringing me down."

Mitch swung up in his saddle. "Bye, Edie. I should be back by seven or seven-thirty. Love you, dear. Even when you're not being very ladylike." With a laugh, he spurred his horse away before she could throw something at him.

1:17 p.m.

There was a knock on the bedroom door. "May I come in, girls?" a voice called out.

Edie was braiding Winnie's long dark hair into a single strand down her back while Louise watched closely to see how it was done. Lou jumped to her feet and opened the door. Her mother was standing there.

Edie looked up. "Do you need us?" she asked.

"Yes, but go ahead and finish." She looked down at Winnie. "Moroni Bailey just came by. His father has asked him and our William to help him mend his corral where the cows kicked it down. That will take them the rest of the day."

Winnie and Lou both nodded. William, who was fourteen, was their older brother. Everyone else called him Will, but his mother always called him William. "So you need us to take the cows out to pasture?"

"Yes. Your father wants them west of town, up near where the cedar trees begin."

"We can do that, Mama," Lou said eagerly, "can't we, Winnie?"

"Of course."

Their mother nodded thoughtfully, still holding back. Edie guessed why. Winnie was only twelve; Lou was eleven. Pretty young to be sending them out alone. "If you don't need me to help here, I could ride out with them, Emma."

Emma's face relaxed. "That would be wonderful. I'll fix you a basket of food." She started to back out of the room but then had another thought. "Ed doesn't want you going north of the Horsehead Peak road, though. That's Carlisle territory."

Edie shuddered. Latigo Gordon was someone she did not want to meet. "We'll stay far away from there." Emma turned to Louise. "Lou, why don't you saddle your two horses while I finish Winnie's hair, and then we'll come out."

"I'll saddle Edie's, too," Lou said as she got up and followed her mother out.

2:05 p.m.—Foothills West of Monticello

Edie finished the last bite of her ham and pickle sandwich and drank the last of her cold chocolate. She returned the glass and plate to the picnic basket. Leaning back on her elbows until her hair brushed the blanket, she sighed with contentment. "That was good. I'm ready for a nap. How about you two?" She reached down and slipped off her shoes. They did the same.

Winnie, always the more serious of the two sisters, closed one eye and looked up at the sun through the trees. "It didn't take us that long to get here. Mama doesn't expect us back until after four. A nap sounds good to me."

"Or we could just lie here and talk," Lou suggested as she put her dishes in the basket.

"And what would you like to talk about?" Edie asked, pretty sure that she already knew the answer to that question.

Lou blushed slightly. "Oh, I don't know. People, I guess."

"Like one with the name of Johnnie Westland?" Winnie teased, poking her with her finger.

The color in Lou's cheeks deepened. "No!"

Edie lay back and closed her eyes. "No? So you don't want me to tell you what he said about you the other day in his letter?"

Lou's face instantly infused with joy. "Did he really talk about me?" Then her face fell. "Are you teasing me, Edie?"

"Nope."

"So tell me. Tell me."

"Well," Edie said slowly, "he said that he thought that you were both too flirty."

Winnie's face flamed bright red. Lou jerked bolt upright. "He did not!" she yelped.

"Did he really?" Winnie cried.

Edie laughed. How she loved these two sisters. Mitch had been right. This was good medicine for her. "No, he actually said he thought you were both really cute." Her smile deepened. "And coming from Johnnie, who thinks that girls are just boys with different haircuts, that's saying quite a bit."

"Really?" they both asked dreamily.

"Yes, really. Now, no more until after we've napped. Then we can talk some more."

Winnie lay back. "Lou, if you dream about Johnnie, try not to talk about him in your sleep, like you did the other night."

Then she rolled away before Lou could hit her. And with that, all three settled down and were soon asleep.

2:32 p.m.

When they woke again they debated about starting back, but Lou vigorously opposed the idea. "So what do you want to do?" Edie asked.

"Can we ask you questions, Edie?"

"About Johnnie?"

"No. Just girl questions."

"Ah. All right. On one condition. When we're through I get to ask you questions too."

"Fair enough," Lou said eagerly. Winnie's head was bobbing up and down too.

The three of them sat up, wiggled themselves into a circle, and began. "So," Lou said, her face quite earnest, "how can you tell when you are in love with a boy?"

And that began it. Edie very quickly learned, as they both peppered her with questions, that in their eyes, she, having been so recently married, was an expert on love, courtship, marriage, and men. And the questions came in rapid-fire succession. How old was she when she first knew she loved Mitch? When did she know for sure that it was true love? What did it feel like to be in love? How did you let a boy know you liked him without being too brazen about it? What was it like to be kissed? When had Mitch first kissed her? What had it been like for her?

When Edie described their first kiss and how Mitch had lost his nerve at the last second and then walked away, they howled in protest.

"He did not!" Winnie exclaimed.

"He did," Edie said. Then a slow smile curled at the corners of her mouth. "But he only went about three steps. Then he came back to me with this look in his eyes, and I could see he was going to do it."

"So what did you do?" Lou cried.

"I didn't know what to do. It all happened so fast, I just kind of stood there, stunned." Her eyebrows went up and down twice. "And then—" She let out a long, slow sigh. "And then I let him kiss me."

Lou threw up her hands and fell back on the blanket, pretending to swoon. "Ohhhhhh," was all she said.

"And then what did you do?" Winnie asked eagerly.

"What do you think I did?" Edie asked in a low, sultry voice. "I kissed him back."

They shrieked with laughter and clapped their hands.

Finally the questioning died out and they sat back, each lost in her own thoughts. Winnie looked around. "We probably ought to be going."

"Oh, no you don't," Edie cried. "Remember, I get to ask you questions."

"What?" Lou asked eagerly.

"But we don't know anything about boys," Winnie reminded her.

Edie hesitated, debating within herself whether she dared do what she was thinking or not.

"What?" Winnie pressed.

She decided to go for it and leaned forward, rubbing her hands in anticipation. "Okay, first, before I ask my question, you've got to swear that you won't ever tell anyone. Okay? This is just between us three. No parents. No best friends. Not Mitch. No one. Agreed?"

She had them with that. Their eyes were wide with excitement as they nodded eagerly.

"You've got to swear." And she demonstrated by making an X mark on her dress before she intoned, "Cross my heart and hope to die, stick a finger in my eye, if I ever tell a lie."

In unison they all did it together. "All right," Winnie exclaimed. "What?"

Edie took a quick breath and let her eyes narrow mysteriously. "Have you ever wondered what it would be like to ride a horse like men do?"

That was hardly what they had expected, and for a moment they stared at her dumbly.

"Not perched on one of those girl saddles where both of your legs are on the same side."

"*Edie Westland!*" Winnie gasped. "Don't say 'legs.'"

"So what are you suggesting?" Lou asked slowly, clearly intrigued by what appeared to be a possible conspiracy.

"I'm saying, I want to try riding like the men. Where you hold onto the horse with your knees and . . . your 'lower extremities,' and then you ride like the wind."

Winnie was still aghast. "But . . . but. . . ."

"But what, Winnie?" Edie prodded, keeping a straight face.

"How can we—" her face was a scarlet red, "maintain our maidenly modesty?"

"Well, actually," Edie said, glad for the question because it meant that they weren't rejecting the idea out of hand, "I have given that some thought." She reached down and pulled the hem of her skirt up about three inches to reveal the bottoms of the white bloomers that she wore under her skirt. They came clear down to her ankles. "I am assuming that you both are wearing bloomers too, right?"

They both nodded, still half in shock, but clearly intrigued.

"Well, aren't bloomers essentially like a pair of men's trousers? They cover our—"

Winnie's hand flew up and waved frantically. "Don't say it, Edie."

Edie smiled demurely. "They maintain our maidenly modesty." She looked around. "So here we are, two miles away from town. No one is anywhere around. No one can see us." She stood up. "So, I cannot speak for you girls, but I am going to pin up my skirts around my waist and—"

"We don't have any safety pins," Lou cried.

"Ah," Edie said. She reached into the pocket of her dress and pulled out a handful of safety pins. "Look what I brought with me from your mother's sewing basket."

Winnie's hand came up to cover her mouth as she gave a soft, "Oh."

"So, are you with me or not? I say we start a sisterhood of the wind. What say you?"

Lou was up in an instant, gathering up her skirts. Winnie watched her for a few seconds and then leaped up. "Yes. Me too. The Sisterhood of the Wind. I like it."

Lou's face suddenly fell. "But we have only sidesaddles. I'm not sure I can ride bareback."

"Then let us ride straddle in spite of our sidesaddles," Edie intoned solemnly. Smiling, she reached down and began lifting the hem of her skirt. "Are you with me, girls?"

"Yes!" they cried as one.

6:25 p.m.—Hyde Home

They said nothing, of course, about their adventure when they returned to the Hyde cabin, but set to work immediately to help. Lou and Winnie started dinner while Edie went over to be with Oma and Angeline. She saw that Emma kept giving her daughters strange looks as every now and then they would look at each other, whisper something in the other's ear, and burst into peals of laughter.

Mitch returned about an hour earlier than he had expected, and Emma asked him to stay for supper. Edie went into the kitchen part of the room and pitched in to help the girls get things ready. When Sister Hyde stepped away for a minute and Edie saw that Mitch was engaged in conversation with her grandmother, she leaned in close to Lou and Winnie. "Do you think it would it be wrong to thank Heavenly Father for such a glorious experience today?" she whispered with a knowing smile.

Winnie, trying hard not to laugh, said, "I think the better question is, is it all right to pray that no one ever finds out about this?"

They nearly choked as they tried to hold back their laughter. When Edie turned and saw Mitch giving her the same strange look that Sister Hyde had given them, she nudged Lou and Winnie and said something that sent them into more paroxysms of giggling.

Half an hour later, Ed Hyde returned and they sat down for dinner, even though Will had not yet returned from helping Moroni Bailey. The presence of their father had a dampening effect on the two sisters, and thereafter they were able to maintain a sober mien.

7:51 p.m.

Mitch retrieved his hat from the pegs on the back wall, twirling it as he came over to Emma. "Sister Hyde, you and your girls make a right fine dinner. Thank you for letting us share with you." He motioned to Edie. "Let's saddle up and ride."

At the word "saddle" her head jerked up. Lou and Winnie had to clap their hands over their mouths to stop from exploding with laughter. "Yes, dear," Edie finally managed, fighting to keep a straight face.

Mitch's eyes narrowed. "Are you three sure that you're all right?"

Winnie nodded gravely. "Yes. Just be sure that you and Edie don't ride home like the wind," she intoned. And that did it. The three of them almost doubled over with laughter.

The other adults looked at each other, rolled their eyes, and brushed it off to adolescence on the part of the two sisters, although not sure how Edie fit into all of that.

As they started to say their farewells, there was a sharp rap on the door. Brother Hyde, who was closest to the door, got up and opened it. To everyone's surprise, President Jones and Brother John Rogerson were standing there. And more surprising, they were dressed in their Sunday suits and ties.

"Evenin', Brother Ed," President Jones said solemnly. "Brother John and I wonder if we might trouble you folks for a few minutes."

Edie had gone stock-still as her heart leaped up into her throat. These men were both close friends and neighbors, but this was clearly not a social call. Not when they were in their Sunday best. They had come as a branch presidency, she guessed, though George Adams was the other counselor and lived in Verdure so he was not with them. Could it be that this was about . . . ? She shook her head. There was no way they could know about that.

"Sure," Brother Hyde responded, He stepped back and motioned for them to come in.

President Hyde looked around the room, his eyes taking in Grandma Zimmer and the rest of the Hyde children. "Uh . . . perhaps it would be better," he said, his voice low, "if we met outside."

"Whatever you wish," Ed said with a shrug and started out the door.

President Jones spoke quickly. "And could we have Sister Hyde and Brother Westland join us too?" Then his eyes turned and looked directly at where Edie, Lou, and Winnie stood together. "And you three sisters as well," he added slowly, beckoning with his finger.

Edie glanced at Winnie and Lou and saw that they too were looking very pale. And at that moment, Edie knew why they had come. They knew. It wasn't possible, but they knew. She could see it in President Jones's eyes. And suddenly she felt a great need to sit down before her knees buckled beneath her.

7:54 p.m.—Backyard, Hyde Home

Edie felt as though her feet had taken root in the ground. She felt like she might be sick. Beside her, she could see that Winnifred and Louise were not doing any better.

President Jones was walking back and forth in front of them, his hands clasped behind his back, his eyes daring the three of them to look at him. "So you do not deny these charges?" he finally asked.

None of the three spoke, but all three shook their heads.

There was a long, weary, and disgusted sigh. "Then this shameful act must be fully rectified as soon as possible. Therefore, on Sunday next, the three of you are to appear at church—"

"No!" Winnie gasped.

Edie's shoulders slumped. She felt like she might throw up. Could he be serious? Confess in church? But she knew it was a ridiculous question. He was more serious than she had ever seen him before. She raised her head. "President, I am the one who proposed this activity. I am the one who persuaded Winnie and Lou to join me. I am the one most responsible. Therefore, let these two young and impressionable girls go and I will do as you ask." She risked a quick glance at Mitch. He was staring at the ground, his face implacable.

President Jones stopped directly in front of Edie. "Since you are older and a married woman and should have set the proper example for these two young sisters, who, as you note, are young and impressionable, you, Sister Westland, shall be the first to confess your actions to the congregation."

"Yes, President," Edie whispered meekly.

"And you, Miss Winnifred and Miss Louise, shall follow immediately afterwards. Got it?"

"Yes, President," they said as one. And with that, he and Brother Rogerson stalked away.

8:02 p.m.

Mitch walked quietly beside Edie, close to her but not touching. He did not reach out and take her hand as he usually did. Edie bleakly wondered what was going through his mind. They were walking toward the Hyde barn, where Edie's horse was still tied to the corral fence. She saw that he had tied Pinter beside her mount.

As they reached their animals, she stopped. "Mitch, I—"

He cut her off with a wave of his hand. "We can talk when we get home."

On the verge of tears, she moved toward her horse. But she had only gone two steps when he put both hands on her shoulders and turned her around. "Stop right there," he said, his voice low. Surprised, she looked around at him, but he was looking back at the house, which was fifty or sixty feet away. There was no one there. Everyone else had gone back inside. When he turned back to her, she let out a long breath. "Go ahead," she murmured. "Say it."

"All right." His hands dropped down and he gripped her around her waist. "Hold on."

"What?" But then she gasped. In one smooth, seemingly effortless movement, he swept her off her feet, hoisted her up, and plopped her astride of Pinter. Startled, she gave a little cry.

"You're all right," Mitch grunted. "Just hold still." As he spoke, he started tugging at the folds of her skirt, pulling them out from under her seat and legs until they were spread neatly across Pinter's back and over the saddle horn in front of her. Edie was so taken aback that all she could do was gape at him.

He went around to her right side and adjusted the stirrup up about six inches. Then he slipped her foot into it. "How's that?" he asked.

"What are you doing?" she whispered.

He checked the stirrup again, and then, satisfied, he ducked under the horse's neck and adjusted the left stirrup. "How's that?" he asked again.

By now Edie's shock had turned to wonder. Was he doing what she thought he was doing?

Mitch gave her a quizzical look, as if to say, "Well?"

"Perfect," she murmured, a smile starting to form on her lips.

He untied the reins and handed them up to her, his

expression never changing. Then he walked over to her horse, untied the reins, gripped the smaller horn of her woman's saddle, and threw himself up and into her saddle. He grunted as he settled into the saddle. "Ugh! You weren't kidding about this miserable thing, were you?" Then he finally smiled at her. "Are you ready to ride like the wind?"

Edie was incredulous. "Mitch, you crazy, impetuous fool. Are you insane? You'll get us both excommunicated."

"Serves me right," he drawled. "I'm the one who told you to go have some fun. And besides, that's only if we get caught." He grinned and motioned for her to lead out. "Last one to the barn has to unsaddle the horses."

By the time Mitch rode sedately up to their barn, Edie was dismounted and had Pinter tied to the hitching rail. When she turned to him, she burst out laughing. In the dim light, she saw that both of his legs were on the same side of the horse. He was riding sidesaddle and his expression was one of pure agony.

When he jumped down, Edie hurtled herself at him, nearly bowling him over. Before he could recover, she grabbed his face with both hands and smothered it with kisses.

He was able to recover his balance sufficiently to kiss her back, though somewhat more restrained.

Notes

The experience of the three girls who decided to ride their horses in a manner other than sidesaddle comes from the life story of Emma Louise Hyde Walton. Louise, or "Lou," had this experience with "two friends." Her sister Winnifred is not named as being involved. No year is given for this event, but it was probably a few years later than is shown here.

The concept of the "Sisterhood of the Wind" is my idea, but much of the narrative is built around Louise Hyde's account as given to her descendants. As they report:

"At that time no woman ever exposed her lower extremities (legs), it was immodest even to refer to their lower 'limbs' as legs, let alone say that word. . . . Emma [i.e., Emma Louise] wanted to feel the security of 'straddling' a horse and to ride like the wind without fear of having your womanly modesty assailed with your do-right neighbors looking down their noses at you. Emma and her friends could not resist this temptation. . . . They used safety pins to fasten the skirts into some semblance of cowboy paraphernalia; they then 'straddled' their horses and rode carelessly [i.e., without any cares]" (Joyce Ann Hunt, "Emma Louise Hyde: 27 November 1879 to July 6, 1954, 3–4," in Family Search archives, copy in author's possession).

No explanation is given as to why the three girls were told they had to confess their "transgression" in a public church meeting. That is not the practice today. How common it was back then, I could not ascertain.

CHAPTER 39

October 12, 1890, 10:22 a.m.—Meetinghouse—Monticello

The typical attendance at Sunday services in Monticello was about ninety percent, because there was always someone who was sick or some of the brethren who were away from town for whatever reason. As Edie glanced around, she was sure attendance was at about 125 percent, even though that was statistically impossible. That did nothing to lessen the dread she was feeling.

Edie had wanted to sit in the back. Mitch had persuaded her otherwise, suggesting that not only did it make her look guiltier, but then she would have to walk all the way up to the podium to make her penance and all the way back again, with every eye upon her. So they came early enough to get the front row of benches. The Hyde family had done the same. Edie couldn't help but notice that Winnifred and Louise were seated on the opposite end of their bench. To keep them as far away from her corrupting influence as possible, she guessed.

Mitch, seeing where she was looking, reached out and took her hand. "Just tell the truth," he said. "It'll all blow over in a little while."

"I'll be grateful if that happens by our fiftieth wedding anniversary."

He chuckled. "It's tough to be a living legend."

Edie raised her fist to pop him one, but then decided that considering their circumstances, that was not a wise thing to do. And besides, Mitch was what was getting her through this. She still felt a warm glow every time she thought of the other night. That glorious, straddle ride home, with Pinter running flat out and her hair blowing back in the wind, was not just Mitch's way of saying that he stood by her and was not ashamed of her, but also his way of letting her know he was actually proud of what she had done. And that was a very big thing for her.

Emma Hyde had sent word via Mitch that all was forgiven and that Edie was still a welcome guest in her home anytime. She also said that Ed Hyde had fought very hard not to burst out laughing after they had gone back into the house.

Oma brushed aside Edie's attempts to apologize for shaming her good name. "*Sie machen aus einer Mücke einen Elefanten*," was all she said, which was the German version of "They are making a mountain out of a mole hill." That had also done a lot to lower Edie's anxiety.

Now, all that was left to do was the most humiliating thing of all. She could feel the eyes of the whole congregation burning a hole in the back of her neck. There were a few sympathetic expressions behind her, but there were far more who had seemed to glare at her as they walked in. The only good thing about today was that once she and Winnie and Lou made their confessions, it would squelch the wild rumors that were being passed from mouth to ear all through the village. Including the one that said there were boys present when all of this had happened.

As the sacrament was finished, Edie crossed her fingers. *Please let us be first.*

To her great relief, that was President Jones's plan. He thanked those who had administered the ordinance of the sacrament and then announced that there was a matter of business to be dealt with before the speakers would begin. "We shall begin by inviting Sister Edna Rae Westland to come to the stand," he went on, and then he gave her a warm smile as he motioned for her to come up.

That was encouraging. It was much different than how he had looked the other night.

When Edie reached the pulpit, she gripped it tightly with both hands for a moment and then slowly raised her head and looked out on the faces of the congregation, desperately trying to ignore her heart, which was thumping so hard that she thought it must be visible for all to see.

Faces jumped out at her in sharp relief for a few moments. Evelyn Adams was near the back but was smiling warmly at her. Suddenly, Nean stood up beside her and waved. Ency Butt had tears in her eyes, but as Edie looked at her, she mouthed, "Be strong." Mitch's face was calm, reassuring. He smiled at her too. One of the newer sisters, seated with her family near the center, glared at her with open condemnation. To Edie's surprise, several of the men looked more amused than anything. Oma gave her a brilliant smile and clasped her hands together. Most importantly, Emma and Ed Hyde also smiled their encouragement.

Edie took a deep breath and began. It was not what they expected. Nor was what came out of her mouth anything that she had planned. "Brothers and sisters, I am the wife of a cattleman. I am married to a man who plans to spend his life as a cattleman. And I am determined to stand by his side and be a partner with him in the cattle business. And I want our children, including our daughters, to be the children of a cattleman."

The reaction ran across the spectrum. Surprise. Bewilderment. Approval. Disapproval. But they were listening, and listening intently.

"On Wednesday, Winnie Hyde, Lou Hyde, and I were asked

to take some cattle out to pasture. As has been noted, each of us rode sidesaddle, as is the custom for women. It was about two miles out to the pasture. As I sat perched on my saddle, sitting sideways, hanging on to the small saddle horn with one hand and the horse's mane with the other, I asked myself: 'Could I rope a calf from this position? Could I chase down a maverick calf racing across a hillside without falling off? What if my horse were startled by a rattlesnake? Would I be thrown off?'"

No one moved. Every eye was fixed on her.

"And so, while the three of us were resting and talking, I wondered what it would be like to ride a horse in the same way a man does. 'Could that be so wrong?' I thought. 'How could I ever help Mitch in fulfilling the primary purpose of our ranch from a sidesaddle?' I wondered. And so, after making certain we were completely alone, I made up my mind.

"Yes, brothers and sisters, *I* made the decision. I want to make that perfectly clear. This was not Winnie's nor Lou's idea. It was mine and mine alone, and I did it without considering the possible consequences of my actions. And for that, I ask for your forgiveness.

"The thing I feel the worst about is this. I, who was the oldest, who was married and supposedly the mature one, willfully persuaded my two young friends to join with me in this decision to answer those questions that were buzzing around in my mind." She looked down at the Hyde family, who filled most of one bench. "Brother Hyde, Sister Hyde, Lou, Winnie. I am sorry. I regret having caused you pain and embarrassment. And I ask for your forgiveness specifically, because if it hadn't been for me, your daughters would not be getting up today."

She looked directly at Mitch now. Her voice went soft. "And I also publicly ask for my husband's forgiveness, though he has already privately given it to me."

Edie paused for a moment; then, deciding there was nothing more to be said, she moved away from the pulpit and, with lowered head, came down and rejoined Mitch. The room was silent. There was no audible reaction to her confession. Was that good? She didn't know, and she wasn't about to turn around and see if she could discern what they were thinking.

Winnie was up and to the pulpit in a rush. She was crying before she reached it. Ignoring her tears, she looked down at her parents. "Mama. Papa. I am so sorry that I have shamed you. I am sorry that we rode with our skirts pinned up."

She looked down at Edie. "It wasn't just Edie's fault," she cried. "Yes, it was her idea. But she didn't force us in any way. As she talked about it, I had some of those same questions. If it isn't bad for a man to ride straddle, why would it be for a woman? I wanted to know what it would feel like to ride like the wind. And so I did it. I did it willingly. We did think we were alone. I'm sorry. I ask you all to forgive me and not to blame my family."

Sobbing, she went back to her seat. As Edie watched, her mother and father reached out and put their arms around her. They were both smiling at her. Edie felt remorse flood over her. That was what the people were looking for. Sorrow. Repentance. Contrition. Humility. For a moment, she thought about going up again and starting over.

But Louise was already up and moving to the pulpit. Edie couldn't help but smile at her as she did so. What a delight this one was. Petite, bubbly, impish, impetuous, giggly, silly, insightful, with a wit like a rapier. Behind the pulpit she looked even tinier. And she was frightened. Edie could see it in her eyes. But they were dancing with excitement, too.

Lou went up on tiptoe, as if she had to do that to see over the pulpit. "Brothers and sisters," she began. "I too want to ask for your forgiveness for being so . . . so wanton as to pin up my skirts and ride straddle on a horse."

Edie gulped. *Wanton* was not quite the word she would have chosen.

But Lou had realized that too. "Uh . . . not wanton. I didn't mean that."

Someone guffawed behind Edie. And that did it. Lou started to giggle.

For a moment, everyone was shocked. But there's something about a giggle that is infectious. One giggle tends to trigger another, and that's what happened now. Several children in the congregation sniggered out loud. So did a woman somewhere behind them. Edie saw that Mitch was fighting hard not to laugh.

That was too much for Lou. She laid her arms across the pulpit and put her head down on them, laughter rippling from her like the music from a player piano that had been wound up tight.

Turning her head slightly to the left, Edie looked at the Hydes. Emma had one hand up to her face and her head was bowed. She looked as though she was dying of embarrassment. Ed, however, was glowering at his daughter, hoping she would look up at him so he could end this right here and now.

Unfortunately, the rest of the Hyde children, with the exception of Winnie, were giggling now too. Winnie looked horrified, but even Will was fighting hard to hold it in.

As for Lou, she was unsuccessfully trying to regain control. She would finally get it stopped only to see her siblings laughing, or adults who were trying hard not to smile, and she would lose it again. "I'm sorry," she would gasp and then collapse again as laughter shook her body.

A movement out of the corner of her eye caught Edie's. Ed Hyde was up, his face like a thundercloud. Lou saw him too and paled. He stuck out his index finger and shook it at her. His eyes were crackling with anger.

"I'm sorry," Lou began again. "I know we done wrong and . . . uh . . . did wrong and—"

But correcting herself set her off again.

"Emma Louise Hyde!" roared her father. "That is enough!" And he started forward.

The look on his face was enough to have sobered anyone or anything, and it instantly sobered Louise. With a look of sheer panic, she blurted out. "I did wrong. I shouldn't have pinned up my skirts and rode straddle. I am terribly sorry. Please forgive me." And she backed away from the pulpit. But then, that irrepressible spirit came flitting back. She bent down, cupping her hand to her mouth, and then, as if speaking to conspirators, she blurted out, "But it sure was fun."

As she darted back down to sit beside her mother, President Jones quickly got to his feet and came to the pulpit. He had to wait there for a few moments for two reasons. There wasn't anyone in the congregation who wasn't laughing now. And he himself was having a hard time keeping a straight face. After a moment, he got some control, held up his hands, and the hall gradually quieted.

"Well, brothers and sisters," he said, trying to look solemn, "I'm not sure that is quite what we had in mind when we asked these girls to confess. But I feel that all three of them have expressed true remorse. They have asked for our forgiveness. All in favor of extending that forgiveness to them, please show by the raise of hands."

Every hand in the hall shot up, including that of the bachelor who had reported their transgressions to the branch presidency.

Notes

Here, from Louise Hyde's life story, is a description of the day the three girls were brought forward to confess their "sins" to the members of the branch:

"As usual, Louise got the giggles, uncontrollable giggles. The other two girls, scared sick, wept, stood, and between sobs, told their shameful stories and humbly sued for forgiveness from the congregation. Whether it was a form of hysterics or not, each time Louie attempted to speak, she was assailed by a fit of giggling. The patience of those in authority was tried and they were losing patience. At this time, Louise saw her father arise in the congregation, and start toward her, and this was instantly sobering to her. To forestall him she quickly spoke. 'Please forgive me,' and then added 'but it was lots of fun anyhow.' As she hastily sat down, overpowered again with giggles, the congregation of course, voted to forgive them" (Joyce Ann Hunt, "Emma Louise Hyde: 27 November 1879 to July 6, 1954, 3–4," in Family Search archives).

CHAPTER 40

December 25, 1890, 6:45 a.m.—EDW Ranch—Monticello

"*Frohe Weihnachten*," Oma said. "Happy Christmas to the both of you."

"And to you too, Oma," Edie said. Then she jumped up. "Okay, then. I am going to make us waffles with the new waffle iron Mitch got me for Christmas."

"Whoa!" Mitch cried. "Not quite yet." He went to the tree, reached around to the very back, and brought out a roundish bundle wrapped in brown paper and tied with a string. He handed it to Edie.

Her face registered both pleasure and surprise. "*Was ist das?*" she asked. "You already gave me my present."

"It's not from me." Mitch looked at Oma. "What's the name of that guy who comes around with St. Nicholas in Germany and helps him distribute gifts to the children?"

"*Knecht Ruprecht*," Oma replied.

"*Ja, ja.* Ruprecht." Then to Edie, "This must be from him."

Amazed at how much like a little boy Mitch was at the moment, Edie tore into the package. When she saw what it was, her face fell. She unfolded a pair of new Levi's and shook her head. "I think there is some mistake. These must be for you."

Mitch stood up, took them from her, and held them up against himself. "Uh . . . I don't think they're gonna quite fit me."

That was painfully obvious. The legs came only to the middle of his shins, and the waist was about two inches too short on both sides. Edie gave a little yelp. "They're for me? You bought me Levi's?"

"Yeah, but you'd better try them on." He colored slightly. "I had to have the man at the store find a clerk who was about your size 'cause I had no idea what size you would take."

"But—" With a cry of delight Edie yanked them from him, gave him a quick kiss, and darted into the bedroom. Three minutes later she came strutting out. She was wearing one of his shirts and the Levi's.

Mitch gave a whistle. "Whoo–ee, you fill those out real good, Mrs. Westland."

Now it was Edie that colored.

Mitch looked at Oma. "What do you think? Shall we give her the rest of what Ruprecht brought for her?"

"*Ja, ja. Das ist gut.*"

"Another present!" Edie cried in dismay. "No, that's not fair. All I got you was a new holster and belt for your pistol."

Mitch ignored that and started for the back door. He looked over his shoulder. "It's kind of bulky. Can you help me bring it in?"

"Bulky? Mitch, what have you done?"

He beckoned with his finger. "Come and see."

Edie looked at Oma. "Come. Let's go see what this man of mine has done."

Oma smiled. "I've already seen it. You go ahead."

Since first light was barely lightening the sky, Mitch grabbed the lantern from off its hook as they went through the kitchen and out the back hallway. He gave a little bow and motioned for Edie to go first. "After you, dear."

When they stepped outside, Edie was taken aback. She had

expected to find whatever it was on the small back porch. It was empty. The only thing in sight was a saddled horse at the back hitching rail. She looked around again while Mitch watched her, looking as though he were the one who was getting the gift. Then suddenly Edie realized that it wasn't Pinter tied up at the rail. "Whose horse is that?" she asked.

Mitch took her by the hand and led her off the porch. He walked around, holding up the lamp so she could see the animal more clearly. "Does he look familiar to you?" he asked.

It was a black horse with white stockings and a white blaze on its face. "No, I've never seen it before."

He lifted the lamp higher. "Sure you have. Many times, actually."

Her perplexity deepened. "I have never seen this horse before. I'm sure of it."

"Remember that day we went with Maggie and Leona to the mountains for gooseberries?"

Edie was still blank. "But . . . we took President Jones's buckboard and his horse that day. It was a sorrel mare. I remember it . . . very—" She gasped and then grabbed the lantern from his hand and went up to the horse's head, looking it up and down." When she turned, her eyes looked as wide as wagon wheels. "Bally?" she asked in awe.

Mitch laughed in delight. "Yep, it's Old Bally of Horsehead Mountain."

Edie set the lamp down and began rubbing the horse's nose. "He's perfect, Mitch. Perfect! Wherever did you find him?"

"I found him at Thompson Springs. The instant I saw him I thought, 'There's Bally.'"

"So you've had him since October?"

"Yup. I sent him south with Fred Adams. Fred brought him up yesterday with George and Evelyn." He laughed. "It's been all

Evelyn and I could do to prevent Nean from coming and telling you. She's more excited than you are, I think."

Edie turned back to the horse. "That's not possible. Oh, Mitch. You promised me you'd find me a Bally someday, but I had completely forgotten about it. I'm so excited." Then her eyes lifted. "And you even put on one of *your* saddles. Are you trying to get me in trouble with President Jones again?"

"That ain't my saddle," he drawled.

For a moment Edie was puzzled, but then she grabbed the lamp and peered more closely at the saddle. "This is for me?"

Mitch grinned. "*Ja, ja!* Vee cannot haf you riding in voman's saddle no more," he said in a pretty good imitation of Oma's accent.

Edie turned, the tears spilling over. "It's really my saddle?" she asked again.

"Well, let's make sure." He took the lamp from her and held it up. As he did so, his finger ran across some hand-tooled lettering on the skirt of the saddle. Edie moved in and gave a low murmur. "Oh, Mitch." With a cry of joy, she set the lamp down on the ground and threw her arms around him and kissed him. Then she turned and looked again.

Clearly visible in the lamplight she read what was inscribed there: *Sisterhood of the Wind* was printed for all to see.

Mitch pulled her close and gave her a quick kiss. "Merry Christmas, Edie."

"Thank you." She could barely get it out. "Thank you, my dearest Mitch."

He stepped back. "Let's go in and have some breakfast, and then I'll saddle Pinter and we'll go for a ride." His smile broadened. "Probably not down into town quite yet. Don't want you being brought up before the congregation again."

He started for the porch, but she pulled him to a stop. Her

face was suddenly radiant through the tears. "I lied," she said, her eyes sparkling. "I do have one more present for you."

That took him aback. "What?"

She took his hand and moved it down until it rested on her stomach. Then she put her hand over his and went up on her toes and kissed him softly. "You're going to be a father, Mitch. Merry Christmas."

Notes

Knecht Ruprecht, or Farmer Ruprecht, is a big part of the Christmas traditions in Germany. He accompanies St. Nicholas, typically wearing a brown coat, to determine if the children have been bad or good. If bad, he leaves them a lump of coal or a switch (a hint that they need more discipline), but if good, he leaves treats of various kinds. The children polish their shoes and put them by the fireplace on Christmas Eve, and that's where the gifts are placed. Some families substitute a man's large stocking for the shoes and hang it on the fireplace mantle.

By the early 1890s, women who lived on farms and ranches had begun wearing their husbands' or brothers' Levi's jeans because they were so rugged and practical. It wasn't until 1934 that Levi Strauss began making jeans specifically for women.

CHAPTER 41

January 31, 1891, 7:50 a.m.—EDW Ranch—Monticello

As Mitch walked into the kitchen, rubbing at his chin to make sure he'd gotten all of the whiskers off, he stopped. Edie and Oma were standing shoulder to shoulder in front of the table, and they were looking like two little girls who had just done something naughty.

"All right," he growled. "What are you two imps up to?"

They stepped back, Edie to the left, Oma to the right, and opened up a view of the table. Hiding behind a large stack of waffles, a bottle of Log Cabin syrup, a heaping plate of bacon and eggs, and a pitcher of milk was a two-layer cake covered in white frosting.

"Happy birthday!" they both sang out.

"Well, well," he said, grinning. "Thank you." He went over and gave Edie a quick kiss and then kissed Oma on the cheek. "Why didn't you wake me sooner?"

"It's your birthday, silly," Edie said. "There ought to be some privileges on your day."

"Well, I appreciate that, but I've got to go out and get the cow milked or she'll be busting her udder. It will only take me—"

"Already done!" Edie sang out. "And the milk is in the ice house."

He came back and took her in his arms. "Aren't you the

energetic one?" Then as he bent down to kiss her again, he added in a whisper, "How are you feeling?"

Her laugh tinkled merrily. "The same as I am every morning now. Wonderful. Not bad morning sickness. Right now I'm so hungry I could eat everything on the table, so let's sit down and say a blessing on the food so we can eat."

Fifteen minutes later, Mitch pushed his chair back and groaned. "That was wonderful, ladies. Thank you very much."

"Oh, no you don't. You have to have a piece of cake."

He groaned louder. "*Ach!* I'll burst like a bubble."

Picking up a knife, Edie started cutting the cake into small slices. "You'll survive. Oma baked this cake for you, and her feelings will be deeply hurt if you don't eat it. Right, Oma?"

"*Ja, ja,*" she said with a chuckle.

"All right," he conceded. "If I must. But why are you cutting those pieces so darned small?"

8:35 a.m.

After breakfast, Mitch saddled up both Pinter and Bally while Edie changed to her jeans, one of Mitch's woolen shirts, a leather jacket and cowboy boots. "Do you think this will be warm enough?" she asked as he came back into the house.

"It's a bit brisk out there right now, but we are in the middle of one of the warmest January thaws that we have seen in years. I'm guessing the temperature might even hit into the fifties today. So I think you'll be fine."

"And you're sure this is what *you* want to do? It is your birthday, remember."

"It is. What could be better? A beautiful day. A beautiful woman. Two fine horses. No sidesaddle to be seen anywhere."

He turned. "Oma, if we're not back by next week, send someone looking for us."

9:48 a.m.—Horsehead Peak Road, West of EDW Ranch

When Mitch gave Edie the choice of where to ride, she, of course, chose the road to the mountains. It was a place she never tired of, and it always pleased her deeply to be riding a horse who looked so much like the giant horse's head on the mountain. They let the animals take their own pace, walking closely enough together that occasionally Edie and Mitch could reach across and hold hands.

Their days of unusually warm weather had left the lower part of the road all but dry. Farther up it would get muddy, and eventually it would be covered in snow too deep for the horses, but Mitch didn't plan to go that high. Though Edie was doing remarkably well, he remembered Aunt Jodie's counsel to not overdo things. They would ride for an hour or two and then turn back.

"I've got a question for you," Mitch said after a while.

"What?"

"Uh . . . maybe it's too early to ask this question, but I was wondering, when I'm in Colorado, would you like me to buy some things for the baby?"

"Oh, my! I wasn't expecting that. Of course I would." Edie smiled. "As long as you let me have input and don't just try to surprise me." Then she gave him a strange look. "Why would you think it's too early?" But even as she asked it, she guessed the answer. Her eyes softened with love. "Are you worried that if we lose the baby, having baby things would only make it harder for me?"

Mitch nodded. "Something like that."

Edie leaned across to him and took his hand. "I want you to listen to me. I know you're worried, and I love you for that. But I'm not going to lose this baby. I'm not. I can feel that it's different this time. I . . . I can't explain it to you. But everything is going to be fine. So yes, I have a whole list of things we need."

"Will you give it to me before I go?"

"It's not a written list." She tapped her head. "At least, not yet. It's up here." She pulled Bally to a halt. "But if you want, we can go back and we'll make a list."

He reined in Pinter. "That's okay with me."

She reached over and punched him on the shoulders, her eyes impish. "The proper answer is, 'Oh, Edie, making a list of baby things that you want me to buy while I'm in Mancos is the very thing I most wanted to do on my birthday.'"

Mitch gave her a teasing smile. "You took the words right out of my mouth."

February 11, 1891, 7:55 p.m.

Wednesday, February 11th

This is my first entry in the new journal that Mitch bought me while he was in Mancos. My previous one is now full and put away in a safe place.

Yesterday afternoon the men returned from Mancos. As always, I was very happy to see Mitch return. However, I must admit that this trip was not as bad as some. Mons Peterson went to Mancos too, so I asked Emma if she wanted to bring Ellie and Little Mons to our place and stay with us until they got back. She was very pleased, and so was Mons. It also gave Oma company when I went down to help Sarah with the school.

In spite of my reminders that we have a limited budget, Mitch spent over $50 on baby things in Durango. I tried to appear to be angry, but that's hard to do when you're so delighted. So we now have several little nightgowns, a snowsuit for next winter, two packages of flats (cloth diapers as they are calling them now), two boxes of safety pins, and some other small stuff, like a baby rattle and a teething ring. It pleases me that Mitch is as excited about the baby as I am.

Monday, February 23rd

Today was a perfectly awful day. Horrible in every way. The weather is nice again, so I invited Emma Peterson to bring Ellie and Little Mons up to be with Oma again so I could go help Sarah at school. When the weather is warm like this, the children get restless and want to be outside. As it happened, Sister Cedenia Foy, who is our Primary president, was also there. The plan was to finish school early and begin Primary immediately. As I am a called Primary teacher too, that worked out nicely for me.

But we didn't count on the cowboys, though I guess we should have. Mitch had told us that when they were in Mancos, they had seen some of the Carlisle hands there getting supplies too. Only their idea of "supplies" always includes a generous allowance of liquor.

Well, unbeknownst to Sarah and me, two of our young male students—I shall not list their names here but leave it up to the angels in heaven to record their deeds—had gathered up two or three empty beer bottles that the cowboys had left behind on one of their weekly drunken rides through town. Somewhere they found a ladder, and while we weren't looking, they climbed up on the roof and tied the bottles in the meetinghouse belfry. They thought they might provide a tempting target for the cowboys some time.

Well, that's exactly what happened. About an hour later, three or four cowboys came riding into town. We could tell right away they were pretty much liquored up, so we had all of the children gather up on the stage where there are no windows that look out on the street. We hunkered down and told them to be very quiet until the cowboys passed by. They passed by without bothering us. Where they were going, we couldn't tell.

At two o'clock, Sister Cedenia came with the younger children to start Primary. The children always like that time because they don't have to do schoolwork, so they were all very happy and we forgot about the cowboys. However, to our great horror, about a quarter of an hour later, they returned, drunker than before. We heard them coming and had all the students crouch down so it would look like the building was deserted, but suddenly the riders started blasting away at the schoolhouse. We thought they were shooting at us. We later learned that they had seen the bottles dangling in the belfry and decided they were perfect for target practice. The result was instant panic and pandemonium. When we heard the bullets hitting the logs on our end of the building, the children began to scream and cry. We were pretty scared too. We knew the cowboys weren't shooting at the children, but when they saw the children through the windows running to the other end of the room, they started blasting away down at that end. By that time, children were hiding under their desks or clinging to each other. Older brothers and sisters huddled over their siblings to protect them. Sarah, Cedenia, and I crawled around, telling the children to stay down. (I am now about four months along, and it is no longer comfortable for me to be crawling around on my hands and knees on a hardwood floor.)

The cowboys thought that all the pandemonium was hilarious and decided to "make them little chickies scatter," as we heard one of them yell. So they started shooting some more. I was where I could see out to the street, and

I think they were mostly shooting at the roof, not trying to actually hit the children, but they were so drunk they didn't know what they were shooting at. We could hear the bullets hitting the logs. Then one window pane was shot out, which only terrified the children all the more.

About that time, the cowboys ran out of ammunition. Off they trooped to Mons's store. He wasn't there, so they shot off the locks and helped themselves to more bullets and whatever else struck their fancy. Seeing our chance, we opened the windows on the back side of the building and had the students crawl outside. There is a ditch right behind us and we had them crawl along that, staying out of sight.

Or so we hoped. However, one of the men saw us and came running, shouting at his buddies to follow. He shot a couple of times into the air and shouted for us to show ourselves. A minute later they had all of the children and the three of us women lined up in a double line in the street. "School's out," one of them chortled. "Let's march 'em home."

Roaring with laughter, completely oblivious to the terror they were creating in the children, they lined us up on both sides of the road and started marching us down the street. If anyone even stepped a foot out of line, they'd fire at the ground in front of them. If one of us women tried to help a child, they waved their pistols in our faces and threatened to shoot us directly. It was a very frightening experience. Through it all, I kept thinking, "This could cause you to lose the baby." And that frightened me far more than the shooting. I nearly fainted.

And then, a little miracle happened. Sister Foy called out in a loud voice. "Children, we're going to sing a Primary song now. Let's all sing, 'Love at Home.'" And without waiting for the astonished cowboys to react to that, she began: "There is beauty all around, when there's love at home."

Sarah and I saw immediately what she was doing, and we joined in: "There is joy in every sound, when there's love at home."

The older children understood and started singing, urging the younger ones to do it too. Soon all were singing: "Peace and plenty here abide, smiling sweet on every side, Time doth softly, sweetly glide, when there's love at home."

What happened next was astonishing. The men were baffled for a moment, but then they stopped shooting. They actually stepped back, watching the children marching past them, singing as only children can. "Love at home, love at home."

One by one they began holstering their pistols. One man started to yell at the children to shut up, but the man next to him cuffed him hard, nearly knocking him down. I couldn't believe it. After a minute or so, they turned and started walking away, heads down, shoulders slumped. I think I even saw the one who had lined us up reach up and wipe a tear from his eye.

About then, our brethren, who had been out east of town plowing, were seen coming hard on their horses, having heard the gunshots. In panic, the cowboys mounted up and disappeared in a cloud of dust.

It was a good thing. Mitch and the others were so furious when they learned what had happened that I thought they were going to go after them. But finally Mitch took me home and made me rest for the remainder of the afternoon. That evening I was okay again, and there were no complications with the baby.

The last letter I got from Aunt Jodie told me that I should feel the "quickening" between the 16th and 25th week after conception. Though I continue to feel good and am having only an occasional queasiness, I have been eagerly awaiting the first signs of life as confirmation that everything is all right. If my calculations are right, this is the fifteenth or sixteenth week. Tonight, we had another small miracle. As I was telling Mitch about what had happened, I felt the baby give me a good swift kick with his foot. I started to cry because I knew then that everything was all right.

Friday, March 13th

Joy! Joy! Joy! This is about the 18th week. I am feeling life every day. Mitch lay beside me on the bed tonight with his hand on my belly. He actually laughed out loud when he felt it for the first time. I told him that I'm sure that it's a boy and that he's gonna be a bronc buster when he grows up. It is an incredible thing to feel that little life within me and know that this will be our child. I remember the story from the first pioneers who came through the Hole in the Rock to Bluff. Up on San Juan Hill, after their last push up a difficult grade, someone chiseled five words in the face of a rock cliff. WE THANK THEE OH GOD.

That is what I say this night. My heart is full. I thank thee, oh God.

Thursday, March 26th

Big surprise today. Mitch and Johnnie brought in about forty head of cattle this afternoon. My joy was short-lived, however, for they leave again in the morning to go back and round up the rest. Mitch said the herd was getting too big to handle and that he and Johnnie were low on food and wanted to get a hot bath and a hot meal before they headed back up. In reality, I know that he came down to make sure everything was all right with me.

What did I ever do to deserve this man? I thank thee, oh God.

Saturday, April 11th

President Jones, Charles Walton, and Edward Hyde came out to see me today. They are thinking ahead to this summer and the Pioneer Day parade. Their wives are the overall committee for the holiday's preparations, and they asked if I would help Maggie and Leona Walton prepare games and contests for the children. And here is what warmed my heart. I will only be expected to help plan the games and not to actually carry them out, since they know I may be in my confinement by that time. (Aunt Jodie thinks I am due between August 1st and August 10th. It startled me to think that by that time I could actually have a baby. It is clear that everyone now is convinced everything is going to turn out all right with my little bronc buster.

Notes

In those first early years in Monticello, trouble with the cowboys was much more frequent than problems with the Indians. I have blended what appears to be three separate encounters with drunken cowhands into one incident, though one actually occurred while Primary was being held at the meetinghouse. However, the other details, including the beer bottles in the belfry, the children running back and forth inside the building while they were being shot at, climbing out the windows to escape, being marched along as the cowboys shot at the ground to keep them in line, and the effect that their singing "Love at Home" had on the cowboys, are all mentioned in the sources (see *Saga*, 107; *Anchored Lariats*, 100–01; Inez Foy Barker, "History of Thomas Bingham Foy," Ancestry.com).

CHAPTER 42

July 23, 1891, 10:20 p.m.—EDW Ranch—Monticello

The ropes beneath the straw mattress squeaked as Edie turned over in bed. Yet again.

"Can't get comfortable?"

She snorted in disgust. "You try getting to sleep with a pumpkin inside your stomach."

Mitch chuckled. "A pumpkin with little hands and feet?"

Edie took his hand and pulled it over to her stomach. He immediately felt something hard jab the palm of his hand. He laughed in delight. "Well, two more weeks at the most."

She groaned. "No, Mitch, don't say that. Cedenia said it could come anytime from *now* up to two weeks from now."

"But," he chided her gently, "she said she believed it was more likely the latter date."

"You're no fun," she grumped. "Then I *am* going to the dance tomorrow night."

"Edie, you are to take it easy. That's what Sister Foy said."

"I am taking it easy. I'll go to the parade and potluck picnic, but nothing else in the afternoon. I promise I'll come home and rest until the dance." She reached out and took his hand, interlocked her fingers with his, and brought his hand up against her cheek. "Please. I am so sick and tired of being stuck in the house."

"We'll see what Oma and Sister Foy say after the parade. Okay?"

"Okay, just so you remember that I get the final say."

July 24, 1891, 11:50 a.m.—Main Street, Monticello

Like cities and towns all across the United States, Monticello celebrated America's Independence Day with great gusto and activities that started in the morning and went until late in the evening. But all across Utah and in scattered settlements in Arizona, Colorado, Nevada, Idaho, and Wyoming, three weeks following the Fourth of July, an even more robust celebration took place to honor the arrival of the first Mormon pioneers in Utah forty-four years earlier.

This was their "founder's day," though they called it "Pioneer Day." Having it so close to America's birthday allowed them to use all their decorations and preparations twice. On their last freight run over into Colorado, the men had bought a double portion of fireworks—firecrackers, Chinese rockets, and sparklers, a favorite of the young children—sacks of hard candy to distribute during the parade, red and white bunting, and dozens of miniature American flags.

The children had decorated their little wagons and wooden tricycles, dressed up their dogs and cats to look like Lady Liberty or the flag itself, made whistles from willow sticks earlier in the spring when the bark was still soft, or made clapping boards that cracked as loud as a gunshot.

The children, up early for the festivities, weren't waiting for the formal games to start after the parade. They had started gathering at the meetinghouse by ten, once their chores were done. Some of the girls were inside playing jacks on the hard wooden floor. Outside, other girls were jumping rope or playing hopscotch. The boys played marbles or mumblety peg on the grass with their pocketknives. Any boy who was anybody had to have his own pocketknife.

Mitch, Edie, and Oma had come about an hour early so that Mitch could park the buckboard in the shade of a cedar tree along the parade route. He had then unhitched the horse and put it into Mons Peterson's corral. Edie and Oma had gone off to visit with the women. Mitch had joined the men at Fred Jones's corral to look at the various horses that had been entered into the race that afternoon.

Now, as both sides of the street filled up and children zigzagged back and forth, jockeying to find the best place to catch the candy, Edie, Oma, and Mitch headed for the buckboard. As they reached it and Mitch helped the ladies up into it, Edie turned to him. "I'm feeling fine. I'm definitely staying for the picnic," she declared, "and maybe for the games as well."

Mitch and Oma exchanged glances, and then Oma said. "Vee vill see, *ja?*"

"*Ja,*" agreed Mitch firmly. "We will see then."

1:45 p.m.—EDW Ranch

"Thank you for letting me stay for the picnic, Mitch."

"I'm glad you felt up to it. Thank you for coming home to rest now."

"I am tired. But I am determined to go to the dance, so I'll lie down for a while." She turned to her grandmother. "But, Oma, go back with Mitch for the games and races. I'll be fine."

Oma Zimmer shook her head. "I do not have great interest

in seeing old men racing horses around and around like crazy little boys. I vill stay and rest also."

"Okay," Mitch said, "I'd better get back. Me and Charlie Walton are in charge of the gunnysack, the three-legged, and the wheelbarrow races for the kids." He came over and gave Edie a peck on the cheek and put on his hat. "The afternoon activities are supposed to be done by five or five-thirty. I'll be back about then. That will still give us plenty of time for supper and to get back in time for the dance."

"Good. *Auf Wiedersehen, Schatzi. Ich liebe dich.*"

"And I love you too. See you around five."

1:57 p.m.—Main Street

As Mitch tied Pinter behind the Waltons' barn and came around to the front of their cabin, he saw that several men were standing together across the street in the yard of the Peterson store. They were in a tight huddle, talking quite animatedly with each other. Curious, Mitch started across the street. Something was definitely up. "What's going on?" he asked as he joined them. Fred Jones answered first. "We just got word that Tom Roach had a flask of whiskey delivered to his house yesterday for today's celebration."

"What?" Mitch cried. The others nodded somberly. Charles Walton looked particularly depressed by that. And no wonder. Tom Roach was one of the cowhands that worked for Carlisle. He was one of the few that was married. He and his wife, Minnie, lived in town in a small cabin next to the Waltons. Tom was in his mid or late twenties. Minnie looked like she was not yet twenty. Because Tom was gone a lot of the time out riding the range, Jane Walton had made a special effort to befriend Minnie, and they had become friends.

"Who brought it for him?" Ed Hyde demanded to know.

President Jones shrugged. "One of his cowhand rowdies, I'm sure. Carlisle brought in two wagons full of freight from Mancos day before yesterday. Knowing Tom, he paid one of the drivers to pick up a flask just for him. That way he doesn't have to share it with his buddies."

"He can't do that!" Mitch exclaimed hotly. "Especially not if he's going to be part of the festivities today." But he knew there was no law against having liquor in the town. More to the point, in the eyes of the cowboys, bringing in liquor was no great offense because drinking was not a sin. And if a man got in trouble or things got out of hand, as the men often did when they got drunk, it was not seen as great crime, because the man was "under the influence" at the time. Like that time they had ransacked Mons's store and made two little girls "dance" as they shot at the dirt in front of them. On that day, a drunken Roach had been the ringleader.

Charles spoke now. "Minnie came over earlier and told Jane that someone had delivered some whiskey to the house. According to her, it is a large flask. Tom was out at the ranch and wasn't home, but she didn't dare refuse to take it because Tom knew that it was coming. Minnie was in tears when she came over. Tom didn't go to the ranch today. He's been in his room drinking all morning. Minnie is frightened because he gets so mean and violent when he's drunk. She's worried that he might hurt someone else. That's why she warned Jane."

"Is it true that he's murdered six men?" Charlie Walton asked.

"That's what they say," Charles Sr. said. "Back in Texas, supposedly in barroom brawls."

"Seven," Mitch corrected him grimly. "The last time I took cattle up to Thompson Springs, on our way back we stopped in Moab overnight. When the locals heard I was from San Juan they asked me if I knew Tom Roach, who worked for the Carlisles. When I told them yes, they told me to steer clear of him. Said one night when he'd been drinking hard, he took insult at something an Indian said. Tom shot him down in cold blood and then jumped on his horse and hightailed it out of there. They sent for a marshal, but one never came."

John Rogerson was nodding. "He's two completely different men—one when he's drunk, one when he's sober. He can be a real gentleman when he hasn't been drinking. But like his wife says, when he's liquored up, he's meaner than a dog with rabies." He shook his head. "She's a nice young girl. Not sure how she ended up with a lowlife like him."

"Oh, he's a charmer when he's sober," Mons piped up. "I know more than one of our girls who nearly swoon when he smiles at them."

"Then I say we go over there and take that flask away from him before he gets himself drunk," Charlie said angrily. "We can't have him coming out here with all these kids."

"Can't do that, Charlie," Charles Sr. said. "As long as he's not making trouble, he's not breaking any law. We can't go busting into his house just because we don't like what *might* happen."

They all turned to their leader to see his reaction. President Jones was pulling at his lower lip. "Nope. Not one thing we can do except prepare for whatever contingency develops." He turned to Mitch. "Mitch, can you handle the games this afternoon if we take Charlie away from you?"

That was an easy one. "Sure, the ladies always pitch in too. We'll be fine."

"Good. Then Charlie, I want you staying close to your house.

Look like you're staying busy, but keep a constant eye on the Roaches' front door."

"It's a small cabin," Charlie nodded, seeing where this was going. "There is no back door."

"If you see him come outside, you immediately alert the rest of us. We'll shadow him and make sure he doesn't make any trouble."

"The dance is going to be the problem," Mons said. "There won't be no keeping him away from that."

That sobered them all. There was no question about that. The president turned to Mitch again. "You know Bill McCord, don't you?"

"Yeah. Helped him pull a couple of his cows out of a bog a couple of months back."

"Good. Why don't you watch for him tonight, take him aside, and tell him what's going on? I understand that Roach is afraid of McCord, is that right?"

"That's what they say. Supposedly, one of the men Roach killed back in Texas was McCord's cousin, so Roach is terrified that McCord is going to try to get even with him sometime. But that's a good idea, President. McCord's one of the most level-headed of the whole bunch out there. He'll help us keep him in line."

"In a way," Hyde said, "the dance will be easier. We have strict rules for the dance. No liquor inside. No one comes in if they're drunk. You can only dance when they call your number. And any rowdiness gets you thrown out of the hall. And those rules are the same for everyone, so Roach can't say we're picking on him."

Mons agreed. "I say we have two men at the main door at all times. Intercept him before he gets in. If he's drunk, we don't let him in. That's the rule."

President Jones looked around. The others were nodding. "Okay then, that's our plan. Let the other brethren know what's going on, but quietly. We don't want to alarm the women and children."

7:40 p.m.

"My, my! You are *wunderschön, Schatzi.*"

Edie gave Mitch a dubious look. "You're playing a little loose with the truth here, aren't you, sir? This is a 'hard-times' dance, remember? We go in our everyday clothes. Isn't that why you're in your Levi's and a work shirt?"

He didn't back down. "Well, it's a new dress, and I still think you're beautiful."

"And I agree vit Mitchell," Oma said.

"*Danke,* Oma. *Danke, Liebling,*" she said, clearly pleased. It was a new dress, which Sarah Rogerson had made for her and finished two weeks ago because Edie could no longer fit in any of her other dresses thanks to her bulging stomach. This one had an extra panel sewn in, which Edie would mostly conceal under a light summer jacket.

"I appreciate your gallantry, Mitch, but I still look like a woman who's hiding a medicine ball under my dress, and that's not my idea of beautiful. And, by the way, don't you dare ask me to dance tonight. I'll not be waddling around the dance floor."

"Dat's right," Oma said sternly. "You vill not dance tonight. Absolutely not. You must not strain yourself."

"Why not?" Edie shot back. "Maybe that would jar this little guy enough to get things started." Then she smiled sweetly at Mitch. "And by the way, you, mister, are limited to dancing with women who are married or girls under the age of ten."

"Yes, ma'am," he said, touching the rim of his hat in salute.

Edie's expression softened. "Except for Lou and Winnie Hyde. I promised them you'd dance with them so they could dance with at least one handsome man tonight."

"That will be my pleasure," he said. He moved forward, turned around, and offered them both an elbow. "Then, ladies, your buckboard awaits. Let us be off."

Notes

Two different sources refer to this Pioneer Day dance as a "hard-times" dance. It took some searching before I was able to discover what that meant. Since a ball or more formal dance required fancy dresses for the women and suits or Sunday clothes for the men, they called a "come-as-you-are" dance a "hard-times" dance, probably from the idea that in hard times there wasn't enough money to spend on fancy clothing.

CHAPTER 43

July 24, 1891, 11:35 p.m.—Community Hall—Monticello

Handing them both glasses of lemonade, Mitch sat down beside Edie and her grandmother.

"Thank you, dear," Edie said, cupping her hand to her mouth to make herself heard over the music and the rhythmic clapping of the crowd as they kept time to the fiddle.

"*Ja, danke*, Mitchell," called Oma, who was on the other side of Edie.

"*Bitte*." He leaned in close and spoke into Edie's ear. "Are you sure you're not getting tired? It's almost midnight, you know."

"No. I'm having too much fun. I just wish you and I were up there dancing."

"Yeah, me too," he deadpanned. As she laughed at that, he leaned across her and raised his voice. "And what about you, Oma? Isn't this a little late for you?"

She flashed him a chiding smile that for a moment looked just like Edie's. "Are vee keeping you up past your bedtime, Mitchell?"

He gave it up and turned back to watch the whirl on the dance floor. At the moment, the floor was filled with couples dancing a Virginia reel. The Waltons—father and son—had the room jumping with an energetic rendition of "Ragtime Annie." Charles's bow was moving so fast that it was almost a blur. Charlie was at the small organ, his fingers racing as he chorded in time with his father. Kneeling on the floor behind the organ, fifteen-year-old Will Hyde worked the foot pumps with both hands, sweat dripping from his forehead and face. The organ rested on a cradle made of polished hardwood and was open to the back. Having someone else do the pumping for him allowed Charlie to concentrate on keeping up.

Standing next to Charles, Fred Jones had put aside his branch president's hat for the night and was calling out the dances. *Singing* out the dances might be a better term, Mitch thought. President Jones had a deep, rich voice and kept perfect time to the rhythm of the music, but he was always embellishing the traditional calls with little innovations of his own. For example, "Forward two and a three and a bow, back again and a smile right now. Swing your partner, do-si-do, move on back, don't stub your toe. Change it now and see-saw round, back again and don't fall down."

He kept the dancers and the audience smiling continuously, and, late or not, the crowd was still having a grand time. Off in the corners, the younger children were doing their own version of the dance, trying to keep up as best they could. The older folks sat on the benches that defined the dance floor, stomping their feet and clapping to the music but otherwise content to leave the actual dancing to the young.

All of the windows were open to provide at least some circulation, and four lanterns hung on hooks driven into the log walls up and down both sides of the hall. Mitch sat back, willing himself to relax. So far Tom Roach had behaved himself, but he had disappeared again ten minutes ago. Gone home to sleep it off? Mitch doubted that. Not being Sunday tomorrow, the dance wouldn't end for another hour.

Just then Mitch saw Jane Walton making her way toward them. When she saw that he was watching her, she inclined her head slightly to one side, a silent indication that she wanted to talk. Mitch got up, telling Edie he needed to ask Jane a question, and moved over to join her.

As he came up to her, she took his elbow and turned so they were facing away from Edie and Oma. "Tom's back out front," she said in a low voice. "He's pretty drunk. Ed thinks he's got that flask stashed out back in the woodpile somewhere. He's demanding that he be allowed to come back inside the dance."

"Who's out there watching him?"

"Ed, Mons, John, and Willard Butt."

"I'll go out too," he said.

"Good. They're hoping that since he knows you, maybe you can reason with him. Willard asked me not to tell President Jones or Charles, because he wants the dance to keep going. If they stop, that could set Tom off."

"All right." He touched her arm. "But you stay inside here too, Jane."

She smiled bleakly. "That's what Mons said, too. I'll go over with Edie and Oma."

"Thank you." They turned together and walked back to where Edie and Oma were sitting. "Hello, Jane," Edie said as they came up. "Come and sit for a while. You look tired."

"I'll be right back, honey," Mitch told Edie as Jane settled into a chair.

Once Mitch plunged into the crowd, he increased his pace and headed for the door. He saw Bill McCord off to one side talking to Parley Butt and nearly changed directions but decided it was better to see what was going on outside first.

As he stepped out, the sight that greeted him was not good. Tom Roach and a young woman faced a small half circle of men who blocked the way to the door. Mitch pushed his way through the circle, noticing that there were two or three cowboys there as well. He didn't know them by name, but he was relieved to see that they were standing off to one side, staying out of it for now but definitely not siding with Roach yet.

He focused on Roach, sizing up the situation. He was wearing a pistol now, something he didn't have earlier. One hand was hovering just above the butt. His face was flushed and his eyes had a wild look in them. Though his feet were spread in a wide stance, he swayed back and forth like a willow branch in a breeze. His left hand was gripping the hand of the girl, holding her in place beside him.

Mitch recognized her. Eliza Holyoke. Her name came to him as he saw how frightened she was. She was from Moab, but her family had lived in Bluff for a time a few years back. Now she was visibly trembling and was as white as a sheet.

"Hey, Tom," Mitch called easily, taking a step forward, holding his hands away from his waist so Roach could see that he wasn't wearing a gun.

Roach was momentarily startled and fell back a step.

"It's Mitch Westland, Tom. How ya doing?"

Tom's eyes narrowed. "Stay out of this, Westlake," he said, his voice heavily slurred.

Mitch raised his hands to shoulder height and took another slow step forward. "Actually, it's Westland, Tom. Had a couple of drinks too many, have we?"

He shook his head and raised the pistol. "Stay back," he commanded again. Then he launched into a string of profanities in which about every third word was *Mormon* and about every fifth one was *dancing*. Mitch took a deep breath and eased forward another step. "That your wife, Tom?" he called.

There was a guffaw, as if Tom found that ridiculous. "Are you some kind of idiot, sod buster? My wife's at home, where she belongs." He pulled the girl forward. "But Eliza here promised me a dance. And now these pig farmers won't let us in."

"Well," Mitch said, deciding he had gone about as close as he dared, "Eliza looks a little tired to me, Tom. Why don't you let her sit down a minute while we work this out?"

"This ain't none of your affair, Westlake. So butt out." But to Mitch's enormous relief, he let go of Eliza's hand and waved her away. With a sob, she darted forward. The men opened ranks and let her pass and then closed in again. Eliza stopped behind Mons and turned back to watch.

Looking confused and dangerous, Roach eyed Mitch suspiciously, cursing steadily under his breath. "Them hillbillies won't let me in the dance hall. How can I dance with Eliza here if they ain't gonna let me in?"

"Well, Tom, there's a small problem. You're wearing your gun. The rules say no guns in the dance hall." Mitch gestured toward his waist. "See? I'm not wearing a gun." He waved toward the men behind them. "None of them have a gun. Tom, those are the rules. And they're the same for all. Mormon and non-Mormon. No guns inside. You can see that, can't you?"

Roach lunged forward, causing the men to gasp and Mitch to fall back a step. Tom was waving the pistol back and forth but keeping it mainly pointed at Mitch's head. "I got this," he shrieked. "That means you and your rules can be damned. Now get out of my way."

Just then the music from inside stopped. There was a smattering of applause, and then they heard Charles Walton's voice call out, "All right, folks. Next dance will be the quadrille. This is dance number nineteen. So find your partners and sashay back onto the dance floor."

The men behind Mitch turned and looked inside. That was all Roach needed. He leaped forward, knocking Mons out of his way, and grabbed Eliza's wrist. "Come on, girl. We gonna dance." And he started for the door, pulling her behind him before anyone could stop him. Cursing himself for not anticipating that, Mitch went after Roach. The others fell in behind him.

When the door slammed back with a loud crash and Roach staggered in dragging a terrified girl in his wake, every head inside the meetinghouse spun around to stare, and for a moment no one moved. They had not witnessed what had happened outside, so to see a drunken man enter the hall wearing a pistol came as a deep shock.

The quadrille got its name from the fact that four couples stand together so they form an open square facing each other. Enough couples had already taken to the dance floor to form six or seven squares. There wasn't room for any more, and a few couples were returning to their places when they were stopped by the sudden activity at the front door.

As Roach jammed his pistol into his holster and pulled Eliza toward the floor, Mitch jerked his head to look over in the corner. In a glance, he saw that Edie and Oma and Jane Walton were still seated in the same place. Their faces had drained of color, pretty much like everyone else's in the room, but he saw that where they sat was about as safe as one could be inside the hall. He turned back, looking for Bill McCord. He saw him pushing his way through the crowd, his face grim. Before Mitch could reach him, McCord broke free and went straight for Roach. "Tom," he called sharply. "You can't come in here with a gun. You know that."

Roach's hand dropped to the butt of his pistol like a striking snake. He swore at McCord, his face twisted into a contemptuous sneer. "You ain't the boss here, Bill. Ain't givin' up my gun." The slur in his voice had disappeared, and he was as cold as a block of ice.

Mitch and President Jones reached McCord at about the

same moment. "It's all right," Mitch spoke low. "Let's give him his dance. Then we can get him out of here."

McCord saw the wisdom in that instantly. "Agreed," he said.

The branch president turned and called to Charles, who was on the stage, his fiddle in one hand, the bow in the other, stunned into immobility. "Charles," President Jones called, "Mr. Roach did sign up for the quadrille. So let's get started."

Roach swore loudly and looked at the two musicians. "You heard the man, hayseed. Let's hear that fiddle start to sing."

As Charles recovered and lifted the fiddle to his shoulder, one of the cowboys Mitch had seen outside came up and joined the three of them. "Bill," he said in an urgent whisper, "when me and the other boys saw how drunk Tom was earlier, we unloaded his pistol. He's only got one bullet in the chamber. Couldn't get that one out before he came back. But we got the rest."

Mitch felt a jolt of relief. *Wonderful!* But he immediately shook his head. But was it true? Cowboys had a code of sticking together. And even if there was only one bullet, firing it into a crowd of women and children was not something they could let happen. He looked at McCord and President Jones. "Watch things. I'll be right back."

Mitch moved quickly over to Edie, Oma, and Jane and sat down beside Edie, whose eyes were wide and whose color was gone. "It's all right, Edie. They're going to let him dance one dance, and then we'll get him out of here."

"Can't we just leave?" she asked. Her face was almost ghostlike.

He looked around and made up his mind. "Yes. We'll go out the back door as soon as the music starts. Then I'll take you home." He turned to Jane. "And you too."

"No, I'm all right. But I'll stay back here out of the way."

And at that moment, things began to unravel.

CHAPTER 44

July 24, 1891, 11:44 p.m.—Community Hall—Monticello

Ed and Emma Hyde had come with their family to Monticello in the summer of 1888 along with Mitch and Edie. The following summer, two other Hyde brothers and their families came up to join them. Frank Hyde, who was younger than Ed and of a more serious nature, was the designated floor master for tonight's dance. It was an assignment he took very seriously. Just as the squares were getting into position, he strode over to Roach. "Hold on," he snapped.

Mitch was dumbstruck. What was he doing? Couldn't he see how drunk this man was? Did he not see the pistol strapped to his waist? Of all the times to be a stickler about the rules. His jaw set, he started over to try to intercept Frank and cut this off. Ed, looking equally astonished, was moving toward his brother too. They weren't fast enough.

Frank thrust his face right up next to Roach's, clutching the master sheet in one hand. "You are number seventeen, Mr. Roach. That number was called two dances ago and you weren't here, so someone took your place. This is dance number nineteen. Please leave the floor."

Astonished by this unexpected interruption, Roach took a step back. "I . . . I had to go to the bathroom," he stammered.

Yeah, Mitch thought, *out to the woodpile for a drink, more likely*. He was still several feet away, so he called out, "Frank, it's all right. Let him dance."

If Frank heard this, he ignored it. Charles was dumbfounded too. He had stopped stroking his fiddle and was staring down at them.

"I'm sorry, Mr. Roach," Frank said primly, "But you have lost your turn. You'll have to wait until your number is called again."

"No!" Roach roared. He lowered his shoulder and thrust Hyde out of his way, still dragging Eliza behind him. He moved onto the dance floor, his head swinging back and forth, glaring balefully at the faces around him, daring them to intervene.

The nearest dancers to him were a young, single couple, Peter Bailey and Stella Hyde. Peter, oldest son of Nephi and Annie Bailey, was a strapping boy of seventeen. Stella, who was sixteen, was Ed and Frank Hyde's younger sister, a pleasant girl with an enchanting smile. At the moment, they were like two statues, shocked into immobility by this sudden turn of events.

Roach fixed his eye on them and jerked his thumb over his shoulder. "That's my place," he roared. "Get out of there." And, not waiting for a response, he stepped forward and gave Peter a hard shove. Stella screamed as Peter crashed backwards into her and they both went down hard.

Peter was up in an instant as the hall erupted. Women and children screamed. Those seated leaped to their feet. The people on the dance floor were scrambling backwards. But Peter was in a fury. He came at Roach, his fists cocked and ready for battle. Roach's left hand streaked down. When it came up again there was a flash of light on steel. He had a hunting knife with a six-inch blade in his hand. He lunged forward, slashing at Peter. Peter jumped to one side and barely escaped the vicious strike.

Pandemonium exploded in the hall. Mitch whipped around and darted back to the corner, planting himself in front of Edie and Oma and Jane. "Get down," he hissed. "Crawl back underneath the chairs. And stay down." Eyes wide, they scrambled to do what he said.

Just then, a movement caught Mitch's eye. To his left, several of the young couples who had been in the squares were crawling on their hands and knees toward the back wall. Mitch recognized the nearest person. It was Jacob Adams, whose family had come to Monticello just a month or so earlier. Following right on his heels were the two young daughters of Ben and Mary Ann Perkins. Not sure what they were doing or where they thought they were going, Mitch just gawked at them for a moment. They had reached the back wall and were scuttling along it. When they reached the nearest window, the boy looked back for a moment and then urged the girls to go out the window. He followed the moment they disappeared, but then Jacob's face popped up again. He was waving frantically at Mitch. "Brother Westland," he said in a panicked whisper. "I know where there's a gun. I'll go get it."

"No!" Mitch shouted, but the boy was gone again. He nearly went after him. The last thing Tom Roach needed was to see someone with a gun. But then Mitch pushed the thought away. What was going on behind him was far more urgent. Satisfied that the women couldn't be seen, he ran back to the dance floor, where Roach and Peter Bailey were facing off, Roach with his knife, Peter bravely shielding Stella with nothing but his fists.

By this point, men were cautiously moving in on Roach from every side. Roach saw them and screamed at them to stay back, slashing at the air with his knife. Everyone stopped, and for a moment the scene seemed frozen.

Everyone except for Frank Hyde. He was livid. Not only had the man violated every rule of dance etiquette, but this madman had knocked his little sister to the ground and now was coming at her with a knife. With a roar of his own, Frank went after Roach, fists flailing. The knife flashed, and flashed again. Frank screamed in agony and dropped to his knees. He was staring at his hands, which were suddenly covered in blood.

Things were happening so swiftly now that they registered only momentarily in Mitch's mind. In the melee, Roach had finally released his grip on Eliza Holyoke. She was frantically crawling away from him on her hands and knees, sobbing hysterically. Roach's head jerked back and forth, his eyes crazed like a trapped animal's. Realizing that he was surrounded, he dropped the knife and clawed for his pistol. "Stay back!" he screamed. "Stay back or I'll shoot!"

For one split second, Mitch considered hurling himself at the drunken man. *If there really was only one round of ammunition in his pistol. . . .* He instantly rejected the thought. A wild shot could hit anyone.

Whatever it was surging through Roach's body now—whiskey or adrenalin or both—it had cleared his mind of any fog. "Everybody outside," he shrieked. "Now!" He swung around to another terrified couple and thumbed the hammer back. "*Now!*" he roared as he started backing toward the door. He grabbed the nearest man—Mitch couldn't tell from this angle who it was—and jammed the pistol in his back. "If anyone tries to get away, I'll shoot this hillbilly, you hear me?" he screamed shrilly. "So help me, I'll shoot him down like a dog. Now, outside. All of you."

President Jones and Bill McCord, who were still together, assessed the situation and reacted in a flash. "You heard him!" the president shouted. "Everyone outside."

Dazed and numbed, the people started following Roach as he dragged his hostage outside into the night. The moment Roach was out the door and the crowd blocked his view back inside,

Mitch ducked down and raced back to the corner. He dropped to one knee, bending down until he was looking into the very terrified face of his wife. "You three stay right here and—"

"No, Mitch!" It was sheer terror. "Don't leave us."

He reached in and touched Edie's cheek. "I have to. Roach knows me. I was talking to him just a few minutes ago. If I don't come out, he'll start shooting people. Just don't move. He can't see you in here. I'll come back for you as soon as I can." Then he walked swiftly over to join President Jones and Bill McCord and the last of the crowd pushing through the doorway. McCord leaned in closer to Mitch. "You with me on this?" he asked softly.

"Yes. But you'd better take the lead. I've already confronted him once, and he's not happy with me."

McCord gave him a curt nod and turned to President Jones. "Keep everyone else back. No one does anything stupid, okay?" It was superfluous counsel. Roach was shouting and swearing at the crowd as he waved his pistol at them. They were too shocked to do anything but what they were told. McCord waited until the crowd's movement stopped, and then he stepped forward. He wore no pistol, but he still held his hands high, palms forward.

"Tom," he called, his voice even and calm, "it's Bill McCord."

Roach whipped around. "Get out of here, Bill. This ain't none of your affair."

As Mitch had done earlier, McCord starting moving very slowly forward. "Come on, Tom. I know you've been wronged, but you don't want to shoot anyone here tonight. These people have treated you no differently than they treat their own people. They've been fair with you. Come on. I'll take you home and you can sleep it off."

"Stop!" Roach screamed as McCord took another step forward. The two men were just six feet apart now. Roach's pistol was pointed directly at McCord's chest. "Back off, Bill, or I swear I'll blast a hole in you."

McCord stopped and turned his head to the crowd. "Folks, Tom here means business. There's no need to panic. Just do what he says. Everyone stay back and stay calm."

It was clear that Roach was on the brink of losing control. He had backed himself into a corner, and he knew it. He glanced to one side and saw a fellow cowboy nearby. "Bart," he yelled. "Get my horse. Now!"

"Go, Bart," McCord called. "Do what he says."

As the man turned and darted away, Roach swung back to face the group. "All right," he said, voice still unnaturally shrill, "give me all your money. Empty your pockets. Toss me your bill-folds. Anything you have. Everybody! Do it or I start shooting."

President Jones turned. "Do what he says, folks. We don't want anyone getting hurt here."

There were probably thirty-five or forty people outside now, and all were held at bay by a single gunman, who possibly had only one bullet. Mitch's mind was racing. McCord knew that too. Should he suggest that they rush him? But again he pushed the idea aside. Give him a horse. Let him leave and perhaps they could end this without anyone getting hurt. Mitch reached in his vest pocket, drew out the five or six dollars he had there, and tossed it forward.

Seeing that the crowd was complying with his commands, Roach seemed to settle down a little. "That's right," he said, almost talking to himself, "give me your money and you'll never see me again."

Suddenly, to Mitch's surprise, McCord started forward again, moving very slowly. "Tom, no one means you any harm. Put the gun down, take the money, and ride out of here. Let's end it right now."

Roach stiffened, his eyes narrowing into tiny slits. "I'll end it right now, you—" He raised the pistol. "Get back!" he screamed, spittle spraying from his mouth.

"Okay, okay," McCord cried. "I'm moving back, Tom, just settle—"

BLAM!

The shot, fired from no more than four feet away, caught McCord full in the chest and slammed him backwards. Screams, shouts, and cries broke out all around them. People dropped to the ground. Men threw themselves in front of their wives and children. One woman fainted. McCord lay on his back in the dirt, his eyes filled with surprise, a red stain spreading across his shirt. He wasn't moving.

"I told you to get back." Roach was like a wild man. "I told you, McCord! I told you!" He turned around, cupped his free hand to his mouth, and screamed, "Bart! Where's my horse?"

Inside the deserted hall, Jane Walton had crawled out from her hiding place and crouched down, trying to see what was going on outside. She could see the backs of the people in the lamplight streaming through the open door, but it was too dark to see what was happening. She could hear Roach yelling but couldn't make out what he was saying. She too had seen the young people go out the windows and decided that her first priority was to get Edie to safety. She could not lose another baby. But as Jane turned back, the blast of a gunshot exploded in the night. With a cry of alarm, she turned and sprinted for the door. Her husband was out there. Her children were out there.

Mitch was standing off to one side, about four or five feet away from McCord's body, still shocked into immobility. That also gave him a clear view of the door and into the dance hall. When a figure appeared there, silhouetted by the lamplight behind it, he gave a low cry. For a moment he thought it was Edie and his knees went weak, but as the figure came through the door, pushing through the crowd, he saw that it was Jane.

"No, Jane," he cried. "Don't come out here."

By that time she had pushed her way through the people and saw McCord's body on the ground. Her eyes took in the scene in an instant. Jane Walton had been stake Relief Society president for about three years now. She had traveled by horse and buggy to every ward and branch in the stake, in all four seasons. Though she had never before faced a man with a gun, she had dealt with nearly everything else: blizzard conditions, sandstorms, torrential rain, flooded washes, quarreling spouses, sick children, diseased Indians, women giving birth prematurely, fractured bones, gruesome cuts. It was not in her nature to blanch at such things and turn away. To Mitch's horror, she took a step forward, extending her hands in supplication.

"Tom, it's Jane Walton. Your neighbor and friend. Minnie's friend."

"Get away!" he shouted.

She took another step, very slowly, her expression not changing. Mitch nearly leaped in front of her, dove at her to pull her down to the ground, but he feared any movement would panic Roach. So he watched in horror as she took another step. She spoke in perfect serenity.

"Tom, I want to help you," she said. "Let me help you. I'll get you some food for the trail."

Roach was nearly sobbing now as the muzzle of his pistol lowered a little. "No, no! Stay away, Miz Walton. Stay back."

But she didn't. She took another step. Then another. He kept yelling at her, but her face was composed and had a soft smile on it. "I'm here to help you." He backed up a step. She kept coming. She stopped only when she was about three feet in front of him. Everyone was watching in horror. No one dared breathe. There wasn't a whisper of sound. "It's all right, Tom," she soothed. "It's all right. Let me help you."

Off to Mitch's left, someone cried out. It was a hoarse voice, a boy's voice. "Drop the gun, Tom Roach! I've got you covered."

Mitch spun around. A solitary figure stood just inside the circle of lamplight. Mitch gasped when he saw that it was Jacob Adams. Then he saw the glint of lamplight on steel. Jacob had a long-barreled rifle or shotgun up to his shoulder, pointed at Roach.

Roach's reaction was instantaneous. With an animal howl of betrayal, he leaped forward. He seized Jane and yanked her around so she was in front of him. At that same instant, he raised his pistol and fired. Mitch heard the distinct CLICK of the hammer falling on an empty chamber.

KABOOM! A split second later a heavy caliber rifle blasted off with a flash of gunpowder.

Jane Walton's body jerked violently as the bullet passed beneath one arm and went all the way through her body and out the other side. She turned her head and looked up at Roach as she slumped in his arms. "Tom," she gasped, "you have hurt me." Then her head fell to one side and she slipped from his grasp, dead before she touched the ground.

Inside the hall, Edie had crawled out from beneath the benches and was walking in a daze across the room. "*Nein,* Edie. *Nein!*" Oma's voice was calling to her. But Edie, blinded by tears, dazed by the gunshot she heard outside, and sick that it might have been meant for Mitch, moved forward. She also had to stop Jane. This was the woman who had taken her into her home when she had nowhere to stay. This was the woman who had welcomed her into her family and became, quite literally, a second mother to her.

Edie spied the top of Jane's head and saw that she was

standing next to the drunken cowboy. Her heart all but stopped. "Jane! Jane!" She broke into a lumbering run for the door, cradling her stomach in both hands. Before she had gone two steps, the blast of a heavy gun rocked the night and Jane's head disappeared. With a shriek of horror, Edie leaped forward.

When Mitch heard Edie's cry, he froze for a moment, not comprehending. He swung around and saw her figure coming rapidly toward him across the dance floor.

"No, Edie!" he screamed, racing forward. "No!"

He was not quite fast enough. As she reached the doorway, running hard now, she didn't see the threshold across the doorway. Most cabins and buildings put a six-inch board across the bottom of a doorway to discourage mice and other critters from coming inside. It was an automatic thing to step over it without giving it a second thought. But Edie's eyes were fixed on the spot where Jane had been a moment before. The toe of her left shoe caught on the threshold, and she went down face first. Her hands jerked away from her stomach to break her fall, but not quickly enough.

Mitch uttered a low, guttural cry as he heard Edie cry out and saw his wife go down hard, face first. He sprinted forward. When he reached her, her face was twisted with pain. She was sobbing and clutching at her stomach with both hands.

Notes

Virtually every history of San Juan County describes the tragedy that happened on Pioneer Day, 1891 (see *Saga*, 108–09, 338; *Anchored Lariats*, 102–03; *Indians and Outlaws*, 107–09; *History*, 80–82; *Life of Parley Butt*, 16; *Monticello*, 113–14; and "Jane McKechnie Walton," *SJR*, 1–2). In the history of the San Juan Mission, Jane Walton, who was serving as the San Juan Stake Relief Society president at the time, is the only pioneer woman known to have been murdered. She was the first person to be buried in the Monticello Cemetery. Bill McCord was buried a short distance away from her grave site.

Since no detailed eyewitness accounts were recorded at the time, the various reports contain minor contradictions. For example, one source says the Adams boy was named Jacob; another says it was Frank. One source says that Roach tried to attack Peter Bailey with a knife; others say he attacked Frank Hyde when he tried to intervene, probably to help his sister Stella. The biggest question is who actually fired the shot that killed Jane Walton.

It is agreed that during the panic inside the dance hall, Jacob Adams snuck out a back window with some other young people. He evidently knew that Charles Walton kept a loaded rifle above his fireplace in his house, which was just a short distance away. He got the rifle and returned with the intent to shoot Tom Roach before he hurt someone. He did fire at Roach, and it was at that time that Sister Walton was hit and killed. As one source summarizes it:

"Opinions differ as to which was the fatal shot. Some eye-witnesses think Roach had no bullets left in his gun. Others disagree. Frank Hyde stoutly maintains because of where the young boy stood, [that] it would have been impossible for his bullet to have reached Mrs. Walton without first hitting Hyde himself" (*Saga*, 109).

In an article written for *Blue Mountain Shadows*, Jane Walton's great-great-grandson wrote this: "Some say Roach pulled Jane in front of him for protection. Some say he jumped behind her. Others say Tom Roach had no bullets left in his gun. But a shot was fired, which hit Jane in the upper torso. Roach fled, left the country and was never heard from again. Jane was carried to her home where she died. . . . As to who actually killed Jane Walton . . . the only tangible evidence was the hand-written diary of Charles E. Walton Sr. who recorded: 'Between twelve and one o'clock, Roach started a row and killed a cowboy. Jane was accidentally killed by Jacob Adams, a drunken Mormon boy, with my own gun, a 35–70 caliber. The ball passed through her body, just under the arms, killing her instantly'" (Buckley Jensen, "Jane McKechnie Walton: Early Pioneer Martyr" in *San Juan Record,* Mar 23, 2011).

Jacob Adams was not a child of George and Evelyn Adams from Verdure. I could not find to which Adams family he belonged. The Charles Walton diary entry is the only one that speaks of him as having been drunk.

CHAPTER 45

July 26, 1891, 10:18 a.m.—EDW Ranch—Monticello

Edie's eyes fluttered open when Mitch opened the door a crack and peeked into the room, even though he had oiled the door hinges so they opened and shut without a sound. "Come in," she said, so weakly that he could barely hear her.

"I didn't mean to wake you."

"You didn't. I'm just lying here."

He moved over and sat down in the chair beside their bed. He took her hand in both of his and squeezed it softly. "Can I get you anything before I leave?"

She shook her head. Her face was so pale and wan that he wanted to gather her up in his arms and lend her some of his strength, to let some of his energy flow into her body.

"Thank you for going," she finally said. "I'll be all right."

"I don't feel good about leaving you," he whispered.

To his surprise, she raised up on one elbow, her face filled with a determination so fierce that it was almost frightening to him. "You have to go, Mitch. You have to!" Edie fell back, gasping and panting for breath. "You have to go for me," she finally managed. "Be there for me. Say my farewells to Jane."

Mitch bent down and laid his cheek against hers. He could feel the fever in her body. "I am going, Edie. But I still have a few minutes before I have to leave."

The fight in her was gone as quickly as it had come. "Good. Stay with me until then."

He sat back as she closed her eyes and began to relax again. Suddenly, though they were still closed, her eyes brimmed with tears. Turning her face away, she wiped at her eyes with the back of her hand. "Why do the people I love so much have to die? Eliza. Little Bird. Now Jane." Her voice choked in her throat. "If I lose the baby too, I—" Her words were cut off by a sob from deep within her. "I can't lose the baby, Mitch. I can't. If I do, I think I shall die as well."

What could he say to that? *You're not going to lose the baby? I won't let you die?* The bleakness settled in on him, knowing how empty those words would sound to her. At that moment the bedroom door opened and Oma was there, and he was saved from answering. She beckoned for him to come out. "Somevun is here, Mitchell," she whispered.

Edie's head jerked around. "I don't want to see anyone," she croaked.

He nodded. "I know. I'll be right back." He left swiftly and pulled the door shut behind him. As they moved away from the bedroom, he touched Oma's shoulder. "Who is it?"

She smiled briefly. "Come and see."

Two minutes later, he opened the bedroom door and stepped back inside. Edie's eyes opened. "Who was it?"

"Someone I think you'll want to see, dear." He stepped back and pushed the door open wider to let his mother enter the room.

For a long moment it was as though Edie didn't comprehend, but then she started and held out her hands. "Oh, Gwen," Edie cried as she burst into tears again.

Mitch's mother rushed to her bedside, sat down beside her, and took her in her arms. Both were weeping now, clinging to each other as they cried. Mitch turned to his father, who had come up behind him. "I don't understand. How did you find out? How did you get up here so fast?"

Arthur stepped back out of the room and lowered his voice as Mitch followed. "Yesterday morning, just about this time, Willard Butt rode into Bluff. His horse was heavily lathered and nearly dead. Willard left here right after Jane was shot. He rode all night to bring us the news."

"Willard? But—"

"He told us that you didn't know that he was going. By that time, you were bringing Edie here. Well, you can imagine how shocked we were with the news of Sister Walton's death. The whole town of Bluff could barely speak. And when Willard told us about Edie, that shocked us even more deeply."

"But how did you get here so quickly?"

"By noon we had several wagons loaded. Almost everyone wanted to come up for the funeral. We knew it would take all night to get here in time, but we were determined to do it."

"In the rain? That was a terrible storm we had last night."

"Yes. We had to send men ahead with torches to find the road. At one point Bishop Nielson's wagon went off the grade and tipped over, but we righted it and kept on coming."

"Oh, Papa, I am so glad you did. Mama is just what Edie needs."

Oma was standing nearby listening to them. "Tell him the rest, *Bruder* Vestland," she urged.

Arthur nodded and laid a hand on Mitch's arm. "Aunt Jodie came with us."

Mitch felt his body slump at that news, and he had to steady himself against the wall as relief flooded through him. "Really, Papa? Really?"

"Yes. She stopped at the Waltons' for a few minutes to pay

her respects because she won't be at the funeral. Then she's coming here. Johnnie's got President Jones's buckboard and will bring her up."

Oma moved over to the big window and peered out. "I think they are coming now. They are almost to the lane."

"Wonderful." A sob burst forth from somewhere deep inside Mitch. "This is an answer to prayer, Papa. A miracle."

Just then they heard Edie cry out with joy from the bedroom. Arthur smiled and laid a hand on his son's shoulder. "I think your mother just told Edie about Aunt Jodie."

Oma came over to Mitch, reached up, and pulled him down enough that she could kiss him on the cheek. "You go to funeral now, Mitchell. Dat is very important for Edna Rae. Vee vill take care of her now. All vill be vell."

12:55 p.m.

Aunt Jodie slipped out of the bedroom as Mitch, Arthur, and Johnnie came into the house.

"How is she?" Mitch asked anxiously.

"She is resting at the moment."

"And the baby?"

She took a quick breath. "The baby is clearly under stress. I spoke to Cedenia Foy at the church before I came up. She told me about the bleeding and the contractions that followed Edie's fall. She also told me that she thought the baby was turned somewhat, probably from the severe jarring it took when she fell. My examination confirms Cedenia's diagnosis. If it weren't for being turned, I think the baby would have come by now."

At the anguish on Mitch's face, she touched his hand briefly. "It's not breech, or backwards. That would not be good. I'm hoping we can turn it back. But we can't wait any longer. Edie is exhausted and so is the baby. Now that you're back, it's time to see if we can get her started."

"What can I do?"

"Go in and be with her for a few minutes. She's anxious to hear about the funeral." She gave him a wan but encouraging smile. "After that, we'll have you men wait outside. Keep us supplied with hot water. That's about all you can do for now."

When Mitch opened the door and stepped into the bedroom, Edie turned and then quickly raised her head up. "Oh, Mitch. I'm glad you're back. Did Aunt Jodie talk to you yet?"

"She did. She told me where things are now."

She fell back on her pillow. "I can't believe she's here, Mitch. And your mother. It's a miracle."

"That's what I said too."

She pointed to the chair. "Come. Tell me about Jane's funeral. I understand half of Bluff came up this morning."

"Yes." He took both of her hands in his. "Aunt Jodie wants to start in a few minutes, so I'll just say this. The funeral was wonderful. A marvelous tribute for a remarkable woman."

"Who spoke?"

"I'll tell you all of that later. But there is one thing that was really significant. Charles was the last speaker." He sighed. "I don't know how he got through it, but President Jones said that it was his request to speak. And it was a wonderful, touching way to honor her memory. He talked about their courtship and some of the things that they went through together—" He glanced at Edie quickly and then away. "Including the fact that she could only have three children."

He stopped again, close to tears now. "But then he shared something that I think will help you as you struggle with her loss."

She had been looking up at the ceiling while he spoke. Now she turned to him. "What?"

"He told us that when Jane was a young mother with her three children—so about fifteen years ago now—her father came and visited her."

Edie nodded.

"Her father," he went on slowly, "who had died when she was two years old, the father that she had never really known, came to her."

Her eyes widened. "Oh."

"Yes. He told Jane that he had been sent to tell her that she was needed on the other side and that he had come to bring her home."

"Oh my word," Edie breathed.

"But Jane told him that because her children were still small that she could not agree to go with him until they were grown. Her father said that he couldn't force her to go, but then said . . . now listen to this. He said that he would come back for her when she was forty-five years old."

Edie gasped. "She turned forty-five on the sixteenth of this month. Remember? They invited us to come and have some cake to help her celebrate."

"I do remember," Mitch said softly.

The tears had started again and trickled sideways down Edie's cheeks. "So it was her time," she whispered.

"Exactly." He was finding it hard to speak too. "I'm glad Charles shared that with us. As horrible as this whole thing has been, that does bring a sense of peace."

"Yes. Thank you, Mitch. That helps very much."

He got to his feet, bent down, and kissed her gently on the lips. "Now, I have strict instructions to leave. But I'm right outside. And though we men aren't good for much right now, we are good for praying, and we'll be doing that."

"I love you," Edie whispered through her tears.

"And I love you, Edie. I'll be back in later to see you and the baby, all right?"

She smiled through her tears. "I will be here. And so will he."

9:15 p.m.

Mitch reached out and with the back of his index finger softly stroked the pudgy cheeks. "He is so tiny," he said in wonder.

Edie groaned. "Aunt Jodie thinks he weighs close to nine pounds. That's not tiny. It was like giving birth to a colt."

The baby was lying between them, his eyes closed, his features in repose as he slept. Mitch touched a red mark on his cheek. Edie smiled. "He got kind of beat up getting out of there."

"So was he turned to one side?"

"Yes, about a quarter of the way, but Aunt Jodie—" Her voice caught. "Dear, wonderful, marvelous Aunt Jodie was able to turn him back, and once she did that, he came out without too much trouble."

Mitch reached across the baby and laid his hand against her cheek. "I was so afraid that I was going to lose you, Edie. I've never prayed so hard in my life."

"Well, He heard you. It was a miracle. Cedenia told me that she had never dealt with a baby that was turned. She wasn't sure what to do. If Aunt Jodie hadn't been here, I think we would have lost him."

"And you too," he said in a bare whisper. "Aunt Jodie said we could have lost you, too."

"But that's not the only miracle," Edie said. "Did Aunt Jodie tell you what happened when he was born?"

"No, she just said that you were all right and that I was to get in here and be with you."

With an effort, Edie turned partway onto her side so she could look at him directly. Her eyes were dark in the dimness of the room, but he could see that they were shining. She began, her voice barely audible.

"I was so exhausted there at the end that I couldn't push anymore. Aunt Jodie and your mother kept telling me to push harder, that he was almost out. Then suddenly, there was one last, really hard contraction, and out he came. I wanted to shout for joy. But when I lifted my head to see him, I nearly fainted. He was black. And the cord was wrapped around his neck. Probably from when Aunt Jodie turned him back around."

Mitch stared. "Black?"

"Yes, not jet black. But a dark grey. All over. I thought he was dead. It was awful." She shuddered. "Horrible."

Taken completely aback at this news, Mitch leaned closer. "So what happened?"

"The instant she saw him, Aunt Jodie dropped the surgical scissors she had in her hand—she hadn't yet cut the umbilical cord—and grabbed the baby from Cedenia. She took the baby by the heels and held him upside down. And then I heard her saying, 'Breathe, baby, breathe.'"

She was staring at her hands now. "I was terrified. All I could think was, 'Not another one.' In a panic, I tried to sit up, but Oma and your mother pushed me back down again. They said I had to lie still. By now Aunt Jodie had unwrapped the cord. She was still holding him upside down with one hand and was rubbing his arms and legs with the other, all the time crying, 'Breathe, baby. Breathe.' And I heard someone else shouting,

'Breathe! Breathe! Breathe!' and realized it was me. I think I had stopped breathing by then too."

Edie's hands came up and covered her eyes as her shoulders began to shake. "It was so awful. More horrible than anything I have ever experienced. I finally had to look away. I couldn't bear to watch."

She fell silent, reliving it all over again in her mind. He waited. "But I had to see," she finally continued. "So I opened my eyes again. Just as I did so, Aunt Jodie gave him a smack across his bare bottom with the flat of her hand. I mean, she really hit him. It sounded like a gunshot in the room."

The tears were overflowing now. "And then came the miracle. Where she hit his bottom, the skin turned instantly pink. And it was a perfect imprint of her hand. And then—" She choked back another sob. "And then from that spot, pink started to flow outward in every direction. It went across his back, up his legs and into his feet. I even saw his tiny toes turn pink. Pink spread down across his chest and neck and across his face."

She turned to him, her cheeks soaked with tears now. "When the pink reached the crown of his head, he suddenly gave this little gasp—" A cry that was half laughter and half a sob burst from her. "And he started to howl. Oh, my," she cried joyfully, "did he howl. He was mad. He was howling, I was bawling, your Mom and Oma were jumping up and down and hollering like crazy. And I think that was when Aunt Jodie finally started breathing again too."

She had to stop and take a breath. "And thus it was that your son entered into mortality, kicking and screaming and fighting for his life. And I shall never, ever, not in my whole life, forget that sound or have the image taken from my mind of that tiny grey-black body turning a rosy pink."

Mitch was overcome with emotion, the image she had just

described now vivid in his own mind. And he felt a sense of gratitude unlike anything he had experienced before. He slipped out from under the sheet and knelt down beside the bed. He reached out and found Edie's hand. "I should like to pray," he said. "I should like to thank God for the gift of our son."

August 20, 1891, 7:40 p.m.—Church House—Monticello

Mitchell and Edna Rae Westland had their baby blessed and gave him his name about a month after his birth. On the first Thursday of each month, a fast and testimony meeting was held by each ward or branch, and it had become a tradition to have babies blessed as part of that worship service. In addition to virtually every family in Monticello being there, all four families from Verdure had also come up, along with Mitch's family and Aunt Jodie and her husband.

In the circle with Mitch were two other men—President Frederick I. Jones and Arthur Westland. The husky boy with lungs like a blacksmith's bellows was given the name of Mitchell Arthur Westland Jr. In addition to the baby blessing, two recently baptized children were confirmed members of the Church.

When those ordinances were completed, President Jones came to the pulpit. "Brothers and sisters, it is time for our testimonies. In keeping with our custom, we invite all who feel so inclined to come forward and share the feelings of their hearts and to bear witness of their testimonies. The time is now yours." And he sat down.

Edie was immediately on her feet. She had made up her mind yesterday that if she wasn't the first one to stand, she would never get up. Ignoring the astonishment on Mitch's face, she walked slowly to the pulpit, mindful that she was still pretty tender.

"Brothers and sisters," she began, her voice quavering with nervousness, "I pray that the Lord will help me to express the feelings of my heart. It is filled with joy, and it is filled with sorrow. Just a few weeks ago, sometime around midnight, a terrible tragedy took place within a few feet of where we now sit. Sister Jane Walton was taken from us. We deeply mourn the loss of her presence, her friendship, her love, and her compassion."

Her head lifted and she spoke more firmly. "Yet we do not grieve for her in the way that the world grieves for their dead, for we know that she is not dead. Though her body lies lifeless in the grave, we know that she has started a new life in the spirit world. It is my testimony that she continues to live, more glorious, more vibrant, more alive than ever she was here. It is only this testimony of the reality that she still lives that makes her loss bearable.

"While we mourn her loss, we also think of the joy of those who were waiting to greet her, including her father who had come once before to bring her home."

As she stopped, she looked down at Charles Walton and his family, who were seated three benches back. Charles had his eyes fixed on her, and she could see that his eyes were shining. Charlie, who sat beside his father, stared straight ahead at nothing. Maggie and Leona were openly crying. That nearly did Edie in. She took a handkerchief from her pocket and wiped quickly at her eyes and then her nose. Then she took a deep breath and went on.

"We call these losses tragedies, and in a way that is what they are. But consider this. Less than eighteen hours after Jane's death, something of quite a different nature also happened in our little town. A baby was born. Instead of death we had birth;

instead of sorrow we had joy. As I thought about that contrast, I thought to myself, 'Isn't that the story of life itself, of our mortal existence? Life is sometimes easy. At other times it can be very hard. And that's life.'

"And now I realize that a great part of my frustration these past two years as we have tried to start our family was that I forgot that basic principle. I became frustrated with God because He wasn't making life conform to my expectations, to my desires, to my will. Fortunately, one early morning, I was alone, reading the Book of Mormon. And the Lord reminded me in a small and insignificant but profoundly important way that His tender mercies never fail."

Edie looked around at the faces that were watching her with complete concentration. "I know I am taking too long, but there is one more thing I would like to say. As I was contemplating the events of these last two weeks, something came into my mind. Out to the west of Bluff, there is a place known as San Juan Hill. I see many of you nodding, because you know firsthand what hill I am talking about it. It was the last test of those forging a trail here, the last brutal, punishing grade on a long trail filled with many brutal and punishing grades. But this one came at the very end of their journey—a journey that they had assumed would take them only six weeks but instead took six months. This one came when they were trail weary, were low on supplies, and had teams that were as utterly spent and jaded as they were. But there was no choice. Between them and their new home lay San Juan Hill, and there was nothing to be done but to go up and over.

"So they hitched seven span of animals to each wagon—fourteen horses or mules to take each wagon up that impossible grade. Men wept as they lashed their exhausted animals forward, watched in horror as they stumbled and left smears of blood and hair on the slick rock as they fought their way upward.

"I've seen some of those bloody smears, and I've seen the scars that still exist on the legs of many of the animals down in Bluff, but that is not what I was thinking about as I thought this morning about the death of Jane Walton and the birth of Mitchell Arthur Westland Jr. No, what I was remembering about San Juan Hill was something I saw off to the right of the road, just below the crest of the hill. There, chiseled into the smooth rock face of a small cliff were five words. How many of you have seen those words for yourselves?"

Half of the adults raised their hand.

"The inscription reads, 'We thank thee, oh God.' That is astonishing to me. Knowing what these pioneers had been through, knowing what they still faced, knowing how much their faith had been tested, and that's what one of them wrote? They didn't exclaim, 'We did it!' or 'This was awful,' or 'Why did you make us do this, oh God?' They simply said, '*We thank thee.*'"

Edie lowered her head as the remembrance of her feelings from the other night swept over her and finally the tears did come. She didn't care. She didn't try to stop them. Raising her head again, she looked only at Mitch, though she spoke to the congregation. "My brothers and sisters, Mitch and I are just at the beginning of our lives together. We cannot see what lies before us. But based on what we have already seen, I think it is safe to say that there will be other deaths in our future, and hopefully, other births. There will be marriages and there will be funerals. There will be floods and there will be droughts. Some days will be filled with jubilation and some nights will be filled with weeping. But we have come here to stay. We have come here to plant our roots in the red soil of San Juan. We hope those roots go deep enough to bind our children and our grandchildren and our great-grandchildren to this same soil. San Juan is our home. Here we shall live, God willing. And here, God willing, we shall die. And through it all, we are determined to lift our heads to heaven and cry out with joyful voice, 'We thank thee, oh God.'"

Edie was barely aware of the tears, or of how many others—women and men and youth—were weeping too.

"One last thing," she said softly. "None of us knows what races there are yet for us to run, what trials there are yet for us to face, but my husband showed me a scripture in the book of Isaiah the other day. It gives me great hope for the future. It says this: 'But they that wait upon the Lord shall renew their strength; they shall mount up with wings as eagles; they shall run, and not be weary; and they shall walk, and not faint.'

"I thank God for the privilege of running that race, and I testify to you from my own experience that if we wait upon the Lord, we too shall rise up as though on eagles' wings. Of that I bear my solemn witness, in the name of Jesus Christ, amen."

Notes

We are not told who rode to Bluff to spread the news of Jane Walton's death, but someone did ride all that night, and several wagon-loads of people drove all the next day and night so they could attend her funeral on July 26th (see *History*, 80).

The story of Jane Walton's father coming to her from the other side when she was a young mother is told by her great-great-grandson. It was just eight days following her forty-fifth birthday that her life ended so abruptly (see Buckley Jensen, "Jane McKechnie Walton: Early Pioneer Martyr," in *San Juan Record*, Mar. 23, 2011).

EPILOGUE

CHAPTER 46

October 15th, 1919, 2:35 p.m.—EDW Ranch—Monticello

"Mama Westland? Are you here?"

"Yes, June. I'm up in the attic."

A moment later Edie heard footsteps coming up the narrow stairs, and then a figure appeared at the door. June Westland, Edie's daughter-in-law, appeared. She stopped, taking in the scene before her, and shot Edie a quizzical look. "What are you doing?"

The attic was a long, clutter-filled, narrow space under the V shape of the roof. There was only one small lightbulb hanging from a cord, which partially illuminated the room. Edie was sitting on a three-legged stool beneath the light with a book opened on her lap. Wearing her winter coat and gloves, she motioned for June to come forward. Her breath showed as light puffs of silver in the light from the single bulb. "Come, sit. I decided I was going to clean the attic before Mitch gets back from Germany. Then I found my old journals in our trunk."

"You kept a journal?"

"Three or four of them over the years, actually."

"Does MJ know this?"

"I think so. They go up through the end of 1910, after Frank and Tina were born and Oma Zimmer died. So Mitch Jr. would have been . . . um . . . almost twenty by then."

"Oh. He's never said anything about it. Do you still keep one?"

Edie shook her head. "No. After Oma's death, Frank and Tina were getting to be a handful, and it was about then that I was called as the Relief Society president. I guess I just never got around to it after that. But I haven't looked at these in years." She motioned again. "Come, let me show you."

June glanced at the cobwebs that were everywhere evident. "Ugh. There are spiders up here."

"It's too cold for spiders right now, dear," Edie said with a dismissive wave. She stood and walked back to the far end of the attic, where a battered old wooden chair had a box on it. She set the box down, brushed off some of the dust, and dragged the chair forward and motioned for June to sit. "Come on. I was just reading about the night when Jane Walton was murdered and when Mitch Jr. was born two days later."

June came forward, bent over, blew some more dust off, and sat down. When she looked at her mother-in-law, her eyes narrowed a little. "Have you been crying?"

Edie laughed, a little embarrassed. "Of course I've been crying. It was like I was back there on that horrible night as if it were only yesterday, not twenty-eight years ago." She brushed at her eyes.

June reached across and laid a hand on Edie's knee. "Will you read it to me?"

That startled Edie. "You mean now?"

"Yes. MJ took the children and the twins with him down into town. Grandma Westland is in her room. I think she's taking a nap. I finished my ironing, so I thought I'd come over and see what you were doing."

Edie still had her finger in the book. She opened it and smoothed the pages down. "It's several pages long."

June hesitated. There was no heat up here and it was chilly, but she had not removed her coat before coming up, so she nodded. "MJ won't be back for a couple of hours," she said with a shrug.

And so with that, Edie took a quick breath, turned back a few pages and began.

2:53 p.m.

For almost a full minute, June sat there with her head down, tears streaking her cheeks. When she looked up, she made no effort to brush them away. "Oh, Mama Westland. I've heard you tell that story more than once, of course, but there are so many details here I've never heard before."

Edie nodded. "I know. There were things that even I had forgotten."

"You are an amazing writer, Mama. I felt like I was right there with you." She wiped at her eyes. "As you can see. You have to read that to the family."

"Oh, June, I don't know. . . . I. . . ."

"I'm serious. Rena and Rowland are coming down from La Sal on Saturday to help us put in enough firewood for winter. They're already planning to stay Saturday night and go to church with us on Sunday. We usually do family night on Sunday afternoon between morning priesthood and Sunday School and afternoon sacrament meeting. So share this for our family night."

Edie liked the idea except for one thing. "I think the story of Jane Walton's death is too grim for the young ones. Maybe we could send them down to your house to play and let Frank and Tina watch them."

June was shaking her head before she finished. "I agree that the little ones shouldn't hear it, but Frank's fifteen now, and Christina is twelve. I think they need to hear this too. For just that part of it, we could send the young ones in another room and let them play games. I think they'll be all right for a while. My kids beg MJ all the time to tell them the story of when he was a tiny baby and got spanked real hard by that 'mean old lady.'"

"Is that what they call Aunt Jodie?" Edie chortled.

"Edna June does. I can't convince her otherwise. But they both think it's hilarious that Daddy got a spanking when he was so little. But the part you read to me just now, about how her hand left a pink handprint and then how the color spread throughout his whole body. Even I hadn't heard that from MJ before. And that's my point. This is a wonderful part of their heritage, and I'd like them to hear you read it to them. And for that matter, I'm not sure if Rena's two children have heard MJ's story at all."

Edie was clearly intrigued with the idea. June's mind continued racing. "If we did the Jane Walton part first, then they could join us for the rest of it. You have to do it, Mama Westland. For your children and your grandchildren."

Edie was actually very pleased with the idea and finally nodded. "All right."

"I'll call Rena and tell her," June said. "She'll be very excited."

As Edie closed the book and started to get up, June waved her back down again. "Mama Westland, can I ask you another question?"

She settled back again. "Of course."

"Did you know that Rena is starting to worry about whether she's going to have the same difficulty you had when it comes to having babies?"

That totally caught Edie by surprise. "She is? Why? She had Charles only ten months after they were married, and Lemuel seventeen months after that. That's hardly a problem."

"I know, but Lem is almost three now. She weaned him almost a year and a half ago, and she's still not pregnant. She's not panicked yet, but she is worried. I think it would relieve her a little to know that even though it didn't come easy for you, it didn't mean you were barren. The last time Rena was here, she and I were trying to remember the details. How long you had to wait. How many miscarriages you had."

That brought Edie's head up with a snap. "Has Rena had a miscarriage?"

"No, no. There's been nothing at all. She was going to ask you about it, but then they returned home before she could. So I told her I would ask. If you'd rather not talk about it, that's fine too."

Edie shook her head as she got to her feet. "I don't mind at all. If you think it will help Rena, I'm happy to. But let's go downstairs. It is getting a little chilly up here. And we need to check on Grandma Westland."

"I agree." June stood too. "Let's go make some hot chocolate."

"And if the twins didn't clean out the breadbox, I've got a few cinnamon rolls left."

"All the better."

3:15 p.m.

"Okay," Edie said as she pushed back her empty plate and cup and licked the frosting off of her fingers. "Where do you want to start?"

"Right at the beginning," June answered. "You were married in early January 1889. Were you able to conceive right away?"

Edie turned to her mother-in-law. "Grandma, you pitch in here too. There'll be things you remember that I don't."

Gwendolyn Westland chuckled. "Oh, I'm not sure my memory is that good." Which wasn't really true. Mitch's mother had turned seventy-nine in February. She had come to live with Mitch and Edie after Arthur had died in 1912. Her body was growing increasingly frail now, but her mind was still sharp, and she was an active part of the family.

Then, turning back to June, Edie answered her question. "Yes, I did conceive right away, within a month or two. I was ecstatic, of course. But then I miscarried at three or four months. That was a huge blow to me. I cried for two or three days, as I remember it."

"Was there any specific reason why you lost it?"

"No. Aunt Jodie said it just happens sometimes. But she assured me it didn't mean I would automatically have problems. And she was right. I found I was with child again a month or two after I had miscarried. That was very encouraging. And there were no problems this time. By the time I was six months along, Aunt Jodie said that the chances that I would carry the baby to full term were excellent. I was feeling life, and everything was good."

Edie stopped, turning to look out the window, her face showing pain now.

Seeing that, Gwen broke in, speaking quietly. "When Edie passed the six-month mark without any problem, we were all very encouraged. And then. . . ." She looked at Edie again.

"And then I had the accident with the buckboard," Edie said in a bare whisper. "Mitch felt awful, but it wasn't his fault. We were in town for some ward activity as I remember it. When we saw that a storm was coming in, we decided to get home before it got too bad. I was climbing up into our buckboard when the first raindrops started. Then suddenly, lightning flashed overhead and there was a tremendous crack of thunder. The horse reared, jerking the buckboard pretty violently. And I went down. I landed on my side, with my arm underneath me. It really jolted me, and I screamed out in pain."

Her eyes were shining now. "That night I started into labor. The next morning, I gave birth to a perfectly formed little girl who never drew a breath. Aunt Jodie guessed that the fall had been so hard that the baby probably died soon thereafter."

June was shaking her head. "I can't imagine how hard that must have been for you, especially after losing one and getting your hopes up so high."

"I came up and stayed with Edie for a time," Gwen added. "She was totally devastated. Mitch even talked about sending her to Richfield to stay with her mother, but she wouldn't hear of it."

"My life was with Mitch, and the tragedy didn't change that," Edie agreed. "There was one tiny ray of hope, and that was that this had been caused by an accident. It wasn't my body rejecting the baby. But as the months went by and nothing more happened, that hope began to die. That was a pretty bleak time for both me and Mitch."

"So how much longer before you conceived MJ?" June asked.

"Well, before we get to that, there was the whole thing with the Indian girl, Little Bird."

"Oh, yes. And that was after you lost the baby?"

"Yes. Not long after, actually. By then, I was convinced that I was never going to be able to have children of my own. So when Little Bird came along, Mitch and I began to talk about adopting her. We even talked to President Jones about it. Since the other sisters who had taken her into their homes already had children of their own, the plan was that we would adopt her. So when she disappeared and we found out what had happened to her, I completely fell to pieces."

"If there's time," June said softly, "I would like you to read that story to our family, too. A few weeks ago, I saw Frank and Tina out at her gravesite there in the cedars. Frank was trying to explain it all to Tina, but he couldn't remember all the details."

Edie was shaking her head. "If we do read it—" She turned and looked at Grandma Westland. "You'll have to read it. I'll never get through that. I think that was the darkest day of my life." Gwen nodded. "I will, but I agree with June. This is something the children need to hear too."

"And is that when Dad gave you that blessing?" June asked.

"Yes. Nothing else he said or did could pull me out of it. So he went off into the mountains for two days and nights and fasted and prayed before giving me a blessing. The whole branch fasted with us, and the blessing that he gave me was really beautiful. Though he didn't specifically promise me that I would have children, this great sense of peace came over me as he spoke." Edie smiled. "And it was a short time later that, to my great surprise, I was with child again."

June leaned forward. "Okay, this is the part that really interests me. I've heard you say that right from the beginning you knew you weren't going to lose MJ."

"Yes, that's right. I'm not sure why. But from the beginning I was filled with peace and surety that everything would be all right."

"Until that night at the dance hall," June added.

"Yes. I was due within a few days, but Aunt Jodie's fear after I tripped and fell was that the baby had been injured too. But I knew it would be all right, even when I went into hard contractions a few hours later. Mitch was absolutely beside himself, of course. How would I cope with yet another loss? That was his worry. But even though I was in pain, I sent him off to attend Jane's funeral, because I knew that everything would be okay."

"I was there that day," Gwen came in. "Willard Butt had come to Bluff to tell us about Jane's death, and a whole group of us came up for the funeral. Aunt Jodie and I were up here with Edie. We were all pretty certain that Edie was about to lose another one. But not Edie. She was at peace. It was amazing. And it turned out that she was right."

"As I look back on it," Edie said, "I think that peace was Heavenly Father's way of helping me cope with the shock and loss of seeing Jane gunned down before my eyes."

They fell silent for a time, and then Edie continued her narrative, speaking quietly, but at peace now. "Two more years passed. I was nursing MJ during that time, so I didn't expect I would get pregnant again right away. But a few months after I weaned him, we learned that I was carrying Rena. I knew it was a girl this time. I told Oma Zimmer that we were going to name the baby after her, and she was so thrilled. And sure enough, Rena was born three years after MJ. With no complications of any kind."

A shadow crossed Edie's face. "Then I went through the same pattern again. A few months after weaning Rena, I found myself with child again. And the pregnancy went perfectly. I felt life early. My health was good and I was strong." Her shoulders lifted and fell as she sighed. "But from the moment the baby was born, we knew something was wrong." She looked away. "We named her Caroline Gwendolyn, for my mother and Mitch's mother. She died in my arms two days later."

Tears formed in the corners of Edie's eyes and trickled down her cheeks. Gwen was crying too. "I had thought my previous losses had toughened me, but I was wrong. To have held this precious little one, to have nursed her, and cuddled her, and sung to her—and then to watch her die. Mitch wept like a child that day. And it was almost more than we could bear."

They were silent for a time, and then June ventured a guess. "You didn't have Frank for another seven years. Were there miscarriages during that time?"

"None after that. It was like I had gone into menopause early, so we assumed that there would be no more children."

"That must have been especially difficult for you."

"Actually, it wasn't, even though I expected it might be. We had two beautiful, delightful children, a boy and a girl, which was more than I had expected when I was younger. So we felt blessed, and that helped us accept what the Lord had chosen to give us."

Edie smiled. "So Frank came as a big surprise. We named him Franz Arthur for my father and Grandpa Westland, but everyone called him Frank, just as they did my father."

"Frank was a surprise in another way," Gwen said, smiling now. "He was the one to break the Westland-Zimmer mold, that's for sure. With his carrot-red hair and that mass of freckles, he doesn't look like anyone in either of our families. And, as you know, he is quite unlike either MJ or Rena. He has a gentle heart and a patient disposition. He has been a welcome respite in this family of very strong-minded individuals."

"I love Frank," June said quietly. "I love to watch his face as he's thinking a problem through. He's like a dog wrestling with a bone. He just won't let it go. And the grandkids adore him. He is so patient with them."

Edie nodded and said, "And that became the new pattern in our lives."

"What?" June asked.

"Surprises," she laughed softly. "Three years later, I was pregnant with Tina. Again, totally unexpected. The midwife figured her due date was around the first of February of 1908, but Rena was absolutely convinced that she would be born on Christmas Day. Nothing we could say would change her mind. So for fun, as Christmas drew closer, I knitted a large red-and-green Christmas 'stocking,' which was actually a baby sack, like the Indians use for their newborns, but without the cradle board. The birth was still six weeks away, but Rena insisted that we hang it by the fireplace just in case."

"I remember this story now," Gwen said. "Do you still have that baby sack?"

"Yes. It's somewhere in the attic, I'm sure."

"I'll help you find it," June said. "My kids would love this story, too, and we could show it to them then. I think we're going to have several family nights doing this."

"All right. Anyway, hanging the sack up as a stocking was more for fun than anything, but to our surprise, at about two in the afternoon on Christmas Day, just as I was getting Christmas dinner on the table, my water broke and I started into labor. Mitch raced down to town to bring back Cedenia Foy. At 12:16 the following morning, December 26, 1907, we had another little girl. She was tiny, being six weeks premature, but she was healthy in every other way. We named her Christina Rae Westland."

"Which means 'follower of Christ,' right?"

"Yes, which is what we hope for all of our children. And having been born so close to Christmas, it seemed especially appropriate."

A smile stole across Gwen's face. "Later, Mitch pointed out that she was a follower of Christ in another way. Her birth followed Christ's birthday by just sixteen minutes, and so in that sense she 'followed' Him."

"And little did we know how fitting that name would be," Edie said. "Tina, as we quickly began to call her, proved to be our dreamer. She was always off in her own world, lost in some fantasy or another. And so she was perpetually late for things. She would stop to smell a flower, chase a butterfly, or watch ants carrying grains of wheat across the road. Mitch always tells people that she was sixteen minutes late for Jesus's birthday, and she's been sixteen minutes late ever since."

"What's funny," June said, chuckling, "is that she doesn't mind being teased about it. It certainly doesn't hurry her up any."

Edie straightened. "Well, I'm taking longer than I intended. Our last surprise was the twins, of course. And perhaps they were the biggest surprise of all. After Tina, I was really sure that was it for us. First, of all, we went another six years with nothing. Second, by that point, I was thirty-seven and sure I was done. Third, in the summer of 1913, Mitch got called to be a missionary in Germany, with his term of service being three or four years."

"I remember how shocked you both were," June commented. "MJ and I were engaged by then, and it meant Dad Westland wouldn't be here for the marriage."

"I *was* shocked," Edie replied. "But I was very pleased, too, even though I knew how hard it was going to be to have him gone for that long."

Gwen spoke up again. "We were both sure that it was Oma Zimmer's doing. She'd gone on to the other side by then, but we were sure she was still working on getting that promise in her patriarchal blessing fulfilled."

"We always thought it would be Mitch Jr. that fulfilled it," Edie added, "not my Mitch."

"I remember it very clearly," June said. "I was sick when we thought the call was for MJ, for we were engaged by that time. I have to admit, I was glad when it turned out to be Mitch Sr."

Eddie nodded. "Then the Great War broke out, and Mitch was sent home after a little more than a year. That next Christmas, my present for him was to tell him that we were going to have one more child."

June was smiling in remembrance. "A child who would be a year younger than your first grandchild, because Noah was born by then."

"Yes, and the surprises just kept rolling in. A couple of months later, Dr. Remington called us both in and told us that we were going to have twins." Her eyes were glistening again. "At first we thought he was joking. But sure enough, on May 13th, 1915, which was my forty-fifth birthday, we had Abigail and Benjamin."

June was smiling. "MJ thinks that was the Lord's way of letting you know that He had never abandoned you."

"I agree. I absolutely, totally, joyously agree."

"So, let's talk about all of this on Sunday between meetings. My kids love these stories, and we do too."

"I think it's a wonderful idea," Grandma Westland said.

"I hope so," Edie said mischievously, "because you're all stuck now. We're going to do this even if I have to hogtie you all down to make you listen."

June tossed back her head and laughed. "I'll bring the rope."

Notes

The initiation of the program that we today call family home evening was actually in 1915. No set night was designated, and no Church-prepared materials were furnished then. It was typically called "family night" or "family hour" in those early years.

CHAPTER 47

October 19, 1919, 12:45 p.m.—EDW Ranch—Monticello

Edie stood up and rapped the table to get everyone's attention. When the noise quieted, she spoke. "All right, everyone. Let's clear the table. Dishes go into the sink, but they can wait until tonight to get washed. We'll do dessert before we leave for sacrament meeting. So let's take the chairs out into the living room. We need to be done with our meeting and dessert so we can leave for town about 3:30."

June stood up beside her mother-in-law. "My children and Rena's children, along with Abby and Benji, are excused from cleanup. We're going into the back guest room, where we're going to play some games. Then we'll join family night a little later."

"Hey!" Christina cried. "Can I go with them, Aunt June? I can tend them."

"Nope," Edie said, looking at her daughter. "You and Frank are part of family night this time. So let's get to it."

1:25 p.m.

Edie put a marker in her journal and then closed the book and set it aside. Instantly hands were up all around her. She looked to Mitch Jr. "MJ, will you go tell June we'll be about ten more minutes, then we'll be ready for the children?" As he nodded and got up, she pointed to Frank, whose hand was waving wildly back and forth. "Frank?"

"Did you actually see Sister Walton get shot?"

Edie nodded somberly. "Yes. When I heard the first gunshot, which killed Bill McCord, I got up and ran to the door to see what was going on. I was terrified because Mitch was out there, and Jane had gone out to see if she could help. As I reached the door, I saw that Jane was moving toward Tom Roach, trying to calm him down. I think my heart literally stopped for a moment. I went to shout at her, but at that instant, there was the boom of the rifle, and I saw Jane jerk and fall into Tom Roach's arms."

Rowland Redd, Rena's husband, was leaning forward, watching Edie intently. "So it may not have been Tom Roach that actually shot her?"

Edie shook her head. "No one knows for sure. But Charles Walton was pretty certain it was the Adams boy who shot at Roach to try and stop him but missed and hit Jane instead. Not that it really mattered. Roach was the cause of the whole thing, whether he fired the actual shot or not."

"And that's when you tripped and fell?" Rena asked in a low whisper.

"Yes. I think I tripped on the doorsill. But I went down face first. I don't even think I had time to reach out my hands and brace the fall. I hit pretty hard."

"How soon after that was MJ born?" Tina asked. She had heard this account before, but hearing it described in such detail had left her both fascinated and horrified.

"Well, the shooting was right around midnight. By the time Mitch and Grandma Westland and Aunt Jodie got me back here, I was starting into labor. But it wasn't until the following day that Mitch Jr. was actually born."

The questions continued for another few moments, and then MJ came back into the room. "June says they've just started a game of duck, duck, goose. They'll be about five more minutes."

They fell silent for a moment, contemplating what they had just heard. As MJ sat down again, he said, "I wish Dad were here. I'd love to hear his side of that whole thing again after hearing all the details."

Edie sighed. "I wish your father were here too, and for a lot more reasons than that." A frown creased her forehead. "I really thought I would have heard something from him before now. The last letter we got said that he and Elder Reissner would be leaving Switzerland before the middle of the month and that he would let me know his travel plans as soon as they got the details. Since then, there's been nothing."

"Well, you be sure to call us the minute you hear anything, Mama," Rena said. "We want to be here when he arrives."

"I will."

Rena's husband leaned forward. "My Grandpa Redd had told us a little of that story, but he wasn't there that night. Our family had moved to La Sal by that point, and he didn't come down for the Pioneer Day celebration. So this was fascinating to me, and it raises a question in my mind. Those of you who first came to San Juan had challenges with both the cowboys and the Indians. Which would you say gave you the most trouble?"

"The cowboys," Edie answered without hesitation. "Without question." She turned to Gwen. "What would you say, Grandma?"

That caught Gwen off guard, but she immediately responded. "No doubt about it. And this was a great surprise to me. When Arthur and I answered the call to join the San Juan Mission, we knew we would face two great challenges. The first was to make friends with and help the Native American peoples. The second was to bring law and order to a region where the violent and lawless—mainly the cattle ranchers and their hired hands—acted with impunity. And I was sure that the Indians would be far and away the greater of the two challenges. But I was wrong.

"Oh, we had our problems with them, of course. They were constantly stealing our horses or cattle or anything else of value they found lying around, but that was part of their culture and traditions. They don't view personal ownership in the same way as we do. If they see something they like, they simply take it. But except for a few bad apples, which every society has, their nature is basically peaceful. They value their families deeply and have a sense of fairness and justice worthy of emulation by a lot of white men. And, for the most part, we quickly learned to get along with them. We helped them, fed them, helped to educate their children, treated their illnesses and injuries, and learned to live in peace together. In turn, they reciprocated and taught us many things that benefitted us. For example, their knowledge of herbs and other plants that have medicinal properties have blessed many a family in the mission."

"But the cowboys were another matter entirely," Edie said as she sat back. "Only a few of the hands hired by the big cattle outfits were married. They were mostly young men and boys, some as young as sixteen, who had left home for various reasons to make their own way in life. They had received at least some education, and most had been raised in Christian homes. I know for a fact that a few even had fathers that were ministers. But when they left home, they tended to kick over all of the traces and give themselves over to smoking, chewing, cussing, drinking, stealing, rustling, and visiting houses of ill repute. Their morals were more like those of the wolf or the coyote—take whatever you can get away with. Including our water, even though we had legal title to it.

"And one will ever know how many of the Mormons' cows and sleeper calves were stolen by the cowhands. Certainly hundreds, and more likely thousands, over the years. These men could be pretty resourceful in their thievery. Willard Butt, who was our county sheriff for many years, reported that one set of rustlers actually shod their horses with horseshoes put on backwards to make it look like they were going the opposite direction. It didn't work. He caught them.

"Worst of all was what happened to them when they were drinking, which basically was anytime they could get their hands on whiskey or other liquor. Invariably they would come to town so drunk they could barely stay on their horses, shooting at anything that moved, even making women and children 'dance' to the blasting of their six-guns. The title cow-BOYS is appropriate, for they were often like little boys looking for any mischief they could stir up. They were always playing tricks on each other, only their practical jokes could be deadly.

"One of the Carlisle men, by the name of Pat Murray, was known to love his whiskey. One day his 'friends' decided to see just what his capacity for drink was. They held him down and poured whiskey down his throat until he passed out. He died a few hours later. When they buried him in the Monticello Cemetery, one of his supposedly penitent buddies slipped a full bottle of whiskey into his casket so he could be happy on the other side."

Rena was shaking her head. "I can't believe that."

"Oh, believe it," Rowland said. "Even some of the men we have to hire are like that."

Down the hall the door opened and June came out. "We're just finishing up," she called. "Be there in just a minute."

So Edie finished. "Mitch used to say that it took a blizzard and a full eclipse of the sun to get me to marry him, and—"

"And those are two more stories I want you to share with us and our children, Mama," MJ said.

"Okay."

"But finish your sentence," MJ added. "I didn't mean to interrupt."

Edie picked up where she had left off. "And when we couldn't get the cowboys to leave, Mitch said that the Lord sent a drought to drive them out. It started in 1893, as I remember, and continued off and on for several years." She looked at Rowland. "I remember your great-grandfather, Lemuel H. Redd Sr., lost half of his herd in those years. We lost at least a third or more. But anyway, that was too much for the big cattle outfits. Carlisle, the ranch down in Recapture Canyon, the Elk Mountain bunch out on the Rincon, and other smaller outfits finally gave up. They sold what was left of their herds to the Monticello and Bluff co-ops and went back to Texas or. . . ." An impish smile flashed across her face. "Or hell or wherever it was they had come from."

"Mama!" Tina cried, feigning shock. "Did you just profane?"

"I did not," Edie said, fighting to keep a straight face. "Hell is a place described in the scriptures."

"But it doesn't say it was in Texas," Frank quipped.

"Doesn't have to," Gwen shot right back. "We know where it was, because we met the devils who lived there."

As they all busted out laughing, there was a whoop and the younger children came running down the hall to join in the fun.

As the four grandchildren gathered around Edie, she reached down and opened her journal to the place where she had left her marker. "All right, children," she said. "Find a seat. Let's talk about something a little more pleasant. She bent down and looked into Edna June's eyes. "Like that day when that mean old woman spanked your daddy's bottom and started him yowling like a bunch of hungry coyotes."

Edna June's eyes were dancing. "Yeah, Grandma. I love that story. Was Daddy really, really bad?"

"Well, let's read it and find out, shall we?"

4:50 p.m.

Edie removed her coat and hung it in the closet and then took Grandma Westland's and did the same. She turned and looked at the rest of the family, who were still coming in the house. "All right, children, as soon as you're out of your Sunday clothes—and they're hung up—you can have another piece of pie or cake, whichever you want."

Rowland's and Rena's four-year-old turned around, a plaintive look on his face. "But, Grandma, we don't live here. We don't have a place to hang up our clothes."

Edie dropped into a crouch and took him into her arms. "That's all right, Charles. Give them to your mother. She has a suitcase for them."

Rena came forward. "But no dawdling, Charles. Or you either, Lem. Daddy wants to get on the road for home as soon as you have another snack."

He shot off, following Benji, who was about his same age.

"You could stay the night if you'd like," Edie said to Rowland. "We have plenty of beds between the two houses."

"Thanks, Mama Westland," he said, "but the forecast is calling for rain on Tuesday, so I've got to get some tarps over a few more of our haystacks."

"Then let's get our clothes changed too and get you on your way."

5:11 p.m.

The six younger children took both pie and cake, covered it with ice cream, and were still done before the adults had really gotten started. Without asking permission, they trooped off to Benji's bedroom to play some more games. In spite of having a forty-five mile drive ahead of them, Rowland and Rena didn't say anything. They didn't seem to be in too much of a hurry. Rowland kept asking Edie questions about what she had read to them from her journal. To Edie's surprise, Frank and Tina stayed around to listen.

Rowland, who hadn't grown up in Monticello, had the most questions. "Earlier, Mama Westland, you made mention of that time when Washington was trying to give San Juan County to the Utes. Did you know that it was my great-grandpa Redd who was the one that took that committee from Washington around San Juan County?"

"Of course I do," Edie said. "In fact, I was right there when the group of them came into Monticello after their tour, with Lem Redd leading them. And rightly so—everyone in the country agreed that no one knew the county like he did, because he ran his cattle all through it."

"Really? You were right there?"

"Yes. It was just before noon on October 17th, 1888."

"Wow!" Tina said, clearly impressed. "Your memory is amazing, Mom."

Edie frowned. "Actually, I remember the day because it was the following day that Eliza Peterson, my best friend, died. Just before the group arrived, I had been trying to comfort Eliza. She knew she was dying and wanted so much to say good-bye to her parents. But her mother was in Mancos, and her father had been assigned by Salt Lake to accompany this group from Washington, and no one knew where they were."

"Why was her father with Lem Redd?" MJ asked, surprised by the detail.

"Her father was Francis Hammond, our stake president. The First Presidency had assigned him to be the Church representative."

Frank was watching this interchange intently. "So she did get to see her father before she died."

"Yes, she got to spend her last day with him. It was a great comfort to her. She said it was a miracle of sorts."

"I think so too," Frank said, his voice tinged with awe.

"Anyway," Edie went on, turning back to Rowland, "I was with Eliza in what we called the Peterson Store then—it was their house and store—when your great-grandfather and President Hammond knocked on the door."

"Wow," Rowland said. "I don't know that Grandpa Redd ever told us that. So was it after that commission came that Washington decided to give the county to the Utes?"

"No, no. Actually, the committee told us that they were going to recommend that the Utes not be moved here. The land was too desolate and isolated for the Indians. It would be too much of a sacrifice for them."

MJ hooted. "They actually said that? Even though they were in Monticello and had seen Bluff? They had seen our homes and our buildings and our farms, and they said it wasn't good enough for their Indians?"

"Exactly," Gwen spoke up. "They told us that, too, when they passed through Bluff. But then they went back to Washington and recommended to the Senate committee that the tribe be moved here."

"How could they do that?" June asked in disgust. June

Westland was not a San Juan girl. She was from the town of Hyrum, in Cache County. She and MJ had met and started courting while MJ was attending the Utah State Agricultural College in Logan, getting a degree in animal husbandry and range management. There had been no significant Indian population that far north, so this was all fascinating to her.

"Because they were two-faced liars," MJ growled. "They had absolutely no integrity. I think they really meant what they said when they came here, but when they got back to Washington, the big cattle interests got to them and they rolled over and played dead."

"Do you have that written up in your journal, Grandma?" Rowland asked.

Edie hesitated. "Well, not all of it. Remember, this issue was unresolved for years. In fact, it wasn't until 1894 that it was finally settled once and for all. I hadn't started keeping a journal when Lem Redd arrived with the committee, so I only summarized that part later. And as things developed, I would write a few snippets about it here and there. But in 1893 and '94 when it all boiled over and we nearly went to war, I wrote quite a bit about it."

Everyone was staring at her now, even Gwen. But it was MJ who spoke first. "Would you read that to us?"

Edie reared back. "Now?"

"Why not?" MJ retorted.

"Because Rowland and Rena have to leave. It'll be dark in an hour, and—"

To everyone's surprise, Rowland cut her off. "I'd love to hear it."

Rena's head jerked around. "You would?"

Grinning, he nodded and took her hands. "Yes. This stuff fascinates me." He glanced down the hall. "The kids are being good. We could take another half an hour or so. Don't you think?"

"I grew up with these stories," Rena said. "But I've never heard Mom read it from her journal. If you're fine with it, then so am I."

MJ slapped a hand against his leg and jumped up. "Tell me where your journal is, Mama, and I'll get it for you."

Notes

Lemuel Harrison Redd Sr. and Lemuel Harrison Redd Jr., along with some additional family members, came to Bluff via the Hole in the Rock with the original pioneer company of 1880. Thus the Redds are one of the founding families of the San Juan area. Eventually, some of the Redds moved north and started ranching in the area around the La Sal Mountains, which is about thirty-five miles south of Moab, Utah. Many descendants still live in that part of Utah.

I chose to have Rena Westland, a fictional character, marry into the Redd family, since there were many such "local" marriages in those early years. So I created Rowland Redd and made him a descendant of the original Redd pioneers, even though he is also a fictional character.

CHAPTER 48

October 19, 1919, 5:17 p.m.—EDW Ranch—Monticello

"Is everyone ready?" Edie asked, looking around at the others in the room.

"I think we are," MJ said.

June nudged him. "Do you think we should have the children here for this?" Then she turned to Edie. "Is it too grim for them?"

"Not in the same way as the account of Jane's death, but it's probably not something they will understand."

"Then let's not bother them," Rena said. "They're happy back there."

"Would you rather be back with them?" Edie asked Tina.

She seemed surprised by the question. "No. I want to hear this too."

With that, Edie opened up the book to where she had inserted a piece of paper. She glanced at it for a moment and then looked up again. "This entry is dated February 23rd, 1895. That was about a week after things had begun to settle." Her head lowered and she began to read.

A Reservation in San Juan.

It was Charles E. Walton who first told us there was talk about putting an Indian Reservation in San Juan. That was as early as spring of 1886, but I don't remember

> hearing any talk of it until we came up to Monticello in the spring of '88. Then it suddenly surfaced with a bang.
>
> We learned that a group of influential cattlemen in southwest Colorado had convinced the Indian agent of the Southern Ute Indian Reservation to petition the Bureau of Indian Affairs to close the reservation and move the Utes to another location. Their reservation is a strip of land about 15–20 miles wide and about 75 miles long, which lies along the border of Colorado and New Mexico. Cattlemen from Texas and New Mexico wanted the land because there were several rivers running through it and it included a lot of good grasslands. It was such an egregious land grab that everyone assumed the proposal would be instantly rejected. But to our consternation, the BIA convinced the U.S. Senate to form a committee to look into the matter.

Edie looked up. "That's the committee that came out here that I was talking about a few minutes ago. Even after that, we weren't overly concerned. With the negative comments the committee members had made, we were all pretty confident nothing would come of it. What we were too naive to realize was that this proposal was never about finding a better place for the Indians to live. It was about finding a legal way to give their lands to the cattle interests."

MJ spoke up. "I remember Dad saying that some of our people were actually in favor of the proposal."

"That's true. A few of our settlers were happy with the prospect. Remember, we were experiencing an extended drought. We were losing cattle by the hundreds to the drought or to rustlers. The cowboys were still shooting up our town on a regular basis. If the trade was approved, it meant that, one, the San Juan Mission would be closed and we would be released from our callings. Two, the government said we would be reimbursed for our property if it went through. This meant that we'd get a significant amount of cash to help us start over again in a more hospitable place."

"But Dad wasn't one of those who liked the idea, was he?" Rena asked.

"No, not at all. He went right on as if nothing would come of it." With that, she turned back to the journal.

> Not long after the commission reported back to Congress, somehow the Utes learned about what was going on. They were excited by the possibility, of course. They were told that they would get everything that we had built here—nice homes, barns, sheds, irrigation systems, and established crops. Some of them even came to Monticello and began "shopping around," seeing which properties they would be interested in if it happened. I remember one day in the summer of '94. A Ute brave with his woman and four or five children stopped by one day when Mitch was away in the hills. That wasn't unusual. They often stopped and asked for food. Mitch Jr. was three then, and Rena was just a baby. But the man didn't ask for food. He walked right into the house with his family right behind him. He looked around and grunted in satisfaction. When I asked him what he was doing, he just sneered at me. "Soon this will be my wickiup. You go away. I come here." I was so flabbergasted, I didn't know what to do. I walked over to the fireplace, pointedly looked up at Mitch's rifle that hung there, then turned and told him to leave. He got the message and left, promising that he would be back soon.

"I remember that day," MJ said. "I thought it was real neat that Indians had come to visit us."

"Oh my gosh," Rena said. "I don't remember you ever telling me that. Did you just die?"

"I was pretty shaken after he left," Edie admitted before she went on reading.

> The thing that was maddening was that nothing was resolved. The issue just wouldn't go away. The committee was here in '88. But it wasn't until the next year that they made their official report to the Senate subcommittee. And to our utter surprise, after all their negative comments to us, they recommended that the reservation be moved to San Juan County. So the Senate opened hearings on the proposal. The Church asked President Hammond to represent our interests in Washington. The various Ute tribes also sent their chieftains to represent their case. But when President Hammond returned, he reported that a lot of senators saw it for exactly what it was, a naked land grab by the big cattle barons, and he was convinced it would never pass.
>
> Another year went by. Then another. No official action either way took place. Finally, President Hammond wrote to the Secretary of the Department of the Interior and asked him to make a decision one way or another as quickly as possible because everything was up in the air here. But still there was no decision. We grew more confident that it was a dead issue and moved ahead, focusing our efforts on surviving the drought and saving our cattle.
>
> Then came shocking news. Later in the summer of '94, eight years after it was first discussed, we received word that Congress had voted to approve the transfer of lands and that we were going to be evicted. As it turned out, that wasn't true. The subcommittee had approved the recommendation and voted to send it to the full Congress, but we didn't know that. That was a terrible day. It was like a great pall descended on our settlements.

By this time, Mitch and I had enlarged our ranch house significantly and put in a lot of new fencing. Mitch had purchased more grazing land. We had even gone into a loose partnership with the Carlisle Ranch to build some dams in several of the washes to create small reservoirs for our cattle. Now it looked like it would all be for naught.

Governor Caleb West, our territorial governor, was furious that he had not been alerted to this development. Telegrams flew back and forth between Salt Lake and Washington. Finally, we learned that it hadn't been passed by Congress, only the committee. That was a huge relief, but it seemed like a terrible omen of what was coming.

We sent delegations to Salt Lake from both Bluff and Monticello to present our case to the governor. The cattlemen also sent three of their leading men with us to show that we were united in our opposition to the plan. Mitch was one of those who went. The governor called a mass meeting, and thousands turned out for it. The whole territory was aflame over this issue.

What we didn't know at first was that over in Colorado, Mr. Dave Day, the Indian agent on the Ute reservation, had also gotten that same erroneous report. But under tremendous pressure from the cattlemen, he had told the Utes that it was a done deal in Washington. San Juan County was now officially their new home.

"Even though he knew that wasn't true?" June cried.

"Maybe not at first," Edie answered, "but soon after. But it was the excuse he had been looking for. I think he decided that if the Indians came here, then it *would* be a done deal and nothing we could do would stop it."

"And did the Utes come then?" Frank asked.

"Oh, yes." And again Edie let the journal answer the question for her.

CHAPTER 49

October 19, 1919, 5:45 p.m.—EDW Ranch—Monticello

I clearly remember one day shortly after Mitch got back from Salt Lake. This would have been around the last of September, 1894. Mitch was going down into town to participate in a meeting of all the brethren to discuss the situation, so Oma Zimmer, MJ, Rena, and I rode down with him and went to visit Emma Hyde and her family. On the way down, Mitch suddenly stopped the buckboard. I saw him peering directly to the east. It was a beautiful, early fall day and the San Juan Mountains were clearly visible to us, even though they are about a hundred miles away. When I saw him staring in that direction, I asked him what it was he was seeing.

"Look at that dust cloud way out there, just slightly to the south of straight east," he said.

I had already noticed it, but it was so far away I kind of dismissed it. "It's probably just a big dust devil," I suggested.

He didn't seem to buy it, but not knowing what else it might be, we continued on. He dropped Oma, me, MJ, and baby Rena off at the Hydes' home, then went on to his meeting. Ed Hyde and his son, Will, were not at the house, having gone to Verdure to get some lumber from the sawmill. While the younger children watched the littlest ones, Oma and I went into the main room, where Emma and her two daughters, Winnifred and Louise, had a quilt set up. I was especially happy to have Winnie and Lou there with us. Ever since our "sisterhood of the wind" experience and the resulting confession of our "sins," the three of us had grown especially close. About an hour later, there was a knock on the door. Winnie got up and answered it. When she gave a low cry, we all turned to see who it was. It was Old Wash, one of the Ute chieftains, along with several other Ute men, mostly older men like he was. They were decked out in their finest regalia, with beaded shirts and trousers and feathers in their hair.

Wash quickly assured Emma that no harm would come to her or any of the rest of us, but he and the other chieftains needed to powwow and were going to use her house to do so. He didn't ask if he could. He just declared that was why they were there. Trying to remain calm as they herded us all into the kitchen, Emma asked Wash if he and the others were hungry.

"Yes hungry! You fix food. We powwow." That was all he said.

As soon as the Indians began talking, Emma set Winnie, Lou, and me to cooking some food for them. Emma slipped over to the door where she could listen to the Utes' conversation without being seen. Ed had dealt with the Utes enough that he could speak their language pretty well, and Emma had picked up quite a bit herself. What she heard turned her as pale as a ghost.

The men with Wash were other chiefs of the various tribal subgroups, so this was a tribal council of some sort, but what they were discussing shocked her greatly. They were in the process of dividing up the cabins, houses, stores, and other buildings of Monticello among their different groups. They were familiar enough with the town that they named some names of property owners. In other cases, they described buildings in detail. They were also talking about who got which pasture lands around the town. Then Emma heard Old Wash arguing with the others angrily. He was telling them that the house where they were right now was to be his, and they didn't like that one bit.

Emma must have let out a startled cry, because Old Wash suddenly strode over and yanked open the door. He thrust out his lower lip, which is the Indian way of showing great anger. "This my wickiup now. Great Father in Washington say you go. So this my house now." Then, ignoring her protests, he started pointing out items of furniture and knickknacks that he would give to his wife and children.

We stood back, watching with great apprehension as they ate the food we had prepared and continued their conversation along those same lines. They were still arguing with each other over who got the choicest properties. Emma stayed back in a corner with Oma and me and the children and translated as much as she could for us in a quiet voice.

Then she gasped. Wash was talking about how their people were already on their way here and would probably arrive with their flocks and herds the next day. When Emma told me that, I told her about the dust cloud Mitch and I had seen.

That really upset Emma. She turned to Lou and told her to get down on her hands and knees and slip out the side door. Keeping the house between her and the line of sight of the Indians, she was to go to the meeting and alert the men to what was happening.

What a horrible night ensued. The meeting broke up immediately and the men returned to their homes. By then Ed was back from Verdure and confronted the chiefs. Mons Peterson and Charles Walton, who also spoke pretty good Ute, joined the powwow. They tried to convince the chiefs that Washington had not made a final decision and that Agent Day had jumped the gun. The Utes didn't like that one bit and got angrier and angrier. President Jones, who was outside listening to all of this, immediately slipped away and found two riders. He told them to ride as fast as they could to Thompson Springs, changing horses at ranches along the way, and to send a telegraph to Governor West and tell him what was happening, that we were in a crisis.

We learned later that they rode the 100 miles to Thompson Springs in fourteen hours, stopping only long enough to change horses. By that time, we saw for ourselves what had made the dust cloud. A line of Indians at least two or three miles long was coming up the road from Mancos. This wasn't a war party, which was good. They had brought their families and everything they owned, which was not good. There were old, toothless grandmas, mothers with cradleboards strapped to their backs, angry-looking young bucks with rifles or bows and arrows. There were dozens upon dozens of children, the little ones often naked, and more dogs than I had ever seen together in one place. They were darting in and out, nipping at the horses' hooves and barking furiously at one another. It was utter chaos!

And with them came their herds. The Utes and the Navajo keep some cattle, but the largest herds were of horses, sheep, and goats. There were literally thousands of them. By nightfall, their flocks had filled every pasture, every street, every yard in and around Monticello. Flower and vegetable gardens alike were eaten or trampled under. A land already parched by drought was suddenly stripped bare. Some of the Utes moved their larger flocks of sheep north about twelve miles into Dry Valley. Mitch rode out with them and said he could actually see what little withered grass there was disappearing before his eyes. By the next day, what few springs and meager watering holes that were still available were churned into muddy bogs.

Tina raised her hand timidly. "If there were that many animals, how many Indians were there?"

Edie's face was grim now. "That was the most chilling thing. The men did a quick count of the humans. We figured that we had a total of about a hundred and twenty able-bodied men—that was counting Monticello, Verdure, Bluff, and any scattered homesteads. But the Utes had brought an estimated five hundred people with them, with more coming in every day. About half of them were braves who were ready to fight. The greatest surprise, and a most sobering one, was that about three hundred Navajo, mostly angry young braves, had come up from the south and joined their Ute cousins. If it came to war, the numbers were sobering. Counting only the braves of fighting age, we figured our men were still outnumbered by four or five to one."

Rowland gave a low whistle. "My word," he said. "I had no idea it was that bad."

"I'll tell you how bad it was," Gwen spoke up for the first time in several minutes. "This is one of the few times that the Mormons and the ranchers worked together. Being men of action, these cowhands were not content to sit back and wait for the government to come up with a solution. The ranchers called for a meeting out in Hatch Wash. Dozens of cowboys came in, armed to the teeth and spoiling for a fight. Some of our people went out and listened. The hotheads argued that if they started a fight with the Indians, that would get a much quicker reaction from the army forts to the east and north of us. Fortunately, others were more conservative and argued for patience, reminding them that we had women and children who would be in danger.

"What was finally agreed upon was that a letter should be written, printed up, and distributed as quickly as possible. It called for all whites to stay off the roads and to not travel alone or even in small groups. Those living on isolated ranches or homesteads were urged to move into Monticello or Bluff or the Colorado settlements for protection. Riders then took those letters out all across San Juan County and southeast Colorado."

"So it was almost like martial law," MJ said, shaking his head.

"Yes," Edie responded, "only not just *almost*. All normal activity in our town came to a halt. School was canceled. All children were kept in their houses. Women only went out in groups or when accompanied by adult males. The biggest challenge was feeding the mobs of Indians. That sounds strange, considering the circumstances, but we couldn't let them starve. So every morning, the women would start baking bread as the men and young boys kept them supplied in flour, lard, sugar, salt, and the other necessities. Our men slaughtered several head of beef to help feed them. Fortunately, the tribal chiefs told their people to contribute some of their sheep as well. And every day, more Indians kept coming in from the east."

Edie looked around, but no one else said anything. They were deeply subdued. So she began to read again.

> The two riders returned late that following afternoon with word that Governor West had wired Washington and apprised them of the situation. He also told Washington to wire Dave Day and tell him to pull his Indians back to the reservation until this could be resolved. They did, but Day ignored them.
>
> Brother L.C. Christensen, a former Indian missionary and a skilled and trusted translator, came to help try to calm the situation. Nothing seemed to help. The Indians had been told by their agent that these lands were theirs, that these houses now belonged to them. A rider was sent east with an urgent letter to Day, explaining the situation and begging him to pull them back while the government sorted this out. He refused and sent word back to

> the Indians that they were in the right and that the white man had lost all claim to the land. The Utes grew increasingly angry and belligerent. When they started sending the squaws and children away from our settlements and more and more armed young bucks kept arriving, we knew the situation was critical.
>
> Finally, Willard Butt, as sheriff of San Juan County, sent a message to Governor West. He described the urgency of the situation. He said there would be a catastrophic loss of stock, both Indian and white, if something wasn't done immediately. He closed with this statement: "If you do not immediately convince the U.S. government to waive all red tape and immediately send troops, then you must call out the territorial militia to help us. Further delay may mean the slaughter of women and children."

Edie looked up briefly. "And that was not in any way an exaggeration. We were all terrified of what might happen next. We kept guards posted at virtually every house. Men slept with their rifles at their sides. We began to secretly fortify the schoolhouse." She turned back to the journal.

> Willard's message finally got some action. This time the governor sent a very blunt telegram directly to the Secretary of the Interior. Letters and telegrams were sent to Day, but he continued to stonewall. Finally, according to one report, someone handed him one of the warning letters that had been distributed by our cattlemen. Evidently that convinced him that if he did not respond, he might be responsible for a bloodbath. He sent a terse telegram to Governor West: "Hold back your long-haired Armenians [I guess that meant us Mormons] until I can get the squaws and people out of your God-forsaken country. We'll meet you in Monticello to confer on February 8th."

Rena spoke again in a hushed voice. "He's the real villain in all of this, isn't he?"

"Yes. Him and the Texas and New Mexico cattlemen who had made him their stooge."

"Did the government respond?" Frank broke in. "I mean, I've never heard you or Papa say anything about actually going to war."

"Well," Edie said, "Day's telegram quieted things for a time. He did manage to get the Indians to pull back away from town, but they didn't go far. We were still surrounded by their camps on every side of us. And they were angrier than ever now. They had been betrayed by their own agent on the one hand, and they were being denied by us on the other." Her head lowered again.

> Finally the night of February 8th came. The great powwow began that night in the log meetinghouse. A Ute chief called Mariana was spokesman for the Utes, with L.C. Christensen interpreting. All who wanted to speak for the white men—farmers, storekeepers, ranchers, cowboys, miners, and villagers—were allowed to express their concern. Agent Day spoke too, finally admitting that he had acted hastily. That was met by much anger and muttering from both sides, but especially by the chiefs. When all had spoken, Governor West, who had brought two of his militia captains down with him, concluded the meeting by saying, "It is clear that the rights of the citizens of San Juan County have been infringed upon. Therefore, I will do everything in my power to have the Indians removed back to their reservation."
>
> I wasn't there in that meeting, obviously, but Mitch was. He said that when Brother Christensen translated what the governor had said, the chiefs erupted in a rage. It was a tense moment, and Mitch said everyone had their hands near their guns, thinking that open battle might break out any moment right there inside the hall. Sensing

how tenuous the situation was, the governor issued two orders to his militia chiefs, speaking in a loud voice so that all could hear. One militia captain was told to send riders at full speed to Thompson Springs, and to send off two telegrams to Denver and Salt Lake asking for three troops of fully equipped cavalry to be dispatched and the Utah Militia to prepare for immediate deployment to San Juan County.

As the riders left, L.C. Christensen spoke to the Ute chieftains and told them what the telegrams said. "That is nothing to us," Chief Mariana shouted angrily, "We are stronger than all of the cowboys and the bluecoats, too."

Mitch said that Christensen was amazing. He spoke calmly and slowly, as if reasoning with a friend. "You are right, Chief Mariana," he said. "There are not that many cowboys to fight. And the Mormons do not want to fight their Indian brothers but will if they have no choice. But if they do, there are not that many of them either. And you have many, many braves who fight like the puma and strike like the rattlesnake."

Then he sighed deeply and bent down and picked up a handful of sand. As he started to talk, he let it trickle out of his hand. "But the bluecoats that the Great Chief in Washington will send are as the sands of our great rivers. It is not possible to count their numbers. If you fight against them, many of your people will die. And they will suffer much. But if you go back to the reservation, then the Great Chief has promised that he shall be good to your people and make things right again."

Mariana made no reply, and a short time later the meeting broke up. The next morning, Chief Mariana sought out Christensen, who was with Governor West. He stood in silence for a long moment and then grunted. "Maybe we go." And with that, the crisis was over. It would take months to completely clear up the situation, but Chief

Mariana sent out the word that his people were to gather up their flocks and herds and head back to Colorado.

Edie closed her journal and set it on the table beside her. "And thus, war was averted, we got to stay in our homes, and life returned to normal."

Frank was greatly exercised by now. "I hope someone arrested that stupid Indian agent."

"Frank," Edie chided gently. "It's not nice to call someone stupid." Then she smiled wryly. "Dishonest, maybe. Greedy, definitely. An idiot when it came resolving a critical problem, yes, that too. But 'stupid' seems a little harsh."

Everyone was laughing now. To be so pointedly critical was just not the Edna Rae Westland they all knew and loved.

"So tell Frank what did happen to him," MJ said.

Edie's smile broadened. "Yes, there was some justice in how it ended. Mr. Day was so afraid of what the Indians would do to him if they caught him that he hid in the cellar of Mons Peterson's store for several days and then slunk away to the north like the cur he was. He was never seen in the area after that, and rumors said that he returned to the East and took work where there would be no chance of him meeting either a Ute, a Mormon, or a cattle rancher ever, ever again."

Notes

While some minor details had to be added to sustain the narrative of the novel, the events depicted here are largely as described in the historical sources (see *Saga,* 215–218; *Anchored Lariats,* 109–11). Louise Hyde, daughter of Ed and Emma Hyde, was fifteen at this time. She was present that night when Old Wash and the other chiefs came to their house to discuss the "spoils" they were about to inherit. It is from her life story that we get the details of that part of the experience (see Joyce Ann Hunt, "Emma Louise Hyde: 27 November 1879–July 6, 1954").

CHAPTER 50

October 19, 1919, 6:25 p.m.—EDW Ranch—Monticello

Edie went down on one knee and held out her arms. Charles and Lem Redd stepped into them and she gave them a long, hard hug. "Oh," she whispered, "Grandma loves you two so much. Thank you for coming to see me."

"Thanks for the pie, Grandma," Charles said right back.

"Yeah," Lem said. "It was yummy, Grandma."

"Why don't you two just come and live with me all the time?" she asked, finally releasing them.

Charles jerked around. "Can we, Mama? Can we?"

"Not yet," Rena said with a smile. "Maybe one of these days when you and Lem are being naughty."

"Don't say that," Rowland exclaimed with a laugh. "They'll be naughty every day."

Edie got to her feet as Mitch's mother bent down and gave the two boys a hug. "Great-Grandma loves you too. Come see us real soon, okay?"

As the boys nodded and went back over to their parents, Edie moved to Rena and put her arms around her. "We're always so glad when you come. And not just for the boys. We love having you and Rowland here, too."

"Then let's do family night again, Mama," Rena said, holding her tight. "That was such a wonderful thing today. Not only to hear what you've written but to have you be the one who reads to us. And let us ask you questions. Next time I want to read what you wrote when I was born. And about when you and Dad saw the eclipse and decided to get married."

"And the wedding itself," Tina said as she came forward. "That's what I want to hear. Did you have a real wedding dress, Mama?"

"Kind of."

"She was beautiful," Gwen said. "Her smile lit up the whole town."

"But all that will have to wait," Edie said firmly. "Rowland and Rena have to get going."

"Yes," Rena said, "and you are not to talk about things or read from your journal until we're here to be part of it. Promise me, Mama."

"I promise." She turned to Rowland. "Be real careful, Rowland, especially down through that stretch of cedars going down Peter's Hill. The deer are coming down from the mountains and they'll be out about now."

"I will, Mama Westland," he said, and he kissed her on the cheek.

But as Rowland turned around to get his children, Frank suddenly held up his hand. "Shhh!" he hissed. "Someone's coming."

All instantly quieted. Sure enough, they could hear the sound of an automobile engine, and it was coming up the road that ran past their ranch house. Frank strode over to the window. All six of the young ones darted over to join him, pressing their noses against the window.

"Sounds like a Ford," Frank said. "Probably a Model A."

The adults moved over as well. Frank was right. In the fading evening light they could see the headlights of an automobile coming up the hill from town. It wasn't coming fast, but steadily. "Someone out for a moonlight ride?" MJ suggested.

"Maybe some of the young folk going up to snuggle on Horsehead Peak," June said.

"Not on a Sunday, surely," Edie said, frowning.

"Wait," Frank cried. "It's slowing down. Hey, I think it's coming here." He was right again. A moment later, the vehicle slowed enough to make the turn into their lane. Frank started for the door. "I'll go see who it is."

"No," Edie cried. "You'll wait in here until they come. And we'll not be standing here gawking out the window when they arrive. Come, children. Come and sit down."

There were groans of protest as the parents started herding the children away from the window. To Edie's surprise, Rowland didn't move. He actually leaned forward, staring through the glass. "That's not a car," he said to Frank. "It's a pickup truck." He shook his head in amazement and turned to Rena. "It looks like the same one I showed you the other day. The kind I want to buy for the ranch someday."

That brought everyone forward again, including Edie. As it approached, even she could see the railings on the back that enclosed a small truck bed.

"Wow," Frank said. "That's the first one I've seen in real life."

They all fell silent as the truck pulled up in front of the house and came to a stop. The lights went out and the sound of the engine died. Suddenly Edie was embarrassed. The lights in the living room were fully on, so they must have looked like a bunch of tourists at the zoo to whoever their visitors were. "Come on," she said again as they heard the car door open. "Let's sit down. MJ will get the door, and then we—"

But Tina's cry cut her off. She was right up against the window next to Rowland. She had her hands up shading her eyes so she could see out better. She stiffened, gasped, and then yelped with joy. "Omigosh!" She started dancing up and down and waving her arms. "Omigosh! Omigosh! Omigosh!" she cried again and again.

She looked at Edie. "Mama! It's Papa! Papa's home!"

With cries of joy, everyone stampeded for the door.

6:32 p.m.—Front Yard, EDW Ranch

When Mitch finally set Edie down again and gave her one last kiss, she was quite breathless. "You're home," she said. "I can't believe it. You're home."

"Yes I am," he said. He put his arm around her shoulder and pulled her close. "I am home, and I am home to stay."

He moved over to his mother and embraced her. "Welcome home, son," Gwen whispered, fighting back tears. Mitch buried his face against her hair and hugged her tightly.

Everyone else clustered around him now. The twins were clamoring for his attention. The married adults brought the grandchildren in to greet him. Frank and Tina were pushing in as well. All were laughing and crying.

Dizzy with joy, Edie stepped back and watched as the family welcomed him home. When finally they all stepped back, Edie went over slugged him on the shoulder. "Why didn't you call me and tell me that you were coming? Look at me. I'm a fright. I haven't brushed my hair since we went to church this afternoon."

"I wanted to surprise you." His eyes softened. "And you're not a fright. You look absolutely wonderful to me." He kissed her again.

"Papa," Frank said. He was circling the truck with wide eyes. "Whose truck is this?"

"It belongs to the EDW Ranch," Mitch said with a broad grin.

"Really?" Frank exploded.

"What?" Edie cried.

But Frank was not about to be put off. "Are you serious, Pa? Is this really our truck?"

"It is."

"But," Edie sputtered, "we can't. . . . You bought a truck?"

Mitch laughed. "I did. We've been needing one, so I wired Hatch Walker when I got to Denver. He runs the livery stable in Thompson Springs. I've known him for years. He also has the Ford dealership there, so I asked him to see if he could find me a used pickup truck."

MJ and Rowland were walking around it now too. "It's used?" MJ asked. "It looks like it's brand new."

"A farmer in Green River bought it but couldn't make the payments. It's got less than a thousand miles on it."

"Neat!" Frank said. "Will you teach me how to drive it, Pa?"

"Me too," Tina cried, not about to be outdone by her older brothers.

"Will you at least let him get into the house first?" Edie said. Then she slipped her arm through her husband's and pulled him in closer. "Do I dare ask how much it cost?"

Laughing, Mitch shook his head and stopped. "Not until I've been home for at least an hour." He turned to Frank and Tina. "If you two were to get those suitcases from the back of the truck and take them into the house, I might find something in them for you."

They were off like a shot and arguing over who got to carry the biggest one before they even climbed up onto the back of the truck. Mitch motioned for the twins to come forward. "Benji, Abby. My briefcase and my overnight bag are in the front seat. Will you take them in, too?"

Frank had taken the bigger and heavier of the two pieces of luggage and was struggling a little to keep it off the ground. He stopped as he reached the front of the vehicle and looked at the hood. "This is the 1918 Model T, right?" Frank asked.

"Yes." Mitch was trying hard to sound nonchalant but wasn't quite pulling it off. "Come here. I want to show you something. You too, MJ. Rowland, you'll want to see it too."

Of course everyone else wanted to see too, and they followed Mitch as he walked around to the back of the truck. The truck was a single-seater, wide enough to sit the driver and two passengers. The paint was black, of course, and it had thick rubber tires on wheels with large wooden spokes. There were no doors, and while the windshield was glass, there was no glass in the two side windows. Instead they had leather curtains curled up on rollers on both sides. These could be let down to provide some respite from inclement weather. The truck bed was about five or six feet long and a foot wider than the cab on each side. It was enclosed by removable sideboards and a back gate.

Mitch pointed to the truck bed. "As you can see, we can put ten or twelves bales of hay back here, or carry twenty or thirty bags of grain. I even think we can haul fence posts and lumber if we take the back gate off. But here's what I want to show you."

He stepped forward, reached beneath the truck bed, and pulled a latch. There was a soft, metallic click. Then he walked around to the back of the truck and pushed down on the back edge of the truck bed with both hands. With a creak, the entire bed tipped back until the back edge touched the ground. Benji gave a little yelp and jumped back. He hadn't expected that.

Turning to his oldest son, Mitch said, "Nice, eh? It's counterbalanced so you can tip it up. So, if we need to, we can just dump the whole load off at once."

MJ was impressed. He pulled the truck bed up and down,

marveling at how easily it moved. "When can I drive it?" Frank persisted.

"Can we ride in the back?" Benji hollered.

"Me too, Grandpa," Noah said. "I wanna ride in the back."

Gwen sang out. "Can I ride in the front seat, Mitch?"

Delighted at their reaction, Mitch turned to Frank. "Until my luggage is in the house, nothing's going to happen, that's for sure," he growled.

Frank and Tina leaped into action and the twins grabbed his smaller items and trooped after him. The rest of the family followed.

Edie moved over to Mitch and slipped her arm around his waist. "Well," she drawled, "I can see why you wanted the family to see it. There's no way I'm going to talk you into taking it back now, is there?"

He hooted, swept her up in his arms, and kissed her again. "Oh, Edie, my love. I missed you so much."

She threw her arms around his neck and kissed his forehead, his cheeks, his lips, his nose, his chin, and then started all over again. "Oh," she finally said, a little breathless. "I haven't missed you at all."

CHAPTER 51

October 19, 1919, 6:53 p.m.—EDW Ranch—Monticello

Mitch had Frank and Tina leave the biggest suitcase in the living room and then take the rest of his things into the main bedroom. Any thoughts of Rena and Rowland going back to La Sal that night were instantly forgotten. While Mitch took a few minutes to change out of his suit and refresh himself, Rowland drove their car up the lane a short distance and unloaded their things at MJ's and June's house. Rena and the children stayed behind, of course. Once Mitch told the family that his big suitcase was full of gifts for everyone, even wild horses wouldn't have been able to drag the children away. Or the adults either, for that matter.

When Rowland returned and Mitch came out in a pair of Levi's and a flannel shirt, everyone immediately went quiet. With an exaggerated flourish, Mitch set the large suitcase flat on the floor in front of the fireplace. Necks craned as he undid the leather buckles and opened the suitcase. When he let one side drop, it clunked with a heavy thud on the floor. The children scooted forward, necks craning to see what was inside, but two pairs of trousers covered the rest of the contents completely.

Abby couldn't stand it. "What did you bring me, Papa?" she cried. "Did you bring me a toy?"

He shook his head gravely. "In Germany they don't give toys

to little children that have been bad. They give them a lump of coal." He reached down into one corner and pulled out two lumps of coal. He held them out. "One for you, and one for Benji."

The twins stared at them for a moment, looked at each other, and slowly took the coal from their father. Both looked as though they were on the verge of tears. "Have you both been good for Mama while I was gone?" Mitch's voice was very grave.

Both nodded solemnly. Benji's lower lip was trembling a little. "I only forgot to be good once." He turned to his mother. "Right, Mama?"

Edie nodded. "That's right, Papa. They've been very good children while you were gone."

"Oh?" Mitch seemed puzzled, but then he reached out and took the coal from their hands. He tossed the pieces into the fireplace. "Well, then, that coal wasn't for you." He bent over the suitcase and rummaged beneath the Levi's without showing what was beneath them. He brought out two elongated packages about the size of narrow loaves of bread. They were wrapped in brown paper and tied with string. He examined them. The twins and the four grandchildren edged in closer, trying to see.

"Hmm," Mitch said. "This one says it's for a girl named Abigail." He looked at Edie. "Do we have someone named Abigail?"

Abby was jumping up and down. "That's me, Papa. Don't you remember?"

"Well, bust my britches," he said as he handed it to her. "Don't open it yet," he warned. He looked at the second package. "And this one is for . . . let's see. I can't quite read it. There's a B, and an E, and an N, and a. . . ."

"That's me, Daddy!" Benjamin shouted. "That's my name."

"Oh, good." Mitch handed it to him but said the same thing.

"Don't open it yet." He sat back and looked around at the others. "I know it's a little early for Christmas, but I thought I would bring something so we can have a German Christmas in our home this year. Would you like that?"

"Yes!" All six of the little ones yelled it together.

"And guess what decoration you find in almost every house in Germany at Christmastime."

"A Christmas tree," Abby shouted.

Mitch laughed. "Well, yes. That too. But something else. More of a decoration for the house. Can anyone guess? It's very much a tradition in Germany."

Some of the adults looked like they might know, but they said nothing. The children, including Frank and Tina, looked perplexed. The little ones were mystified. Finally, Tina, who was sitting on the couch beside Great-Grandma Westland, leaned in and whispered something in her ear. Gwen nodded, so Tina raised her hand. "Nutcrackers?"

"Exactly," Mitch said. There were oohs and ahs as he pulled off the clothing and tossed them aside, revealing a suitcase filled with numerous small packages wrapped in brown paper. "All right," Mitch said. "There are names on each of these, but nobody can open them until I say, and then we'll open them all at the same time."

Gwen leaned in to Edie, who was sitting on the other side of her. "I think he's as excited about this as the kids are."

Edie's eyes glowed with happiness. "He loves Christmas."

Mitch began calling out names, letting the twins and the grandchildren deliver the packages to each individual. When they were all distributed, he looked around. "Who doesn't have one?"

They looked around. "Mama!" the twins cried. "Grandma Westland," the grandchildren sang out at the same time.

"That's right," Mitch said. He went over to his overnight bag and withdrew a package that was twice the size of any of the others. He handed it to Abby. "Take this to your mother," he said. Then to Edie, "But, Grandma, you have to wait until after everyone else has opened theirs, all right?"

She nodded and smiled as Abby set the package on her lap.

Mitch let them explore the packages with their fingers, and then he had everyone except Edie line up in front of the fireplace. "Okay," he said. "Let's start with Great-Grandma Westland." He turned. "Mother, go ahead and open yours."

She quickly untied the string and pulled the paper away. One hand flew to her mouth and she gave a little cry of joy and surprise. Her nutcracker was a British soldier in his bright red coat and tall, black fur hat. He stood at stiff attention and held a musket at his side. Gwen clapped her hands in delight and held him up. "Do you know what this is?" she asked the children.

"A soldier," Noah called.

"But not just any soldier," she replied. "This is a guard at Buckingham Palace, where the king or queen of England lives. And that is exactly what they look like." Her eyes were shining as she looked at Mitch. "Thank you, son. It's the perfect reminder of my homeland."

"I thought you'd like it," Mitch said, obviously pleased. He turned to the lineup of children. "All right, let's go from left to right. Lem, you begin. Open it up, then tell us what it is. You can have your mama or papa help you if you need to."

The paper was off in about two seconds. Lem held his nutcracker up and studied it. It was a man in dark brown work clothes with an axe in one hand and pieces of wood all around his feet. Lem's nose wrinkled in perplexity. Rena leaned forward and whispered in his ear. His face lit up. "Mine is a woodcutter," he said proudly.

"That's right," Mitch said, "because who's my very best helper when it comes to chopping firewood?"

"Me," Lem said proudly.

Edna June was next. "Mine is a girl on ice skates," she said, tossing the paper aside. She held it up for all to see. "Because I love to ice skate."

"And she has brown hair just like yours," Mitch said.

Charles got a hunter who had a rifle in one hand and a pheasant dangling from his belt. Noah's was a chimney sweep with a ladder on one shoulder and a tall, stovepipe hat. "Why is this one for Noah?" his grandpa asked. Noah looked puzzled, so June answered for him. "Because he's always playing in the ashes in the fireplace." Everyone laughed at that.

The twins were next, but Mitch cut in as they started. "Abby, Benji. I want you to open yours at the same time."

Eagerly ripping off the paper, they held them out for all to see. Abby's face fell. "Mine's just a girl," she said.

Benji was equally disappointed. "And mine's a boy with no pants."

Everyone laughed as Mitch got up and went over to them. He took Abby's nutcracker and held it up. "This is a young maiden from Bavaria, which is in the south part of Germany. That's where I've been the last couple of weeks. The costume she has on is called a *Dirndl.* It is the traditional dress for women and girls there. It consists of a white blouse with lots of lace and a bodice, which is the upper part of her dress." He grinned. "Or so I'm told by the women who know these things. The dress always has a full skirt and a brightly colored and decorated apron." June and Rena both applauded. "Very good, Papa," they called.

He handed the nutcracker back to Abby. She was studying it more closely now, at least interested. "And do you know what people say about girls from Bavaria?" he asked Abby.

She shook her head.

"They say they are the prettiest girls in the whole world."

That did it. Abby was beaming like a ray of sunshine. Mitch turned to his youngest son. "Now, Benji. This boy does have on pants, doesn't he?"

"Yeah, but they got no legs. He looks like a girl."

"Those are called *Lederhosen,* which is German for 'leather breeches,'" Mitch explained patiently while everyone tried hard not to laugh. He held up the nutcracker. "The short trousers and the suspenders that look like the letter H are the traditional dress for men and boys in Bavaria and Switzerland. As is that felt hat with the little tuft of feathers. Very dapper, son," he said, "which you have to be if you're going to escort the prettiest girls in the world, right?"

Benji was clearly unconvinced, so Mitch tried something else. "In America, who are the only men who wear leather pants? Only here we don't call them pants, we call them chaps."

Benji's head snapped up. "Cowboys?"

"Yup."

"Wow." He took the nutcracker back. "So these are German cowboys?"

"Uh . . ." Mitch was trying to keep a straight face. "I guess that's one way to look at it."

"Let me see them," Edie called, motioning to the twins. When they came over, she took the two nutcrackers and held them up side by side and then turned to Mitch. "These are darling, Mitch. Perfect for these two." Then to the twins she said, "These are not to play with. These are something you want to keep your whole lives, so I want you to put them on the shelves above your beds and keep them very nice."

That seemed to cinch it with both of them, and they returned to their places proudly.

June, who was well known in Monticello for the cloth dolls she made and sold, got a toy maker. MJ, who was skilled with his hands, got a wood carver who was working on a miniature nutcracker. Rena, who was named for her Grandmother Zimmer, spoke excellent German, and loved everything German, got Father Christmas, the traditional German Santa Claus, wearing a brown fur suit instead of red. Her husband's nutcracker was old Father Time, carrying around a large clock. That made everyone laugh because Rowland was forever reminding people of what time it was and what had to happen next.

Frank's nutcracker, to everyone's delight, was a shop mechanic. He carried a large wooden toolbox over one shoulder and had smudges of grease on his clothes and hands. Tina's was a flower girl who held a basket of lilacs in front of her with both hands. She too was dressed in a *Dirndl.*

As the last of them finished, Benji was working the lever on the back of his nutcracker, which moved the jaw up and down. "What's this thing?" he asked. "He looks like he's talking."

"These are all actual working nutcrackers," Mitch explained. "And just as we do, the Germans get lots of nuts in their stockings at Christmas."

Almost everyone was moving the levers up and down now, making it look as if the nutcrackers were talking to each other. Mitch went on. "Since some of the nuts have very hard shells, you need something to crack them open."

June was enthralled. "So they actually use these as nutcrackers, and they're not just decorations?"

"That's right. Typically, every house has several different kinds."

"What about you, Mama?" Rena said. "What did you get?"

The children quickly gathered around her. Mitch nodded for Edie to proceed. When she tossed the paper aside and held it up for everyone to see, there were cries and gasps. This was obviously not a nutcracker. It was an elaborate wood carving about ten inches high, mounted on a polished wooden base of dark walnut. There were four figures in the carving. The central and largest figure was an old woman in a plain dress that reached down to her ankles. Around her waist was tied a dark blue apron. Her face was lined with wrinkles, especially around the corners of her mouth and around her eyes. These were clearly smile wrinkles, for she had a broad smile on her face. Both hands were extended. In one she held a plate heaped with cookies. In the other was a pitcher of milk. All had been carefully painted by hand.

Gathered around her in a half circle were three young children who appeared to be between the ages of three and seven—two girls in *Dirndls* and a boy in *Lederhosen.* Their hands were outstretched, reaching for the plate of cookies. Their faces were wreathed in smiles.

Edie looked up. "Oh, Mitch. This is exquisite. Where did you ever find it?"

Pleased, he stepped over to her and carefully took it from her. Tipping it back so all could see the underside of the base, he kept his fingers over some carved lettering near the front of the base with one hand, but showed them a circle about the size of a silver dollar burned into the wood below it. Inside the circle in gothic English letters was stamped "Black Forest Wood Carvers' Guild." Since the lettering was small and hard to read, Mitch read it for them.

"Let me explain what this means," he went on, "for this is significant for our family. The Black Forest, or the *Schwarzwald*, as they call it in German, is a large region in southwestern Germany that is famous for its beautiful mountains and thick pine forests." He smiled. "And for its highly skilled woodcarvers, who make nutcrackers, cuckoo clocks, and many other wonderful wood carvings, like the one I have here."

He brought the statue up again so they could see the figures. He was speaking to Edie now. "While I was in Germany this time, I learned something about the Black Forest that I didn't know before. At the very northwest corner of the Black Forest is a city called Mannheim, Germany."

Edie's head snapped up, her eyes widening. "Mannheim? Really?"

"Yes. And a few miles to the northwest of Mannheim is a tiny farming village called Sulz."

Now Rena and MJ and Frank and Tina were all staring at him. It was Rena who spoke, and her voice was tinged with awe. "Where Oma Zimmer met the missionaries from America and was given a Book of Mormon, right?"

"Yes, exactly right. And where they were baptized. And where, a year later, they said good-bye to their family and left for America."

Edie's eyes were glistening now. "She always talked about going on holidays to the Black Forest, but I didn't know she actually lived in it."

"Lived on the northern edge of it would be more accurate, but yes, Sulz was their home for many years. And that was where your father was born."

The tears spilled over and ran down Edie's cheeks. "Did you get to go to Mannheim?"

"I did," Mitch said softly. "About a month ago, while we were in Munich, we had to wait for over a week for some of the supplies from the U.S. Army to arrive. So President Cannon gave me and Elder Reissner permission to take a train to Mannheim. And we actually found the little village where the Zimmers lived." His voice suddenly caught. "The locals showed us which house was theirs, and to my utter delight, the woman who is living there now with her family is Oma Zimmer's second cousin, once removed. We had dinner with them one night. I have their address, and we promised to write to each other."

"Oh, Mitch," Edie exclaimed, her voice husky. "Oma will be so pleased that you did that."

"Not will be," he said. "*Was* so pleased," he said. "I'm sure she helped us find the place. Sulz consists of only four or five farmhouses out in the middle of nowhere. Most of the members in Mannheim hadn't even heard of it. It was Oma Zimmer's doing, I'm sure of that."

Now he tipped the woodcarving back again so they could see the bottom of the base, only this time, he did not cover any part of it. The two words he had hidden before were now clearly visible. They too were stamped into the wood. *Die Grossmutter*.

Rena gave a low cry and blurted it out to the others. "Dee Grossmooter," she cried, pronouncing it for the others. It means "The Grandmother."

"But I thought *Oma* meant grandmother," Tina said.

Edie smiled. "*Grossmutter* is grandmother. *Oma* is grandma and *Opa* is grandpa."

"Yes," Mitch went on, "and when I saw this"—he straightened the statue again so it was facing them—"I knew I had to buy it. Look at her; she even looks a little like Oma Zimmer, don't you think." As they nodded, he moved over and set the statue on the coffee table where all could see it. Then he moved back to his place by the fireplace. "Now, let me tell you why I bought it."

He looked down at the twins and his four grandchildren, who were seated on the floor at his feet. "When Oma and Opa Zimmer reached Utah and were sent down to help colonize Richfield, they went to the stake patriarch and received their patriarchal blessings. We have copies of both of their blessings if you would like to read them sometime. But in Oma Zimmer's blessing there was an unusual promise." He looked around the room with deep affection. "The patriarch told her that her posterity—which includes all of you—would be the means of taking the gospel to her extended family."

Mitch was filled with so much pride and love that he could scarcely speak. "So, Grandma Westland and I are going to find a place for 'The Grandmother' where we can all see it every day. It will serve as a constant reminder to all of us that, one, we have family roots that tie us directly to the *Schwarzwald,* and, two, that we have promises to fulfill."

He stopped for a moment, and then he looked directly into the faces of the six youngest members of the family. Their gaze was fixed on him. Their eyes were bright and their smiles were radiant. Tears came and spilled over as he softly went on. "And some of you here today will be the ones who will fulfill that patriarchal promise given to Oma Zimmer so many years ago."

Edie got to her feet and went to her husband. She put her arms around his neck and looked up into his eyes. "*Danke schön, mein Liebchen,*" she whispered. And then she kissed him as all of the family applauded wildly.

AUTHOR'S NOTE

In the preface to *A Generation Rising*, the first volume of the Fire and Steel series, I indicated that I planned to introduce two families to the readers: the Eckhardts, a simple farm family from southern Germany, and the Westlands, a ranching family from rural Utah. The plan was to introduce the Eckhardts in *A Generation Rising* and then bring in the Westlands in the second volume, *The Storm Descends*. And that is what I did. The two families meet near the end of the second volume of Fire and Steel.

However, as I began to develop the story of the Westlands, who were one of the pioneering families of the San Juan Mission that settled southeastern Utah, it became clear that their backstory deserved a fuller treatment. This was done in a separate two-volume set: *Only the Brave* and this sequel, *To Soar with Eagles*. These two volumes further explain how these two families, so widely separated by geography, come together and how their lives become intertwined.

Hereafter, the story of the Eckhardts and the Westlands will continue in future volumes of Fire and Steel, and there will be no additional volumes of Only the Brave.

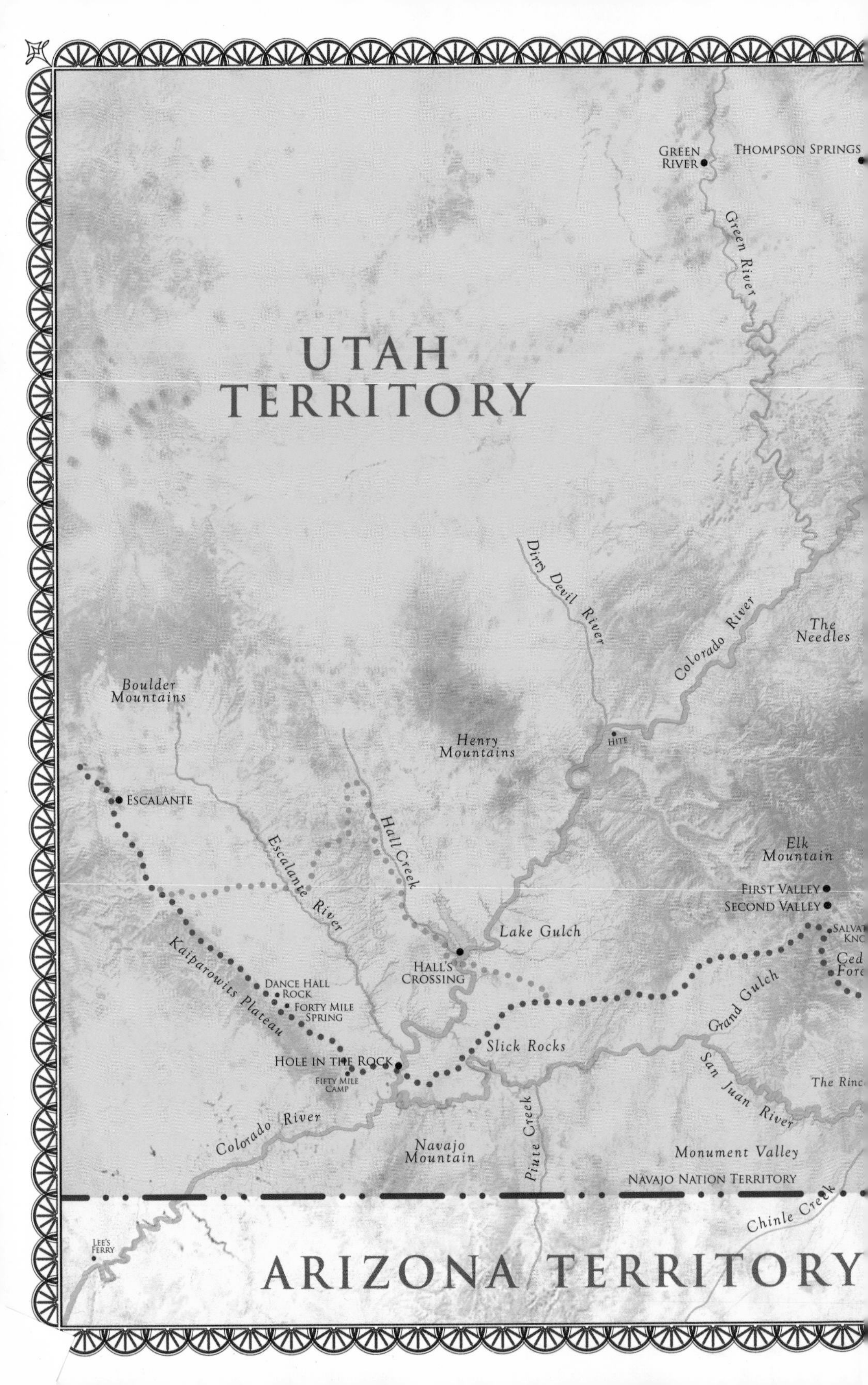
UTAH TERRITORY
ARIZONA TERRITORY
GREEN RIVER
THOMPSON SPRINGS
Green River
Dirty Devil River
Colorado River
The Needles
Boulder Mountains
Henry Mountains
HITE
ESCALANTE
Hall Creek
Escalante River
Elk Mountain
FIRST VALLEY
SECOND VALLEY
Lake Gulch
Kaiparowits Plateau
HALL'S CROSSING
DANCE HALL ROCK
FORTY MILE SPRING
Grand Gulch
Slick Rocks
HOLE IN THE ROCK
FIFTY MILE CAMP
San Juan River
Colorado River
Navajo Mountain
Piute Creek
Monument Valley
NAVAJO NATION TERRITORY
Chinle Creek
LEE'S FERRY